GIVE US THIS DAY

Jonathan Tulloch was born and bred in Cumbria. He was educated by Augustinian friars. He has written three previous novels, *The Season Ticket*, winner of the Betty Trask Prize and filmed as *Purely Belter, The Bonny Lad* and *The Lottery*. He featured on the *TLS* list of the twenty most promising young writers, and recently won the J.B. Priestley Award. His work has been translated into five languages. He is a regular contributor to *The Tablet*, the leading international Roman Catholic weekly.

BY THE SAME AUTHOR

The Season Ticket
The Bonny Lad
The Lottery

GIVE US THIS DAY

JONATHAN TULLOCH

JONATHAN CAPE
LONDON

Published by Jonathan Cape 2005

2 4 6 8 10 9 7 5 3 1

First published in Great Britain in 2005 by Jonathan Cape
Random House, 20 Vauxhall Bridge Road, London SW1V 2SA

Random House Australia (Pty) Limited
20 Alfred Street, Milsons Point, Sydney,
New South Wales 2061, Australia

Random House New Zealand Limited
18 Poland Road, Glenfield,
Auckland 10, New Zealand

Random House South Africa (Pty) Limited
Endulini, 5A Jubilee Road, Parktown 2193, South Africa

The Random House Group Limited Reg. No. 954009
www.randomhouse.co.uk

A CIP catalogue record for this book
is available from the British Library

ISBN 0-224-06169-0

Papers used by Random House are natural, recyclable products made from wood grown in sustainable forests; the manufacturing processes conform to the environmental regulations of the country of origin

Typeset by Palimpsest Book Production Limited, Polmont, Stirlingshire
Printed and bound in Great Britain by
Mackays of Chatham plc

As always for Shirley and Aidan. My home port,
my journey, my destination.

Acknowledgements

I would like to thank the following:

Peter De Bore of Bore Shipping Company for allowing me to sail on his container ships.

The captains of the *Norstream*, Cornelis Fikkert, Jan Peter Bosman and their crew, including Victor Bawalan, Manuel Jr D. Abanes, Eligio Daga-Ang, Coronel Juancho, Isidro Ancino, Nicolas Sanapo, Edwin Rocillio.

The captains of the *Ocean Challenger, Mikkel Tore* and their crews, including Romeo and Xavier.

Joel Sy, long-term seafarer, now with new hope.

The Apostleship of the Sea, the Mission to Seafarers, Friends of the Earth, Colin Worswick, Chris Frazer, Anne Frazer, Anne Burleigh, David Smith, Catherine Fenwick and Joe Galvin.

My editors Shirley Tulloch and Dan Franklin. My agent Robert Kirby.

The Royal Literary Fund.

Jim O'Keefe, who supplied many telling details as well as being a challenging walking companion. Paddy Mackin, big-hearted ship visitor, who has done so much over the years to welcome the seafarers to our shores; film maker and ambassador of Slaggy Island.

Daniel O'Leary, excellent writer and ceaseless giver, his generosity and wisdom have shaped this book.

Chapter One

It had been the hill of God. Now the huge Methodist chapel and the Congregationalist church were derelict. After a brief half-life as a carpet warehouse, the Mount Zion Tabernacle had been boarded up again. Only St Wilfrid's remained. With its tower as high as the chimney of the old cotton mill, recently converted to a mobile-phone mast, the Roman Catholic church shouldered itself heavily from the crowded terraces of mill cottages. Shelving roofs enclosed its horizons, hiding the view of the ancient market town below and the promise of the green dales beyond. Under the smuts of chimneys and then car exhaust fumes, its stones had darkened unevenly over the years, giving the building a mottled look, as of a great whale beached halfway up the hill on some receding tide.

Inside St Wilfrid's it was always dusk. Stone pillars rose to an indistinct ceiling. Even on the hottest days of the year it remained cool. The asceticism of stone and dark wood was softened here and there by tongues of red carpet and kneelers. A rack of votive lights sifted the twilight. Statues peered down from half-hidden alcoves. The marble altar dominated; elemental and immovable, it seemed to occur there naturally, as though the church had been built round a feature on the hillside. Behind the altar loomed the reredos, its exquisitely carved stone figures re-enacting the Passion in perpetual shadow. Except for an hour on Sunday morning, St Wilfrid's was a place of uneasy silences. The revving engine of a car struggling up the hill or someone speeding recklessly down the gradient troubled the stillness without piercing it – a flat pebble skimming the surface of a deep pool. The little screechings of the starlings that nested in the cavities between lead roof and wooden ceiling barely scratched this great stone silence.

On a cold March morning the small congregation was arriving for Ash Wednesday Mass. Pasty faces averted from the wind, the odd greeting was exchanged like drops of drizzle flung on a squall, before the stillness of the chilly interior absorbed them. At ten o'clock precisely the congregation rose as one for the priest.

Middle-aged, he was a tall, almost imposing man. The cobalt of his piercingly blue eyes was noticeable many pews back. Dressed in the severity of purple Lenten vestments, he mounted the steps and kissed the Druidic altar. The aboriginal power of the act was not entirely dispelled by the smile that followed, 'I'm sorry about the cold, but it is the first day of Lent after all.' The congregation tittered a little. 'But seriously,' he continued, 'have a look round you. As befits this most solemn time of the year, our church has been stripped. One might say shriven. From now until the glorious mystery of the Resurrection there will be no flowers, no decorations. My dear people, Lent is a time for us to encounter God, to change our hearts, and to do this we must cast aside some of our comforts.' The priest paused, his posture as unbending as the stone on the altar relief behind him. His blue eyes scanned the mainly female faces looking at him, only one of which was younger than his own. 'Anyway, let's all try and get to know God again a little this Lent.'

The priest moved solemnly about the altar, the church tower a deep space drifting above him. Once in the morning and then again in the evening, as regular as the angelus bell, beams of light poured through the windows in the high turret. On bright days this was like an explosion, a riot of light transfiguring the leaden altar. Even on a grey morning such as this, one or two beams were lowered like spectral ladders.

During the distribution of the ashes, the rain intensified and as the congregation lined up, coats firmly buttoned to the neck, they glanced at the sharp drops driving against the windows. The priest screwed his thumb into the dish of ashes, smearing each forehead with a gritty, meticulous cross. Forty times the precise words rang through the chill air of the church. 'Remember, man, you are dust, and to dust you shall return.'

By quarter to eleven, the congregation was shuffling out. In the sacristy the priest was already taking off his vestments, his fingers moving with the expertise of many years. He fitted the sleeveless purple chasuble on to a hook. He lifted the stole from his neck and kissed it. In one swift movement he removed his alb.

'The new readers' rota, Father Tom,' a woman announced, waving a sheet of paper at him. 'I'll just pop it on the side here.'

'Thanks, Pat.'

'I've pinned another copy on the noticeboard.'

'Great.'

'And are you all right, Father?'

'First day of Lent?' The priest made a mock grimace.

When she had gone, the priest carefully hung up his alb.

'Father,' a second woman said, coming into the sacristy, 'have you remembered that I'm taking the Blessed Sacrament to old Betty Doonan today?'

'Yes, that's OK.'

'And I got these rosary beads for her when I was in Lourdes. Will you bless them for me?'

The priest held the beads up for a moment, the crucifix dangling. His blessing was precise as a spell.

'So what are you giving up for Lent then, Father?' the woman asked.

'A priest friend of mine was asked that, and do you know what he said? I'm giving up *giving up*.'

The second woman left with a laugh.

Under his vestments the priest wore a black shirt against which the tongue of his white Roman collar flickered like a candle.

'And how are you today, Father Tom?' a third woman asked.

'I'm fine thanks, Clare. Yourself?'

'Very well. Very well,' she replied, dancing two bulging black bin-liners into the sacristy. 'Old clothes. I've had a clearout. Can you find a use for them?'

'I can. The Romanian Double-Decker Bus Charity is still asking for things.'

'I'll just leave them here then, shall I?' The priest nodded. The woman made to go but then turned back. 'There's ten thousand in the fund now, Father.'

'Ten thousand, never?'

'For the St Wilfrid's 150th Building Fund.'

'That's fantastic.'

'And shall I tell you something else as well? I shouldn't really; it's a secret.'

'Now you know I'm useless with secrets, Clare.'

'We're arranging a party for you.'

'A party?'

'You are naughty, Father. Why didn't you tell us it's the thirtieth anniversary of your ordination this year?'

'Well, well; thirty years, is it really that long? They'll be putting me out to grass soon enough.'

'Never. What would we do without you, Father? That was a lovely Mass just now. Anyway, I'd better rush. I'll be seeing you.'

'God bless now, Clare.'

After adjusting his Roman collar, the priest took a watch from the top of the chest of drawers and fastened it carefully on his wrist. Opening the wardrobe, he slipped a black suit jacket from its hanger and put it on. He looked at himself in the mirror on the inside of the wardrobe door and conjured out a comb. His short, neat blond hair had not greyed with the years, but faded, like a sepia print. It accentuated the blue of his eyes. His black trousers were creased perfectly; his shoes shone to a sheen and squeaked a little as he walked briskly down the corridor that joined the presbytery to the church.

In the kitchen the plumbing groaned as he poured himself a glass of water. Sipping it, he scanned the headline of the unopened copy of the *Independent* newspaper. It read: *WAR WITH IRAQ INEVITABLE*. The telephone began to ring in the corridor. 'Hello, St Wilfrid's Roman Catholic Church,' he said. During the conversation that followed, the priest took out a slim diary from his breast pocket and wrote in a date. 'No really, that's fine, Chris. We *can* have the deanery meeting here; just as long as I remember to put on the heating. Otherwise I'll be having to thaw you all out. No, Chris, the central heating still isn't all it's supposed to be. I suppose it *will* be by the time we're celebrating St Wilf's bicentenary.' The priest brought out a tube of sweets from his jacket pocket, glanced at it, turned it wistfully in his hands, then dropped it back.

Returning to the sacristy, he suddenly yawned and leant heavily against the chest of drawers. He stayed like that for a while, head bowed as though studying the red, fibrous industrial-strength carpet, then he shook his head vigorously and, whispering admonitions, forced himself upright. Taking a key from his pocket he carefully lifted a heavy hang of chasubles on a hook to reveal a concealed door. With a furtive look over his shoulder he unlocked the door and passed into the darkness beyond. Shivering in the cold damp, he groped his way down a narrow, stone tunnel to where a single chink of light showed. When he reached the light, he pushed his eye against it, and peeped. It was a hole in the stone frieze of the reredos and from it practically the whole church was visible.

The smoke from the extinguished candles was still drifting through the silent air. In the front pew a woman knelt, praying fervently. When she shifted position the wooden kneeler banged against the stone floor, sending a loud crack through the dark hollows of the church. She dropped her hands in a gesture of despair, revealing a heavily made-up face that wore a look of imminent disaster. The priest sighed. Her glossed lips moved in what seemed more like interrogation than prayer. She stared so intently at the back of the altar that the priest pulled away from the spyhole. For a second time he brought out his tube of sweets and fondled them. Pushing his way back up the dank tunnel, he felt for the door handle in the darkness. In the sacristy he brushed a single cobweb from his shoulder before entering the church. 'Marie, good to see you,' he said to the woman who was still kneeling.

'Hello, Father Tom,' she intoned in a voice conscious of its own gravity.

'And how are you keeping this morning, Marie?'

'Not so good this morning.'

'I see. Well, let's go to the presbytery, shall we?'

He'd forgotten to light the fire in the parish room and his breath plumped a little as he said, 'Dear me, it's an icebox in here.' He struck a match and turned on the gas. Flames leapt over the panels of the fire. 'Sorry about that, Marie.' Carefully, he shook out the match, watched the red glow fade and then placed it with other dead matches in a little silver tray on the mantelpiece.

She pardoned him with a waft of her hand. 'The way I'm feeling, I won't notice a little cold.'

He paused just for an instant before saying delicately, 'How's everything at home?'

'I was wrong last time, Father,' she replied quickly. 'He wasn't having an affair. Bob. We've resumed our – *you know whats*. No, this time I'm afraid it's something more important than even that.'

'I tell you what, Marie, I'll put the kettle on. Tea or coffee?'

'How about arsenic?' Her tone was precariously balanced between a heavy humour and an even heavier grief. 'Seriously though, Father, it's Lent. Just make it hot water.'

'You've given up tea and coffee?'

'And *Coronation Street*. But I'll have a hot chocolate if there is one.'

'Well, I'm sure there must be some cocoa somewhere.'

In the kitchen, the priest yawned blearily. Laying his hand on his closely shaven cheek, he shook his head as though surprised by the weight of weariness. Waiting for the kettle to boil, he skimmed the leading story in the *Independent*. The kettle boiled; the milk in the microwave pinged. Reaching into the rather frugal cupboard, he took down the tin of cocoa from its position between a box of porridge and a jar of Hartley's seedless raspberry jam. As he filled the kettle again for the next usage, he caught a glimpse of his reflection in the tap. His face was stretched mercilessly over the chrome, eyes tiny and colourless as an insect's, his nose a probing proboscis. 'Mugs only,' he explained coming into the room backwards. 'If you want bone china you'll have to go to the Vicar. I'm afraid it's not made with full-cream milk either.'

'That's all right. It is supposed to be Lent after all.' As she rose to take her mug, the priest felt her fingers brush his. 'What you need is a woman's touch about the place, Father Tom.' She chuckled. 'Talking about women, did you read in last week's *Universe* about that woman who's been arrested for blackmailing a priest? Put a cushion up her jumper and said he'd made her pregnant. So he hired a private detective. Turns out she'd been blackmailing two other priests as well.'

'She must have been desperate, poor woman.'

'You'd better hide all your cushions.'

The priest laughed loudly, as though trying to conceal a constraint. There was a lull in their conversation. Marie brooded over her cocoa. Feeling himself sink into his armchair, the priest suppressed a yawn. The taint of gas hung on the still, damp air, vying with Marie's perfume. With a deft, scarcely perceptible cock of his wrist, he glanced at his watch. Then she began. As she spoke, he fixed his eyes on her forehead where the grainy ashes adhered to the thick foundation cream. 'I think I'm losing my faith, Father.' She paused weightily. 'Maybe there's no God after all, just a great big yawning hole.'

'When did you start thinking this way, Marie?'

'I'm a good Catholic, Father. All my children have been to the school, and they still all go to Mass with me. Bob even converted. And now he's in the Knights of St Columba. But recently, whenever I try to pray . . . I mean with all this talk of war and famine . . .'

The phone began to ring and the priest half rose as though in response to some conditioned reflex. 'The answerphone will get that,' he said, settling back in the chair.

'What if we're wrong, Father? What if life's just one big nothingness?'

'Yet you came to Mass this morning.'

'Of course I did.'

'Look, Marie, we all have our doubts from time to time.'

'Even you, Father?'

He paused just long enough to sharpen the crease on his trousers. 'Lent is a time when we're called to examine our relationship with God. We may have gone off-centre, wandered away, but at this time in the Church's year we're called back to meet with God.' His stomach rumbled. He risked a second glance at his watch. 'Personally, Marie, I always use this time of year to return to Jesus. It's like a wake-up call I suppose.'

'I don't think I could bear it if I lost my faith.'

'Maybe that's how Jesus felt when he went into the desert.'

'Do you think?'

'And he never lost his way, did he?' The phone rang once more. 'This place can get like a call centre.' A few seconds after it stopped, it rang again. 'I'd better get that. It might be urgent.'

The phone stood on a table in the corridor below a large plaster cast of the Virgin Mary. Under the Virgin's feet a giant snake writhed, fork tongue stiff as a stamen. 'Hello, St Wilfrid's Roman Catholic Church.' The words, though familiar through thousands of repetitions, stumbled slightly on his lips. 'Hello, Joyce. Are you all right? Yes, it must be time for another one of our little get-togethers. There's no one like you for the butterfly cakes. Well, I'm looking forward to seeing Angela as well.

No, no, you're right, we won't be able to have the cakes if it's Lent.' The priest laid a hand on his rumbling stomach. He could picture precisely the woman at the other end of the line. Her eyes, as ever, held his with the tenacity of a hungry dog. It was all there in his mind: the walking stick she kept close, the bandage on her ankle swelling visibly under her wrinkled tights, the room that had remained unchanged through his eight years of visiting, presided over by a stopped clock which made it always ten to four. 'Let me just get my diary out. My life is as hectic as Hollywood at the moment. How about Wednesday week at four o'clock?' He took out his diary and wrote in it, but his thoughts stayed in the room across the telephone wires. The worn three-piece suite with its yellowed antimacassars, the framed picture of a bluebell wood hanging beside a crucifix on wallpaper still faded from cigarettes smoked by a husband dead for twenty years, the coffee table that was brought out in his honour, its grain laden with tiers of home-baked cakes and a teapot covered in a pink cosy; every detail was lodged in his memory. He yawned until his jaw cracked. The thought of the room filled him with a sudden dread. 'It'll be lovely to see you and Angela again, Joyce.'

Marie was waiting for him impatiently in the parish room. 'It was Joyce,' Tom explained.

'Poor old dear,' returned Marie. 'That one's had it hard. With her daughter. Say what you like, the handicapped are no picnic. That's another thing that's been occurring to me. Why is our religion so obsessed with the handicapped?'

'I wouldn't say that it was. I mean we believe in the sanctity of all human life, Marie.'

'But what does that actually mean, Father? I've seen Joyce having to take Angela to the toilet; and her fifteen stone if she's a pound.'

Sitting down, Tom continued to listen to Marie but his mind wandered. He was thinking of Joyce's daughter, Angela, who always took tea with them. A huge, middle-aged woman with the mind of a child, she lived for the days when he came to tea; or so Joyce told him. Small-eyed and heavy, she had the mild, myopic look of an elephant. Once she had been well enough to go out and work for Remploy, but she was growing more and more reserved. You're the only stranger she trusts, Joyce often reminded him.

'Are you all right, Father?'

'What?'

'You seem miles away. Are you hungry?'

'I'm sorry?'

'Your tummy's talking again. I keep on telling you, what you need is a woman's touch. Have you had breakfast this morning?'

'It's a fast day.'

'What blue eyes you've got, Father Tom; did anyone ever tell you that you look like that actor, oh what was he called?'

Tom could not hide the weariness in his voice. 'Not Paul Newman?'

'That's him. Well have they?'

'Not for many years.'

'Those blue eyes. After our little sessions I feel as though I know you well enough to tell you.' She chuckled coyly. 'I used to have an immense crush on Paul Newman.'

'Now, Marie, have you thought about making a retreat this Lent? It could be the perfect opportunity to meet with God in a meaningful way. Let me give you some bible references.'

After three-quarters of an hour, he drew the session to a close. Marie hugged the priest at the presbytery door. As he closed the door behind her, he leant against it. Her scent and the soft impress of her breasts lingered. When he was younger the closeness of a female body would have inflamed him. But he no longer needed scrupulously to avoid the touch of women like Marie, for now it gave him only a deadened little lurch, like the turning over of a flat car battery. He passed back up the corridor and into the sacristy. The fossilised sensuality of Marie's embrace dissipated instantly as he slipped through the concealed door into the dampness and groped his way towards the spyhole to see who was waiting for him next. Yawning again, he shook his head crossly, as though to upbraid himself for the exhaustion that was creeping over him like a fog.

Chapter Two

The prison stood on another hill. Built at the same time as the mill and the church, it loomed over the town like a shadow. Seagulls flew around its dark brick turrets. On top of the high perimeter walls razor wire frothed, like a vigorous climbing plant. Watched suspiciously by the eye of the CCTV camera, the priest pressed the buzzer on the intercom. 'It's Father Thomas Carey.' The door opened with an electronic warble.

The prison officer behind the great slab of the reception desk leafed stolidly through a heavy ring binder. 'Yes, you're down here. ID?' Tom held up his card. 'Worn a bit haven't you, Padre?'

The priest tried to smile. 'Well, I suppose it's five years since that photograph was taken.'

'What you been doing, living the high life?'

He tapped his watch. 'I think I'm a little bit late getting here.'

'Get another photograph done as soon as you can, will you?' The officer looked down at the old-fashioned, battered little suitcase that the priest held.

'Mass vessels,' Tom explained. 'A chalice, a paten –'

'Go through there.'

He walked the few steps to where a pair of officers stood at a metal-detecting machine. Handing over his watch and the suitcase, the priest passed through the machine. 'A chalice, a paten . . .' he began again, blinking in the scalding light of the bulbs directly above.

'What?'

'In the suitcase. They're things we use in the Mass.' The

officer's eyes raged with the silent boredom of a zoo animal. 'The thing is, I'm a bit late. I got held up, I was supposed to be here by half past. I hope it hasn't inconvenienced anyone.'

The early Victorian brickwork showed starkly beneath the white paint. Two-toned security bleeps rang out continually. The officer weighed the chalice in one hand. 'Bit valuable this, isn't it, Padre? I mean the place is full of thieves.'

A female officer passed an electronic arm assiduously over his body. 'He's a bloody priest,' her colleague laughed. 'What's he going to bring in, the body of Christ stuffed with dope?'

'We've got priests in here,' she returned coldly.

'Don't take it personal, Padre. She always double-checks the ministers of religion. What's the matter, Shazza, don't you like religion?'

'Causes trouble doesn't it. No offence, but it does.' She stamped the back of the priest's hand firmly with fluorescent ink, handed him back his watch and ushering him to a security door pressed the button.

He found himself sealed in a perspex chamber. Under a flashing strip light, the stamp on his hand showed a sickly green. He gazed helplessly at his watch. It was two minutes before the second door opened.

The group of officers gathered at the end of a cavernous corridor did not seem to notice his approach. He stood by them, gazing at the stone floor. 'Bloody useless,' one of them was saying to the others. 'They want to sack him. We've gone from challenging for a European place to a bloody relegation dogfight all in six months.'

The officers wore white polyester shirts with black nylon ties. The silver serial numbers on their epaulettes glinted dully. 'What do you make of this war then?' one of them asked his colleagues.

'They want to drop a bomb on all of them. Them Al Qaedas. Before they drop another one on us.'

'They do. They're a right bloody shower, them bloody mad mullahs.'

'Getaway, you can't tar them all with the same brush.'

'Who's talking about a brush? What America wants to do is fucking well bomb first and ask questions later.'

'What I'd do is this,' said one that hadn't spoken yet. 'I'd give them nowt to eat for a week then lay on bacon sarnies.'

There was a burst of laughter, strangled when they looked around guiltily and saw the priest. They peered appraisingly at the Roman collar. One of them picked up an internal phone. 'Someone to take the chaplain, please.'

Five minutes later, the accompanying officer arrived. 'Sorry,' said the priest. 'I think I may be a little late.' Giving him a single, piercing look, the woman prison officer led the way outside. The driving rain of the morning had stopped but it remained grey and windy. The officer's keys jangled as she opened a door in a high wire fence. The priest followed her across a courtyard. Inside the perimeter wall, the gaol was even more drearily imposing. Voices drifted from the cells on the wind that moaned against the brick abutments. Beneath each barred window the walls were stained even darker with a century and a half of emptied chamber pots. Someone was shouting, his words an echoing madness. They passed down the long side of the main block, separated from the lowest cells only by a few yards. 'Hello, Father, how you doing?' A voice addressed the priest conversationally from a ground-floor window. 'What is it this time, caught with your hands in the Lourdes fund, or on a kiddy?' The officer, a few yards ahead, did not appear to hear. The priest caught the fleeting image of a face. 'Don't slip up, Father, because if we ever get you in here then we'll cut your cock to pieces.' He stopped for a moment to stare at the gnomic face leering at him from behind the bars: a teeth-gnashing figure from Breughel's portrait of the damned. 'Don't think that dog collar can save you.'

The keys jarred their atonal arpeggios as the officer opened door after door in the system of wire fences. In a single step they passed from a sheltered area right into the teeth of the wind. The seagulls hung above the turrets like tattered flags, occasionally swooping down on tilting wings, incongruous amongst the motionless horizontals and verticals of wire and bars. Narrowing his eyes to the gusts of grit, the priest followed. He had to hurry to keep up and more than once his old suitcase knocked painfully against his knees.

At last they came to a smaller, more modern block standing on its own. The prison officer led the way up three flights of stairs then, without a word, locked a door behind the priest, sealing him alone on a long, breeze-block corridor. Breathless with the wind and the walk, he stood there. Someone was cleaning in a side room, and the forlorn slop-slop of the mop was audible to the priest as he began to walk tentatively down the corridor, splaying his feet to silence the squeaking of his shoes. 'Hello?' he called uncertainly. 'It's Father Tom Carey.' The air reeked with disinfectant. 'I'm Father Tom Carey.' A head popped round the door of the room being cleaned. Dressed in purple sweatshirt and trousers, the prisoner appeared to stare right through the priest. With his white hair, white cracked skin and red-rimmed eyes, he had the look of an albino. 'Hello,' the priest said, trying to conceal the slight tremor in his voice. 'I'm Father Tom Carey.' The prisoner's mop clanked agitatedly against the bucket. 'I've come for the Ash Wednesday service.' The prisoner blinked then withdrew into the room. The sound of the mop grew more insistent.

At the far end of the corridor a prison officer suddenly materialised. He was a very tall man who stooped gingerly, as though he feared his head might strike the low ceiling. 'Hello, Father T, standing in again?'

The priest relaxed at the sight of a familiar face. 'For my sins. Look, sorry I'm late, Roger.'

'Oh, they don't mind. They're used to waiting.' The two men shook hands. 'Bit of a reduced congregation for you today. Been a fracas. Some of your flock got a tad aerated.' The prison officer led the priest down another breeze-block corridor. 'Do you think there's going to be another war then, Father T?'

'Looks like it.'

'Blair and Bush made up their minds?'

'I'm afraid so.'

'Just as well, if you ask me. Prayers won't stop him. Saddam Hussein. Sadman Insane, that's what I call him. Or Sodhim Insane. That's a good one. I've just thought of that: Sodhim Insane. Him and that bloody Bin-liner, what a pair.'

'Bin-liner?'

'You know, Osama Bin Laden. Well, here you are. They'll be along in a minute: the not-so-meek-and-mild ones. *Hasta la vista*, Father T. Here, I'll just open that cupboard for you in the corner. Oh, by the way, since your last visit there's a new trusty as sacristan. He won't say much.'

The dimpleboard ceiling in the chapel was even lower than that of the corridor outside. The stacks of plastic chairs nearly reached it. There were no windows in the breeze-block walls. A bare bulb ached with light. Posters lined the walls. One showed a white rabbit in grass with the words: FRAGILE, HANDLE WITH PRAYER; another had a clutch of baby chickens and declared: DON'T WORRY, LIFE IS JUST A TEMPORARY SITUATION. The altar was a simple table. On it stood a drawing of the Crucifixion done by one of the prisoners. The hands, powerfully sketched, seemed to be thrusting themselves from the paper. Gazing at the drawing, the priest bit his lip. He lifted his suitcase on to the altar. The clasp stuck. He freed it with a jerk that sent the chalice bouncing to the floor. As he fumbled after it, picking it up whilst it was still rolling, the priest noticed that the red carpet was the same as that in his sacristy.

Reaching into the cupboard in the corner of the room where the wine and hosts were kept, he looked over his shoulder. The albino was standing directly behind him. With a sharp intake of breath, the priest stepped back. He had not heard him enter the room. The prisoner moved soundlessly past him to the cupboard, and as though the priest was not there, began to prepare for the service. He brought out a white cloth. With a single flourish, he opened it out, the linen cracking like a pair of bird's wings, and laid it on the altar, his hands sweeping the creases away. He brought out the hosts and wine, his face still without expression. He placed a single candle on the table and with the exaggerated care of one handling high explosives lit the wick. There was a tape recorder into which he put a cassette. Soft plainchant filled the stark chapel. Slowly, painstakingly, silently, the prisoner began to lay out the chairs. Tom watched him out of the corner of his eye.

'So do you think it'll be United or Arsenal for the title this year then?' the priest asked, with the airy tone of a man forcing himself to make conversation. The prisoner did not reply but continued with his task. 'I think it'll be United,' the priest finished lamely. He looked down at his shoes; there was a single spot of mud from the long walk outside. He wiped it away with a deft, anxious dab against the back of his trousers.

When the seats were in position, the prisoner brought out some vestments from the cupboard. 'It's all right,' the priest replied. 'I won't bother with those.' The prisoner continued to hold out the vestments. The priest pointed at his open suitcase. 'I'll just use my stole.' But still the prisoner did not seem to understand. His expressionless face continued to moon at the priest. He took a few steps towards him until the sleeve of the purple chasuble was brushing the priest's arm. The priest cleared his throat. 'All right then.'

The prisoner took a chair to the furthest corner of the room and sat there. The priest stood awkwardly behind the altar.

The voices that he heard coming down the corridor a little later were deadened by the breeze blocks so that they entered the room like an explosion. He braced himself. 'A flock of lost sheep,' the prison officer announced.

'Who's this?' one of the new arrivals demanded, seeing the priest standing in purple behind the altar.

'Where's Father O'Keefe then?' another said. 'Hasn't swanned off to Rome for another holiday has he?'

'Afraid so,' the priest replied from behind the altar.

'Well, give us five anyway, Father.'

'Five?'

'Here, put your hand up.' The priest raised his hand in ungainly reciprocation. The shaven-haired prisoner darted over and there was a resounding slap. 'He knows how to enjoy himself, Father O'Keefe. Know what I mean?'

The priest tried to grin. 'He's famous for it.'

As the chapel filled with grey faces and burgundy sweatshirts, the stench of unwashed bodies became oppressive.

'So are we in it then, Father?' a black prisoner demanded. 'This war with Iraq. It's the squaddies I feel sorry for. Know what I mean? Stuck out there in the middle of the desert. I used to be in the army, me.'

'Yeah,' drawled the prisoner who had slapped the priest's hand, 'until you killed the sergeant.'

The prisoners laughed: the clanking of a box of nails. The priest could still feel the stinging slap.

'All right, Padre,' the tall prison officer told him. 'You've got six of them?'

'Seven,' the shaven-head hand-slapper corrected.

'Just testing, Jimmy. I'll leave you to it then, Father T. Look at them; what a crew. Just as well God loves them because nobody else will.'

'Tosser. Just because your wife's given it up for Lent.'

'Show some respect, Jimmy, or I'll see you banged up with a nonce,' the officer said, leaving the room with a grin.

'He's all right, that screw,' Jimmy announced, rubbing the bristles of his shaven head. A man much older than the others sat in the front row. He was praying the rosary with a small, metal rosary ring; his shapeless mouth seemed to masticate over the words of the mysteries. 'Hey, Billy. You've left them again.' The old man looked at Jimmy uncomprehendingly. 'Your teeth. You've left them in the frigging cell, you daft cunt.'

The priest glanced at the old man. A dotted blue line was tattooed round his throat with the words *cut here* written along it. The music continued to sound out in gentle waves.

'So do you agree with him then?' Jimmy demanded abruptly.

'Sorry?' the priest replied.

'With Beanpole; that screw. He said God loves us.'

Tom's attempt at a smile was a blink. 'Of course I agree.'

'Do you think he does, though? I mean we're only allowed one pair of undies a week. It might get a bit whiffy for him.' As the prisoners laughed, the priest rubbed his hands together. The palm still throbbed where he had been struck. 'You've been here before, haven't you, Father?'

'Yes. I've stood in for Father O'Keefe a few times.'

'He's a great laugh, him.' Jimmy's nose was prominent as a drawn knife. 'But do you really think that God loves us?'

'Well, yes, I do. It's the teaching of the Church.'

'Loves everyone, does he?'

'Yes.'

'What, even the Ghoul?' Jimmy pointed at the white-haired one who sat utterly motionless. 'You saying God loves *him*?'

'God loves everyone.' For a few moments the priest visibly floundered. Everyone was looking at him. He tried to swallow back his anxiety. 'In fact, the first man to be promised eternal life was a criminal. St Dismus – you know, the good thief.'

'But he hadn't just bloody drowned his wife and kiddy, had he?'

'Well, we don't know exactly what he did.'

Jimmy burst into laughter. 'We know exactly what the Ghoul did, Father Shiny-Shoes. Why don't you tell him, Ghoul?'

The priest coughed. 'I think we should be making a start.'

'This priest I knew once,' said a prisoner without neck or eyebrows, 'he ended up inside as well. Touched up the altar boys.'

'You ever been inside before?' Jimmy asked. 'I mean been banged up. Heard the door close on you and that?'

The priest licked his dry lips. 'No. No, I haven't.'

'We should arrange it for you. We did it for Father O'Keefe.

They let him stay for twenty-four hours. You have to hear the door close on you. Then you know what it's like. And all night the loonies shriek. Don't you, Ghoul? Quiet as a mouse here, wouldn't say boo to a goose, but all night he screams. No wonder. I think I'd scream if I'd drowned me wife and kid.'

'Right, if we can make a start then.'

'They found him in the bath with them, didn't they? 'Course the water had gone cold.'

When the ashes were ready to be distributed the priest looked over his congregation. They seemed hungry as wolves for his meagre words. In their eyes was the terrible relentless patience of the long-term captive. 'Sometimes,' he faltered, 'God feels very far away. That's why we have Lent. It's a time for us to make a bit more effort than usual. An opportunity to come to God face to face. The main thing is that . . . well, the Church teaches that it doesn't matter what you've done. As long as you're sorry and have confessed it then God will . . .' Breaking off, the priest stared at the man they called 'Ghoul', who looked right through him, as though he were not there.

Chapter Three

The phone rang but he did not move. The stiffness in his joints had grown painful. His knees creaked against the uncushioned prie-dieu. The priest turned the beads in his fingers and started another decade of the rosary. A single candle guttered below the statue of Our Lady of Lourdes. The pillars rose above him like an avenue of yew trees. Coming down the corridor from the presbytery through the open door, echoing in the countless stone cavities of St Wilfrid's church, the phone rang again and then fell silent. Allowing the rosary beads to fall slack in his hands, the priest stared at them blankly with the disappointed air of a man who has failed to hypnotise himself. He had been trying to pray ever since his return from the prison.

When he left the church the wick of the snuffed candle glowed for a little while, a tiny eye peering in the gloom, before spending itself in a final plume of smoke that circulated in the darkness.

In his private sitting room on the first floor of the presbytery, the priest lit his gas fire, switched on the angle-poise lamp and taking out his breviary sat in an armchair. '*I shall not fear the sling by day,*' he read out loud. '*Nor the arrow that flies in the night.*' The gilt-edged, skin-thin pages were still crisp despite many years of use. After the readings, he sang compline. His voice was thin but held the tune so that the Latin plainchant fluttered about the room like a moth. Bookshelves lined three of the walls from floor to ceiling. The ancient armchair and matching sofa reinforced the room's institutional look. The sombre details on the large picture that hung over the mantelpiece were concealed in the shadows cast by the lamp.

He tried to sing the *Salve Regina* again, but faltered halfway through. The rain of that morning had come back and in the sudden silence it lashed the window. The emptiness of the huge presbytery seemed to press against the sitting room. He closed the breviary and went over to the bookshelves. Running a hand down the spines, he chose, more by touch than anything else, an old, hardback volume. The uneasiness of a few moments before dissipated. Taking the book to his armchair, he rested it on his lap for a moment, fingers exploring it fondly, like a blind person reading a favourite passage of Braille. He opened it at the frontispiece, a sepia photograph of a heavy, bearded man wearing the half-buttoned jacket of a black soutane and a bucket hat. The man in the photograph peered back at the camera rather severely through wire-rimmed spectacles. His ear was swollen into deformity. The priest smiled as though at the picture of a friend or brother. The book was called *Damien the Leper.*

He had absorbed a dozen pages or so when the presbytery bell rang. The priest tutted with annoyance then went back to his book. The bell rang again. As he walked down the stairs his face was set in a glower that he had only half managed to erase by the time he reached the bottom. Irritably he opened the door on a phalanx of rain.

'Hello, old friend.'

'Frank.' The priest's voice raised itself slightly in surprise.

'Tommy boy.'

'What are you doing here?'

'I'm sorry, I'm breaking into your reading time.'

'Don't be stupid, come in.' Conquering the last visible sign of annoyance, the priest ushered in the man standing on his doorstep. He was slight and dressed in jeans and a woollen jumper. He wore no coat against the rain. His short hair was beaded with raindrops. 'You're soaked, Frank.'

'It's raining, Tom. No, it's not raining. It's pissing down. It's blowing a fucking typhoon.' Hurriedly Tom closed the door. 'What's the matter?' Frank demanded. 'Worried someone might hear me swearing?' There was a smear of blood on his forehead.

'What's happened, Frank?'

'Can't I call on a fellow priest any more?'

'Have you cut yourself?'

'It's nothing.' The visitor waved the priest away peevishly.

Tom stared in confusion at the sodden, abject man. 'Come upstairs, Frank. I'll make some cocoa.' Doubling up, Frank began to laugh hysterically. 'What's going on, Frank?'

'You've got to laugh, Tom, haven't you?' Frank managed to say through his hilarity. He sobered abruptly. 'Forget about the cocoa, Tom.'

They went upstairs. 'Very cosy,' Frank said as he crossed the threshold into the sitting room. He picked up the copy of *Damien the Leper*. 'Ah Jesus, but the old ones are the best, eh Tom? You were forever reading that when we were at Ushaw, weren't you? The perfect seminarian.'

'Let me get you a towel.'

'I'm all right.'

'And that cut wants seeing to.'

'It doesn't matter.'

'How did you do it?'

'I hit my head against a wall. In fact I've been hitting my head against a wall for thirty years.'

'What's going on, Frank?'

'I'm desperate for a piss.'

Standing by his bookshelves, the priest listened bewilderedly to Frank's lurching progress to the bathroom. 'Hey Tom?' he shouted. 'Remember Sister Agnes at Ushaw?' A drunken snigger was followed by a falsetto, '*Tom Carey they can hear you all the way down in the chapel. Do you have to urinate like a horse? Junior seminarians should neither be seen nor heard.*'

The toilet was flushed and Frank came back still chuckling. Tom met him at the door. 'I'd offer you a drink, Frank but –'

'But you think I'm pissed already.'

'No, it's Lent.'

'Screw Lent.' Before Tom could reply, Frank had gone into the sitting room and swooped on the breviary. Following him, the priest reached out for it. 'Don't worry,' said Frank, 'I won't crease the pages. Treat your wife well and she'll treat you well.' With exaggerated care Frank leafed through the gilt-edged pages. He reached the little mark lying between the pages of compline. 'God, but you do it all, don't you? Compline with Complan: the prayer to build up your soul.' He looked at the priest with sudden astonishment. 'You still believe everything they told you, don't you, Tommy? Your breviary is your wife. The whole works.'

Tom stiffened slightly. 'If you mean that I say the breviary then yes, I do. Don't you?'

'Do you really want me to answer that?'

Reaching over, the priest snatched his breviary. 'For pity's sake will you just tell me what's going on?'

Frank collapsed in the armchair. 'I'm in the shit, Tom. I'm in it deep.'

'Do we have to have all the bad language?'

'Yes,' replied Frank simply. 'I think we do.'

'What's happened?'

'What hasn't happened?'

Tom cast about the room in confusion. He went over to the drinks cabinet and after hesitating, brought out the single bottle within, then broke the seal. He poured a measure into a sherry glass. 'Here, Franky.'

'Jesus, what is it?' asked Frank, turning the liquid round in the glass.

'I don't know. It was a gift from a parishioner.' He read the label on the bottle. 'It's Cointreau.'

'As long as it's alcohol. Do you remember Lent at Ushaw? No drinking and no women. Punch and Judy, we called it. I'm surprised at you, mind, Tom. You're the last person I'd expect to break your Lenten vows.'

'I'm not drinking. Anyway, alcohol isn't my vice.'

'Oh no, that's right. The old sweet tooth. The wine-gum priest.'

'Frank, what's all this about?'

For a while Frank seemed absorbed in the liquid. His forehead glistened with blood; a fretwork of grazes surrounded the cut. His eyes narrowed. 'Do you remember that play we did at Ushaw?'

'Play?' The priest's face creased with bemusement.

'It was by John Millington Synge. Not one of his better-known ones but a corker all the same. *When the Moon Has Set.* Do you remember?'

Tom shook his head curtly. 'I was never very theatrical.'

'I know; pity. It wasn't every seminary with its own Paul Newman. We wanted you to play the nun.' Frank tittered. 'Paula Newman.'

'If I remember correctly, we were supposed to be revising for a patristics exam.'

'Here's to Ushaw and John Millington Synge; those were the days.' Frank raised his glass and swallowing half of the sweet liquor exhaled loosely through his teeth. 'Do you know something, Tom, that play is the best thing I have ever done in my entire life. Do you remember the storyline? A man and a woman fall in love; only thing is, she's a nun.'

'I just wish you'd say what all this is about, Frank.'

Frank drained his glass. 'Tommy boy, I'm buggered. Both literally and figuratively.' Sniggering, he dipped a hand into his pocket and brought out a bunch of keys. He held the keys up, staring at them in disbelief. 'You'd better have these.'

'Your parish keys?'

Frank rose abruptly and refilled his glass. Downing it, he tilted up the bottle again for a third glass. 'You keep the old place tidy enough, Tom. Mine's been a wreck since old Mrs Lang retired.' His speech was beginning to slur. 'What's the Catholic world coming to? If I'd known at Ushaw that in my old age not only would I have to do without a curate, but a housekeeper as well, then I think I would have jacked the whole thing in and become a bishop instead.' Frank turned to face the other man with sudden bitterness. 'Oh, it's all right for you, isn't it? You've got no doubts. No rough edges. Not a hair out of place. Look at you. You even wear your Roman collar when you're drinking your cocoa. The Bishop's blue-eyed boy.'

Tom dropped his voice, unable to hide the horror in his tone. 'Have you done something, Frank?'

'You bet I have. Something so fucking big that you'd need a JCB to sweep it under the carpet.' Suddenly Frank dropped the keys. Like a slip fielder juggling for the vital wicket he snatched once and then twice, but they landed agonisingly on the ground. His glass spilled its contents over the carpet. He dropped to his knees. 'Sorry, Tom,' he said abjectly. 'I'll get a cloth.'

'Forget that,' the priest snapped. 'Just tell me what's happened.'

With a groan Frank stood up and went over to the bookshelves. 'All the same old stuff. Hold on, what's this one? Karl Rahner? What was it he said? Jesus was God because he was fully man. Something like that. Bit too unorthodox for a pillar of the establishment like you, isn't it? Living dangerously. If the Bishop found out –'

Tom suddenly flared. 'If you've just come here to insult me then you can take a hike.'

'The bull Carey. Slow to anger, but with a bloody hard punch. Good to see he's still there somewhere. You never know, you might need him one day. I remember no one would mess with you at Ushaw.'

The priest tensed his hands with exasperation. 'What do you keep on going on about seminary for?'

'Because it's all I've got left.' Frank's raw words stung them both into silence. Tom dipped a hand into his jacket pocket and fumbled with the tube of wine gums. 'We used to call ourselves the Apostles, do you remember, Tom?' Frank said at last.

'Yes.'

'Twelve of us all starting together from the same diocese. Ushaw Junior Seminary, September 1958. Now how many are left?'

'Just us two, Frank.'

'Just you now, old friend. The rest of us, we've all left, one by one. After today, they'll want me out. The twelve Apostles? What a motley crew. You're the only one who lived up to your name. St Peter. The rock; the keys of the kingdom and all that. The rest of us have all gone now, like litter in the wind. I don't even know where most of them are. Apart from Matthew. I know where he is, unfortunately. Have you been to visit him, Tom?' The priest shook his head. 'I have. It was horrible. To see him sitting there in the prison. I know he's done a terrible thing. But he was a friend. And now he's a criminal. Matthew, a sex offender. Can you believe it?'

All at once the long weariness of the day engulfed Tom. He sat down on the sofa and lifted a hand to his temple. His head had begun to pound.

'It was like going to see a leper.'

'A leper who brought it on himself.'

'No less a leper.' Frank sat down heavily beside Tom. 'I've become something of a leper myself. There's no easy way of putting it. I've been caught with a man, Tom.'

The priest took his hand from his brow. 'What?'

'I'm telling you what's happened. I was caught with a man.'

'Caught? I don't understand.'

'*With* a man. *With*, Tom, *with*. I was caught *with* a man.' Frank's eyes flared with pain then deadened. Tom could see the ashes still grey under his friend's fingernails from the distribution that morning. 'Aren't you going to say anything, Tommy boy?'

'Are you telling me that you're homosexual?'

'It happened just after I'd distributed the ashes.' Frank's voice broke momentarily. He sobbed, then managed to calm himself. He averted his gaze as though from himself as well as from Tom.

Tom's voice was small. 'I don't understand.'

'For Christ's sake, Tom, what's difficult to understand? I was caught with –'

'No, not that.'

'What then?'

Tom raised his hands in a barrier. 'This is so unexpected. I had no idea, Frank.'

'It's not the kind of thing that you talk about in homilies.'

'But I've known you since we were eleven. Am I really so unaware? All these years . . .'

'It was that interfering bitch Margaret Ellis. An evil cow if ever there was one. She came upstairs into my private quarters. Thought I should know about the new guitarist in the folk group or some such bloody nonsense. Said she came into my bedroom by mistake. By mistake, I ask you. She rang the Bishop straight away. I disgust you, don't I, Tom? There's no need to answer. You can't even look at me. Probably just as well. I've loathed myself for long enough without wanting to see your disgust. You've no idea what it's been like all these years. Always pretending to be someone else. Always hiding. I'd almost say I was glad that it had all come out, if I wasn't so shit scared. I keep on reminding myself of that play.'

'The play?'

'It's my only scrap of hope.'

'For pity's sake. What on earth can you mean?'

'I've really rattled you, haven't I?' Frank laughed sourly to himself. 'The nun thinks that she's going to eternal damnation because of her love for the man. She can't stop herself loving him, but she thinks it's going to damn her. She prays to be forgiven. Can you remember what the man says to her? *How many people ask to be forgiven for the most divine instant of their lives?* That's what he says. You see, she thinks her love has damned her, but in the end it's her moment of redemption.' A hunger filled Frank's features. 'Do you think it's true? That the moment of your damnation might really be the moment of your salvation?'

'Bloody hell, Frank!' Tom said quietly. 'I don't even know what that means.'

Frank rose and went over to the bookshelves. He seemed to be calmer. For a long time he stood there as though looking at the books, round shouldered like an ageing browser in a second-hand bookshop. 'You still don't go in for novels, do you, Tommy? Mind you, that's some travel section. There must be a book on every country in the world here.' When Frank swung round, his face was dirty with tears. 'What's going to happen to me, Old Blue Eyes?' Frank narrowed his eyes with sudden malice. 'Old Bloody Squeaky Clean. All these travel books and you've never been anywhere but Rome. And Damien, Father Damien. Your obsession with Damien. The bloody blessed Damien in the colony of the damned. And you don't even know how he got the disease in the end.'

'I know how *some* people say he got it.'

'He had sex with them. With the lepers. That's how he got it.'

'That's not true. Robert Louis Stevenson denied that –'

'Robert Louis Stevenson,' scoffed Frank.

'I don't recognise you like this, Frank.'

'And I'm supposed to apologise? You always wanted to be Damien, didn't you? Well maybe you're too perfect to be a real saint. Where's that bottle of Cointreau?'

'That won't do any good . . .'

'Don't count on it.' Getting up, Frank yanked open the cabinet and brought out the bottle. Before Frank could drink, a din suddenly filled the room; both men looked up at the ceiling. The liquid shook in the bottle, like a spirit level rocked from the true. 'Tornadoes,' said Frank. 'Flying overhead.'

'Is that what it is?' Tom asked. 'I've been hearing it a lot recently.'

'They're banking over the town. Listen: climbing and falling. Gearing up for the new Gulf War.' The noise became deafening, like the wailing of a traditional Catholic hell. Only after a long time did it begin to fade. 'Those poor bastards in Iraq. They don't know what's going to hit them.'

Weariness struck Tom like a blow. Unable to stop a yawn, he felt his chin wobble. 'My God,' whispered Frank. 'You want me to go, don't you? I came here because I had nowhere else to go, no one else to turn to, and now you –'

'I'm just tired, that's all.'

'I see. Well I won't keep you up any longer.'

'It's not like that.'

Frank grabbed the bottle by the neck and drank deeply. He stumbled over to the door. 'Actually, I'm in love.'

Tom grimaced. 'Is that what you call it?'

Frank looked at his friend sadly. 'Oh Tommy boy, did I really expect you to understand?'

Tom heard Frank's footsteps on the stairs. He picked up the bunch of keys. 'Frank, Frank!' Tom stood at the head of the stairs, the keys heavy in his hand. The slamming of the front door echoed through the presbytery.

Chapter Four

'Another sandwich, Father? Angela, give Father Tom another sandwich. Ham or tuna, Father? The tuna has sweetcorn.'

'Tuna then, Joyce, thanks.'

With both hands Angela carefully lifted the plate and held it out to the priest.

'And another cup of tea, Father?' Joyce urged. 'Tea can't hurt you in Lent. Give Father another cup of tea, Angela.'

'No, thanks.'

But Angela was already reaching for the teapot. 'Angela loves spooning in your sugars, don't you, Angela?'

'All right then.'

'Pour Father a cup of tea then, Angela,' said Joyce. Angela poured the tea slowly and exactly like a scientist conducting an experiment requiring precise volumes. 'Three sugars,' her mother smiled.

The priest glanced over at the stopped clock on the mantelpiece before surreptitiously checking his wristwatch. 'We've ten thousand pounds in the building fund now, Joyce.'

'Ten thousand pounds, isn't that amazing? What are we going to do with it, Father?'

'There's a lot of renovation needed. It's a listed building. Believe me, that ten thousand is a drop in the ocean.'

'But you've worked so hard to raise the money. Angela loved putting all the price tickets on for the fête. Didn't you, Angela? I'm telling Father that you loved putting the sticky labels on the bric-a-brac. She loved it, Father. And that Clergy Revue you did. We still laugh at Father Frank. Don't we, Angela? A wonderful actor. He's your great friend, I know. How is he?'

'He's fine, Joyce.' There was only a moment's pause before he added, 'The Bishop's sent him on a sabbatical.'

'So what's next in the pipeline?'

'How do you mean?'

'The next fundraiser, Father?'

'Let's have a look.' With almost a flourish, the priest brought out his diary. 'There's a race night in April. We should do well that evening.'

Joyce nodded. 'Just think of St Wilfrid's being 150 years old. Angela was baptised there, and so was I. My father was too. And his father before that. Of course, he was one of the bog Irish that came over in the famine. Hard times for our people. When wasn't there a famine? They all came to work in the cotton mill. They were as poor as church mice all right.' Angela reached out and touched the pom-pom on the knitted tea cosy. 'She likes doing that, don't you, Angela?' Angela nodded. 'She knit it herself, Father. That cosy. I helped her with the pom-pom, but it was all her own work. I'm telling the Father that you knitted the cosy, Angela.' Angela smiled. 'It means the world to her, you know, Father, your coming here. Even when there can't be cakes. How are the Lenten vows? I know what you're like with the sweeties.'

He reached into his jacket pocket and brought out an opened packet of wine gums. 'I'm afraid I've broken my fast already.'

Joyce reached out and covered the priest's hand with her own. 'But of course, you're without your mam this year. I'm saying a novena for her, you know.'

'Thank you.'

'I pray that through her intercession we'll get more priests. If there were more like you and Father Frank, then we'd be all right, wouldn't we? And you always so clean and smart. There's nothing like a priest in the black. Are you all right?'

'I'm just a bit tired, Joyce.'

'I always say you work too hard. There aren't many of your like. And now you without your mother. Let me see. We're two weeks into Lent so it's seven months now since Our Lord called her.'

'Yes.' Tom glanced up at the scene of the bluebell wood hanging on the nicotined wallpaper. He had never noticed before how faded the gorgeous blue of the flowers had grown.

'She went in August. Ah, but the summer is no time for a death.' She continued to stare at the priest with her imploring, hungry eyes. 'Angela, go and get me a glass of water.' Joyce watched her daughter's heavy, careful step, the tread of a circus elephant. When she was out of the room, Joyce sighed. She reached for her stick as though she wished to lever herself up on to her feet. 'I'm worried about her, Father.'

'She's fine, Joyce. Look how well she poured the tea.'

'But what happens to her after I've gone?'

'Oh you've ages yet.'

'Don't butter me, Father Tom. I know when the wick's guttering.' Grabbing her stick Joyce groped herself upright. 'What kind of life will she have? They'll put her in some institution. God knows the life she has here is nothing, but that would kill her. Could you ever make sure that there was a Catholic place for her, Father? I know there's fewer and fewer places these days but I couldn't send her away from her own.'

'I'll do my best, Joyce.'

'Will you promise though?'

'Don't worry.'

'I do worry, Father, all the time.' For a moment Joyce's face was stricken with anxiety. Her heavily wrinkled lips quivered. 'I'm like the water on a stone with the worry, drip-drip. To think of her somewhere strange and all alone. And who knows for how many years?'

'I promise,' he said simply.

'They're angels, you know. In disguise. The simple ones like our Angela, they're our guardian angels. In heaven we'll see the truth of it. She'll go straight to Our Lord's side.' Her ecstatic smile lasted until Angela came back into the room and carefully handed over the glass to her mother. 'Well done, Angela. That's great. You didn't spill a drop. Did she, Father? She didn't spill a single drop.'

'No, she didn't spill a single drop.'

The priest left at precisely quarter to five. He was almost back at the church when he realised that he had left his diary in Joyce's house. He retraced his steps through the mill cottages that clustered round St Wilfrid's, built to house the influx of Irish labour a century and a half before. A grainy light was falling over the crowded roofs.

Joyce had not locked the door behind him and having knocked loudly twice he opened it. 'I've just come back for my –' The words died on his lips as he entered the little front parlour. Angela was lying splayed on the floor as her mother tugged off a huge tea towel that served as a nappy. The priest gagged at the stench of the glistening excrement. Angela's eyes were gazing blankly at the ceiling.

Chapter Five

'Father who?'

The priest forced himself to speak louder. 'Father Tom Carey.'

'The Bishop is very busy.'

'I've got an appointment, Sister.'

The woman looked at him severely. 'You're soaking wet, Father.'

'It's pouring outside.' He tried to smile. 'It's April tomorrow and you'd think it was still the middle of winter.'

'Take a seat, Father.'

He sat down. Having nervously tested the crease on his trousers, he reached out and took one of the magazines from the low table, a copy of *The Tablet*. He leafed through the magazine, turning each page carefully so as not to crease it. An article on the recent bombing of Iraq had the headline: STARS AND STRIPES, OR KEYS OF PETER? But he could not concentrate. He glanced anxiously at his wristwatch. Piped music began to play 'Bring Flowers of the Rarest'. He shut his eyes and breathed in deeply.

'Tom, good to see you.' A loud voice boomed through the little waiting room, drowning out the hymn. Tom rose to shake hands with the man who had just entered. Despite his huge voice and huge hands, the Bishop was a small man. Large spectacles emphasised his owlish eyes. 'How are you?' The Bishop turned to the woman who was hovering by the door. 'Tea in my study please, Dymphna.'

The desk in the Bishop's study was as solid as an altar. A large crucifix hung on the wall. The many books were behind glass panels. There was a photograph of the Bishop with Pope John Paul II. The Bishop ushered the priest to one armchair and then eased himself into the other with the wooden nonchalance of a formal man making a show of informality. The priest could see the letter that he had sent the Bishop propped on his desk. 'Tom, so glad you could pop in. Tell me, how's the building fund?'

Tom forced himself to trust his voice. 'We've topped ten thousand.'

'That's good work, Tom, and all down to you. Oh, I know it's a good parish, but it takes the right man to get the juices of Christian charity flowing.' The Bishop smiled. 'Let me tell you a story. A true one, more's the pity. There's a man, who shall remain nameless, a very nice man, in many ways a fine priest, but he doesn't have a clue about money. For some reason my predecessor saw fit to give him practically the richest parish in the diocese. And he hardly gets a penny out of it.' The Bishop switched on the light with a gesture of despair. 'His collection plate is the size of St Thingumajig's in the local sink estate. Oh, I know it's not all about money and we're not talking about squeezing the pips till they squeak, but come on, Tom, you and I know we've got to live in the real world. We have to deal with the whole man.' The Bishop shifted position slightly and broke wind. 'That Clergy Revue you helped organise was brilliant. People still talk about it. A sell-out and the audience wanted more.'

A quiet but insistent knock at the door interrupted them. Instinctively the priest felt his trouser creases. His trousers were cold and wet from the rain, but his hands were hot and sweaty. Sister Dymphna backed expertly into the room with a heavily laden tray. The thick brown liquid flexed like muscle as she poured the tea. 'Milk and sugar? Do you want milk and sugar, Father Carey?'

'Milk and three sugars please, Sister.'

The nun raised an eyebrow. 'Tom's famous for his sweet tooth,' the primate explained. 'Now, Tom,' began the Bishop discreetly when the nun had withdrawn. Lifting a foot on to the opposite knee he expertly balanced his cup and saucer on the angle. 'What's all this about?' Before Tom could answer, the Bishop continued. 'The truth is, you're the last priest that I would expect a letter like this from.'

The priest spoke haltingly, knotting his heavy, moist hands. 'I'm experiencing great difficulty.'

'So you wrote. Before we start let me tell you this, Tom. After you leave me today I'm putting that letter in a drawer until after Easter; only then am I going to take it out and talk about it with you again. Lent can do strange things to a priest, and I want us to look at the matter in a cool and collected moment. Tom, let's use the rest of Lent as a breathing space.'

'The thing is, I don't think I can even last that long.'

'Oh, it can feel bad, I remember that from my days as a parish priest.'

'I've never felt like this before.' Despite all his preparation, Tom's voice cracked. 'Sometimes I don't even recognise myself.'

The Bishop glanced furtively at the priest, his owlish eyes blinking. 'Now I have to ask you this, Tom. Nothing's happened has it? I mean, that's not what's brought this on. There's nothing likely to enter the public domain?' Tom shook his head. The clinch of his hands tightened. In the Bishop's single exhalation was profound relief. He took a large, curiously loud smack of tea then leant forward to put down his cup and saucer. 'I knew it all right, Tom, but I had to ask. It's one of the things that goes with the job these days. Distasteful as it is. Then there's that business of Frank. I don't mind telling you that it's knocked us for six. I mean none of us had any idea.' The smile was belied by a piercing blink behind the glasses. 'Had he told you, Tom, about his *active* persuasion?' Tom shook his head again. 'Thank God the papers haven't got hold of it, that's all I say. We can't take another scandal. Not after Matthew. The media's not finished with us yet, not by a long chalk. And why? They hate everything we stand for, Tom. We're not part of their so-called liberal agenda. But I don't need to preach to the converted, do I? Still, I appreciate what you're going through. You and Frank go back a long way.'

'I let him down.'

'How so?'

'He came to me for help and . . . Well, now I don't even know where he is.' Tom blinked. 'I let Matthew down as well.'

'Matthew?'

'What he's done is terrible, but I should have visited him. Maybe even gone to court with him.'

'That would have been the worst thing you could have done. What would the press have made of it?'

Tom dropped his head and his voice. 'I've known him since we were eleven.'

'Tom, let's not get bogged down in this unpleasantness. Let me shoot from the hip. I've very few priests left like you. One of the old reliables. Popular too. You've kept your numbers up very well at St Wilf's. As it is the whole thing's going to come crashing down on our heads. Not enough hands for the pump. Every church wants a priest but the mathematics won't work. Then when I get someone of your calibre talking this way . . .'

The priest swallowed. 'I'm a disappointment.'

'To whom?' The Bishop's voice rose with professional indignation. 'As far as I'm concerned, you're one of the best, always have been.'

The Bishop stared at him. Out of his view, Tom's hands strengthened their grip until he could feel the pain, then they fell inert on his lap, like something strangled. 'Whenever anyone talks to me, my mind wanders; even when I'm saying Mass. I have such uncharitable thoughts.' The priest blushed with shame. 'Such disgusting thoughts. Last week I . . . This is very difficult for me. During the consecration last week, I found myself doubting.'

'We all have our moments of doubt, Tom.'

The priest shook his head. 'I'm beginning to feel a revulsion for God's world.'

'What do you mean?'

'I mean, the bits you see when you lift the stone.'

The Bishop bobbed, and dissipated his discomfort with a smile. 'Let me tell you a story, Tom. There was once a man who burned to do good, just like you. He didn't want to be any ordinary parish priest. He didn't want to be prey to the little doubts and imperfections that the rest of the world must take on as a cross. No, he wanted to burn with goodness. And do you know what happened because of this yearning? He lost touch with his people. He became *too* demanding of them. This led to his being judgemental, and eventually to his own disillusionment. He had to learn to accept his own limitations. After all, remember what we were taught at seminary. It's as much a sin to be scrupulous as to be lax. Tom, listen to me, we've got great plans for you. Look, I wasn't going to mention this yet, but we've got you marked down as a Monsignor. And that might not be the end. After all, I'm pushing seventy, Tom. I can't go on for ever; there's a salmon river in Ireland that's been calling me for years now.' The Bishop took another fond, loud slurp of his tea. 'Someone like you is what the Church needs at this time. Solid, dependable, and no skeletons in the cupboard.'

The priest's voice tremored slightly. 'I've given it a lot of thought and I just don't think I should be acting as a priest when I'm thinking all these things. It's like something's curdling in me. My parishioners deserve better than that.'

A harshness steeled the Bishop's tone. 'Think about it honestly, Tom. If you left the priesthood, where would you go, what would you do? It's all very well talking, but the reality is quite different. I have to be blunt, Tom. What could a man of your age do for himself outside his vocation? Are you not a bit too long in the tooth to be starting all over again? You're like me, I'm afraid. Good for one thing. Out there, you'd be a straw in the wind.' The Bishop bridged his fingers delicately. His tone lightened. 'We won't let it come to that. If you can hold out for a while, I'll fix you up with something. You need a change. You've been at St Wilf's for nearly ten years. There's a port chaplaincy vacancy on the River Tees. That wouldn't be too onerous. You'd get some time for yourself. You lost your mother last year, didn't you?' Tom nodded. The eyes behind the glasses grew large. 'Tom, are you fasting? It's just that I've known fasting to do funny things.'

The priest smiled bitterly. 'This year I can't even do that properly.'

With sudden energy, the Bishop went over to his desk. Turning on his computer, his hands darted over the keyboard. The printer began to churn. Out came a piece of paper. He handed it to Tom. 'It'll be a perfect stopgap for you. There's an empty presbytery close to the river as well, if my memory serves me. It might need a little renovation. It'll give you time to get a bit of perspective, almost a sabbatical. All you have to do is pop on board the ships with some phonecards, a few holy pictures, have a chat with the crew and say the odd Mass. There's a lot of Filipino seafarers. You've no idea of their thirst for the Mass. It might rejuvenate you. To be with people who really care about their religion.' The screensaver appeared on the computer; it was the ceiling of the Sistine Chapel. The Bishop studied it for a moment. 'What's your screensaver, Tom?'

'I'm sorry?'

'I always think it says so much about the man. You know, a screensaver. It comes up when the computer's idle.'

'I'm afraid I don't have one.'

'You should, they're fun. I use mine to focus. What kind of computer do you have?'

'I haven't got one.'

'I assume you're joking.' The Bishop decided to smile patronisingly. 'No mobile phone, no computer? We'll have to drag you with us into the twenty-first century, Tom. Seriously, the

Church has to use whatever technology it can. I want every parish to have its own website.' He peered at his screensaver. 'Let me tell you a story.' He levered up the height of his office chair. 'Actually it's not a story, it's my vision, if you like, a piece of history.' The Bishop paused for a moment, his hands knotted on the desk in front of him like a penitent. 'Take a parish like yours, St Wilfrid's, Tom. Think of St Wilfrid's, but it could be anywhere in this diocese. Those men who built that church arrived in England with nothing but their hands. They were the scum of the earth, Tom, the bog Irish, those at the bottom of the pile. But in ten, twenty years, they'd built the biggest bloody church in the area. And the only bloody church that people still give a toss about.' The Bishop's voice boomed through the room. He moved the chair so that his body was wedged under the desk. The penitent had become an interrogator. 'Our people, Tom, our blood. That was our strength. We harnessed the power of the oppressed. We collected all the hopes and dreams of the little people and made them into something big, something huge, something that the bastards in power had to respect. That wave is spent now. We're on our last legs. But we've got to hold firm, Tom, people like you and me. We've got to be strong. The Church in Britain is going through a period of change and it's painful. You know how it is for us these days. We're laughed at, scorned, pitied even. Hated in some quarters for certain. Because we still haven't lost that rawness that came from the bog. Because we still remind them that their material world is as shallow and cruel as ever.' His voice fell low, but still vibrated with the power of a thousand pulpits. The knot of hands untied and Tom was surprised by their spade-like size. 'That's why I carry on. The Church will be mighty again. It's up to us. This is our test, our challenge. Now, Tom, don't you feel that way too? Doesn't that just fire you up for the job?'

Chapter Six

As she unhooked her bra she caught herself smiling. Despite everything that she had done and lived for, this simple act of undressing was still hard. With her head bowed slightly, arms crossed over her chest, and her long coil of chestnut hair, flecked with one or two silver strands, resting lightly on a white shoulder, she stood on the cold surgery floor. 'Are you ready?' the doctor asked gently from the other side of the tattered curtain.

'Not yet,' she replied, trying to conceal the worry in her voice.

Lying down on the examining bed she gazed at her body. The harsh glare of the lamp seemed to draw up her ribs against the pale, downy skin. Her single breast appeared meagre and strange. Aside from this, she realised that her body was well preserved. With a sudden incongruity that made her stifle a laugh, she recalled Sister Philomena. At the convent when she was a novice, Sister Philomena, the Mother Superior, had told the young women to blindfold themselves when they were having a bath. Lying here now on the examining bed, although so many years had passed, she felt as though she was still that girl bathing blindfold in tepid water. Only the mastectomy told the truth, its scar the jagged white of a lightning strike. She shifted position and the thin paper sheet slid beneath her. Her blue tracksuit top fell from the chair and she sprang up to lift it back. The movement was lithe and caused her hair to bounce. She settled back on the bed. Into her eyes stole the look of childish anxiety that shows on faces where a smile is the normal expression. 'I'm ready, Doctor.'

The doctor avoided her eye as he conducted the examination of her remaining breast. The hardness of the tissue formed itself unforgivingly under the press of his fingers.

Her voice was calm. 'There is a lump, isn't there?'

'Well, there's something.'

'You don't have to soft soap me. I've been there before, remember.'

'It might just be a cyst, Sister.'

'A cyst?'

'It might not be malignant. We'll get it checked as soon as possible.' The doctor withdrew, his movement feathering the ragged, polyester curtain.

Left alone she stared unseeingly at her pile of clothes. Throwing up a hand to her mouth, she took a single gulp of air.

'Are you all right there, Sister?'

'Yes, yes, I'm fine.'

Waiting for the nun to come out, the doctor tried to hide his desolation in a close perusal of her medical notes, but his eyes swam. He could make out only the vague shape of the desk. The cheapness and flimsiness of it suddenly angered him. 'We can't tell anything for definite yet, Sister,' he said when the woman emerged.

'Don't hide anything.'

'I'm not. I'll refer you immediately. You shouldn't have to wait long.' As the doctor spoke, he averted his eyes, like a man sickened by the banality of his own words.

'And you don't have to call me Sister, you know, Doctor.'

'And you don't need to call me Doctor.'

'All right then, John.'

'OK, Mary-Jo.' The doctor tried to keep the smile on his face, but he could still feel the lump in her breast forming itself under his fingers; here was the dried pea of the textbooks. 'How long has it been there, Mary-Jo?'

'I only noticed it last week.' For a moment she seemed to weaken. 'It's come back, hasn't it?'

The doctor spoke softly. 'If there's anyone I know with the strength to beat it then it's you.'

'I don't feel very strong.'

'No one's saying it *has* come back yet.'

She glanced for a moment at the medical notes then took her eyes away. 'Do you think there's going to be a war, John?'

'I'm sorry?'

'Is there any way we can stop them, Bush and Blair?'

The doctor looked at the nun blankly. 'No, there probably isn't.'

When Mary-Jo had gone, the doctor sat at his desk and listened to the silence of the surgery. Nothing stirred in the waiting room. Once it had echoed with voices, but yesterday he had looked at the magazines on the table and noticed that they had not been disturbed for weeks. He had left fingerprints in a film of dust. With a throb of anger, he brought his fist down on the desk. It creaked flabbily on its thin legs. Is this what fifteen years of hard, grafting practice had brought him? A wobbly, self-assembly desk dating from the days before computers and a waiting room without a full-time receptionist.

He rose heavily to his feet and went over to the examining bed. Mechanically he peeled off the length of paper and thrust it in the bin. The impress of the nun's body could still be made out. Blowing air from his cheeks, he approached the single window. Through this could be seen the fragments of what had once been a thriving community. Beyond the remaining houses were the green miles of the marsh, and framing the marsh, the many petrochemical installations from which drifted smoke of countless colours. The acute angle of the drifting smoke showed the strength of the wind. He waited. Soon Mary-Jo would be walking past, down the deserted parade amongst whose once bustling shops the doctor had first arrived to take up a partnership in a flourishing practice. He rubbed his hands vigorously on his trousers, but the texture of the lump stuck to his fingers, like a barnacle.

Not knowing that she was being watched, Sister Mary-Jo walked down the derelict parade with her usual bouncing step. She flapped her arms in defiance of the cold March wind. Opposite the old post office, a little girl was sitting on the bonnet of a burnt-out car, the bright plastic red of her wellies showing like gaudy butterflies on the rusted, scorched vehicle. 'Sister Mary-Jo!' The child scrambled from the car and sprinted over unsteadily in her boots. Under one arm was tucked a bedraggled doll. From the surgery where the doctor watched, the girl had the look of a bird with a broken wing. He turned from the window, back to the desk on which lay the nun's medical notes.

'Why aren't you at school, Hope?'

'I was waiting for you. Are you poorly, Mary-Jo?'

Still smiling, the nun tried to admonish the girl, 'You know you've got to go to school.'

'I saw you go to Doctor Cassidy's.'

Mary-Jo took the hand nudging hers like the nose of a puppy. As they walked through the ghost township of the estate, the child skipped. Mary-Jo began to skip too. The blue of her tracksuit and the red of Hope's wellies flashed in the grey of the derelict concrete like a kingfisher. A single terrace of houses came into view. One of the houses was painted white. Slipping her hand free, Hope began to run. 'Race you!' Mary-Jo tore after her, her head thrown back with laughter.

They arrived neck and neck. 'Go and get ready for school, Hope. Tell your mum that I'll take you. You've got ten minutes. And don't forget your inhaler.'

Hope disappeared into one of the houses on the terrace; Mary-Jo stared after her. The look of anxiety she had worn in the surgery returned to her eyes. With sudden resolution, she entered the white house. 'Anne? Are you there, Anne?' There was no reply. Mary-Jo went into the kitchen and stood at the sink. Beyond the well-cultivated back garden stretched the marsh. The cattle had just been turned out of winter stalls and despite the wind the first meadow flowers were beginning to bloom. With her hands resting on the windowsill, Mary-Jo closed her eyes.

She found Anne in the garden. Following the sound of her digging, she came across her at the vegetable patch, forking manure into the earth. 'I hope that's well rotted,' grinned Mary-Jo.

Anne took another large forkful of manure from the wheelbarrow. She wore a woollen hat over her short hair. Overalls and a thick jumper flattened the contours of her round body. Red-faced, her breath came in sharp bursts. 'This is the best stuff. From your friends the cows. Have you seen they're back on the marsh?'

'I saw. It must be officially spring.'

'At last. Although it doesn't feel like it.' Anne straightened with a groan, a hand wedged in the small of her back. 'Remind me to get some cod liver oil capsules. I'm not as young as I used to be. Neither are you, although you're wearing a heck of a lot better than me.'

Mary-Jo looked at the expanse of the friable brown soil that Anne was now hoeing energetically. 'What are you planting this year, Anne?'

'The usual. Carrots, spuds, runner beans, cabbages, I thought maybe some maize.'

'That would be good.'

'Just to remind you of Africa. Some broccoli as well. But that won't be ready until the following spring.'

'So long?'

'Rome wasn't built in a day. And neither is broccoli. After ten years I think I'll have leached away the chemicals. But what the heck, the stuff you buy is laced with pesticides.'

Mary-Jo crouched down and took a handful of the soil. She

held it on the palm of her hand and closed her eyes, as though weighing something of great value. It was the soil of the marsh itself, sweetened by a decade of Anne's care. All at once, a terrible sadness dimmed Mary-Jo's sight. To counter it, she bit her tongue and then stood up. Anne was looking at her. 'And what are you smiling at, Mary-Mary-quite-contrary?'

'I'm watching how your garden grows.'

'That smile of yours. I don't know. You'd be laughing at your own funeral.'

'I hope so.'

Just then the sirens of the petrochemical plants began. The eerie wail passed from plant to plant. The two women waited, counting out the code of the weekly practice run – a sustained note followed by three swooping oscillations. 'I don't know what we'd do if it was a real leak, mind,' said Mary-Jo, turning to go back into the house. 'Nobody else counts it.'

'That's why we've got to. Mary-Jo?' Leaning on her fork, Anne studied her friend. 'What's the matter?'

Without looking back, Mary-Jo shrugged in a show of nonchalance. 'Why should anything be the matter? I just wanted to see someone do a proper day's work, that's all. So get back to it. Any news on the war?'

'Not yet.'

Mary-Jo drove Hope along the quiet road to school. They passed only a single, lumbering oil wagon. The petrochemical plants stood behind tall iron fences, their pipelines groping like the exposed roots of a petrified forest. Passing between two giant cooling towers, they reached the primary school and Mary-Jo parked. It was break time and the children were all playing outside. The nun smiled to hear the din of their play.

She was walking across the playground when the thunder began. It did not fade but grew louder. The children stopped playing. The sound quickly became a deafening scream as though the wind-washed blue sky was being ripped in two. Instinctively Mary-Jo began praying. It was the nightmare scenario, a chain reaction of explosions in the chemical works. And still the noise intensified until it became physically painful, as though the whole world was going to explode. The children looked at the nun in bewilderment. The ones nearest the classrooms shouted for the adults. Then they began to scatter, their screams inaudible under the power of the greater blare. It was Hope who saw what it was first. She pointed and those who weren't running looked up. Mary-Jo followed the finger. Instead of the drifting black clouds of a fire in the chemical works, she saw a pair of Tornado jets. They banked repeatedly, playing in the shallows of the sky, their bellies flashing shark silver when they caught the sun.

Even after the jets had passed on, their din fading, the children remained where their panic had taken them: silent, muted faces turned up, scattered over the playground like casualties. The infants' class was cowering under a wooden climbing frame. The sound of their crying carried on the wind.

Chapter Seven

'Welcome to Smith's Dock, as was.' Christy Garbutt stopped the car, a battered Peugeot 205. 'I think they call it Terminal Four now or something godforsaken like that. When I was a lad, Father Tom, this place was an anthill; men working everywhere. Look at it now.' The priest followed the doleful sweep of Christy's hand. There was not a single human in sight. Beyond the solitary Portakabin where they had stopped, acres of flat concrete spread, hardy weeds colonising where the dust had settled deep enough for roots. Huge warehouses stood empty, like giant cloches, daylight visible at their far ends. A soft rain was falling. 'They've turned it into a desert.' Christy's face looked mournful for a second, then he shrugged and broke into a wide smile. He jabbed the horn, which gave a surprisingly loud blare for so rickety a car, and jumped out.

Through the window, which was beaded with tiny drops of rain, the priest watched Christy bound over to the Portakabin. For a heavy man, he moved startlingly quickly. 'Harry!' He could hear Christy's voice calling out. 'Wakey-wakey!'

The sliding windows of the prefab were reluctantly opened and a thin face peered out blearily. A sharp smile carved itself on the woozy features when it saw Christy. The lips threw out a greeting of good-natured abuse. The priest reached into his pocket and brought out an open packet of wine gums. He ignored the black sweet at the top and took the orange one underneath. Popping it into his mouth, he glanced at his watch.

Christy beckoned. With his shoulders hunched against the rain, the priest got out of the car.

The air inside the Portakabin was so thick with cigarette smoke that it was hard to make out the CCTV images on the nest of monitors. A pot-bellied Calor gas heater fumed in the corner of the hut; standing on top of it, an old, squat kettle was growling to the boil. 'Here he is,' Christy announced, his bulk already ensconced in an old armchair. 'Our new port chaplain. Father Tom, I want you to meet a good friend of mine. Harry Hunter. He's in charge of port security . . . and cups of tea.'

'Nice to meet you, Harry.'

The diminutive Harry came over and shook hands with the priest. 'You're going to be working with this troublemaker then are you, Father?'

'Afraid so,' replied the priest, trying to reciprocate the tones of bonhomie.

'You'll have to watch him, mind. I mean I know he's sixty-five year old, but he always has been a bit of a funny bugger.'

'Hey,' growled Christy complacently, scratching his huge stomach. 'Do you mind? I'm still sixty-four.'

'How long have you been a volunteer with the Apostleship of the Sea, Christy?' the priest asked politely.

'Ever since his wife got sick of the sight of him,' laughed Harry.

'Is that kettle not boiled yet?' Christy replied.

'It switches itself off. All this will be a bit different from what you're used to, mind, Father. Christy's been telling me about the big posh parish you were in.'

A pencil of steam began to rise from the kettle. 'Sit down then, Father Tom,' Christy said. 'That's right, just throw his hat there. Mind that mug, there'll be pond life growing in it. If anything moves, hit it. So, how are you settling in at the old presbytery?'

The priest suppressed a yawn. 'I've only been there one night, Christy.'

'Bit draughty, I bet?'

'A bit.'

'And damp. It's been empty for five years. I'll send our Don round to do some jobs.' The steam from the kettle was gathering into a cloud. 'Did you sleep all right, Father?'

The priest rubbed a hand over his face. 'Not brilliantly.'

'But you did get *some* kip?'

'Yes.'

Christy's face grew abruptly serious. 'That's a relief. You haven't come across him yet then, Father Tom?'

'Who?'

Christy shook his head solemnly and, unseen by the priest, tipped a wink at Harry. A grin flashed over his fat face. 'No no, if you haven't heard him then I won't interfere.'

The priest pictured the half-derelict, late Victorian, red-brick presbytery in which he had tossed through the night on the sharp springs of an ancient bed. 'I think the kettle's boiling.'

Christy shook his head solemnly. 'I shouldn't have mentioned *him*.'

'Now don't you be frightening the Father, Christy Garbutt.'

'Ah Harry, the man has to be warned.'

Father Tom tried to feign interest but managed only a fixed half-smile. 'Warned?'

'Well, Father, some call him the Mad Monsignor.'

'The Mad Monsignor?'

'It all happened a hundred years ago. He was a high-ranking fella in the Church, but the Bishop took a dislike to him and banished him to your new home, St Bede's on Southbank. On high days and holidays he still roams the presbytery trying to get out the front door, but it's always locked. People passing by have heard him rattling the great door chain and moaning and screaming: *Not Slaggy Island, not Slaggy Island!*'

Christy and Harry laughed violently, like adolescent boys. Mixing with the cigarette smoke, the steam was now engulfing the Portakabin. Tom could hear the kettle dancing belligerently on the Calor gas heater, like an angry dog on the end of its chain. 'I think . . . the kettle's boiling,' said the priest.

'Beware,' intoned Harry, disappearing into the steam, 'of the Mad Monsignor.'

Christy and Harry burst into renewed laughter.

'I'll tell you something, mind,' Harry said ominously, his bitten features looming out of the steam like a famished will-o'-the-wisp. He was holding three mugs. 'It's not him you have to worry about round Slaggy Island these days. Tea up, lads.'

'Got any sugar?' Christy asked.

'One or two today, Christy?'

'Two, I think. After all this talk of the Mad Monsignor, we'll all need it.'

'Do you take sugar, Father?'

'Three please, if that's all right.'

Harry disappeared into the cloud again. He came back with a bottle. 'One, two,' he said, pouring some of its contents into his and Christy's mugs. He took Tom's mug. 'One, two, three.'

Christy took a gulp of the tea laced with whisky. His chubby face shaped itself into a grin. 'Hits the spot.'

'Bull's-eye,' nodded Harry. 'By God but this Fairtrade tea is the real McCoy, Christy. Sixty per cent proof.'

Smiling weakly, the priest raised the mug to his lips in a pretence of drinking. He tried a proper grin but only managed to set his chin wobbling. 'So what *do* I have to be worrying about then, Harry?'

'What, Father?'

'You said it wasn't the Mad Monsignor that I had to worry about.'

'Nothing at all, Father Tom,' chirped Christy. 'It's great having a priest on Slaggy Island again.'

'Slaggy Island?'

'It's what they call Southbank. On account of the slag heaps from the ironworks that surround the place.'

'We used to produce a third of the world's iron,' said Harry.

'*Pig* iron,' Christy corrected. 'Of course there's none of that now. It's still the best place in God's kingdom, mind. Don't listen to Harry, he can't tell his you-know-what from his elbow.'

'You'll find out what it's all about soon enough on your own, Father,' Harry winked.

Tom raised his mug half-heartedly. 'Well . . . to Slaggy Island then.'

'To Slaggy Island,' the other two agreed resoundingly.

Christy smacked his lips with satisfaction. 'And if it does get a bit hairy, Father, don't worry. I'm just round the corner. Our Don can settle most things with his fists if that girlfriend of his will let him go for two minutes.' Again the two men bellowed. The priest took a furtive sip of his drink, and could not completely hide his grimace of disgust. 'Oh yes,' said Christy. 'Father Tom, I could tell you a few things about the heyday of Slaggy Island.'

'And he will,' laughed Harry. 'He will. Here, lash the fags, will you, Christy. Do you mind if we smoke, Father? Not that we'd mind if you did.'

When they got back in the car, Christy clicked in his seat belt and turned decisively to the passenger seat. Tom winced at the sharp reek of whisky on the man's breath. 'Wonderful fella, Harry. Known him all me life. Only thing is . . .' Christy mimed the tilting of a bottle. 'Always did. Even when he was a lad getting a jug of stout from Barnacle Bill's for his old nana, he used to wet his nose. God knows what would happen if there was a real security alert. He's away with the fairies by lunchtime.' The priest looked at the huge face so close to his; it was red and glistening with what his mother would have referred to as 'grog blossoms'. Suddenly Christy's fleshy features disappeared into creases. His laughter reverberated through the car. 'Paul Newman.'

'I'm sorry?'

'I've been wondering all morning who you remind me of. And now I know. You're the double of Paul Newman. In his later films of course. *Get off your horse and drink your milk.'*

'That was John Wayne,' said the priest wearily.

'You dirty rat.'

'Jimmy Cagney.'

'Here comes that damn train again, Sir.'

'Michael Caine in *Zulu.*'

'What did Paul Newman say then?'

'Too much.'

'Well, it'll come to me. I bet you're a whizz at the pink ones.'

'The pink ones?'

'In Trivial Pursuit.'

'Trivial Pursuit? I've never played it.'

'Are you any good at pub quizzes?'

'I don't really go to pubs, Christy.'

'What do you do then?' Christy asked in genuine puzzlement. 'Bet you're a cinemagoer. I mean you must go to the pictures a lot to know all them films.'

'I suppose I did, in the old days. When I used to be a curate. Making up for lost time. You see, we weren't allowed to go to the pictures in seminary.'

'Many moons ago, eh? Where were you a curate?'

'Close to here actually. Just on the other side of the river.'

'Really? Well, I never; not St Aidan's in Chemical Alley?'

'That was it.'

'So Slaggy Island will be a breeze for you.'

'It was a long time ago, Christy.'

'There's no priest on the north bank either now. Have you been there recently?'

'I haven't.'

'Most of it's been knocked down. Mind you, there's a couple of nuns living there. Doing great work, one's a part-time teacher, the other works with the mentally handicapped in Southbank. Just near you.' Christy chuckled. 'You don't remember old Father Fitz, do you?'

'He was the PP when I was the curate.'

there was a movement in the pipe behind him. He lunged back into the darkness. An instant later Christy was thrust into the light, pinioned in a headlock. 'It's me,' Christy shouted. 'It's me.'

The man in the leather jacket scrutinised Christy, then relaxed his grip. 'Ah, Christy, my friend,' he said rather heavily.

'Captain Cargo, top of the morning to you! Sorry for sneaking up on you, but I couldn't find you. I want to introduce you to this fella.'

'Word of advice,' the captain said, looking now at the priest: 'Do not be doing this at dead of night.'

'Scout's honour,' replied Christy.

'Good,' said the sailor, still staring at the priest. 'And how are your genes today, Christy my old friend?'

'They're fine, Captain Cargo; just fine.'

Captain Cargo smiled at the priest. 'As you can see, my friend Christy and I are having many interesting conversations, especially about genes. What do you make of it?' he demanded abruptly.

'I'm sorry,' the priest replied, 'make of what?'

The man in the black leather jacket punched his own chest. 'You think it is a soul? A human being? Or just machine to carry genes. Let me be putting it this way. When aliens land on our planet what will their first question be?'

'I've never really thought about it,' said the priest.

'Where's the nearest pub?' put in Christy.

'*Have you cracked the genetic code yet?* That will be first question.' The fist, which still lay against his chest, unclenched and offered itself. As he shook hands, the priest noticed that the knuckles were raw and tattooed. 'Are you a man of science?'

'He's a man of God,' Christy explained.

'God?'

'This is the new port chaplain. Father Tom Carey.'

Taking out a packet of American Dream cigarettes, Captain Cargo did not release the hand. The priest felt the weight of the grip growing uncomfortably warm. 'A real priest, so?'

Tom managed to find a grin. 'Yes, I was real enough when I last checked in the mirror.'

The grip tightened. The captain remained serious in the face of the priest's attempted joke. 'But what about women?'

'What about them?'

'Don't you like them?'

'Yes. But as a Catholic priest I am a . . . celibate.'

'Curious. Then you are anomaly in world of genes.'

'Aren't we all?'

'How so?' the captain demanded.

'I mean isn't that the point?' The priest's hand no longer felt as though it belonged to him. It was paralysed in the grip of the other man's hand, a smaller fish in the jaws of a pike. 'Genes rely on mutations; therefore anomalies become the norm. Oh I don't know,' he faltered lamely. 'It's a bit early for all this.'

Captain Cargo stared at the priest for a little longer, then released his hand and laid a heavy arm over his shoulders. He drew him closer. 'That, my friend, I am thinking, is the mark of the seminary. The erudition is – how are you saying – aromatic. You can still smell the incense.' The arm was removed abruptly and the captain sniffed the top of the priest's head. The priest smiled weakly, like a guest overcome by the family Great Dane. With an expansive swipe of his Zippo the captain lit two American Dreams and handed one to Christy. 'And are you also playing chess, my seminarian?'

'Chess?'

'Chess.'

'I have done, in the past.'

'No, no, I mean now. The board is ready.'

'Well, it's my first day at the port. I really should be looking round. I have the Anglican chaplain to –'

'I have just finished playing myself. Not a good arrangement. Of course it means that you always win, but it is also the fact that you always lose: a teleological stalemate. But I cannot resist it. There is something so molecular about a game of chess, yes?

Its ramifications are like the unending string of the human genome, yes? Now Christy is no good as an opponent. He is too predictable. Neither can he discuss the ordinary miracles of modern genetics. Perhaps this is because he did not go to seminary.'

'Give me a game of dominoes any day,' Christy replied.

'Dominoes, agh!' A look of infinite disdain peppered the captain's features.

'Any news on when you sail?' Christy asked.

Wedged in the captain's jaw, his cigarette revealed an array of uneven teeth. His canines were as sharp as a wolf's. He blew a huge and perfect smoke ring. 'No news, Christy my friend. And in this case that happens to be bad news. What good is a seafarer in port? But in these matters we are mere drops in the great ocean of deoxyribonucleic acid.' He turned abruptly to the priest. 'You know what is deoxyribonucleic acid?'

'DNA,' the priest replied.

'The captain's been stuck here for three months now,' Christy explained.

The captain continued to stare at the priest for a while, then threw his hands up in a vigorous gesture of despair. 'Impounded. Essential maintenance required, they are saying. But who will pay for it? Mickey Mouse?' The leather of the captain's jacket crackled as he shrugged his shoulders. '*Ours is not to reason why*, as a poet once said about an insignificant war. All right, my scientific priest, I meet you in Barnacle Bill's with chessboard in an hour?'

'Good idea,' returned Christy.

'I need to have a look round first,' said the priest in a voice which he hoped hid his panic. 'The Anglican chaplain –'

'Look round, my friend, what is there to look round at?' The captain blew another immaculate smoke ring; it drifted through the light rain and over the edge of the quay. 'Once you've seen a single corner of a port, you've seen them all; same all over the world. And once you see me, you see every sailor.'

'But the ships. Really I should see some ships. I'm supposed to be the port chaplain.'

'Well, can he come on board the *Neptune*, Captain?' Christy asked. 'Your ship's just there, isn't it?'

'What a good idea, my friend Christy,' the captain said lightly. 'Unfortunately that is not possible today.'

'Why not?'

The captain's accent seemed to thicken. 'Today all busy, busy. Men swabbing decks and tarring sails as the New Englander Herman Melville might say.'

'Another day then.'

'Another day, Christy.'

The priest cleared his throat and, fighting against a sudden feeling of foolishness, forced himself to say, 'Well, if there's anything I can do, any comfort or support, for you or your crew. I mean in my capacity as port chaplain.'

'He's getting the hang already,' grinned Christy. Just then a wailing siren began to sound from the far bank of the river. The priest looked at the other men for an explanation, but neither appeared to notice it. 'By the way,' Christy continued, 'don't you think he looks like Paul Newman?'

'Better than looking like Cardinal Newman, my friend.'

'You're familiar with English Church history?'

'That surprises you, Father?'

'It just seems so unusual.'

'Believe me, when you've been stuck in a place for three months with nothing to do but contemplate the immortal coils of your DNA, then you read or watch anything that comes in your grasp. The last port chaplain lent me some books. One, as you say, was on English Church history.'

The siren stopped abruptly. The priest found himself quailing under the intense gaze of the other man. 'Well, as I say, if there's anything that I can help you with.'

'For comforts I will have to be content with chess or the girls on Babbington Road. But books, yes, bring me books, and any videos. And very soon we play chess.'

The captain walked away. When the sound of his leather

jacket had faded from earshot down the long sections of pipeline, Christy and the priest headed back to the car. The gentle rain abruptly intensified and Christy broke boyishly into a sprint. The priest lumbered after him self-consciously. It was not Christy who was breathless back in the car. 'Well, Father Tom, you've already met one of the fixtures here. Captain Cargo, or whatever his name is.'

'Quite a character.'

'Oh yes.'

'And he's really a ship's captain?'

'What were you expecting, Horatio Nelson?'

'He just looked –' The priest broke off and looked about him. 'This is the last place I'd expect someone to mention a Victorian English cardinal.' The wailing of another siren could be heard. 'What's that?'

'It's the chemical plants.'

'Why do they have sirens?'

'For a leak.'

'A leak?'

'That stuff they keep in them metal beehives is enough to make Saddam Hussein look like a ten-year-old with a chemistry set.'

'The siren goes off to alert against a leak? Forgive me if this sounds naïve, but shouldn't we be driving away at about a hundred miles an hour?'

Christy waved away his concern. 'It isn't a real leak. Just a practice. They have them all the time. No one takes any notice. If there was a real leak you'd be dead before you heard it. There, it's stopped now.'

The priest looked over the emptiness of the vast site. 'What's security like here?'

'You've met him.'

'Apart from Harry Hunter.'

'There's the bobby. Nice fella, you'll meet him.'

'Does he have much to do?'

'He picked up some asylum seekers last week.'

'Asylum seekers?'

'They come in on the boats. This lot were just walking down the main road bold as brass. Mind you, they were half frozen. They'd come from West Africa and just spent a night hiding outside. He gave them a drink and a fag each back at the centre before locking them up. I suppose for them it was like finding themselves in the Siberian taiga. Talking about security, if Saddam or Al Qaeda wanted to make a proper splash then this place is about as well prepared as a sandcastle on Saltburn beach.'

'I see.' The priest stared gloomily at the grey skies and concrete. 'Christy, what did he mean about Babbington Road?'

'That's the local red-light district.'

'But isn't that the presbytery's address, 119 Babbington Road?'

'Don't worry about it, Father. It's not anything like there is in London. Anyway, you always get a few women of the night where there's a port. Goes together like a horse and carriage. Remember, Mary Magdalene was a whore and she stayed with Jesus to the bitter end.'

'I wondered what all those cars were doing last night.'

'Cheer up, Father. After a few days you won't even notice them.' Christy's laughter rolled out as he flicked his cigarette away. It hissed in a puddle. He took the packet out and immediately lit another. 'By the by, did you see the boat moored just where we were standing? You wouldn't believe that it could float, would you? That's the *Neptune's Booty*. The captain's ship.'

'But it looked like a piece of scrap.'

'There's a lot of that goes on, Father. They call them coffin ships. Nobody knows who owns them or who makes the money from them. Nobody counts how many poor souls go down when they sink. Trade is trade, and goods must move. Come on, I'll take you on board a decent ship. He turned the engine on. The *Ocean Princess* should be in. She's a bulk carrier. You haven't seen big until you see the *Ocean Princess*. Now come on, are you going to lash them wine gums you've got stashed away?'

The moving car filled quickly with the smoke from Christy's

cigarette, which he smoked right past the filter as he chewed Tom's sweets. Discreetly the priest tried to open the window but the handle came off in his hand. He broke into a coughing fit. 'Sounds like you're a forty-a-day man, Father.'

'I assure you, I'm not.'

'Well do you want one? I don't know what they're called. We get them off the boats, duty-free. Go on, clear the tubes.'

'I don't smoke, thanks.'

'If you want to start I can get them cheap for you.'

'I think that's unlikely.'

'You never know.'

'I think I can safely say I do know. What are those ships over there?'

Christy slowed down. 'Cable-laying vessels, Father Tom. In beautiful condition, aren't they? See that giant plough and the winding gear? It can dig up to a thousand metres down. They laid the cable that brought the last soccer World Cup from South Korea to our televisions.'

'What are they doing here?'

'Waiting for new orders. See this dock? I remember when it was a forest of cranes.'

The river itself came into view, a muscular limb of grey water. On the far bank squatted the silos of the chemical terminals. They parked alongside the *Ocean Princess*. 'Some size,' grinned Christy, getting out.

'It's massive,' said the priest, stepping on to the quay, 'like a whale. Leviathan.'

'Bigger than that. I worked it out. Middlesbrough Cathedral would fit three times into the *Ocean Princess*. Here, Father Tom, a new set of vestments for you.' Taking the fluorescent bib and yellow hard hat, the priest put them on.

They walked along the dock, two tiny figures beside the immensity of the *Ocean Princess*. 'Careful, Father Tom!'

'What's the matter?'

'Watch out for that.' The priest, who had been about to step over the rope, retracted his foot. 'When the tide moves, that rope can suddenly tauten. Friend of mine, another volunteer ship visitor, parked his car over a ship's rope once.' Christy clapped his hands together. 'Flipped up like a pancake. If it can do that to a hunk of metal I'd hate to think what it could do to you, Father Tom.' Warily the priest looked up the length of the rope from the bollard to the deck. 'Look out!' With a deafening shout, Christy bundled him over the rope. 'Only joking, Father.' The priest didn't even try to smile.

Showing an agility belying his age and weight, Christy bounded up the gangway and disappeared on to the deck. With the uncertain step of one who doesn't like heights, the priest followed him. His eyes looked doggedly up the steep gradient and when the ship lurched slightly with the tide, he clutched the rope railings so hard that his tendons stood out like quills.

The ship was pristine. Its white paint was freshly applied, and there wasn't a single speck of rust on the huge double funnel. The air was thick with the smell of lubricating oil. 'Thought you'd fallen overboard,' Christy said as the priest stepped on to the deck.

'I think I can just about manage to climb up a gangplank, Christy.'

'Now don't be getting riled with me, Father. I just like to have my little joke; otherwise, what's life?'

'Should you be smoking on board? Look it says there: SAFETY FIRST, NO SMOKING.'

'Ee, you've a lot to learn, lad. Come on. The *Princess* is due to sail tonight. Bound for Colombia.' The rivets on the deck were still glistening from that morning's wash. They passed beneath a raised lifeboat. 'You won't get those on *Neptune's Booty*.'

'What do you mean?'

'They don't bother much with maintenance and safety.'

'Is that legal?'

'What's legal in the world of shipping?' Christy paused for a moment to scrutinise the priest. 'You really don't have any idea, do you?'

'No I don't.'

'So, if you don't mind me asking, why did you want this job?'

The priest paused a moment before answering. 'I just got sent.'

They stepped over the raised threshold and entered the deck-house. 'Wait a mo. Common courtesy.' Christy took out two pairs of blue plastic shoe covers from a container. Christy put on one pair and handed the other to the priest. 'Bend the back. You'll have to exercise those hamstrings, Father. If you don't mind me saying so, you seem to be rather uptight. A busy priest's life no doubt, but we don't understand the meaning of the word stress, not in comparison with the lads on these ships. Some of them are away from home for six months at a time, nine months, more than a year even. Let's find Tadeusz, he'll get us a drink.'

'A drink?' said the priest pointedly. 'I should have thought that drinking was the worst problem at sea.'

'Oh,' returned Christy airily. 'These ships are all supposed to be dry, but there's more than one way of turning water into wine.'

The priest followed Christy down intestinal corridors, up sudden stairs and past closed cabin doors. They came through a door and encountered the thick smell of cooking food. 'Hello, all,' Christy announced, going into the galley. 'And top of the morning to you, Tadeusz.'

There was a volley of replies in thick, east European accents. 'Hello, Chrusty. How are you? Good to see you.'

From where he stood awkwardly by a stack of cutlery, the priest heard Christy saying, 'You all right, Tadeusz; your family all well? And you, Karol, still not proposed to that girl yet?'

'Soon, Chrusty, soon.'

The conversation fell out of the priest's earshot until he heard, 'Are you coming in then, Father Tom? Don't be backward in coming forward; shy bairns get nowt.' The priest came into the galley just as Christy was emptying a glass. There was a bottle of cognac on the metal kitchen surface. 'Father Tom, this is Tadeusz and this is Karol.' The men wiped their hands on their blue-checked catering trousers. The priest tried to hide the wince that came involuntarily under the strength of their handshakes. Both men's forearms were the size of a thigh.

'You say Mass for us, Father Tom?'

'A Mass?' The priest stepped back.

Tadeusz nodded vigorously, shaking his sharp knife in emphasis. 'A Mass.'

'A Mass?' put in Christy. 'Of course he'll say a Mass.'

'But I haven't got my suitcase. You know, with the Mass vessels in. The chalice, the –'

'Oh,' said Christy airily. 'We'll be able to cobble something together for you. You can't stand on ceremony now, Father Tom.'

'But will the crew have time? I understand crews are very busy.'

Tadeusz spat into one of the gleaming stainless-steel sinks. 'They are Croats, but even they will want a Mass.' He stepped a little closer to the priest, waving the knife. 'Just don't expect us to make the sign of the peace.'

'There's a bit of an international situation here,' chuckled Christy. 'The Poles and the Croats don't exactly get on.'

Suddenly many voices sounded out from down one of the corridors. The voices came close and then rose suddenly and dangerously, as though in violence. 'The zoo is open,' Tadeusz announced. The swish of his knife startled the priest, who stood there watching the cook as he cut a huge carrot, the pieces rolling free in a blurring rapidity.

'Go on then, Father Tom,' said Christy. 'Go and introduce yourself to the zoo. They're in that room there.'

'What about you?'

'There's something I need to discuss with Tadeusz.'

As the priest walked slowly from the kitchen he heard the

chink of glass on glass. 'Father Tom?' Karol had followed. 'The Croats, they are pigs, really, not proper Catholics. We call them "the Muslims".' Karol tittered. 'Especially when we want to annoy them.' A tall figure with wolf-grey eyes walked past. 'Animals!' Karol hissed. 'Your father did it like a dog with your mother.' He smiled at the priest. 'Don't worry, most of them don't speak English. Do you, you ignorant mullah-baboon?' A Croatian oath was tossed back with a nonchalant shrug of the shoulders as the tall figure slouched into the room indicated by Christy.

The priest followed the Croatian to a packed room where tinny-sounding accordion music blared out over the groans of what sounded like a woman running. The priest stood tentatively on the threshold, coughing with the brackish tobacco smoke. Instinctively, he ran his fingers down the creases on his trousers, but seeing the general unkempt state of the men, he lifted his hands away. He looked at the television. On the screen two women were fondling each other's massive breasts. He was about to back out when Christy appeared behind him, blocking his way. He had to shout to be heard over the film soundtrack. 'Have you introduced yourself to the captain yet, Father Tom?'

The priest looked around the group of men in despair. Suddenly the sound of the video was muted and a radio was turned on. Every single member of the crew sat upright and began to concentrate on a Croatian voice. 'They're listening to the currency reports,' Christy told him. On the screen the two women were now bouncing with silent anatomical abandon as the crew and officers followed the radio with painful intensity. There was a howl of despair from the gathering, and the faces of the men grew murderous. 'Oh dear,' said Christy, 'bad news. They get paid in dollars. A tiny difference in the exchange rate can make a massive difference. I've seen men lose a thousand dollars in a matter of seconds.' The priest turned to say something. 'What?' said Christy. The priest tried again. But the howling of the men was still too loud.

Tom shouted in Christy's ear, 'I don't really think that this is the time or the place for a Mass.'

'Why not?'

'Well –'

Christy looked at the television screen. 'There's no room to be squeamish, Father. These men are far from home. They've got the needs of the body as well as the soul. Only, don't take too long about it, Father, they've got to get back to work, and we've got to visit the *Shanghai Queen*. Captain Chow wants to meet you. You'll love him, a proper gentleman. He'll insist on us staying for dinner. Have you ever had rice wine?'

It was already getting dark when the Peugeot 205 drove off the port. Having skirted a flattened wasteland on which tethered ponies grazed, they mounted a bridge over a fan of railway lines. 'You are now entering Slaggy Island,' Christy announced, holding his nose, 'please get all passports ready.' They wove a tight, winding way through narrow cobbled streets, on which many houses were boarded up. Passing a pub, which stood alone in a rubble of dereliction, they ran alongside a viaduct. 'Babbington Road,' said Christy. In the arches of the viaduct stood shadowy figures, who emerged at the approach of the car, only to recede again as it passed.

'Are those the –?' the priest asked.

Christy nodded. 'Ladies of the night.'

The viaduct gave way to a terrace. Amongst the row of derelict, boarded-up houses was the austere, red-brick presbytery. Pulling up, Christy's tyres grated on fragments of broken glass. 'Right, I'll be round for you at seven-thirty, Father.'

'Seven-thirty?'

'To take you to Barnacle Bill's. We passed it just before the viaduct. Lots of the crews go there. Captain Cargo might be there.'

'I might pass on that if that's all right.'

Christy's features creased with puzzlement. 'What do you mean?'

'Look, Christy, I'm not really the pub sort.'

'What do you do at night then?'

'Read mainly, pray of course. And I'm a bit tired tonight. First day of the new job and all that.'

'Well, have a rest first and I'll pop in about nine.'

'No. I'll see you tomorrow, Christy. And thanks for showing me round.'

'Did you enjoy it, Father Tom?'

'It was a real eye-opener.'

'And are you sure you don't want to come for your tea at ours? Our Pam makes a great shepherd's pie.'

'What we picked up at the Co-op will do for tonight.'

Christy rolled down his window and threw his cigarette end out. 'That's not a proper meal. I tell you what. I'll send our Don round with a portion.'

'I'm OK, really. See you tomorrow, Christy, and thanks.'

The priest got out of the car. He stared up at the presbytery. It loomed over him like a cliff with no footholds. Taking the key from his pocket, he forced himself up the three worn steps to the front door.

Inside, enclosed in darkness, his hand groped the wall. The click of the switch echoed in the hall; the light revealed the black and white tiles of the tessellated floor on which he stood. Motes of dust swam about the bulb. The air was damp and musty with neglect. The priest was aware of a profound silence.

The sharp honking of a car horn shredded the stillness. He opened the front door. 'Don't forget,' Christy shouted from his car. 'Look out for the Mad Monsignor!' Laughing uproariously, he drove away.

The bulbs on both landings of St Bede's presbytery were dead and the two flights of stairs the priest mounted were a narrowing tunnel of darkness. He had chosen the attic as his bedroom because it was the only room with a working light. The ceiling sloped down to a desk standing in a window well. Emptying his carrier bag, he placed the objects on the desk: a tin of tomato soup, a loaf of bread, a carton of milk, a jar of jam and three tubes of wine gums. Through the uncurtained window, half-lit by the intermittent street lamps, he could see the length of the quiet, cobbled road give way to the viaduct. Beyond the arches of the viaduct he could just make out Barnacle Bill's. The presbytery appeared to be the only inhabited building on Babbington Road. There was a loud rumbling; a goods train was labouring over the viaduct.

Foraging through the dark rooms, the priest brought back an old electric fire. The dust on the bars wreathed up in a thick, choking smoke. He began to unpack his books, meticulously dusting each one before placing it on the bookcase he had lugged up from downstairs. When he had filled the shelves and eaten a lukewarm bowl of soup heated in the musty candlelight of the kitchen, he emptied the battered suitcase: Mass vessels, two identical black suits, four black shirts with four collars, and underwear. Then he sat on his narrow bed, propped up against the ancient headboard with three uncovered pillows stained sepia with sweat, and began to read. From time to time his fingers caressed the pages of *Damien the Leper* as though they were letters from a loved one. Imperceptibly, the evening deepened beyond the window to raw night. The street lamp opposite his bedroom began to flash. His head began to nod.

The priest woke with a jolt. A worm of saliva slithered from between his lips and dropped on to his book, which lay against his chest. A bell had been ringing in his dreams. It sounded again. A car drove by, then another; voices drifted from the street. Shaking sleep from his head, he descended the stairs. The bell now sounded out without a break, its old-fashioned clang echoing in the empty presbytery.

Crossing the hall, the priest put the door on the chain and then opened it. Through the crack in the door he could see an arm extended to the bell. There was a foul eddy of stale sweat and urine. 'Hello?' There was no reply. The arm remained extended. The bell continued to ring out, its sound the weary shaking of chains. 'Who is it?' Craning through the narrow gap, the priest caught a glimpse of a thickly-tangled rufous beard. A single small, pig-like eye loomed at him. He stepped back in shock. The ringing stopped. The eye continued to bore through the gap for a moment and then the figure backed down the front steps. The priest could see that his vagrant caller was wearing a thick tweed coat and slippers. His beard was flaming red; the socket of his other eye was a little tumour of dead skin. 'What do you want?' he called. A finger and thumb, yellowed with nicotine, smoothed the beard in a gesture of pondering. The single eye blinked then averted itself. As though cowed, the caller walked away, his blistered heels revealed by the loose fit of the slippers. The chain played a brass glissando as it fell from the lock and the priest opened the door. A car sped by. He watched it slow down at the viaduct. A woman in a miniskirt came out from one of the arches and the passenger door opened for her. She got in and the car sped away. When the priest looked back down the road, the vagrant had gone. He locked the door and carefully applied the chain before trudging back upstairs.

Standing in the window well, his hands resting on the flaking wooden sill, he watched the cars come and go, the women flickering out from the arches. The doorbell rang again. It rang for five minutes then stopped. Down below he saw the figure of the red bearded man, standing on the cobbles beneath the broken street light. The priest did not go downstairs. The vagrant shambled away. The priest stumbled over to the bed and fell to his knees. For a whole minute he tried to pray. When he rose, he calmly took up his copy of *Damien the Leper* and sat on the bed, his back resting against the ancient headboard.

Chapter Eight

When the doorbell rang out again after a long lull, the priest leapt from the bed. With a great grunt of exasperation he managed to yank up one of the sash windows. 'Look, just go away, will you?' he shouted down.

'Is that any way to greet a fellow Apostle?'

'What?'

'Who are you telling to go away?'

'Frank, is that you?'

'Yes, but it's not you by the sound of it, Tom. I can't remember the last time I heard you so het up.'

The priest ran carefully down the darkness of the unfamiliar stairs. 'I'm so glad to see you, Frank. Sorry about the greeting, but someone's been ringing that bell all night.'

'What the hell are you doing here, Tom? There's women selling themselves down the road.'

'Where have you been, Frank?'

'Oh, here and there.'

'Please, come upstairs.'

'Now there's an offer.' Frank followed Tom as they groped up the stairs. 'I thought they'd shut this place down years ago. Is there a black-out or something?'

'Not much works in St Bede's, I'm afraid.'

'I don't suppose I could borrow a bath.'

'If you can heat the water you can have as many baths as you want.' Tom set a wooden chair by the desk in the window well. 'Look, Frank, about that night when you came –'

'Oh, forget it. I didn't exactly choose my moment.'

'No, Frank, I should have . . . I . . . Look, I'm so sorry. I wasn't . . .' He broke off. 'It's just so good to see you. But how did you know I was here?'

'Bush telegraph. Priests can never hide. Who's your friend with the flaming beard by the way?'

'I don't know.'

'Whoever he is, he's watching this house.'

'It's him that's been ringing the bell all night.' Tom stared out the window. The vagrant was standing below the flashing street lamp staring up at the presbytery. 'Maybe it's the Mad Monsignor.'

'What?'

'Oh nothing.' Tom looked at his friend's creased clothes. 'How have you been keeping, Frank?'

'I almost believe you're worried, Tom.'

'Of course I am.'

'Even though I'm "one of those".'

'Frank . . . I didn't know whether I'd see you again.'

'And would that have bothered you, Tommy boy?'

'Yes,' said Tom simply. 'You're my best friend.'

'What's this? St Peter growing sentimental?'

There were black bags beneath Frank's red-rimmed eyes. The priest saw his friend eyeing the four items of food. 'Sit down, Frank, I'll get you something to eat.'

'A room with a view, eh? All you need are a few junkies shooting up and you've got the whole set.'

'This is all I've got; to eat I mean.'

'Jam sandwiches? Thanks, Tommy boy, just like the old days.' Frank smiled. 'I'll always remember the first time I saw you, Tom. It was the first day at Ushaw. We were eleven years old. You'd come on the train with the others. I came in the car with my parents. I'd been crying. Everyone else was already in the ref. *Don't worry*, you said to me, *they've got jam here*. You said it as if it meant that everything was going to be all right.

I can't tell you how much it helped me. *They've got jam here.*'

'And I got punished for talking.'

'Oh yes, breaking the *magnum silencium*. Your one and only punishment at seminary.' Frank sat on the bed, his weariness showing in the stiffness of the movement. 'Where is she then?'

The priest looked up from the jam sandwiches he was making. 'What?'

'Your breviary.'

'Oh, I've still got a couple of boxes to open.'

'Tsk-tsk, Tommy; a cardboard box is no place for the old trouble and strife. And you haven't put your picture up yet either.'

'Eat your jam sandwiches and shut up, will you, Frank?'

Frank ate his jam sandwich in two bites then stood up. 'Ah, here it is,' he declared, picking up a flat object leaning against the wall. It was wrapped in brown paper. Frank undid the knot tied neatly with a string. 'Dead centre.'

'What?'

'Your knot. It's dead centre.' Frank took off the brown paper to reveal a framed picture. It was the print that had hung in St Wilfrid's presbytery: *The Return of the Prodigal Son* by Rembrandt. 'Your only possession,' said Frank. 'Along with your books of course.' He held it up to the light. Out of the painted shadows and the half-lights, watched over by his brother, the squandering son emerged to kneel under his forgiving father's blessing.

'I've had it for thirty years,' said Tom. 'It was an ordination present from my parents.'

'Thirty years, eh? Shall we have a joint party?' Frank tilted the picture slightly so that the rich russet of the forgiving father's robe seemed to shimmer and the contrite son was transfigured in a bright light. Then he looked at his friend. 'What on earth are you doing here, Tom?'

'The Bishop sent me. The thing is, Frank, I . . .' Tom cleared his throat. 'I asked him for a rest.'

'A rest?'

'Yes, I'm here to have a rest. You see, I've been tired.'
'Why?'
'Nothing very dramatic.'
'Don't tell me, you've been caught in bed without your breviary.'
'I'm glad you haven't lost your sense of humour.'
'That's the good thing about losing everything. You get to keep what really matters. But what is it, Tom? It must be something pretty big for you to give up your parish. Are you all right?'
'Yes, it's nothing really.'
'You're not ill?' Tom shook his head. 'What did the Bishop say?'
'It was horrible, Frank. Having to sit there and tell him.'
'Tell him what?'
'I'm losing my faith, Frank.'
'What?' asked Frank in astonishment.
'But it's more than that.'
'What do you mean?'
'It's so hard to describe. When I think of God and the world, then I feel a kind of revulsion. That night when you came to me, you said you didn't want to see my disgust, but that's all I seem to have left.'
Frank stared at his friend. 'How long's this been going on?'
'I don't know. I thought that with Lent I could get through it somehow, get back to how I was. Then I thought by coming here it might help, but already . . . you see, I've been running on empty for a long, long time.'
'You've never mentioned it before. What is it that sparked it all off?'
'I'd rather not talk about it, Frank.'
Both men gazed at the picture again. It was Frank who broke the silence. 'I suppose we're all like the prodigal, aren't we? Longing for unconditional love whilst demanding our inheritance.'

'Are we? I think maybe I might be the brother who remained at home.'

'Yes,' nodded Frank. 'I think that one probably is you. Look at him watching his father welcoming his brother back. You can almost see the white knuckles in the way he's gripping that stick. It looks as though he wants to start laying into them both. Is that how you feel, Tom?'

The bell rang again, its continuous, strident cry echoing up the stairs. Putting the picture down, Frank went to the window. 'It's your friend downstairs, Rip Van Winkle. What are you going to do about him?'

'He'll stop in a minute. Tomorrow I'll see about disconnecting the bell.'

'Have you got any more of that Cointreau of yours, Tom?'

'All I've got you can see here.' Tom swept his hand over the groceries and the tubes of wine gums. 'Not forgetting the prostitutes and a wino lurking at the door, of course.'

Both men began to laugh. When they had sobered they realised that the bell was no longer ringing. They made more sandwiches, ladling the jam on thickly then spreading it with a teaspoon. 'Is there anywhere to go for a drink round here, Tommy boy?'

'At this hour?'

'It's only half ten.'

'Well there's Barnacle Bill's.'

'Are you joking?'

'It's popular with sailors.'

Frank giggled. 'Sounds good to me. Let's go and get a drink.'

'I don't really feel like it.'

'You may not feel like it but I would say you need it.'

'If you must know there are some people from the port who are there and I just don't have it in my heart to see them.'

'I'll tell you what, I'll get a carry-out. Bring back a bottle. Christen the presbytery. A house-warming gift.'

'All right. But if a big bloke with a cigarette in his mouth asks you where you've come from, don't say here. And if a Russian sea captain starts talking to you about genes then run a mile.'

'Jeans?'

'It's a long story and look out for the –'

'The prostitutes? Don't worry, they've got nothing to worry about with me.'

Standing alone in the bedroom, Tom listened to the cars cruising past the viaduct. It was getting busier. From somewhere close by, a bass voice began to moan in the tuneless cantata of loveless sex. As he waited for Frank, he studied the picture of the prodigal son.

Frank reappeared about a quarter of an hour later with a bottle of amber liquid. 'I'd like to introduce you to a friend of mine, Tom. A fellow by the name of Jameson. But how did you know those two blokes would be there? Barnacle Bill's is a dive. Clearly the haunt of criminals. Oh, and by the by, it might interest you to know that there's a man being wanked off by a prostitute in the church doorway.' He took a drink from the bottle of whiskey and held it out. 'Stand up for yourself. Tell the Bishop to move you somewhere more human. Let alone the sex, this place is more like a mausoleum than a presbytery.'

'It was me that left my parish.'

'But you didn't ask to come to a red-light district. Bit late for a Lenten challenge, isn't it? Or are you really going to start trying to emulate the Blessed Damien at last? Well, I suppose there's plenty of lepers for you to befriend round here.' Frank held his arms out wide. 'Me, the bearded wonder downstairs and the whores . . .'

'Don't, Frank.' The priest lifted the bottle of Jameson's, and with the stilted poise of a non-drinker, tilted the bottle back. He swallowed, grimacing.

'Go easy, Tom. It's not lemonade. You don't want to overdo it.'

'That's just it. I don't know what I want to do any more, Frank.'

They drank without speaking, passing the bottle to and fro. A goods train lumbered over the viaduct, setting the glass in the window well shimmering. 'I've done something terrible,' Frank said at last. 'No, not what you're thinking. Something else. Perhaps even something worse.' He turned from the window abruptly. 'I've broken the seal, Tom.'

'What?'

'The seal of confession.'

'The seal of confession?'

'I thought that would shock you. I seem to be making a habit of that recently.'

Frank held out the bottle. Shaking his head numbly, Tom sat on his bed. He exhaled heavily. Frank watched him for a while. 'I'll understand if you'd rather I didn't tell you the details.' The priest did not reply. Frank wandered back to the window well. 'There's ten women down there. Not exactly dressed for an April night. They must be freezing. I wonder how –'

'How could you, Frank?'

'Ah.'

'The seal of confession is a sacred bond –'

'I know, I know, the gift and burden of the priesthood.'

'We're supposed to die rather than break it.'

'You think I don't know that!'

'You obviously didn't!' Tom's loud voice echoed in the sparsely furnished attic room.

'Do you want me to go?'

Reaching up, Frank gently probed where the slope brought the ceiling into his reach. 'Do you remember all the examples they shoved down our throats at Ushaw, Tom? Someone confesses that they've poisoned the altar wine and you've still got to drink it or try and persuade –'

Tom's voice was a murmur. 'You've broken the seal.'

The amber eye of the whiskey winked as Frank upended the bottle. The liquid had fallen halfway down the label. 'It was because of Matthew.'

'Matthew?'

'Do you mind if I tell you?' Frank grinned humourlessly. 'It's been eating away at me.' Tom did not reply. Frank drank deeply. 'Tom, he came to me in confession and said that he'd been downloading things from the Internet. You know, porn. Those pictures of children. He was in a real state.'

'I don't want to know,' Tom whispered.

'There was a wildness in him. I was terrified he might go on and do something worse so I told him to go to the Bishop.'

'Frank, no –'

Frank laughed bitterly. 'The Bishop. I suppose I still subscribed to it all then. I told him that there were treatment programmes he could go on. The important thing was to get him away from where he might . . . get him away from children. He laughed in my face. It was so frightening. So I said that if he didn't go then I would have to inform on him.' Frank closed his eyes. 'He pleaded with me. Then when that didn't work he said he'd implicate me. Tom, he threatened to take me down with him. *Shit sticks*, he said, *and since you're a bender anyway it'll turn you into a walking sewer*.' Frank shuddered as he drank. 'This was a friend of mine once. If ever I come to doubt the existence of God, I'll be slower to doubt the existence of the devil. You see, I've seen hell. Go on then, Tom. Tell me how much you despise me now. But what would you have done? Come on, I've never known you without an answer. What would you have done?'

'I don't know.'

'You don't know?'

'No, I don't know.'

'How the fuck was I supposed to know then?' After the shouting, the sudden clanging of the doorbell seemed almost harmonious. 'They never gave us that example at seminary, did they, Tommy?'

'No, they didn't.'

'He got two years in prison. Because of me.'

'Not because of you.' Tom looked at Frank. 'We used to hold

the keys of the Kingdom, Frank,' he whispered. 'And now look at us.'

'I went to visit him inside, you know. I couldn't believe he agreed to see me. Turns out that no one else would visit him. Oh, I don't blame you for not going. We're all scared, Tom, these days, the innocent as well as the guilty. I reminded him about the play.'

'The play?'

'The one we did at seminary. *How many people ask to be forgiven for the most divine instant of their lives?*'

'How did he take that?'

Frank lifted the bottle. 'Fuck knows. I don't even know what I meant.'

The bell stopped ringing. In the silence that followed, an argument between one of the women and a client raged outside. A car door was slammed and it sped away to a throttle of engine and female abuse. 'Give me that bottle, Frank.'

'You'll have a sore head in the morning.'

'It's my turn to confess.'

'How do you mean?'

'Do you really think that I've been the perfect parish priest all these years?'

'Do you want me to answer that honestly? Then yes, I do. That's why I can't believe you're here.'

Tom no longer grimaced as he swigged the spirits. 'It must have happened about twenty years ago, and I've never told a soul.'

'Look, Tom, don't . . . I mean don't if you don't want to. We've both had a lot to drink. In vino veritas maybe, but there's such a thing as proper reserve.'

'What's the matter, are my sins not good enough for you?' Tom stood up and, going over to the window well, stared out at the road. As he spoke his face flashed orange with the faulty street light. He took a deep breath. 'One evening I took off my Roman collar and suit, put on a pair of jeans and went to a pub.'

'I thought you were going to say nightclub.'

'I was on retreat in Wales. At St Beuno's. Anyway, I began talking to a woman at the bar.'

'Never.'

'Look, Frank, be serious.'

'I am.'

The throbbing rumour of a goods train rumbled along the viaduct, sparks flickering from wheels groaning on the track. The glass in the rotten frame of the window well shook slightly again. 'We talked all night. It turned out that she was this divorcee. She was a loose woman, I suppose. Anyone's for the price of a few drinks and a bit of sympathy. But I liked her. I mean, something about her touched me. She was big-hearted. I listened to her. Then I started telling her about myself.'

'What did you tell her?'

'Nothing true of course.'

'Of course, there's other ways of observing the *magnum silencium* than just keeping your mouth shut.'

'I told her . . . I told her that my wife had jilted me on our wedding day.'

'Tom!'

'It was out before I could stop myself.'

'What did she say to *that*?'

Tom shrugged. The long goods train evaporated; the pane of glass fell still. 'A whole world of possibilities seemed to open up, Frank. She was just a normal woman, but to me what she promised was something completely extraordinary. She was like some kind of bird of passage, a visitor from a different continent. Just before closing time, she went, I don't know, to powder her nose or something. We'd agreed to go on to a club she knew.'

'What happened?'

'I left before she came back.'

'Why?'

'The truth is, I'm a coward to the marrow of my soul. That's the real mainspring of my morality. That's the really disgusting thing. I was too frightened to sleep with her, that's all. What's the matter?'

'I'm just trying to picture you in a pair of jeans and trainers.'

Tom stared at Frank. 'Actually I Brylcreemed my hair as well.' The two friends began to chuckle. 'Oh yes and she said that she could drown in my blue eyes.' The chuckles became louder and louder until they were helpless. Tom was still shaking with hilarity as he took the bottle and drank. 'Look, Frank, why don't you stay here for a while? Until you find your feet. There's loads of space. I mean, it was built for a priest, at least two curates and a housekeeper. There's a kitchen table big enough for the Last Supper. Have a whole floor if you want. Have the bloody west wing.'

Another car revved on the road outside. There was a cacophony of bickering voices. The bell began to ring.

Frank tittered. 'Not much in the way of the *magnum silencium* round here is there? Still, you don't want quiet. We've both had quiet all our lives. Time enough for being quiet when the spade digs in soil over your head. Tom, I can't accept your offer.'

'Why not?'

'Think about it when you're sober. Your reputation. What will people say?'

'I think I've cared too long what people say.'

Finding a hook on the wall, Tom hung the print of *The Return of the Prodigal Son*. He straightened it exactly, and then standing back, gazed at its shadows and light. The bell sounded out through the rambling presbytery, like an unanswered petition.

Chapter Nine

The flowers of Pentecost were blooming on the marsh. It was the first hot day of the year and the blue sky stretched above the salt pasture, an ocean without a single island. Beneath the lone line of ancient hawthorns, white with may blossom, the herd of cows was sheltering. A kestrel hung high above, like a kite flown by a child. From where she stood in the garden, Anne could just make out the figure of Mary-Jo. Her cotton dress was as blue as the sky. The nun was not alone. She was on the marsh with a slightly stooping figure. The figure appeared to be remonstrating with Mary-Jo, then they separated. Anne only recognised who it was when he neared the house.

'Hello, Doctor.'

'Hello, Sister Anne.'

'Nice day for it.'

'It is.'

'Been having a walk?'

The doctor laughed uneasily. 'I suppose I have.'

'No patients this morning?'

'I've got so few patients that the surgery is almost run-down now. I'm doing three full days over at the port.'

'Is Mary-Jo OK?'

'I'm sorry?'

'I just thought I saw the two of you chatting there on the marsh.'

There was a momentary pause before the doctor replied, 'I was just telling her about the latest findings. You know, the research on the pollution. It arrived today. We've got a meeting with Friends of the Earth. We might just call the chemical companies to book this time.'

Anne gazed piercingly at the doctor and then shook her head. 'You'll never get them to admit anything.'

'We can't give up.'

'There's too much pussyfooting about. Between you, Mary-Jo and Friends of the Earth, you've been playing grandmother's footsteps with those sharks for five years now, and what have you ever achieved?'

'I'm surprised, Sister Anne. I would have thought that your religion counsels faith.'

'In this case I think it counsels a whip and one hell of a temper.'

When the doctor had gone, Anne walked over the marsh towards her friend, a blue figure in the green of the meadows. A shimmer of gold seemed to shine around her. It was the buttercups caught in the heat haze.

Mary-Jo was gazing up at the kestrel. Anne watched her for a while before speaking. Her voice was soft. 'What did the doctor want, Mary-Jo? I saw you talking.'

'I didn't know that our Order still had a rule against talking with men, Sister Anne.'

The kestrel dropped lower so that they could see the slight breeze ruffling its feathers, its sharp eyes roving. Mary-Jo cleared her throat; her voice was a monotone. 'Well, the cancer's come back.'

'What do you mean come back?'

'There's a lump in the other breast.'

'Has the doctor referred you to a consultant?' Anne spoke decisively, without apparent emotion.

'I've done all of that, Anne. The results have just come back.'

Like someone settling down at a picnic, Anne sat down in the long grass. She whispered something to herself.

'Anne?'

'Yes?'

'I've decided something. This time I'm not having any treatment.'

'What do you mean?'

'I mean, I'm not going through it all again.'

'Don't be ridiculous,' Anne's voice cut through the heat stridently. Then by a massive dint of will, she calmed herself. 'Are you saying it's inoperable, Mary-Jo?'

'I don't know.'

'I don't understand, Mary-Jo.'

Still Mary-Jo spoke without tone. 'I couldn't face it a second time, Anne, the operation, the chemotherapy; and for what? To find out that it's spread to my bones, my lungs? I mean, it's probably already there.'

Anne's voice broke. 'So you're just going to die, is that it?'

'Yes,' whispered Mary-Jo. 'I'm just going to die.'

For a moment Anne's nerve deserted her. She raised a hand to her mouth and gnawed at a knuckle. 'I thought you were a fighter, Mary-Jo. I thought you never gave up. I thought you never said –' The word died on Anne's lips. The kestrel swooped.

'Anne, listen to me.' Mary-Jo came over and sat by her friend in the long grass. 'I watched my mother die. Anne, surely you understand that I can't want . . . Hey, don't cry. Please, don't cry.' Mary-Jo took her friend's hand. 'We all have to go some day. You nursed with me at Nazareth House. How many people did we see die there all alone, old and lonely? I've got you to be with me, all the other Sisters. Our neighbours, little Hope next door.'

'But what about . . . the pain?'

As Mary-Jo looked away a single tear exploded on a buttercup. She did not know whether it was her own or Anne's. 'Anne, we have to think of all the good days left. The doctor says that I could have months.'

'Months?' The word was a choke. 'You could have years if you have treatment.'

'I'll have the spring and the summer. And only feel pain near the end. No, Anne, you mustn't cry. I've lived with the fear that this might happen for a long time. And now I feel relief.' Mary-Jo broke off as though in amazement. A small blue butterfly meandered by; landing for a while on a flower close by, it spread its tiny wings. 'Look,' whispered Mary-Jo to herself. 'Look.'

Chapter Ten

A knock on his door summoned Tom from sleep. For a while he lay disorientated, the darkness splashed with a lurid orange from the faulty street lamp. Then he recognised Frank's voice on the other side of the door. 'There's someone wanting to talk to you, Tom.'

The priest groped for the wristwatch on his bedside table. He looked at the luminous hands. 'It's four o'clock in the morning.'

'Says he wants the port chaplain. Someone from a ship; some kind of foreigner, definitely not British.'

'And he's at the front door?'

'No, he's on the telephone.'

'I didn't even know we had one.'

'It's downstairs, in the west wing, so to speak. The parish room. I had to take it out of a drawer. Hurry up, Tom, it sounds like an emergency.'

The priest shivered as his feet touched the ground. With his suit jacket over his pyjamas, he descended the stairs, guiding his way with a torch. 'I thought you were going to get some more bulbs,' he snapped at Frank.

'You always were a bad-tempered so-and-so after midnight, Tom. I used to dread the Easter Vigil with you when we were curates with old Fitz over in Chemical Alley. I thought you were going to punch me once.'

'Don't be ridiculous.'

Tom picked up the telephone, an old black model with a

dial. 'Hello? Yes, this is Father Tom Carey. That's right, the port chaplain.' Tom yawned. The torch, held loosely in his hand, picked out a picture on the wall. It was a black and white photograph of an old priest in a biretta and cassock; his austere features glared down. 'Sorry, it's a poor line. You're cutting up. Yes, yes, I'm a Catholic priest. Have you any idea what time it is? Are you having me on? You ring me up at this time just to tell me that you want me to say a Mass?' Putting down the torch, he brought out the diary from his jacket pocket. He calmed himself and spoke slowly. 'Go on then, you might as well tell me now.' Taking the pencil from its spine, he began to write. 'All right, I'll be there.' The caller rang off, leaving the priest with the void that follows the cutting of a phone line.

'Nothing serious?' Frank asked, coming into the parish room.

'Someone wanting a Mass.'

'At this time of night?'

'I'm afraid I was a bit abrupt with him.'

'What did he expect, ringing at this time? Who was it, that Captain Cargo you've been telling me about?'

'Someone from his ship, *Neptune's Booty*.'

'And he wants a Mass?'

'Tomorrow morning at eight o'clock. Or should I say, this morning.'

'Is it some kind of joke?'

'He was very precise. It had to be at eight exactly.'

'Are you going to do it?'

Tom paused for a moment, then shrugged. 'Of course.'

'He sounded oriental.'

'Lots of them are Filipinos. I shouldn't have been so offhand with him.'

'I thought you were very restrained, considering.' Seizing the torch, Frank shone it around the room, resting the beam on the photograph. 'Your man up there wouldn't have been so reasonable.' They looked at the photograph of the cleric staring unblinkingly at them. 'Shh!' Frank put his finger to his lips.

'Don't say a word, we're being watched. At last we've found him. Christy's Mad Monsignor.'

'Give me that torch, I'm going back to bed. I've a Mass to say in four hours. One of us might as well do our priestly duties.'

'Look at him, though, the old bloke, you'd think he ruled the world.'

'He probably did, his part of it anyway.'

'I wouldn't like to meet him on the wrong side of a confessional. The arrogance of the man, he's wearing that biretta as though it were a crown.'

'Different times, Frank.'

'That's what we were being prepared for, wasn't it? Arbiters of the absolute. No shades of grey, everything as black and white as the clerical dress.'

'It's no good getting bitter, Frank. People just did what they thought was for the best.'

'We were made for a world that doesn't exist any more.' Frank turned the photo of the priest against the wall. 'It's probably better that he doesn't see what it's all been reduced to.'

Tom yawned again. 'Well, I'm sorry for disturbing you, Frank.'

'That's all right. In fact, I wasn't asleep. Insomnia. I've suffered from it ever since seminary days. Those prostitutes are at it all night, aren't they? They deserve to be millionaires.'

'There must be something you can do. About the insomnia, I mean.'

'You name it, I've tried it. No, I missed my calling in life. It should have been me in Gethsemane with old JC. He wouldn't have caught me sleeping. Are you OK, Tom?'

'Yes. I'm just tired.'

'I mean, are you really all right? It's just with what you said that night I first arrived. We haven't really had time to talk about it with you so busy at the port. You know, when you said about feeling disgust.'

Tom looked away from his friend. 'It's funny, I've just remembered. What I was dreaming of when you woke me.'

Frank followed Tom up the stairs. 'What was the dream, Tom?'

'Faces.' Tom stopped on the landing to his attic room. 'It's always faces. I suppose you'd call it recurrent.'

'Who are they?'

'Oh everybody, nobody. Some of them can be quite alarming. They stare but they never seem to see me. They *do* speak though.'

'What do they say?'

'I'll tell you in the morning. It's not the kind of thing to talk about at night.'

Back in his attic room, with the ceiling sloping across the orange darkness, Tom tossed and turned, the springs groaning beneath him. The flow of the cars stopped when the sun rose. Its rays filled his room. Dressing quickly but meticulously, having shaved his face to a shine, he left without any breakfast.

Neptune's Booty lay high in the full tide. The dock seemed as deserted as it had been the first time he saw it, and even more dilapidated. With a deep breath he forced himself to mount the gangway. Reaching the top, he stood there uncertainly, clutching his battered suitcase. The deck was strewn with smashed wooden pallets, frayed coils of metal rope and the glinting chips of broken asbestos boards. Open hatches yawned like mouths. Sow thistles had germinated where rivets had fatigued. The portholes on the towering deckhouse were opaque; a flight of metal stairs clung weakly to its side. There wasn't the usual, all-pervasive ship smell of lubricating oil. Tom looked helplessly at his watch, like an explorer with a broken compass. 'Hello?' his voice called over the destitute vessel. 'Is there anyone about?' A couple of terns flew overhead. At the far end of the slack water, a cargo ship was on the river, going out on the tide, its engines churning the dredged mud of the riverbed. 'It's Father Tom Carey. Port chaplain.' More and more seabirds were gathering above the seagoing vessel's brown wake. Screeching, they began to dive. The priest undid the buttons of his black jacket and ran a finger under his Roman collar. Although it was early, the sun was growing warm.

'Hello, Father Tom Carey?'

'Yes.'

'Port chaplain?'

'Of course.' Tom searched in vain for the person talking to him. 'Are you the one that rang me up?'

'I am bosun. Please to come this way.'

'Where are you? I can't see you.'

'Hello, Father Tom Carey. Up here.'

The priest looked up and saw a face staring down at him from high up on the top deck. 'Did you ring me up early this morning?'

'Yes, Father Tom Carey. I am sorry for disturbing you.'

The terns, returning with the tendrils of sand eels writhing in their beaks, took his eye for a moment. The metal of the stairs creaked as a slight figure stepped off them. 'Father Tom Carey, please to come with me.'

'Where's the captain?'

'Please to come.'

'I should see the captain first. It's a courtesy.'

'I am bosun.' The figure spoke unwaveringly. 'Please to come.' He was wearing ragged shorts, a torn T-shirt and flip-flops. Small of stature and fine featured, his smile belied an obvious anxiety. He averted his eyes from the priest.

Pressing his suitcase to his breast, the priest followed the seafarer over a raised threshold. The door gasped shut behind him and he found himself in a dark corridor. A terrible heat engulfed him. 'Please to come, Father Tom Carey, port chaplain.' A pair of white eyes glinted ahead of him.

'I really ought to see the captain first.'

'Is not possible. He is not here. Gone to casino. Please, take care, is stairs here.' Gingerly, the priest made his way up a number of flights of stairs, following the sound of the flip-flops in front of him. His calves began to ache with the climb, and his breath came heavily. At last he found himself on level ground; another corridor shimmered its shape from the darkness. The flip-flops began to pitter-patter down its length and he followed. Something soft brushed against his cheek. He clawed it from his face. Then he realised that it was a line of washing. Already he was sweating profusely. 'Please to come.'

'I can't see the hand in front of my face.'

'Electrics is not working.'

'I really should see the captain.'

A cloying fug thickened the air as they passed through the lines of washing. The priest's eyes were growing used to the dim and he could see the figure ahead of him moving gracefully through the lines of clothes. His own back stiffened as he stooped his way onward. Thrusting aside a pair of dripping trousers, he found that he was alone. 'Hello?' he asked, then with rising annoyance, 'Where are you?'

'Father Tom Carey, please to come this way.'

A door was thrust open and light beckoned. There were eight of them standing in the small room, all dressed in worn T-shirts and shorts. It was even hotter than in the corridor. The priest threw up his hand to protect his eyes from the stinging light of the countless candle stubs standing in bottles. As the priest stood there squinting, a cockroach scuttled across the floor. With a gentle lift and kick, a flip-flopped foot crushed it and flipped it apologetically from sight beneath the scattered row of plastic chairs. Fumbling inside his suitcase, Tom brought out a thin book. He cleared his throat. 'I will say the order of Mass for seafarers,' he said.

Instantly the candles were snuffed. The heavy, waxy smoke drifted on a sluggish current in the darkness. Then a cigarette lighter brought to life two large, immaculate church candles, which had been placed carefully on a table laid with a pristine cloth. Beside the candles was propped a *Stella Maris* picture: a pastel portrait of Jesus as the Star of the Sea standing behind a seafarer at the wheel of a ship, hand on his shoulder. From the shadows one of the men began to play a guitar. The song was mournful. Tom opened his old suitcase and arranged the vessels of the Mass on the table: the paten full of round white hosts, the chalice with a little wine, and a crucifix. He kissed the stole and placed it round his neck.

The plaintive singing finished, and he faced the silhouettes of his congregation gathered on the edge of the circle of light. Raising a hand to his mouth, the priest suppressed a profound sigh. He looked at the *Stella Maris* and at the worshippers gazing so intently at him. He made the sign of the cross, then for the first time in thirty years he could not remember the opening words of the Mass. His mind had gone blank. He fumbled his missal open.

When the Mass was over, he hurriedly packed his things away. Having closed his suitcase, he found that the congregation remained standing, like people who have not been given what they came for. 'Please, Father Tom Carey,' whispered the bosun, 'now you must drive away bad spirits.'

'Bad spirits?'

'Yes.'

The priest felt the sweat drip down his back. 'How do you mean, bad spirits?'

'Please to come this way.'

They took him through the darkness down into the silent, cavernous reaches of the ship. After the stairs, the priest found himself descending ladders. Despite the enervating heat, the metal rungs were cold in his hands. The suitcase was an encumbrance. He tried to control the tremor in his voice. 'It seems a long way down.'

'Is not much further.'

'The thing is, I forgot my hard hat and the captain –'

'I take case for you?'

'No, no thanks. I've got it.'

After the last ladder, a hand gripped his wrist tightly, and the priest was helped down a steep slope. He felt scabs of rust lifting from the metal under his scrabbling feet. His own progress produced a deep metal reverberation whilst the flip-flops all around him kept only the hint of a beat. 'Where are we going exactly?' His voice was suddenly loud. There was no reply. He could see the eyes of the crew glinting at him. At the bottom of the slope he crawled after his guide into what seemed to be nothing more than a hole gnawed in a steel skirting board. The sweat was dripping into his eyes. Lifting his head, he banged it resoundingly against metal. His heart began to beat queasily. 'I'm sorry, but are you sure this is safe?'

'Nearly there now, Father Tom Carey.'

'You really don't have to say my full name like that. Father Tom will do fine.'

He came at last to a cavity where the rest of the crew was standing waiting for him, their faces lit by daylight which came in from somewhere above in the crevasse of rusting metal. The priest hauled himself to his feet. Way above he could make out a patch of blue sky. 'Bad spirits here,' the bosun explained.

'How do you know?'

'Bad things to happen here.'

Tersely Tom brushed off the shreds of rust from his jacket. As though trying to reassert himself, he meticulously hardened the crease of his trousers. He could feel the sweat at the back of his knees. 'Now come on, we've got to be clear about this. The Church teaches that exorcisms –'

The men began talking to each other in their own language. Their voices were anxious, strained. To the priest it seemed that every seafarer spoke a different dialect, but they fell silent all at once. 'Bad spirits,' insisted the bosun. 'Father Carey, you must drive them away.'

Tom's shoulders sagged a little. 'But I don't have any water.'

The bosun reached into the tight group of men and brought out a big bottle of water. 'Now please to bless.'

'Has something happened down here?'

The bosun looked uncertainly at the rest of the crew, who were bunched fearfully in the constricted space, then nodded once. 'Accident, very bad.' Eager faces pressed round the priest, staring at the bottle of water. Unscrewing the cap, the priest blessed it with his hand, then dipping a finger in he flicked the water out. The seafarers shuffled awkwardly; another discussion flared amongst them. 'Please, Father Tom Carey,' said the bosun, 'we primitive people, want big blessing.' He mimed emptying the bottle with the expansiveness of a Grand Prix winner shaking his champagne.

'The thing is, none of this is strictly orthodox.'

'We desperate.'

As the water cascaded over the walls, the crew leapt into its shower, and with beaming faces running with drops, blessed themselves.

When the priest emerged back on deck, the sun blinded him. He stood there for a long time, waiting for the spots to clear from his vision. From the chemical works across the river, the practice sirens wailed. He looked behind to the deckhouse, but could see no one. Still squinting in the sunlight, he carefully walked down the gangway.

At the Flying Angel Club, he found Christy waiting for him. 'We were just about to send a search party out for you, Father Tom.'

'Well, there's no need to bother now.'

'Tsk-tsk, a tad touchy today, aren't we?'

The priest walked through the bar area into the little office he shared with the Anglican chaplain. He sank heavily into the chair at his desk. 'Good to see a bit of order in here,' said Christy from the doorway. 'You should have seen the way the last chaplain had it in here, papers everywhere and never to be found when we needed them. Still, he was very popular with the seafarers. And that's what it's all about. Are you all right? What have you done to your head? I see you left your hard hat.' Christy pointed at the yellow hat on the chair. 'And how's everything at the presbytery, Father Tom?'

'Don cleared the drains. I tried to pay him.'

'He wouldn't have taken anything. He's got a heart of gold, that lad. And is Father Frank all right?'

'Yes, Father Frank is fine, Christy.'

'He was saying that he might come and do some more ship visiting. He's very popular with the seafarers.'

'Good.'

'No more problems with the Mad Monsignor? Or old Kevin? You know, the one-eyed chap with the red beard.'

'Kevin rings the doorbell all night, Christy. And when he's not ringing it he's standing under that blessed street light. I don't even notice him any more. As for the council –'

'The council?'

'I've been ringing them about the faulty street light.'

'Poor Kevin. Did you know he was the winner of the county hundred-yard dash for five years running?'

'You told me. Anyway, I thought it was three years.'

'He always was a gentle soul, not an ounce of badness in him. Then he let himself go.' Christy mimed the upending of a bottle. 'And all because he –'

'Witnessed his ferret being run over by the drayman's wagon. Yes, I know, Christy. He must have been very young when that happened.'

'Oh, we had draymen's wagons on Slaggy Island for many years after they'd gone from the mainland.' Christy lit a cigarette. 'Bit edgy today, Father Tom; what's the matter, had an argument with Father Frank?'

'And what's that supposed to mean?'

'Come on, lighten up, Father. I'm only joking.'

'No, *you* come on. If you've got something to say about Father Frank then spit it out.'

'Word gets about.'

'Does it?'

'He was thrown out of his parish, wasn't he?'

'Father Frank is staying at the presbytery until he finds somewhere else.'

'I know that, Father Tom. But I wouldn't let it become public knowledge.'

'Why not?'

'You know what people say.'

'What do they say?'

'That he's batting for the other side. You know, that he's stolen the family silver.'

'And what do *you* say?'

'I say, good on you, for not turning your back on a mate.'

'Well thank you,' said Tom.

'Even though people might think you were a fudge packer as well. Go on, Father Tom, crack a smile, that's better.'

'Christy, it's not a matter for great humour. And if you've got to smoke I'd rather you didn't do it in the office. You know how the Anglican chaplain feels about smoking.'

'It's solidarity, Father. All the seafarers smoke.'

Going into the bar area, Tom put the kettle on. Christy followed him. 'Have you remembered about tonight, Father?'

'Look, how many times do I have to tell you, I'm not going to Barnacle Bill's.'

'Hold your horses.'

'I'm sorry, I am a bit snappish, aren't I?'

'You're not as bad as my uncle used to be – old Fitzy. He once slapped a sacristan for putting too much wine out.'

'Ah yes, the good old days, when priests were king.'

'And the rest of us peasants. Actually, they weren't all like that. You won't remember Father Larkspur.'

'What a name. Do you want a cup of tea, Christy?'

'Please. Did you know old Father Larkspur?'

'I think you're just inventing him.'

'Would I do that? He was the parish priest at St Bede's for many years. He lived in your presbytery.'

Tom dropped a tea bag in each mug. 'Is he that fellow in the photograph on the wall in the parish room?'

'That's him. He baptised me and all my brothers. And married my mum and dad, even though she was three months pregnant, *and* he knew it.'

The water came to a boil. 'How many sugars, Father?'

'None, thanks. I mean no whisky and three real sugars.'

Christy's bottle kissed the rim of his cup. Tom lifted the tea bags out with a spoon. 'He died the year England won the World Cup. He loved football, did Father Larkspur. Used to watch the Boro religiously. My mum was desperate when she went to see him about the baby. She'd already been to see Old Ma Turney.'

'Old Ma Turney?' As Tom took his first sip of tea, his interest rose slightly.

'Old Ma Turney, the vermin extinguisher, and back-street abortionist.'

'Another Slaggy Island character?'

'They don't make them like they used to. Haven't I told you about Old Ma Turney?'

'Just in passing.'

'Well, she used to live above the old slaughterhouse. You know how the first bomb to land on British soil in the Second World War landed on Slaggy Island?'

'I didn't.'

'It came down on the slaughterhouse. We all had chops for a month. Except for Old Ma Turney.'

'She wasn't in the mood for meat presumably, having just been blown up.'

'There, I knew you had a sense of humour, Father Tom.' Christy followed the priest to where he sank into one of the soft chairs that lined the lounge. Above them was a huge *Stella Maris* poster. 'As it happens, Father Tom, she was out killing a rat that had been raising its litters in a crack in young Spam Smithson's U-bend.'

'Do you make these names up, Christy?'

'As if I would.' Christy slurped his tea. 'Another sugar I think.' The bottle was tilted again.

'Put us out of our misery then. Why didn't Old Ma Turkey eat any meat?'

'Old Ma *Turney*. Well, that's easily explained. You see, Old Ma Turney had no teeth and she swallowed her falsies when she heard the blast.'

'Christy, you should be on the television. You know, one of those programmes, *Christy Garbutt Remembers*, or *Down Our Old Ways with Christy Garbutt.*'

'That's not a bad idea. Anyway, where was I?'

'Somewhere with the Mad Monsignor.'

'Oh yes. He looks like a proper martinet I know, in that photo in the parish room. By the way, I've turned that photograph back the proper way. I'm surprised at you not showing respect to the cloth, Father Tom.'

'When were you in the presbytery?'

'Oh, I've got a set of keys. Now, where was I? Yes, Father Larkspur could give out the stare when he wanted. Hated the Church of England with a vengeance; used to laugh openly whenever he saw a vicar, threatened as many Presbyterian ministers as you could shake a stick at, but our mam would only ever speak about him as though he were a saint. You see, he saved my life.' Christy broke off and drank his tea meditatively. 'He really did save my life.'

'What happened?'

'When my mum was pregnant with me she went to see him. Told him about the situation. About her being sixteen and the father just being a sea coaler from Hartlepool. Now, a sea coaler is a raggedy-arsed fella with a horse and cart who shovels up the coal that the tide brings in and goes about the houses selling it. She said how her parents would kick up a holy rumpus if they knew; how she'd even been behind the old slaughterhouse to see how much it would cost for the old gin and knitting needles. Father Larkspur listened to it all and then asked her one question, *Will you marry this lad?* He married them the next day. Didn't bother with all the red tape. It was a Saturday, and he missed the Boro match. My dad took his bride away from church in his horse and cart to Saltburn for the honeymoon. There wasn't a dot of coal in that cart, and the nag's tail had even been plaited. And do you know what, that horse didn't shit once between the church and Saltburn, nor so much as fart.'

'Have you ever thought about writing a book, Christy?'

'Now that's not kind, Father.'

'I'm not joking.'

The smoke drifted from Christy's cigarette over the No Smoking sign that Tom's Anglican colleague had placed prominently on the wall. 'They settled down together on Slaggy Island,' Christy continued, 'our mam and the raggy arse from Hartlepool. And that baby was the first of many, all loved and looked after as though they were the most precious things in the world. They were their wealth, you see. Didn't have two ha'pennies to rub together, but what did that matter when they had us kids?'

'Were you a folk singer in a past existence, Christy?' The priest looked at Christy. His eyes were glistening.

'That baby was me.' He took a draw on his cigarette. 'Oh, our mam. I can just hear her voice now if she could see me standing here with a fag in my mouth. *Christy, chuck away that disgusting thing before I knock it from you with a cricket bat.*' Loud peals of laughter thudded about the room.

'She sounds like some woman.'

'She was on forty Woodbine a day when she could get them, but she *never* smoked in the presence of a priest. A Slaggy Island character. Not many left now. And Kevin himself, he's one.'

'I feel honoured that it's my bell he's ringing.'

'Yes, the last of a dying breed. How are you finding living there, Father Tom? Must be different from what you're used to.'

'It is, Christy. It *is*.'

'Where were you born, Father Tom?'

'I was raised on a farm; on the moors.'

'The moors? I bet it's lovely there; bit isolated, mind.'

'We never noticed that.'

'Far cry from Slaggy Island. Do you miss it?'

'I left for Ushaw when I was eleven.'

'Have you any family left there?'

'Not since Mam died. There's still the farmhouse. Actually I should go up there and sort it out. I haven't been there since the funeral. I keep putting it off. We sold most of the land when it became too much for her. There's still an orchard; it doubled as a ewe paddock. My dad was Irish. He died young, just when I went away.'

'The Church is your family now then.'

'Yes,' said Tom. 'I suppose it is.'

'You're bleeding, Father Tom.'

'What?'

'The side of your head there. It didn't look too bad at first, but it wants seeing to.' The priest lifted a finger to his head and winced. 'That's what comes of not wearing your hard hat. What were you doing?'

'A crew wanted a Mass saying. That ship. I've never seen anything like it in all my born days.'

'A rust bucket?'

'More like a rust colander. They wanted a potholer not a ship visitor.'

Christy ducked out of view for a moment, coming back with a first-aid kit.

'Really, I'm OK, Christy.'

'We'll just put a dressing on it. We don't want an infection.'

'Aren't you going to wash your hands first?' Tom demanded.

'You haven't got one of those obsessive-compulsive disorders have you, Father?'

Tom closed his eyes, tensing when the antiseptic cream was applied. 'You're only supposed to *dab* it on, Christy. What's that you're doing now?'

'Putting the lint on.'

'A simple plaster will do.'

'You look like you've been in a fight out the back of Barnacle Bill's. What's all this stuff in your hair? It's rust. Where *have* you been, Father Tom?'

'With Jonah, into the whale's stomach.'

'Well, as long as you're OK for tonight. You've remembered, I hope. It'll be nice grub. We've been invited for a candle-lit supper, you and me, Father.'

'Who by? Kevin or the Mad Monsignor?'

'Nice to see you trying for a laugh. They've invited us because you're the new port chaplain, and because, I suppose, I've got a reputation as a great table companion and raconteur. It's the nuns over in Chemical Alley. Did I not tell you they'd invited us?'

'No you didn't.'

'Oh, I must have forgotten. Have you met them yet?'

'No.'

'Look, I know what you're thinking, Father Tom.'

'How on earth do you know what I'm thinking?'

'Well, a dinner date with a bunch of nuns isn't exactly on the list of all-time great nights-out, but these two are different.'

'Two?'

'There's just the pair of them.' Christy chuckled throatily. 'By God but they've been putting the wind up some of the big boys. You know, the chemical companies in business around the marsh. They've been polluting for years. Only the nuns keep on badgering them with research. There was a fire here a few years ago and when people woke up it was still dark. In fact we didn't see the bloody sun all day. Thick palls of smoke hung over everything. It was like something from a sci-fi film. The day the sun stopped shining.' Christy's voice boomed out in an American accent, 'Darkness covers Teesside, strange things grow in the smoke.' Both men laughed. 'Are you sure you won't have some sugar in your tea, Father? It's Fairtrade.'

Tom paused for a moment. 'Go on then, as long as it's Fairtrade.'

'And I'll join you.' The bottle clanked against the lips of both mugs. 'Congratulations, Father Tom, you're getting a sense of humour for yourself. As Father Frank likes to say, you've got to laugh.'

That evening they crossed the river on the Transporter Bridge: a huge web of girders from which a ferry platform dangled. Slowly the platform was hauled across the river, a few yards above the current. Downstream, vast ships hulked the docks, their hulls caught in the westering sun. 'Not much left of this place,' remarked the priest as they drove down the quiet road.

'Didn't you know that Margaret Thatcher's nom de plume was Terminal Decline?'

'It can't just be her, Christy. I mean, she hasn't been around for over ten years.'

'I'm just preparing you for Sister Anne.'

'What do you mean? Bit of a lefty is she?'

'A bit? If she was any more to the left then she'd be a communist.'

'Look, Christy. I don't feel like this. I'll just drop you there and go home.'

'What's the matter, Father Tom?'

'I just don't feel like it.'

'Bit intimidated are you?'

'What do you mean by that?'

'By these modern nuns?'

'Of course I'm not.'

'So what are you frightened of then? It's not like you to be so rude. After all they'll have gone to the trouble of cooking a meal.'

They arrived on the shrunken estate without passing a single vehicle. They parked outside the white house. Christy opened the little gate and approached the front door. After the grey of the chemical works, the flowers in a hanging basket were a kaleidoscope of colours and when the priest came up behind Christy, their sudden fragrance filled his nostrils.

'Christy, how are you, you old reprobate?'

'All the better for seeing you, Anne. This is Anne, Father Tom.'

'You must be the port chaplain.'

'Father Tom Carey,' Christy announced. 'England's finest. Seriously, I'm thinking of nominating him as priest of the year, for services to Fairtrade tea and sugar.'

'Come in.'

'Hello, Sister.'

'Really Tom, just call me Anne. There's no need for formalities. After all, it's forty years since Vatican Two.'

Christy winked at Tom. 'And it just feels like yesterday. Ah, yes, the good old days; Latin Mass, the priest with his back to the congregation and the fear of hell and damnation.'

'Mary-Jo's just in the kitchen. Come on, Mary-Jo, come and say hello to Christy and Tom.'

They were ushered into a room filled with the brilliant light of a late spring evening. Vases contained wild flowers from the marsh. The window was open and a pleasant breeze blew from the open acres. 'Been in the wars, Tom?' Anne asked.

'I'm sorry?'

'The field dressing on your head.'

'Oh that, it's nothing.'

Mary-Jo appeared at the kitchen door. 'Hello. How you doing, Christy?'

'Very well, Mary-Jo, and all the better for the seeing of you.'

'Hello, Sister,' Tom greeted her.

'I've told you, we don't have labels in this house,' Anne returned.

'I'm Mary-Jo, Tom. Do you want a glass of wine?'

'That would be nice, thank you.'

'And I don't need to ask you, Christy.'

An embroidered screen stood in front of the gas fire. A loose accordion of books played itself across a shelf. 'I've never been able to work out what that was,' Christy said, laying a hand on the terracotta statue standing in the corner.

'Oh, it can be what you want it to be,' Mary-Jo replied, bringing in the wine.

'What do you reckon, Father Tom?'

'Yes, it's very . . . unusual.'

Christy roared with laughter. 'Mind what you're saying, the artist is among us. Mary-Jo created it.' Hunkering down, he ran a finger over the statue. 'Last time I was here I thought it was a mother and a child, now I look at it, it seems more like someone dancing.'

'What do you think, Tom?' Anne asked.

'Isn't it Mary and Jesus?'

'Bit of a traditionalist, are you?' Anne shook her head. 'You tell us about it, Mary-Jo.'

But already she was halfway to the kitchen. 'There's a pan on the hob.'

They sat down at the table, the wine in their glasses a swimming ruby filtered by sunbeams. When Mary-Jo brought in the starters Christy winked at the priest. 'What's this then, Mary-Jo, bite-size pizzas?'

'Feta cheese, spinach and pine-nut galettes,' replied Anne.

'With a spring of basil, I see,' said Christy. 'Well you nuns certainly live well.'

Anne laughed. 'What's the point of belonging to one of the richest organisations in the world without eating well? Now, Tom, would you say something?'

'Sorry?'

'A few words.'

'A grace,' Christy put in.

'Oh yes, of course.' The priest laid down his napkin and closing his eyes made the sign of the cross. 'Bless us, O Lord, for these thy gifts, which we are about to receive from thy bounty, through Christ Our Lord, Amen. In the name of the Father, and of the Son, and . . .'

'Thank you, Mother God, for drawing us together,' Anne put in, 'to share food and friendship, Amen.'

'Munch munch, crunch crunch,' said Christy, 'bless the bunch who made the lunch.'

With a single scissor of knife and fork, Christy separated a third of the pastry and popped it in his mouth. Anne watched him. 'Actually it's Delia. You know, Christy, a Delia Smith recipe.'

'Yes, I'm sure we're all entitled to eat, even religious orders,' said Tom, his knife and fork carefully incising the dish, 'and Delia Smith is a good Catholic, isn't she?'

'Is she?'

'Yes, in fact I think she won Catholic Woman of the Year some time back. Or was it even a papal award?'

Flakes of pastry sprayed from Anne's mouth as she hooted with laughter. The priest's knife clanged on the plate as he dropped it. The tip of his tongue probed discreetly at the loose pastry flaking his lips.

'Don't mind her, Father Tom,' grinned Christy. 'She's a bit of an iconoclast, is our Anne. She says novenas for the demise of the clergy.'

'My prayers are obviously working. But seriously, that Pope has set things back thirty years. Don't you think so, Tom?'

'I'm not really sure what you mean.'

'I mean he's plunged us into the Dark Ages. It's the vision of Mary this, and Our Lady that, but when it comes to a real woman it's *get out of here*. Talking of awards, I hear some groups of Papal Knights or other are going to give Margaret Thatcher their highest honour at Westminster Cathedral.' Christy winked at Tom. 'God help me,' Anne continued, 'but sometimes I pray for a schism; something dramatic to jolt the real Church back to life. Have you been reading in the *Catholic Herald* about the Pope's plans? Not only does the idea of women priests make him reach for the holy water but now he wants to ban girls serving on the altar. What is that old man in Rome so angry about?'

'You tell him,' laughed Christy, finishing the rest of his food in a single prong of his fork.

'It really gets us down, doesn't it, Mary-Jo?'

Standing up, Mary-Jo reached for the bottle. 'More wine anyone?'

'I think we'd better have after that,' said Christy.

'Think about it,' Anne continued. 'They allow anyone, even paedophiles, to be priests before women. And I wouldn't mind if the priests were any good, but talk about low calibre . . .'

'Still,' Tom cleared his throat, 'the Holy Father's in poor health, we can't . . .'

'He's wrecking our Church.' Anne spoke with a sad calm; different from the bantering tone she had shown so far. 'And what's more he's broken its wheels so that after his time, it still won't move. Look at all the cardinals he's appointed, toadies to the right wing, every last man of them. This Pope is so authoritarian.'

'Whereas you,' said Tom, taking a deep gulp of his wine, 'would never tell anyone what to do or think.'

Christy roared with laughter. 'He's got you there, Anne. That's what she wants, someone to stand up to her. He's a bit shy is our Father Tom but once he gets going I've a feeling he'll really go for it. He might even be a match for you, Anne.'

Anne beamed. 'Come to my defence then, Mary-Jo.'

'I'll just go and open another bottle of wine.'

Anne found Mary-Jo standing against the sink in the kitchen, gazing at the dusk falling over the marsh. 'What's the matter with you?' Her voice grew abruptly concerned. 'Are you all right? You're not feeling any ill effects, are you?'

'I told you, Anne, you've got to stop worrying. I feel fine. I've just come to open a bottle of wine.' Mary-Jo held up the wine and corkscrew.

'But the other bottle's still half full.'

'I thought we might want more.'

'We're not a bunch of alcoholics. Well, Christy might be if his wife let him. Why are you being so quiet? You've hardly said a word.'

'Don't you know?'

'What is it, Mary-Jo?'

'You don't recognise him, do you?'

'Recognise who? What's got into you, Mary-Jo? Are you blushing?'

'It's Blue Eyes.'

'Blue Eyes?'

'You know, Father Paul Newman.'

'Who?'

'Don't tell me you've forgotten Father Paul Newman.'

'What, Father Paul Newman who used to come to Nazareth House?'

Leaning against the sink, Mary-Jo giggled. Anne strode back to the door.

'Where are you going, Anne?'

'Just to have another look.'

'Don't, he'll see you,' Mary-Jo hissed.

'We're not in a closed convent any more, Mary-Jo. I'm not going to be on bread and water for a week for looking at a man.' Anne opened the kitchen door a crack and peered through it. She came back and threw her hand to her mouth. 'You're right, it is him.' Coming over to the sink, they both began to laugh, a high girlish sound bubbling irrepressibly through the kitchen.

'Shh, he'll hear you.'

'Father Paul Newman. Who would have thought it after all these years.'

'Anne, keep your voice down.'

'What's got into you? It's not such a big deal, is it? He doesn't know us. He couldn't tell us from Eve. Even you've changed a bit in thirty years. He's certainly changed. You'd think he had the woes of the world on his shoulders. Anyway, when he used to come to the convent we had full habits on: veil, wimple, the lot. A colony of identical penguins. He's a bit of a stuffed shirt, isn't he? Who's his mentor, Cardinal Ratzinger?'

'You've been a bit hard on him, Anne.'

'Oh, they deserve it. They've had too much deference over the years. They need it squeezing out of them.'

'You've put him through the mincer.'

'Did I? Mind you, as I was talking part of me was wondering what old Sissy Philomena would have made of it.'

'She'd have died of apoplexy if you'd dared to breathe when a priest was in the same room.'

'Well maybe I'm just redressing the balance a bit. Come on, Mary-Jo, we'd better go back.'

'I can't.'

'What?'

'I need a few minutes.'

'Why? Look, maybe you're right. I was a bit hard on him, I mean hate the sin, love the sinner and all that. Let's tell him we remember him from the years behind the veil and all have a good laugh.'

'No way!'

'Mary-Jo, what's the big deal?'

'Well at least let me get a few glasses of wine down first.' Mary-Jo shook her head wonderingly. 'Father Paul Newman. You just never know what life's going to throw up next.'

'What are you on about? Come on, let's go and tell him.'

'No!' Mary-Jo's voice rang through the kitchen. 'I mean, let's save it until we're on to the coffee. When I nudge your elbow that will mean you can tell him. But don't bring it up until I give the sign.'

'How old are you, Mary-Jo? You're acting like a teenager. I mean, what did the two of you actually do apart from hold hands for two seconds?'

'That *was* a big deal in those days.'

'It was, wasn't it?'

'Anne, I –'

A cough from the door froze the words in Mary-Jo's mouth. The women looked over to see the priest standing there with the dirty plates. Christy came in behind, thrusting Tom forward. 'Get the rubber gloves and squeezy out. Don't let it be said that we Slaggy Island lads won't do our bit for Women's Lib.'

The main course was gnocci with sage butter and Parmesan. 'Not got any chips?' Christy winked.

'Look Tom, I'm sorry if I was a bit heavy-handed before,' Anne said. 'I've had a difficult day.'

'In that case, apology accepted,' Tom nodded stiffly.

'He's actually got quite a good sense of humour if you can get under the prickles,' Christy put in. 'He's a nice kind of gruffalo.'

Anne chuckled. 'So you're staying on the other side of the river, Tom?'

'Yes, in the old presbytery, St Bede's.'

'Patron saint of writers.'

'I don't seem to have had much time for books since I got here.'

Filling her mouth, Anne asked, 'And what do you make of the prostitutes?' Anne flinched as under the table Mary-Jo kicked her. 'Why are you living there? Doesn't the Bishop like you?' There was a second kick.

'What are you insinuating?' Father Tom laid his knife and fork on his plate.

'Whatever you do, don't ask him about his partner,' Christy laughed.

The priest sighed. 'I seem to have become an easy target.'

'Well I think it's wonderful,' Mary-Jo put in. 'Come on, Anne, what other priest would live in a place like that?'

'There's two of them,' Christy said.

Almost playfully Tom snatched Christy's glass. 'I'm afraid it's going to be a very long night if you give Christy any more wine.' Evading Christy's grab, the priest drained the glass for him.

'No, Mary-Jo's right,' said Anne. 'Fair play to you, Tom. Most priests wouldn't go anywhere near a place like that. So why have you?'

Tom shrugged. 'I'm port chaplain. The presbytery was empty. And before Christy says anything more, I happen to have a colleague staying with me temporarily.'

'A gay icon actually,' said Christy, refilling his glass.

'Rubbish.' Tom pressed his napkin against his lips for a second. 'This is very nice. Thanks for inviting us over.'

'Christy said you used to be the curate at St Aidan's.'

'Yes, I did, Anne.'

'So you used to go to Nazareth House?' Ignoring the kick she received under the table, Anne stared steadily at the priest.

'The old people's home? Yes, many moons ago. I shared the duties with Father Fitz.'

'My uncle,' beamed Christy, lifting his wine glass up to an equally rosy cheek. 'I can't imagine he did much.'

'And the other curate Father Frank.'

'They're back together,' Christy giggled.

'Do you remember much about Nazareth House?'

'Anne, don't interrogate Tom.'

'I'm not, Mary-Jo. I was just wondering whether Tom could remember Sister Mary-Philomena.'

'I can,' laughed Christy. 'She was the only person who could stand up to my uncle.'

'Are you all right, Mary-Jo?'

'I'm fine, Anne, something just went down the wrong way.'

The conversation lagged for a few moments as Anne and Christy ate wholeheartedly. 'Has this . . . house been a convent for long?' the priest asked politely.

'There's just the two of us,' replied Mary-Jo.

'What do you do here?'

'I work in mental health. Art therapy sessions, that kind of thing.'

'Near Babbington Road,' put in Christy. 'But she's had exhibitions in London.'

'I teach part-time,' Anne said. 'And do community work here. We both badger the chemical companies in our spare time. Not that it makes any difference. I'm sick of writing letters to them when I want to pour hot lead down their trousers.'

'You seem to have a lot of grievances, Anne.'

'I'm a nun living on the north bank of the River Tees, do you think I should pretend everything's rosy? If the Pope doesn't get me then ICI will.'

Tom took a deep draught of wine. 'Still, this place is very comfortable.'

'It was being used as a shooting gallery before we moved in, Tom.' Anne pushed her empty plate decisively away. 'And I don't mean grouse.'

'A shooting gallery?'

'We had to practically push them out the door. People think Mary-Jo's all sweetness and light but they haven't seen her confronted with a drug dealer.'

'Still,' said the priest weakly, 'the flowers are lovely.'

'Mary-Jo picked them. They're from the marsh, or her garden as she calls it. You love the marsh don't you, Mary-Jo?'

'Yes. Anyone for more wine?'

'Look, Tom,' said Anne gently. 'I really am sorry if I've been a touch spiky but sometimes priests don't seem to understand what we're up against. When we were in an enclosed convent – are you OK, Mary-Jo? Well, when we were in the convent we weren't even allowed to be in the same room as a man, and I'm not sure that much has really changed.'

'Oh, come *on*,' Tom remonstrated. As he took another gulp of wine he could feel the heat rising in his cheeks. His head was growing light.

'Think about it, Tom. Priests were held in such high esteem that when they came to the door we weren't even supposed to look them in the eye, let alone talk to them. When we entered the convent we even had to change our names. I became Sister Mary-Bernard. When I went to vote I'm sure the electoral clerk was expecting a big Swiss dog to walk in. We were kept completely in the dark about everything. I mean, I was twenty-five before I even knew who Paul Newman was.'

Mary-Jo rose quickly and began to stack up the plates.

'Take this war,' Anne continued, suppressing a giggle.

'You can't pin that one on the Pope,' said Tom quickly. 'He made it quite clear that the Church was categorically opposed to the action in Iraq.'

'He didn't do anything to stop it though, did he?'

'He's favourite for this year's Nobel Peace Prize.'

'And what does that mean? He didn't do anything radical. Once again the men in suits strangled us: Bush, Blair and Bumsfeld.'

'Get her on about Thatcher, Tom.' Christy roared with laughter. '*Thatcher-Thatcher-the-Milk-Snatcher.*'

When the nuns were out making the coffee, the priest stared at the door. Christy watched him. 'What's the matter, Father Tom?'

'I'm sorry?'

'You're staring at that door like a dog at a butcher's shop.'

Tom stood and went over to the books. He picked two up. '*A Woman's Bible Commentary*,' he said, reading the title. 'And *Praying Your Goodbyes*.'

'They're all right really, aren't they, Father Tom? Anne rides a high horse, but mostly she just likes a laugh.'

'A laugh? If I treated her the way she treated me I'd be arrested for sex discrimination. It's only thirty-odd years of training that keeps me polite.'

'Oh, she's just having her little joke.'

'A joke like a sledgehammer.'

'Now don't go all hoity-toity on us just when you've started to thaw.' Both men drained their wine glasses. Christy filled them again. 'You're a dark horse, mind, Father.'

'In what way?'

'Here's me thinking you were teetotal and look at you tonight, knocking your wine back like it was Ribena. It warms the heart to see it. By the way, did you ever come across them at Nazareth House?'

'What's this book called?' Tom selected another from the shelf. '*Travelling Light* by Daniel O'Leary. He'd have to be here, of course. You know, Christy, he has the nerve to say that the era of the priest is coming to an end.'

'And is it?' Without answering, Tom went over to the corner of the room. 'You like that statue, don't you, Father Tom?'

Tom scrutinised the statue. 'A mother and child, do you think, Christy? Maybe two adults, a man and woman.' The priest narrowed his eyes. 'Or is it the prodigal with his father?'

'Or the prodigal with *her mother*, Father. You can't be sexist in this house.'

Reaching out, the priest laid a hand on a contour of the figure, gentle as a caress. 'Yes, I can see that.'

'Can you remember Anne and Mary-Jo from your days at Nazareth House, Father Tom?'

Tom straightened up and looked coolly at Christy. 'In those days we never looked women in the eye, Christy.'

'Not even the pretty ones?'

'Especially not those. Now tell me more about this statue.'

When the women came back with a laden tray, the room was filled with the fragrance of coffee. The four of them sat back down at the table.

'What were you doing?' Anne demanded.

'I'm sorry?' Tom replied.

'To earn that field dressing on the side of your head.'

'I was right at the bottom of a ship. I had to literally crawl on my hands and knees.'

'Sounds like dedication,' said Anne.

Christy nodded. 'This fella visits every single ship that comes in. Even the chemical tankers that are only here for a few hours.'

'What do you do on the ships, Tom?'

'Well, usually it's just to welcome the seafarers. Extend the hand of friendship, you know. See if they want anything. Take them to the mission centre or into town sometimes. I could start bringing them here, if you want. To get a lecture on the evils of the male-dominated Church.'

'Touché,' laughed Anne.

'Actually today some seafarers wanted an exorcism.'

'An exorcism?'

'Yes, Anne. They wanted an exorcism but they would have been better with a new ship.'

'Which ship was it, Father Tom?' Christy asked.

'Neptune's Booty.'

Christy sat upright. 'Captain Cargo's?'

'That's right.'

'I'm surprised he allowed you on board. He's been here for months and he won't let anyone within a hundred yards of it.'

Tom's fingers straightened the creases on his trousers. 'Actually he didn't know.'

'Didn't know?'

'That's right, Christy. The men rang me up for a Mass, and when I got there the captain wasn't there.'

'You know we're supposed to clear our presence with the shipmaster, as a matter of courtesy.'

'I know. But they seemed desperate. There was a bosun.'

Anne clapped her hands. 'God, there's hope for the world. A *priest* breaking the rules.'

Christy shrugged. 'Rather you than me.'

'What do you mean by that?'

'There's lots of rumours about him, you know, Father Tom.'

'Who? What are you on about, Christy?'

'Captain Cargo, or whatever his real name is, he's a bit of a tricky customer. Some say he's a smuggler, others that he's a member of the mafia.'

'Oh, come off it.'

'I'm only saying what people say.'

'He's not Italian for a start.'

'The Russian mafia, I mean, or one of the former Soviet

republics. They control shipping in that part of the world, you know.'

'You've been watching too many thrillers, Christy.'

'No, Father Tom, I've been a ship visitor for twenty years, that's all. I talk, I listen. I go to Barnacle Bill's with the seafarers.' He turned to the nuns. 'You've no idea of the murk at the bottom of the world of shipping, and now Father Tom's gone and stirred it up.'

'Don't you think you're being a shade melodramatic, Christy?'

'No, I don't, Father Tom.' Christy stared solemnly at the priest. His gaze grew piercing. Then all at once he spluttered with laughter. 'You should have seen your face, Father Tom. You were crapping yourself!'

'I was not,' the priest countered pettishly.

'What did you think?' Christy hooted. 'That the mafia were going to throw a horse's head on your bed for muscling in on their wine-gum smuggling racket? That's his vice. Father Tom loves wine gums; never without a packet. Here, no hard feelings, let me fill your glass.'

Anne poured the coffee. 'Well, don't worry, Tom, we'll hide you if the mafia come looking for you.'

'Actually,' said Christy thoughtfully, 'there *is* a lot of eastern European organised crime in shipping. So you never know. Then there's the Snakehead gangs. The Ulo ng Ahas, as our Filipino friends call them.'

'Now,' Anne announced, 'Mary-Jo and I have got something to say, haven't we?'

Mary-Jo drained her wine glass. 'It's nothing really.'

'You don't remember us, do you, Tom?'

'I'm sorry, Anne?'

'I told Mary-Jo that you wouldn't. She would have been Mary-Joseph when you knew her. We were all Mary, with a saint's name tagged on. She chose Joseph because she thought she'd miss her dad, didn't you, Mary-Jo? She was only fifteen when she entered the convent. It still hasn't penetrated, has it?

We were nurses at Nazareth House, the old people's home.'

'Oh, I see.'

'I was just telling him that,' put in Christy.

'You *don't* remember us, do you?' Plucking up a tea towel, Anne placed it over Mary-Jo's face like a wimple. 'Surely you remember Sister Mary-Joseph, the belle of Nazareth House? I mean, how many other pretty faces were there amongst all those old dears?'

Mary-Jo pulled the tea towel down. 'Stop it, Anne.'

'But you must remember her, Tom. It was your fault that she sinned against Holy Poverty.'

'Anne!'

'Oh come on, Mary-Jo. He can't even remember, look at him. It's such a funny story.'

'Oh, good,' said Christy, clapping his hands.

'Wait till you hear it. You'll think I'm exaggerating. You can't believe what life was like for us when we first joined the Order.'

'It wasn't all bad,' put in Mary-Jo from behind her wine glass.

'Every week we used to have to confess our sins to Sister Philomena, Mother Superior. In front of the whole convent, mind you. Some ordeal; it kept the bowels moving, I can tell you. Mary-Jo was the golden girl but she still had to confess. And it was all your fault, Tom.'

Tom lifted a hand to his chest in a gesture of puzzlement. 'Me?'

'Yes you, Father Paul Blue Eyes Newman. Did you know that we called you Father Paul Newman?'

'No, I didn't.'

'Someone *must* have told you,' grinned Anne. 'I mean, you're a touch grizzled now, but in those days you were almost his double.'

Christy clicked his fingers. 'Dead ringer.'

'To be perfectly honest I've *never* thought that I looked like him at all.'

'Take it from me, a whole convent of nuns thought you did.'

'Don't be ridiculous,' said Tom.

'It's true, isn't it, Mary-Jo?' Giggling, Mary-Jo spilled some of her wine. The stain spread quickly over the cloth, like a haemorrhage. 'Now if you'd done something like that,' Anne explained, 'you would have had to confess it on Sunday evening in front of everyone.'

'Really?' asked Christy.

'You had to confess all your sins in the week. Usually it was something like running down a corridor. You weren't allowed to run anywhere, but you weren't allowed to be late either. And after you'd made your confession, you'd get your admonishment from Mother Superior. Then a bell would ring and you'd kiss the floor. Just like this.' Stepping clear of the table, Anne dropped to the ground. She flattened herself and kissed the carpet.

'Anne!' Mary-Jo remonstrated.

Bellowing with laughter, Anne negotiated herself back into her chair. 'But the worst thing was if there was a silence after you'd admitted your fault. You see, there was usually something that you'd been seen doing but couldn't remember. The silence meant that you had to admit to something else. And there was no prompting from Mother Superior. She wanted to see you stew. That's what it was like, wasn't it, Mary-Jo?'

Nodding, Mary-Jo laughed. 'We'd be standing there racking our brains to think of something. You'd end up admitting to all sorts.'

'But the worst thing was being on door duty. We took turns. You see, you weren't supposed to talk to anyone, a bit difficult if they've just said hello to you. And if it was a priest at the door then you weren't even allowed to look them in the eye. Every single time Father Paul Newman came, Mary-Jo broke the *magnum silencium*. One day, he made her break it twice. But that was nothing to what he made you do with the crockery, was it, Mary-Jo?'

'I'm sure nobody wants to hear about all of this, Anne. It's water under the bridge.'

'Go on, go on,' said Christy, urging proceedings by filling everyone's wine glass. 'It's a fascinating piece of history. Reminds me of the time my uncle refused the sacrament to Bernie Chomondley. He ran the Regal, you see, and they'd been showing an Elvis Presley film that week. Threatened to throw him in the midden.'

Mary-Jo half rose from the table; gently Anne restrained her. She turned to the priest. 'You'd just said hello to her when she answered the door and when she came over to the refectory later, she was on washing-up duties, she was in such a tizzy that she dropped all this crockery.'

'What a word to use. I wasn't in a tizzy.'

'A real tizzy. Not only a cup but the saucer as well; a plate, a sugar bowl, and a little milk jug, all of them smashed into pieces. You should have heard the gasp when she admitted that little lot in the public confession. Mother Superior, I have to confess that I have sinned against Holy Poverty. *And how did you do that, Sister?* I broke a cup. *I see.* And a saucer. *And a saucer? Tsk-tsk-tsk.* And a plate. *A plate as well, never?* And a sugar bowl. *Not a sugar bowl, heaven preserve us.* Then there was a milk jug. *How could you? It seems that you not only broke your vow of Holy Poverty, Sister Mary-Joseph, but smashed it. We will pray for your gross act of rebellion with very heavy hearts.*'

'It wasn't as bad as all that.'

'Of course it was, Mary-Jo. I haven't mentioned the time they prayed for your conversion yet. And all because of Old Blue Eyes, or Young Blue Eyes as he was then.'

'Look, he's blushing,' Christy laughed. 'What's the matter, didn't you know you were a heartthrob all them years back?'

'I was nothing of the sort,' the priest replied irritably.

'You still don't remember us, do you, Tom?' Anne asked.

'I'm afraid not.' As Tom sipped his coffee, his eyes glanced quickly at Mary-Jo. 'You see, we had our own, equally draconian rules about talking to or even looking at nuns. There was the *magnum silencium* at seminary as well.' As though to hide the awkwardness that had suddenly come over him, the priest spooned sugar into his cup and stirred it thoroughly.

They caught the last ferry over the river. Christy slumbered as the platform crossed the water. The priest got out of the car and stared downstream. The light of day was just fading over the land, it would not be long before the first rays of dawn rose from the sea. Above him the machinery of the Transporter Bridge whirred; below, the water murmured. The ships were no longer visible in dock. The bright lights of the endless chemical installations flared, like a chain explosion.

Chapter Eleven

Having taken Christy home, the priest drove slowly through the old slag heaps, mounted the bridge over the railway lines, and felt the vibration of the cobblestones beneath him as he entered Slaggy Island. He was passing the viaduct when a figure flitted out from the shadows of one of the arches on to the road. He braked sharply. The young woman wore white leather boots to the knee, and a hugging short skirt. Her exposed midriff was as pale as the moths shimmering in the car headlamps; a pierced belly button glinted with metal. The woman hauled her way round the front of the car to the driver's door. Close up, Tom could see that she was older than he had first thought. Her make-up was badly applied, exhaustion circled her eyes like the age rings of a sawn tree. Her body, propped up in crude allurement, was sagging. All at once, he realised how drunk he was.

A hand suddenly appeared at the window, long false nails drumming against the glass. The fingers curled into a fist and punched the pane. Hurriedly, Tom rolled the window down. The eyes looking at his swam druggedly. 'Looking for business?'

'No,' he managed to stammer.

'Are you sure, love?

'I'm just going home.'

'Oh it's you.' The lurch of recognition on the woman's face made her appear even more exhausted. 'You're a bit late tonight, aren't you? Still, you might want a bit of company, do you?'

'No. No thank you.'

The hand came through the window, the plastic-nailed fingers wriggling like the many heads of a hydra. 'I'll give you a blow job for twenty quid, love.'

'Really, I'm not interested.'

Suddenly the hand opened the door and the woman squatted down. 'I could do it for you in the back of the car. Only take a minute.' The priest tried to clear his throat as the long-nailed fingers walked across his thigh. His head was swirling with wine. 'Give us fifty quid and I'll blow your mind, pet. Come on, you must want it, being a priest.' Unbalancing, she fell on her back and lay sprawled there for a moment like an upended crab. He looked down at her in a paralysis of horror. Her belly-button ring was shimmering. In the sodium light it looked stark, sterile, as though it clamped a surgical wound.

He shot the car forward and with the door still flapping open began to drive away. Getting up, the woman shook a clenched fist. 'So it's like that, is it?' she shouted. 'Don't think the girls haven't noticed. Well, your boyfriend's got his own bit of trouser tonight. He's in there with him now, you'll see him.' Her stiletto heels beat a tattoo as she ran after him.

Having lurched the car into the lock-up garage, Tom stayed sitting in his seat. His hands lay inert on the crease of his trousers. The seat belt was twisted round his neck. He looked at his watch. The luminous face admonished him with its late hour. His mind filled with the newspaper headline of his scandal: DRINK-DRIVING PRIEST IN ALTERCATION WITH VICE GIRL. Only slowly did his breathing return to normal. Yanking the wad of lint from the side of his head, he stared at his reflection in the driving mirror. His face was as pale as the prostitute's belly. His head swam.

The prostitute was just driving away in another car when he sneaked from the garage towards his front door. He heard a step somewhere behind him, and looked over the road. Kevin was watching him from under the faulty street light. The priest stopped. 'What do you want, Kevin?' he demanded, his voice breaking slightly. 'Why do you keep hanging around here?' There was no reply from the flame-bearded man. Kevin stared back, eyes averted, as humble and unpredictable as a stray dog. 'I've nothing to give you.' Hurriedly, the priest mounted the three steps to the presbytery door.

A smell of cigar smoke greeted him as he crossed the tesselated tiles of the hall. A droning voice could be heard from one of the upper rooms. The priest shook his head vigorously to stop its swirling. Climbing the stairs, the fug of blue smoke thickened; the voice resonated, it did not belong to his friend. Tom went first into Frank's room, but it was empty, then slowly he mounted the stairs to his own attic room. A volley of laughter hit him on the threshold. He saw the chessboard first. It stood on the desk in the window well. Then he saw the players. Frank was sitting at the chair, whilst an unshaven man in a black leather jacket and with a gold earring crouched opposite him. They were both smoking cigars. 'Tom, so you're back at last,' Frank greeted him.

'My dear Cardinal Newman,' said the other man, coming over to Tom with the welcoming grin of an intimate friend. 'Have you cracked the genetic code yet?'

The priest's hand disappeared in the large paw of the shipmaster. He blinked. 'Captain Cargo, how are you?'

'Never been better. And for why? Because today I am discovering that instead of consisting of a thousand million million million atoms, I am made up of a thousand million million million *and one*.'

Having pulled his hand free during the captain's laughter, the priest looked around his room. He could tell at a glance that many of the books on his shelves had been pulled out from their usual positions. 'Where've you been, Tommy boy?' Frank asked.

'I had an appointment.'

The blond eyebrows of the seafarer lifted like a pair of grins. 'With a lady?'

'A nun,' the priest replied blandly.

'A nun is still a woman.'

'Two nuns and Christy, if you must know.' There was an empty bottle beside the chessboard.

'It's not like you to be so late, Tom,' said Frank.

The shipmaster touched his earring in his curiously intimate way. 'I have been learning just exactly what *is* like you.'

Tom tightened. 'What do you mean?'

'Frank has been telling me all about your days in the seminary. I have also just been sharing with Father Frank here. You see, I too was a seminarian.'

'Have you cut yourself, Tom?' Frank asked.

'It's nothing.' Tom made no effort to stifle his yawn. 'Well, I'm pretty exhausted actually.'

After a showing of profound deliberation Frank finally moved his knight. Instantly the captain replied with his queen. 'Another game to you,' said Frank, smiling in disbelief. 'Hey Tom, it's been an education listening to the captain, *and* he's won every single game of chess as well. I found a set in the parish room. The Mad Monsignor must have played.' Tom stared at the chequered board. The squares seemed to shimmer, like a mirage. 'Now at last a real opponent's come for you, Captain Cargo,' said Frank standing up. 'Tom's a good player.'

'I'm nothing of the sort.'

'He was the champion at seminary.'

Tom yawned ostentatiously. 'The thing is, I'm pretty tired.'

'But we have so much to discuss, my friend. Now you are knowing that I too experienced the rigours of a seminary, can I not also join the club?'

'There isn't a club.'

'Then we must form one.'

'The seminary club,' laughed Frank.

'I have been hearing from Frank how water in your chamber pots froze solid in winter but perhaps mine was even colder than yours, yes?'

'I don't know, was it?'

'Let me ask you something different, my friend. Are you a Van Gogh or a Stalin?'

Tom glanced about the room. The bookmark in his breviary lay in the wrong page. His copy of *Damien the Leper* was face up on the bed. A pillow had been ruffled. His picture of *The Return of the Prodigal Son* lay slightly skew from the perfect angle it had observed under Tom's eyes for three decades. He rubbed his face with a weary hand. 'I don't know what you mean.'

'It is easy, my friend. Allow me to explain. Both Stalin and Vincent Van Gogh went to seminary. Both men wanted to save world. One of them destroyed it, the other was destroyed. So which are you?'

Frank yawned widely. 'Well I'd better be going. I'll leave you two to your chess and your discussions of life, the universe and everything.'

'Thanks a bunch, Frank,' Tom hissed.

Tom listened to his friend's unsteady descent down the little flight of attic stairs. He missed the bottom step, laughing drunkenly.

'I'm sorry,' Tom explained. 'But I'm tired too. Too tired to play chess. Another time perhaps.' Captain Cargo stood, his leather jacket creaking, and having placed two cigars in his mouth, sparked a heavy Zippo lighter against the huge palm of his hand. His whiskered cheeks pulsed like lungs as he smoked both cigars into life. Their pungent fumes stung the priest's eyes. 'I don't want to be rude, Captain, but I simply must go to bed.'

The captain nodded. 'I understand. We play another night.'

Tom saw the seafarer to the front door then went to the bathroom. Filling the sink, he threw the water over his face. His grazed head stung.

When he came back into his bedroom, the captain was sitting on the bed. He still held the two lit cigars. He rose. 'Why you insult me?'

'Insult you?'

'Yes, my fellow seminarian, you insult me.'

'I'm not insulting you.'

'But I am repaying your compliment and you tell me to go.'

'I don't follow.'

'It is maritime custom. If someone comes to your cabin, you must return visit. But now you turn me away.' The captain's blond eyebrows sharpened interrogatively. Feeling a wave of savage drunkenness break over him, Tom looked away.

'I didn't mean to insult you.'

'Then smoke with me, and tell me about your thoughts.' The smouldering cigar remained stretched out, like a challenge. 'Look at cigar, finger of creation as depicted on Sistine Chapel ceiling.' Quailing, the priest took it. The captain clapped an arm around his shoulders. 'There are many things for us to talk about, my fellow seminarian, not just genes. For instance, did you know that there are no virgins in the Bible?' The captain laughed out a cloud of smoke. 'Of course I am referring to misnomer of Christ's mother as Virgin Mary. It is only when the Hebrew word for *young woman* was translated by Greek Septuagint as *virgin* that all that nonsense began. But you will know all this. Here is an interesting idea. How about God as Platonic hermaphrodite?'

'As what?'

'Let me show you.' With his arm still round the priest's shoulders, he guided him to the Rembrandt print. 'What you see?' he demanded.

'It's the return of the prodigal –'

'I know, I know. But what do you *see*?' Sparking his Zippo, the captain held it up to the print. The light fell on the hands of the forgiving father resting on his son's shoulders. 'One wide, one narrow. One shaped for a hoe, the other perhaps a needle.'

The priest looked at the picture and then at the sailor. Wonder narrowed his eyes. 'Yes, I see. In all these years I'd never realised. One hand is a woman's, the other a man's.'

'Exactly, my friend. But why? Consider this. What has the son done to his father? By asking for inheritance he has publicly wished his father dead. But not only this. The father waits for him to return every day and when he sees him at last he is unable to contain joy. He runs to greet him. By doing this he acts like a woman, and brings another disgrace on himself. The act of forgiveness is one that destroys the father in the eyes of the world.'

'You have this print, Captain Cargo?'

'I have seen the *painting* many times. In Leningrad. Sometimes I like to look at it, at other times not. It is like story from Herman Melville. A sailor falls overboard; in the time it takes to rescue him, he has lost his mind in immensity of ocean. It interest you, this picture?'

'Yes, very much,' whispered the priest.

'You give it thought?' The priest nodded. 'Then think of this, my friend,' said the seafarer with abrupt intensity. 'Despite all the evil he has done, the prodigal son's journey will be shorter than that of his elder brother.' The captain continued to stare for a moment then closed the Zippo. He danced the priest away from the print. 'Here is being an interesting question. Science seems to be a matter of numbers, but is it any different from theology? Six-six-six is number of beast, and a cockroach can live for nine days without head before dying of starvation. Six-six-six and nine days without a head; when it comes down to it both these numbers are signifying same thing. What are they both signifying? They are all two signifying Armageddon.'

Tom stared at the shipmaster through the clouds of their cigar smoke. Despite himself he began to laugh. Cargo shared his humour until their voices became lost in mirth. The seafarer was the first to recover. 'By the way, my fellow seminarian, thank you for the books. You say I borrow. In your capacity as port chaplain.'

'Yes, of course. Let me just write down –'

'I will not forget.' The captain tapped the large, bulging pocket of his jacket. The hard covers of a book showed like the ears of a small animal. 'I am finding this one especially most interesting.' He brought out the book.

'*The Imitation of Christ,*' said the priest with a single glance. He drew on his cigar, coughing back the black smoke.

'What does it say life is, my friend? *A shadow's shadow – a world of shadows.*' Tom's head swirled again; when it cleared he found himself under sharp scrutiny. 'I think tonight that you have had a great shock in the shadows, my friend Van Gogh.'

'A shock?'

'You pale as ghost.'

Without meaning to speak Tom heard himself replying. 'Yes, actually I did.'

The captain drew in a lungful of smoke with abrupt energy. Then released it slowly: a Buddhist exhaling in meditation. 'Life is uncertainty, my fellow seminarian. Sometimes I am finding myself agnostic even in theology of science. Let me be explaining. Two add two equals four. I know this, but sometimes I yearn to throw off yoke of genes and knowledge.' Without warning, the shipmaster screamed at the top of his voice. The cord of his neck thickened like a ship's rope: 'Two add two equals five!' Shrugging he went over to the chessboard and began to lay the pieces on the board for another game. He scooped up two of the pieces and held them one in each huge fist. 'Black or white; good or bad; Stalin or Van Gogh?'

With his ears still ringing from the captain's shout, the priest gazed at the fists held under his nose. Images of the evening throbbed in time with his ringing ears. He saw the house set on the marsh amongst the chemical silos, the statue in the corner of the light-filled room, the red wine in his glass, the face of Mary-Jo, and the drunken eyes of the prostitute gazing at him through the car window, against which her fingers scrabbled. He saw too the mysterious hands of the forgiving father. The urge to laugh again suddenly enveloped him. The captain began to laugh too, his sharp canines revealed by the lift of lips. 'My fellow seminarian, chess later. First you must be my guest at Barnacle Bill's.'

'Now? It's past midnight,' said Tom weakly.

'They know me in Barnacle Bill's. They will give me, how are you saying, lock-in. Until nine o'clock in the morning if I want.'

Lifting both hands in what he hoped was a steady barrier, the priest shook his head. 'Look, I appreciate the invitation, but I'm just shattered. I'm out of it.' The thoughts of a moment earlier seemed to drift with the smoke of his cigar. The urge which had brought laughter cooled into dread. 'Actually, if you must know there's just been a rather ugly incident.'

'Not with your woman?'

'My woman?'

'Sorry, I am meaning the nun.'

'No, no, nothing to do with the nuns. It was something else.' The priest paused for a moment. The seafarer's earring seemed to spin of its own accord. 'One of the women outside harangued me.'

'Harangue?'

'It means abused, behaved very aggressively.'

'No?' The captain lifted a finger to caress his earring and the priest noticed how long he kept his thick nails. 'One of the whores, she ask you want jig-a-jig?'

Tom's face tightened with disgust as he felt again the fingers of the exhausted prostitute creeping over his thigh like a snake. 'She didn't say that. Actually, she asked me if I was looking for business.'

'Looking for business?'

The priest smiled with sour incredulity. 'Looking for business.'

'And what you say?'

'I told her no of course. She started swearing. You won't believe it but she chased after me.'

'Why she get angry?'

The priest stared at the man on the other side of the chess-board. The earring seemed to begin spinning again. All at once it annoyed Tom. 'I don't know why she got angry. How should I know why she got angry?'

'She not friend of yours?'

'Friend?'

'Shh,' coaxed the captain with drunken suavity. 'Do not *you* be getting angry.'

'I wasn't angry. It's what you're implying.'

'I implying?'

'That she had a reason to be angry. That I knew her somehow. Look, Captain, it was hardly anything really. I'm just making it sound dramatic. I think she was just angry because I nearly knocked her down. You see, she stepped out right in front of the car.'

A small bottle materialised in the sailor's hand. He flipped the cap off and held it over the chess pieces. 'What's in the bottle?' the priest asked.

The captain shrugged. 'Whatever you are looking for.'

The liquid was red and seemed to froth as the bottle was lifted. It seared the roof of Tom's mouth. Just as he was about to gag, the spirit suddenly became smooth. Mellowness suffused his veins. The priest took a second, almost extravagant draught, and smiled broadly. Taking the bottle back, the ship's officer drank also. He did not flinch as he lifted the bottle. Neither did he smile after swallowing. 'Father Carey,' he said with abrupt seriousness, 'I would not advise you to drive car in red-light district in your state. It would be scandal if anything got out. And if you kill someone with car, could you live with yourself? I don't think so.'

'Oh, God,' murmured Tom under his breath.

'But do not worry, my friend. Nothing happened. Your guardian angel was there. Just be careful you not do what Blessed Damien did to save his soul.'

'And what was that?'

'He reach out and kiss leper.'

After a moment's silence their laughter boomed out again. Although he had been fighting against it a grim joy was overwhelming the priest. The chessboard bounced between them as their bodies jerked. 'So you come then, my friend? To Barnacle Bill's? The lepers will not come to you.'

'What do you mean?'

'I mean, if you want to be holy man like Damien then you must go to where the lepers are.'

'I don't want to be a holy man.'

'I think you do. Yes, I think you do. Unless you are too frightened to meet with God.'

Kevin had gone when Captain Cargo and the priest emerged from the presbytery. A couple of figures lurking in the arches bobbed out hopefully as the men drew near, then melted away again when they had passed.

There were no lights on at Barnacle Bill's. It was a red-brick house, its lower levels glazed with green tiles. Once one of a terrace, it now stood alone, like a huge crab stranded on a beach. 'You see I thought it would be closed,' the priest said, adding with the precise enunciation of the drunk, 'so I'd better just be getting back. I have port duties early tomorrow morning.'

'Agh!' the captain waved away his scruples. 'You always work too hard. Frank told me. What you hoping to achieve? My friend, have you not learnt yet, the world will always lie just beyond your grasp? How can it be any different for a survival machine in a world of genes?'

Clenching a huge fist, the sailor punched the locked door of the public bar. After a few moments light from an upper room flushed the night. The window was thrust open angrily. 'Piss off, it's way past closing,' a voice called down. The captain punched the door again. 'You'll fucking smash it down, you mad bastard.' The shipmaster lifted his face to the light. The voice changed. 'Oh, is that you, Captain Cargo?'

Less than a minute later locks could be heard turning on the public bar door, tight bolts were withdrawn. The publican was obese and obsequious. 'Third time, it's not door I punch,' the captain declared with bad humour.

The publican tried to laugh but found only a rasping grunt.

He tugged at the folds of fat rippling from his neck. 'And what can I get you, gentlemen?'

'Cognac,' returned the seafarer with the air of one giving the only possible answer. 'And could you have word with those girls. They give priest a scare.'

'Priest?'

'Allow me to introduce. Father Tomas Carey.'

'A priest? Fuck off, Captain Cargo.' Almost managing a laugh, the publican squinted at Tom. He saw the Roman collar. 'Stone the crows, he is as well. Well I'd heard there was a priest back.'

'Nice to meet you,' Tom returned. His own words seemed to echo ludicrously in the empty bar room.

'Which one was it then? What was she called?'

'Excuse me?' said the priest.

'Which one of the girls has been giving you grief?'

Tom swatted away the question. 'It's nothing.'

'No, no,' insisted Captain Cargo obdurately. 'You must sort it out for him.'

'He doesn't have to at all,' Tom returned.

'My friend, you want her to slander you in newspapers?'

'Why on earth should she do that?'

The landlord's folds of face flesh stretched into a salacious grin. 'What you been doing with her then, Reverend?'

'Nothing,' the priest replied. 'What are you talking about? Nothing happened.'

The grin unfolded into a suspicious leer directed over at the door. A bearded silhouette showed in the smoked-glass panel. 'Get out of it!' the publican suddenly cried. 'I've told you not to come round here, you crazy retard.'

'Kevin is with Father Tomas,' the captain said in a dangerously quiet voice. He laid a finger lightly on the publican's chest. 'Wherever he go, Kevin go. Three cognac, please.'

The landlord tried to grin away his fear. 'Cognac for Kevin?'

'Open the door and welcome him.' The finger tensed slightly

and the publican bustled to the door. The red-bearded Kevin shuffled in.

'I declare open first meeting of seminary club,' said the captain arranging three stools round a table. 'Now tell me, Kevin, what seminary did you attend?' Kevin stared from the doorway. 'Come in, come in.' Sitting down himself, the captain beckoned. 'What you say, Kevin?' As Kevin inched towards the table, the sailor nodded as though listening to sage words. 'Perhaps you are right, my fox-haired friend. There is no seminary as good as the gutter. Good, now you are sitting. Come, come, Father Tomas. Why you not sit? But what is matter? You not look as though you are enjoying yourself. Imagine this is confession box. Maybe I am a man deeply in need of spiritual guidance. Perhaps I have terrible thing on conscience; could it be that my soul is in mortal danger?' As Tom sat, the ammoniac smell of the vagrant assaulted him. He stared at the thick coat and slippers. This close the priest could see that the blisters on his heels were raw. The vagrant's one good eye was staring widely, the tumour of flesh wept slightly in the socket.

The landlord brought their glasses on a tray. Cargo shot out a hand and gripped the publican's wrist for a few seconds before allowing him to withdraw. 'There,' the sea captain beamed. 'Where two or three survival machines are gathered in my name.' He took a sip and smacked his lips with a show of great satisfaction. 'Now, my fellow seminarians, what is topic for club's first debate? I know: is the human race founded on an error?'

The priest reached for his drink with an air of abandonment. 'Yes,' he said.

'Ah, our first speech. He will be contending that human race is founded on error. How so? You mean replicator genes making copying errors in the primordial soup?'

'I'm not talking about any of that,' Tom said, drinking half of his measure. 'I'm not even talking about original sin.'

Cargo nodded. 'In moment we hear more, but first, Kevin, you must state your position.'

Kevin lifted a hand to stroke his beard then scooped up his drink and tossed it down in one. The sudden movement wafted ammonia. The captain spluttered with laughter. 'An excellent opening statement.' Kevin's beard was beaded with drops of cognac. 'Why are you smiling, Tomas?'

'I can hardly believe I'm here.'

'And what *are* you doing here marooned on this Slaggy Island amongst fallen women in a falling down house on a falling down street on the edge of the world?'

Tom drained his glass and grabbed hold of the side of the table as though he feared it might slip from his grip. He giggled with astonishment. 'There's nowhere else for me to go.'

'A fine man like you? I no believe it.'

'I'm beginning to think I'm a piece of driftwood, like one of your chromosomes that's wandering loose. A rogue gene.'

'Like a sailor, like a vagrant?'

Tom nodded. 'I belong to nobody and nobody belongs to me. That's a cold fact when you see it square. I'm drunk, Captain Cargo, but perhaps it's the truth.'

'The truth sometimes lurks in a bottle of cognac.'

'You see, just this moment I've come to realise something. It doesn't matter what happens to me. I make no difference to the balance of the world.'

'Maybe it make difference to beautiful nun you love.' The captain's hand came over and rested lightly on the priest's wrist. 'Your secret is safe with me. I knew from moment I first saw you that we were brothers.' With a sudden flex of his arm, the captain pulled the priest over the table to him so that Tom could feel his breath on his face. 'I not know why, but I have concern for you. I worry. For instance, is your head all right?'

'My head?'

'You gash head.' Tom raised a hand to his temple. Another wave of drunkenness broke over him. The seafarer's dark whiskers chafed his own well-shaved cheek. 'Tell me, brother Van Gogh, how did such a terrible thing happen?'

Tom found himself whispering in return, 'I was on a ship.'

'A ship?'

'Yes.'

'Was it a good ship?'

'I don't know.'

'You don't know? What ship was it?'

'I think you know, Captain.'

'Do I?'

'It was your ship.'

'My ship?'

'The *Neptune's Booty*.'

The whiskers grazed the priest like barbed wire but the captain held him. Kevin suddenly reached over the table under them and taking the captain's glass drained it. Roaring with laughter, the captain released Tom. 'My friend, if you and I are Van Gogh or Stalin then who is our flaming fox here?'

'Rasputin?'

'Perhaps, or is he Gustavus Adolphus?'

'Why do I never understand what you're talking about, Captain?'

'You not know Gustavus Adolphus? He a Swede. He burn many Catholics.'

'Why on earth should Kevin be Gustavus Adolphus?'

The sea captain looked in puzzlement at the priest for a few moments, then tutted softly. 'I am worried that worse accidents might happen to you.'

'Accidents?'

'You gash your head first; what next? A ship is a dangerous place for someone who not know what they are doing. Without hard hat a little knock can be fatal.' The captain picked up his empty glass and studied it absorbedly. Tom ran a hand over his face. When he removed it both of the other men were staring at him. 'And now,' announced the captain, 'the seminary club will be reconvening on *Neptune's Booty* for Father Tomas's first official visit.'

'Captain, I only went on board *Neptune's Booty* because they wanted a Mass.'

Without warning the captain crashed his glass down on the table and shouted, 'Two add two equals five!' Glass sprayed over the floor. Vaulting the bar the sailor ripped a bottle from the optics rail. He drank deeply. From behind the bottle he stared long and hard at Tom and Kevin. 'We were wrong, you and I, Cardinal Newman. Kevin is not Rasputin, nor is he Gustavus Adolphus. He is your guardian angel. Under stinking coat are folded wings.' A strange sincerity bloomed in the shipmaster's eyes as he touched his earring.

When the priest emerged from the deserted pub, Captain Cargo was urinating against a lamp-post. Tom breathed out very slowly, desperately trying to claw back his ebbing sobriety. Unbuttoning himself he too began to urinate. The relief flowed through him instantly. 'Cargo,' he called over, 'you're a horse.'

'What?'

'I'm saying you piss like a horse.'

'A horse?'

'It's just something they used to say to us at seminary.'

They walked down the viaduct, and the captain lit two more cigars. A potash train rumbled overhead. No faces showed from the arches as the leather-jacketed figure passed, but Tom thought he could make out the lurking shapes watching them warily, like mice at the passing of a weasel. The pair crossed the wide railway bridge whilst the potash train still passed underneath, bringing the fertiliser to the docks from the mines many miles beneath the Cleveland sea. The walkers moved over the grassy slag heaps that ring Slaggy Island beyond the littoral of railway tracks. When he found the ground spinning beneath his feet, Tom gazed up. The stars were a weak glimmer whose constellations could not be told. The potash train lumbered away into silence. 'Don't look now,' the captain suddenly said, his whisper loud on the quiet air, 'but we are being followed.'

The priest managed to turn round. 'It's just Kevin.'

'Behold, the faithful Fool! Here we are on this blasted heath and your Kevin, he is the Fool in our little play. Only one question is remaining. Is it you or I that is Lear?' Not replying, Tom walked on. 'Why the Fool follows you?' the captain demanded with sudden intensity.

'How do I know?'

'I see him standing by your house.'

'The Church always attracts people like that. No one else will take them.'

'Yet it is *you* he has chosen.'

'Utter nonsense. It would be anyone who was there.'

'Perhaps you are not Lear after all but a great saint, like your Father Damien with the lepers. Or maybe it is *you* that follow *him*.' Cargo dug a hand in his jacket pocket to expose the pricked ear of Tom's well-loved book. 'I borrow this as well,' he explained. 'Maybe one day you *will* be saint. Father Tom, the Slaggy Island Saint. And then people will write book about you, with picture in front. Only, without disgusting deformities of leprosy, and *with* your guardian angel.' As though his legs had been cut out from under him, the priest slumped lifelessly. Only the captain's arm kept him upright. 'What is matter?' The alarm in the shipmaster's voice became a grin. 'I have said something funny?' he demanded of the priest whose laughter gripped him in its paralysis. The captain's grin grew into laughter until he was unable to bear the weight of his companion and both men subsided helplessly to the ground. 'What I say funny? What I say funny?'

'Yes,' Tom managed to say in jerks. 'What you say is *very* funny.'

When the priest's laughter deserted him abruptly, he decided to close his eyes. It seemed to take an age before he realised that he was flat on his back. The ground beneath him was lumpy, the texture of the spoil heap discernible through the grass. He opened his eyes and saw that a single star had dislodged itself from the pale urban night and was orbiting him. A wave of nausea came over him, and he was unable to move. At last, with a shock, he realised that the star was just the prick of a cigar. Captain Cargo was standing above him. Suddenly nauseous, Tom clambered on to his knees. 'Praying to Bacchus, my friend?' Tom's body bucked as the jets of vomit flailed out horizontally.

The next thing he knew he was being supported by the captain and Kevin. 'I can walk,' he heard himself insisting.

The port was utterly silent. The captain's voice lit the stillness for a moment like a flare as he greeted the figure in the security cabin. They had reached the huge sections of the pipeline when the priest saw that Kevin was gone. The sight of the rusting hulk of *Neptune's Booty* seemed to half sober him. 'I've been meaning to ask you something. Are you a Russian, Captain Cargo?'

'Me? *I* am the Fool. Otherwise what would I be doing standing here many miles from home on a dock with a drunken priest?'

'I'm sorry, I appear to have been ill. I'm not used to –'

But the seafarer was not listening. 'I know that I am the Fool, but you . . . who are you?' He sighed grandly. 'You have no idea how I am yearning for friendship. Let me tell you a story. Once I transported a live cargo of sheeps down the Suez Canal. It was no fun. When we got there no one would have them. They had to be slaughtered in the boat. Sometimes I am feeling as lonely as one of those sheeps. Tell me, my fellow survival machine, do you love or hate the world?'

'What questions you ask.'

'Answer then. Are you wanting to save or destroy?'

'I suppose I've always wanted to preserve the world.'

'So? A kind of saving, but not heroic.'

'And you, Captain, which did you want to do?'

'I can't remember.'

A fox passed no more than five yards away from them, its pads silent on the wooden jetty of the dock. No sooner had it appeared than it vanished, its tail stitching back the small rent in the fabric of the night its nose had made. '*They* are no sheeps you know, Tomas.'

'Who?'

'We have tradition at sea, we call "Bosun's Tradition". It mean all new seafarers must go with bosun to the first brothel they dock at. These Filipinos of yours, *they* have their own traditions. Oh yes, they full of God and priests, but they biggest at jig-a-jig. Why you think whores on Babbington Road and every other port? So your altar boys can fuck.'

'Are you trying to be offensive, Captain?'

Cargo smiled disarmingly. 'The Fool has licence to joke. So what if your holy men love whores? Love's small change, but still something. A beggar does not throw away a kopeck. Only a starving man can appreciate a crust.' The seafarer broke off. 'What you thinking about, my friend?'

'Thinking?'

'All evening you are thinking. All night your mind is being distracted. Is it the beautiful nun you love? Or can you not choose between the two?' The shipmaster rasped his whiskers with a thoughtful finger. 'But come. Now let us go to my cabin and continue Socratic dialogue. For start I need to know what you think of Bush and Blair's war.'

'What's your real name, Captain Cargo?'

'Why you want to know that? Not even my own father know that.'

The ship's hawser twisted suddenly under the flow of the tide. With a startling spurt of speed Cargo ran up the gangway. The priest realised that drunkenness had increased his fear of the gangplank. As he stepped on to it his heart began to thud.

He had almost reached the top when he found his way blocked. Captain Cargo stood there. 'Why you come on board my ship without permission?'

'You weren't there. I looked for you, but you weren't there.'

'You expect me to believe that?'

'I really have no idea what you will believe.'

The captain's eyebrows flattened, giving his face a dull, blunt look. His head lifted back like a poised hammer. The priest was forced to step back. 'In sea, predators come from left, right, up and below. Three dimensions of danger. So it is on ship.'

Below him, Tom could just make out the slack water churning between the hull and the quay. He gripped the rope rail until his hand stung but Cargo's huge body was pushing him back now. He could feel the gold earring cold against his cheek. His words were breathy, his canines glistened. 'You should not come on ship when Captain Cargo not here. Otherwise how is Captain Cargo to help you if you slip?' Tom's feet scrambled for traction on the smooth metal of the gangway but a powerful kick knocked them away. For an instant he felt himself falling into a maelstrom of rust, simmering water and darkness, then, just at the last moment, something plucked him free. With a gasp he realised that the shipmaster had placed him back squarely on the gangway. In a confused whirl he saw the cold metal of the gangway, the captain's earrings and the figure of Kevin looking up from the pipeline on the quay. 'We are understanding each other now, I think, my fellow seminarian. Representatives of science and religion have come to agreement.'

Dawn was breaking when the priest woke. His head was throbbing, his mouth was sour, his whole body ached. A fly buzzed fatly about him, repeatedly landing on his sleeve, which was encrusted with vomit. He was lying in a section of the pipeline. Below the wharf the slack water was silent. There had been the ship's bridge, a bottle of cognac and the rest was an uncertain haze.

He walked through the port seeing no one. The reversing tone of a stevedore wagon began to sound out from some hidden dock. A line of heavy-goods lorries queuing at a distant cargo terminal started their engines one after another. On the grass of the old spoil heaps, where a pony had just been tethered, he saw a huge cigar butt flattened by the powerful grind of a heel.

In a pocket he found a packet of wine gums, the tube as crushed as the cigar end. He put three of the sweets in his mouth and chewed, like someone trying to rid themself of a foul taste.

Barnacle Bill's stood like the last tooth in old gums. The arches were deserted. A used condom lay in a doorway, like a fish head. The sign on the boarded-up church beside the presbytery was faded and had been scratched over by countless vandals, but the original gilt words were still visible: ST BEDE'S ROMAN CATHOLIC CHURCH, MASS TIMES: SATURDAY EVENING (VIGIL MASS) 6.30PM. SUNDAY: 8.00AM, 11.00AM, 6.30PM. CONFESSION: SATURDAY 10.00AM AND BEFORE EVENING MASS. The sun was rising above the roofs of Babbington Road.

In the hall Tom sent the wooden coat stand clattering to the tiles. He picked it up clumsily before mounting the stairs. In the bathroom he drank deeply from the tap then gazed at himself in the mirror. His face was drained of colour; grazes webbed the side of his head. His Roman collar was askew; the lapels of his black suit jacket were sprinkled with cigar ash. He breathed in and caught a rank dander of alcohol, tobacco and vomit. He began to cough.

The priest went up to his attic room. He picked up the chessboard. Halfway down the stairs he dropped it. The pieces rattled their way down to the hall. Sunlight was pouring into the parish room. His head flashing with pain, Tom opened the old chest. Placing the chess set inside, his fingers brushed against something. He brought it out carefully. It was a precisely folded cassock on which lay a black biretta. Tom looked up at the old black and white photograph. This was the biretta the old cleric was wearing. And the cassock too. Tom sneezed with the release of long captive dust. 'Thinking of taking on the role of the Mad Monsignor permanently?'

'Hello, Frank. Sorry, did I wake you?'

'I thought it was Kevin kicking the door in, coughing himself to death and then throwing himself down the stairs.' There was incredulity in Frank's eyes. 'Have you just got in?' Tom nodded.

'Tom Carey out all night? I can't believe it. Were you with Captain Cargo? What's the matter, Tom? Has something happened?'

'I can't really remember. All I know is that I nearly fell off the ship.'

'You went on his ship?'

'There was some kind of struggle. For a few moments I really thought he was trying to push me off the gangplank.'

'You're joking.'

'I don't know, Frank. I'm confused. I probably got it wrong. The thing is, I was completely legless.'

'Smells like it. What have you been doing, sleeping in a dust-bin? Are you all right?'

'I can't believe what I've done, Frank. First of all I drove across town pissed out of my skull. What if I'd been stopped by the police? Or I'd knocked someone down? Then I had a run-in with a prostitute. And after that I went to a lock-in at Barnacle Bill's and somehow nearly ended up being thrown off a ship.' Tom cradled his head. 'What's happening to me?'

'I'll give you this much, Tommy boy, when you go off the rails you go off big time.'

Tom laid the biretta and cassock on the arm of a chair. The sunlight blanched his face. 'Frank?'

'Yes?'

'Are you as lonely as me?'

A loud knocking reverberated through the presbytery. 'Right, that's it,' said Frank. 'I'm going to sort him out this time. When we dismantled the bell we didn't mean he could just start knocking at the door instead.'

'No, leave it.'

'What?'

'I said, leave Kevin alone.'

'It's usually you that wants to sort him.'

'Not this morning. Let him be.'

The knocking started again. 'Tom, are you all right? Tell me what it is, otherwise how can I help you?'

'How can you help someone who has lost the person they thought they were? How do you help someone who has lost God?'

'You're just going through a hard time now. It wasn't always like this.'

'Shadow of shadows, a world of shadows.'

'What?'

'I don't understand, Frank. I did it all as I was supposed to.' The priest closed his eyes and quoted: '*Remember all the time that you are a stranger and a wanderer on the earth.*'

'The Imitation of Christ?'

'I gave everything up for the Church. Everything, do you understand? You see, I too had my secret sacrifice, Frank.' Tom's voice became a husky whisper. 'I feel so guilty about her, Frank.'

'What?'

'I don't think a day has gone by when I haven't thought about her.'

'Who are you talking about? That woman you met in the pub?'

'No, no, no. That was just a chance encounter.' Tom sat heavily on one of the old armchairs. 'Maybe we should turn that photograph round again, I'm not sure he'll want to hear what I've got to say.'

'I don't follow you, Tom.'

'It's lain over me like a shadow all my life.' Tom looked up at his friend in agony. 'Would you get me a cup of tea, Frank? I think I'm going to need one.' Immobile in the chair, the priest listened to Frank in the kitchen: the cupboards opening and shutting, the tap, the flick of the switch, then the long toil of the kettle to the boil. Bringing two cups back into the parish room, Frank handed his friend one of them. 'Did you put in three sugars?'

'Of course.'

'Is it Fairtrade?'

'I didn't notice. Do you want me to look?'

'I'm only joking, Franky.' Frank watched Tom drinking gratefully. 'I needed that, Frank, thanks. My throat's a Scotsman's crutch I think the expression used to be at Ushaw.'

Frank grinned. 'A little less on the graphic side please.'

'At the time she was hardly a woman and I was hardly a man.'

'Who, Tom?'

'She was nineteen and it was my first year after ordination.'

'When we were at St Aidan's together?'

'Yes and I haven't seen her for nearly thirty years, until last night.'

'She was on the boat with Captain Cargo?'

'Now that really would have been too much.' Tom's laughter brought on another coughing fit.

'I'll say one thing,' said Frank, 'you're laughing a hell of a lot more than you ever did.'

'All night I kept on thinking about her. When I was with him, with Captain Cargo, her face kept coming back to me. Even when I thought I was going to fall from *Neptune's Booty*, I could see her.'

'Did you *love* this person, Tom?'

'Until tonight I'd only ever seen her face . . . and her hands.'

'This is getting very bizarre.'

'The whole bloody Church is bizarre, Frank! Maybe it's only now that I'm seeing that.'

'Are you still drunk?'

'After what I put away last night I should think I bloody am!' The sudden raising of his voice seemed to exhaust Tom and he sat there for a while without moving, his eyes tight shut, the cup motionless on its saucer. 'You only ever used to see their hands and their face. All those veils and wimples.'

'I see, she's a nun. Where did you meet her again?'

'With Christy over on the north bank. She's one of the Sisters there.'

'What did you say to her?'

'When her friend asked me if I remembered her, I said that I didn't.'

'What the hell did you do that for?'

The priest shrugged slightly. 'I thought it would be easier.'

'Easier?'

'I don't think I need to talk to you about silence, Frank. Silence, reticence, extreme reserve, sweeping yourself under the carpet, whatever you want to call it. It becomes a habit early on, doesn't it? Maybe that's what seminary is all about. Self-erasure. From a habit it becomes a friend, a need. You don't realise until it's too late that all along it's been your bitter enemy.'

'What happened between you, Tom?' Frank whispered.

'Nothing.'

'It must have been a big nothing for you to remember her all these years later.'

Sitting upright, Tom finished his cup and laid it down on the ground. He picked up the biretta. 'We held hands for nothing more than three seconds and it was like discovering a new world.' The priest stared at the biretta turning in his hands.

'Who was she, Tom?'

'She was at Nazareth House.'

'One of the nurses?'

'They called her Sister Mary-Joseph. She's called Mary-Jo now. God, my head's pounding.'

'The wages of whisky . . .'

'. . . is truth. The hangover of truth anyway.'

Frank tried to grin. 'You were right. Let me turn the Mad Monsignor over. I'd hate to think of him watching us right now.'

'Leave him. He should hear it.'

'But what would he say?'

'*Beware of women.* That's what he'd probably say. *Especially those of the female kind.*'

'That's what they did say, at seminary. Not the advice *I* needed.' Frank whistled softly. 'A nun, fair play to you. How did it happen? Convents were like Fort Knox in those days.'

'You remember Nazareth House. It's hard to totally seal an

old persons' home. There's always a reason for a priest's presence. You know how it is, confessions, last rites . . .'

'They had daily Mass in their chapel as well.'

'One of us used to go there practically every day, sometimes twice.'

'Was it that often?'

'Maybe you didn't notice so much because I tried to go as often as I could. God, how I fought against it.'

'How did it all begin?'

'The nuns had a rota for answering the door. I'd been in the parish about a month when I found myself wanting it to be her turn.'

'Mary-Jo, did you say?'

Tom nodded. 'What did I know about this young woman? Practically nothing. Not even her name, until last night. *Custos oculorum*. We weren't even allowed to look in the eyes of a woman. But I couldn't help seeing her hands. *Custos oculorum?* The only way I could have stopped it all would've been to have blinded myself.'

'Christ, Tom.'

'They weren't what you'd call beautiful. Her hands. Rough and reddened with all that scrubbing; coarsened with soap and changing bedpans. But there was something in the way she opened that door. So gentle and . . .' Tom blushed like a boy. 'Love at first hand. Pathetic, isn't it?'

'No, Tom. It's human.'

'I recognised her last night as soon as I saw those hands.' He laughed self-deprecatingly. 'Old habits die hard. *Custos oculorum. Custodian of the eyes*. Even now I find it hard to look a woman in the eye, but by God I can flirt with a pair of hands.'

Frank smiled sadly. 'What have they done to us, Tom?'

'It had to happen and it did. How can one human being not look another in the eye when they meet day after day? So one morning I looked up from the hands. Until then I don't think that I had ever broken a single rule and until that day I didn't really know what it felt like to be alive.' He broke off and stood abruptly. He walked wearily to the door and began to mount the stairs.

Frank found him in his attic room, gazing at his books. He did not turn round. 'In the east, poets often use hyperbole, Frank. They compare the eyelashes of the woman they love to butterflies. When the rest of the body is hidden, I suppose it's even easier to be mesmerised by the eyes.'

'What happened between you?'

Still without turning, Tom spoke matter-of-factly. 'Each time I arrived we looked at each other a little longer until one day I heard myself speak to her. *Good morning*, that's all I said. I was breaking my own rules as a priest and enticing her to break her rules of silence, but I still said it. The next time she answered the door I said: *Good morning, Sister, and how are you this morning?* And she replied. I couldn't believe it.'

'What did she say?'

'*Fine, thank you*. What did you expect, Frank, some great romantic declaration?'

'Oh, you know me. I've grown used to living in hope.'

'I'd gone from the hands to her face and now it was the sound of her voice which haunted me.' Tom smiled sadly. 'They say the human voice is the finest instrument. So you see, they would have had to have made me deaf as well. Giving out Communion became unbearable. To see her lining up with all the others at the altar rail and me wondering how I could stop myself from dropping the whole paten. *The Body of Christ* I would say and she would reply *Amen*. To watch her lips move as they spoke and to see her hands held in prayer was like . . . I'm not describing it very well I'm afraid, Frank.'

'On the contrary, Tom.'

The priest turned abruptly from his books and faced his friend. 'Of course it had to come to a head. There was an emergency one night at Nazareth House. An old woman was dying. She wasn't expected to last until dawn. I answered the phone. In a lifetime of endless phone calls that was one that actually meant something. It was the Mother Superior, Sister Philomena. She was asking for Father Fitz, but when I woke him he told me to get lost.'

'That wasn't *all* he said. I remember that night, Tom.'

'It all came back to me when the bosun rang.'

Tom was suddenly convulsed with a coughing fit. Frank brought him a glass of water from the bathroom. 'We're funny friends you and I, Tom. We've kept ourselves hidden from each other.'

'It's been a long time since I did this much talking. The past twenty-four hours feel like a year.' Tom paused to drink thirstily. 'I soon found out the reason why Sister Philomena had been so adamant Father Fitz came. The nurse on duty was there alone in the room with the dying woman. It was Sister Mary-Joseph. Oh Frank, I'll never forget how she smiled when she saw me. She couldn't help herself, it was a reflex. A small thing perhaps but it was something that would change my life for ever. It's only tonight, seeing her again, that I've realised what it meant. I've spent my life in flight, Frank. I've got the soul of a bird in the bush.'

'No, Tom, no –'

'It's too late to pretend any more. Last night, despite the drink and everything, I realised something. I've got nothing. Maybe it was the drink that let me see. Maybe that's why I went with Cargo last night. When you've got nothing you'll do anything to try and find something. You see, the emptiness aches.' Tom went over to the window well. The sun was rising higher over Babbington Road. 'I'd come too late for the old woman. She was already dead. I gave her the sacrament anyway. She was called Rose. See how I remember it all? We sat there together all night; sat at the deathbed, Mary-Jo and I. At some point, I don't remember when or why, I reached out to her and before I knew what was happening, we were holding hands. That touch, Frank, that touch. Oh Christ, but even without eyes or ears I would still have loved her.' Tom leant his head against the cool of the pane. 'There's more, Frank; I'm afraid there's more. I found out that she used to take one of the catatonics to the coast on Monday mornings. The coast at Saltburn.' A goods train trundled over the viaduct. The glass trembled against the priest's forehead. When the train had gone he straightened, saying softly, 'That's enough for one night.'

'Did it end badly, Tom?'

'It was as though someone had died and I couldn't mourn. *Remember all the time that you are a stranger who must wander the earth alone.*'

'Thomas à Kempis again.'

'When she went away I tried to live by Thomas à Kempis. *You must crush your own nature and never be familiar with any woman.* It became my rule of life, Frank. The memory of her hands, her face, her voice became a torment. I learnt to be revolted by my own thoughts, to see myself as some kind of defective, depraved individual.' Tom nodded to himself. 'I said that it was like not being able to mourn a death. But it was worse than that. You see, it was as though I had done the killing. When I chose not to love her, it was like I had killed someone. And you know what? That person turned out to be me.'

Frank blew the air through his cheeks. 'What are you going to do now?'

Tom looked at his friend through bloodshot eyes. 'What do you mean?'

'I mean, isn't this a second chance?'

'No. It turns out that it hadn't meant much to her anyway. Something in the nature of a joke. Just as well really. Why ruin more than one life?' Tom went over to his bed and picked up the black leather volume lying there. He ran a finger down the gold-tipped pages. 'Now if you'll excuse me, Frank. I'm going to say my morning breviary.'

Chapter Twelve

The sun blazed in the June sky. The world rippled from her feet in widening horizontals: the bench on which she sat, the esplanade, the beach with its pebbles giving way to golden sand, and the sea whose blue merged with the sky. Toddlers flitted over the sand, digging and paddling, bustling with buckets. A group of surfers bobbed in the big waves breaking at the foot of the pier. At the far end of the bay, half a mile of gleaming foreshore away, the rocky escarpments frothed with nesting seabirds, whilst behind her the cliff trams passed up and down from the little town, one rising as the other descended. A child walked past Mary-Jo, licking a huge, melting ice cream, leaving a trail of drips. 'Lovely day,' said the child's mother.

'Yes, it's beautiful.'

'Who needs Lanzarote when the sun's shining in Saltburn?'

The house martins were feeding nestlings in their mud-and-daub nests under the eaves of the wooden amusement hut. Although it was only mid-morning, already the aroma of chips frying drifted from one of the concessions. Directly below Mary-Jo, just on the tideline, a father was teaching his young daughter how to hold a cricket bat. 'It hasn't changed, you know.' Mary-Jo looked up to see a round, elderly woman standing above her, leaning against the railings. 'Not really. They chopped a bit off the pier and cleaned the water up, but it's still the same. Do I know you, love?'

'I don't think so.'

'Let me have a good look at you.' The old woman came over

and lowered herself with some difficulty on to the bench beside the nun. For a moment the effort rendered her breathless, then, with a smile, she stared at Mary-Jo. 'No, maybe I don't. I'm not usually wrong with a face, mind. It'll come back to me.' The woman opened her large, white handbag; the clasp clicked audibly, bringing a scavenging gull towards them. 'Want a sweet, honey? I've got a few in here.' Mary-Jo looked into the handbag. Its capacious depths were filled with bags of sweets, the kind that used to be bought by the quarter pound. 'There's some black bullets and wine gums as well. Do you want one of the black ones? Are you all right, pet?'

'You've just broken my dream.'

'You what?'

'I used to come here.'

'Did you? So did I. Everybody did. Who did you come with, love?'

'Someone who ate sweets, wine gums. He liked the orange ones best.'

'Orange? Now, you don't hear that often. It's usually the red or black that folks are partial to.'

'It is, isn't it?'

'Well here, have any colour you like, dearie; you look as though you need building up. On a diet are you?' Mary-Jo took a red wine gum and the two of them sat there chewing. The old woman's gums slavered loudly. 'It's not the same, you know, love,' she confided, 'trying to eat sweeties with false teeth. Too much of a faff. No, it hasn't changed. The weather's better though, isn't it?' The woman laughed in a surprisingly high-pitched tone like one of the gulls that passed overhead from time to time. 'Many's the time I remember the rain sheeting down. Cats and dogs it was. Excuse me for a moment, won't you, pet?' Through the corner of her eye, the nun could see the woman take out the upper row of her dentures and remove the sweet that was stuck to the palate. 'I don't know why I bother really,' she lisped, her face misshapen by the removed teeth. 'Can't eat sweets properly without your own teeth.' There was a tiny sprout of white whiskers on the woman's chin. 'You know what, dearie?' she said with sudden desire. 'If there's one thing I'd love more than anything else in the world it would be to chew a chocolate eclair with my own teeth again. Can you eat them?' Mary-Jo nodded. 'There, but you've got lovely teeth. Mind you, when I had them it was just one lot of fuss. And the pain you got. I once got toothache so badly that I was fit to jump off the pierhead. What did you say you were called, pet?'

'Mary-Jo.'

'That's a bonny name. And I bet you were a bonny lass. In fact, you still are.' The woman seemed to be repeating the name to herself a number of times, then she sighed. 'No, you're better off without them, that's what my Billy said. And, on the whole, I would say he was right.'

Mary-Jo stared out over the sparkling sea to where the ships were laying off at anchor. A chemical tanker was caught directly by the sun, its red warning colours blazing. From the sea the nun's gaze returned slowly to the land. It retracted itself up the beach, finally coming to rest on the next bench from where she sat with the old woman. What she saw there caused her to lurch as though under the force of a punch. 'Things don't change, you know, pet,' the woman was saying. Having placed her teeth back in, her face regained its shape. 'It's us that do. There, that's the way it is. It's just us what changes. What you looking at, dear?' Mary-Jo forced her gaze away from the next bench along the esplanade, but not before the old woman had seen what had just caught her eye. 'Know him, do you, that priest?'

The nun spoke quietly, as though struggling to keep an even tone. 'He's a priest, is he?'

'Course he is, can't you see the dog collar? I thought my eyes were bad.' As the old woman laughed good-naturedly her dentures worked themselves loose. 'He'll be hot in that black suit. You don't see so many of them that smart any more. Do

I know him? Let me have a proper look. No, I don't. He reminds me of someone though.' The old woman peered at the nun in confusion, as though suddenly remembering that they were strangers to each other. 'What are you doing here? Are those your bairns on the beach?'

'No.'

'Grandbairns?' The old woman's voice was uncertain.

'I don't have any children or grandchildren. Actually I'm not married.'

'Aren't you?'

'Never have been.'

'Pity.' The confusion was gone. The woman reached over and laid a hand on Mary-Jo's. 'You'd have made a lovely mam. I can see it in your eyes. You'd have been good for your bairns. You'd have made a man happy as well. Anyway, I'd better push off. You'll excuse an old woman bothering you, won't you, pet?' The old woman struggled to lift herself and Mary-Jo rose to help her. She clutched at the nun. 'Let me have another look at you. I'm sure I *do* know you.' She stared for a little longer then, blowing heavily, straightened her dress. 'My, what a hot day. And to think I've seen the rain on this esplanade like you wouldn't believe. But nothing changes; one tram goes up, another comes down.' With an air of baffled disappointment that evaporated after a few yards, she shuffled away, her bag of sweets held before her.

Mary-Jo sat back down on the bench and gazed unseeingly at the figures on the beach below. Movement in her peripheral vision showed that the priest had stood and was moving away. 'Tom?' she called. He did not seem to hear her. He was walking even quicker. She stood up. 'Tom?' He did not stop. 'Tom?' Her shout cut through the lazy hum of the seaside summer. The priest stopped.

'Oh, hello, Sister,' he greeted her as he came back. 'I'm sorry, I didn't see you there.' He hovered uncertainly at her bench.

'I didn't know it was you either,' she said.

He spoke briskly. 'I've brought some crew from a cable-laying vessel. They've got a couple of days at Teesport so I thought they might like the beach. The captain's given them a couple of hours of shore leave.'

'Good idea.'

Tom wafted a vague hand to where the shipping was stacked on the horizon. 'It'll make a change for them to see the world from this angle, from the proper end of the telescope.' There was a pause. He filled it quickly. 'But what are you doing here?'

'Oh, I just fancied a bit of sea air. So how's the job going, Tom?'

'It's tiring, but actually I quite enjoy it.'

'Your head's healed nicely.'

'Sorry? Oh, that.' He raised a finger to the hardened scab. 'It was nothing.'

Another pause opened up between them. This time Mary-Jo occupied it. 'Sorry about what happened, Tom.'

'What do you mean?'

'That night you came round. Anne gave you a bit of a grilling.'

'Oh, that doesn't matter.'

'She can be a bit strong when she gets her teeth into something.'

'Maybe I should apologise myself. I wasn't the best of company.'

'I thought you took it very well.'

'Well, thank you.'

'In fact, as far as I can remember you got a few jabs back at her. That doesn't happen very often.'

'She wasn't that bad.'

'Well, I'm used to her, but you coped with her really well.'

They looked at each other. Simultaneously both placed a hand on the back of their bench. Only a yard of cool, green metal separated their fingers. Further down the esplanade the old woman could be seen approaching another stranger. The priest and the nun spoke the same words: 'So how are you then?'

Each waited for the other to continue. Neither did. The hands were withdrawn. 'Look,' said Mary-Jo impulsively, 'do you want a cup of tea?'

'A cup of tea?'

'Sorry, maybe you haven't got time?'

The priest looked at his watch. 'No, I . . .' he stuttered for a moment before mastering himself. 'Of course I've got time. The lads are meeting me at the minibus in half an hour.'

Another silence came over them. On the beach a kite was fluttering, below it the child who had been learning to bat was now bowling at her father. There was only one café on the esplanade. It was by the pier. Without another word they gravitated towards it. The door was open. The strains of a pop song came from the radio perched on the counter beside a stand of scones. 'Two teas, please,' Mary-Jo said to the woman behind the counter.

'Let me pay,' said Tom, struggling for his wallet.

'No, you sit down.'

'Two teas,' the woman replied, moving over to the urn. 'Anything else?'

'Anything else, Tom?'

'I'm OK thanks.'

Mary-Jo stooped to scan the perspex stacks of cakes and biscuits. 'There's Tunnock's teacakes.'

'I didn't know they still did them.'

Mary-Jo grinned. 'Let's have a Tunnock's teacake, Tom.'

They sat down with their mugs and plates at the table overlooking the sea. 'This place hasn't changed a bit,' remarked Mary-Jo.

'It's cleaner,' Tom returned.

'I don't ever remember there being this many people at Saltburn, do you, Tom?'

'It's a hot day I suppose.'

'Yes, it's warm enough for swimming.'

'For the hardy amongst us.'

'The bracing north-easterly breeze. They'd even heard about that in Africa.' Mary-Jo looked at Tom over the rim of her mug. 'So how are things over on Slaggy Island?'

'Fine, fine. Our friend Kevin is still knocking at the door. Christy's been showing Frank round the port. That's my friend who Christy kept on referring to so subtly when we were at your house. He's doing some ship visiting. In fact he's a good help. He took a minibus-load of crew to the shops yesterday. They hadn't been off their ship for three months . . .' The priest faltered when he met Mary-Jo's eye. To hide his confusion he began to spoon sugar into his mug.

'I didn't realise that you had *such* a sweet tooth, Tom.'

'They say habits get worse with age.'

Painstakingly Tom stirred, staring helplessly at the swirling surface. He gazed across the café. Through one window he could see the people on the pier, through the other the cliff trams were constantly rising and falling, like a pair of scales that will not balance.

'Tom?'

'Yes?'

'Did you really not remember?'

'How do they work?' he demanded with abrupt enthusiasm. 'Those trams, I mean. It must be some sort of hydraulic principle. I've always wanted to know.' He followed the progress of the trams, one to the bottom, one to the top. His voice dropped in tone. 'I'm sorry, but I find it hard to even say your real name. It takes a bit of getting used to, these new ways. Sister Mary-Joseph. There, I managed it.'

'I haven't been Sister Mary-Joseph for twenty years now, Tom,' Mary-Jo said gently.

'Yes, well, suppose I'm a bit of a dinosaur really.'

'A friendly one, I hope.' The trams filled with people. The doors were closed and they began their exchange of height again. 'Tom, you didn't answer my question.'

His voice was nothing more than a murmur. 'Of course I remember you.'

'But –'

'How could I forget?' For a long time nothing was said. The tram rose and fell. The lid of the tea urn bobbed restively as the hot water ebbed and flowed on the tide of its boiling. Taking a deep breath, Tom forced his voice to sound brisk. 'I'm sorry, but I just thought it would be easier if I pretended that I didn't.'

Mary-Jo looked at him with sudden sadness. 'Maybe it would.'

'I mean, a whole sea has passed under the bridge since then.'

'Yes, it has.'

'And with Anne being there. I didn't know what . . . Anyway, I wish you'd let me pay for this.'

'You can pay next time. I mean, we're allowed to have another cup of tea together, aren't we?'

'Of course.'

Together they stared at the trams passing halfway up the cliff. The sunlight caught the stained-glass windows and cast a rainbow colour. Amongst the passengers alighting at the bottom were a young man and a young woman who held hands even as they passed through the turnstile. 'I remember every moment of those Monday mornings, Mary-Jo,' the priest whispered. He paused as though to control his breathing. 'I'd watch you bringing your patient down in the cliff tram.'

'She was catatonic but I know she liked it. Just to feel the sea air on her face.'

'Me too. I loved our walks along the front.'

'We even paddled once. Remember, Tom?'

'I remember.' A smile ached on Tom's face then died. 'I'm so sorry, Mary-Jo.'

'What for?'

He dropped his gaze from her face. It was caught in her hands. They were folded on the table. Like the wings of a bird in flight, they suddenly separated: one to pick up the mug, the other to lift a Tunnock's teacake from the small plate. The grace of this movement, simple as it was, astonished the priest. Her arms were bare. She spoke with a full mouth. 'Are you growing a beard, Tom?'

In confusion he lifted a finger to his cheek. It encountered an unfamiliar roughness. 'I just haven't shaved for a few days.'

'It must be being with all those sailors.'

'Yes, when in Rome.'

'Tom, have you had a good life?'

'A good life?' He looked down at his own hands, the skin smooth and untarnished as a piglet.

'Sorry. What a question to ask on a sunny day in Saltburn over Tunnock's teacakes.' The young couple from the cliff tram entered the café. Still holding hands, they sat down. On the table their fingers formed a single, seemingly insoluble knot. 'Tom, are you all right?'

'You must have seen some changes in your time,' said Tom gruffly. 'In your order, I mean.'

'The stories I could tell, Tom.'

He lightened his tone. 'Go on then.'

'What?'

Tom forced himself to smile. 'Tell me some of your stories.'

'Oh, you'll have heard all that stuff about enclosed orders before.'

'You'd be surprised about what people won't tell a priest. Anyway, I'd like to hear them. *And* you promised.'

'What?'

'That night at your house. You promised to tell me about the time they prayed for your conversion. Sounds like strong stuff.'

'OK. You haven't heard the half of it yet. One of the older nuns was ill, so it was decided we should go on a pilgrimage to Holy Island. It was also decided that we should walk the last ten miles. As we walked Sister Philomena led us in prayer for our sick Sister. Sister Philomena was –'

'I remember. Your Mother Superior.'

'Imagine it, decade after decade of the rosary as we splodged through the mud. We must have sounded like an electric lawnmower as we passed through the villages.' Without warning Mary-Jo's laughter rang out through the café. 'It got on my nerves so much that I asked Sister Philomena if we could have a period of silent prayer. She ignored my request of course. So I asked again. You understand, Tom, it was unheard of to ask for something even once, let alone twice. When she still ignored me I told her that I thought Our Lady would appreciate some silent prayer. Well, if looks could kill. When we got to Holy Island, instead of going to where we were staying, Reverend Mother made us go on to St Cuthbert's Island where our night prayers were said for my conversion.'

'That's going a bit far.'

'Wait for the rest . . . As we were praying the tide came in and cut us off. We had to wade back to the main island. Everyone got soaked, and Sister Philomena caught a cold.' Mary-Jo's laughter filled the café. When it was joined by Tom's, the woman behind the counter looked over smilingly at them. It even impinged on the enclosed world of the young couple, who glanced in their direction. 'That was it as far as they were concerned. Not only was I a soul in need of conversion, but I'd made the Mother Superior get the sneezes. So taken all in all, I was obviously better off out of the way. As far away as possible, Africa in fact.'

Tom had been gazing at her all the while but now he dropped his gaze to his empty teacup. 'I'm so sorry.'

'But why, Tom?'

His tongue laboured to pronounce the continent. 'For Africa.'

'What?'

'It was my fault that you got sent there. Somebody must have seen us together one morning in Saltburn. I've felt so guilty about it.'

'But they never knew.'

'What?'

'No one ever found out. They moved me because of the Holy Island incident. And because I had a habit of breaking crockery.' Mary-Jo smiled sadly. 'Is that what you've been doing all these years, blaming yourself?'

'I don't know what I've been doing all these years.' Swallowing, he risked another look at her, then he rose abruptly. 'Is that the time? Look, I've got to go. Nice to see you again. Send my regards to Anne.'

When Tom had gone, Mary-Jo sat for a while at the table, the mug in her hand long since cooled. The cliff tram rose and fell, taking with it the young couple from the café. The tide was ebbing and the foreshore advanced beneath the pier inch by gleaming inch. 'Are you all right, love?' the woman behind the counter asked.

'I've got cancer,' the nun replied simply.

'Oh sorry. I didn't –'

'That's all right. I shouldn't have said that.'

The woman brought over another mug of tea. 'On the house. They can do a lot these days. New treatments.'

'Thanks.'

'Was that your priest?'

'Sorry?'

'It must be good to be able to talk to a priest.'

'Yes,' Mary-Jo replied softly.

'I saw the dog collar. Can you call it that? Well, he'll be a comfort. Doesn't he look like what's-his-name? You know, him what was in *Butch Cassidy and the Sundance Kid*. Paul Newman, that's him.'

'Yes, he still does a bit.'

The sea was a marble blue as Mary-Jo walked along the esplanade. There were more people on the sand. A woman sat under a parasol, breastfeeding her baby. Up the coast, the steelworks could be seen, its bell tower shimmering in the heat. The ships had not moved. The red of the chemical tankers burnt like a perpetual sunset. Mary-Jo bought an ice cream and sat on a bench. 'Now I remember.' She looked behind her to see the old woman who had spoken to her earlier. She had not heard her approach. 'Yes,' she whispered. 'You were one of the Sisters at Nazareth House. You nursed me mam. I remember you. Me mam loved you. You had a heart of gold. An angel, that's what you were. And it was such a long illness. There, I never do forget a face. But what's the matter, lovie? Here, don't cry. Don't cry; not on a nice sunny day at Saltburn. Eat your ice cream, don't sadden yourself, pet, life's too short to waste on tears. Eat your ice cream before it melts.'

Mary-Jo drove along the road beside the railway lines bordering Slaggy Island and skirted the long desolate wire fence behind which yawned the concrete expanses of the port. She crossed the river on the Transporter Bridge, the cables whirring above her. Terns flew overhead amongst the winching machinery supported by the girders. As soon as she saw the car standing outside the white house, she knew what was happening. Parking hurriedly, she ran on to the marsh.

The tide, which had been ebbing at Saltburn, was draining the marsh, revealing the glistening beds of its creeks. Mary-Jo sat on a creek bank gazing at the footprints of a little bird, pristine in the mud. The wader must have passed that way just moments before she got there. Perhaps she had disturbed it. With a pang she thought of it probing, searching for food, its movements caught up in the ceaseless dance of survival, these footprints its only legacy.

When Mary-Jo heard the voice addressing her, she did not look up. 'Are you running away from me, Mary-Jo?' The voice was Irish and belonged to a slight woman in open-toed sandals. 'Or does the sight of your Mother Superior still make you quake?'

Mary-Jo got up and the two women embraced. 'It's good to see you, Moira.'

'And you, Mary-Jo. As I was driving along the river I hardly recognised the place. Your terrace seems the only one left.'

'They want to knock that down as well.'

'But you and Anne won't let that happen, will you?'

'Well, it'll be up to Anne; I won't be around to prevent it.'

The embrace broke and the two nuns stood looking at each other. 'Now what's all this about?' Moira began gently. 'Anne's beside herself. She says you're refusing all treatment.'

'That's right.'

'But why?'

'Shh.' Moira followed the direction of Mary-Jo's pointing finger. A little marsh bird was coming up the creek. It passed the two women, probing the mud.

'Everyone thinks the world of you,' Moira said quietly when the bird had passed from view. 'We're all so upset. Will you not reconsider?'

'I saw my mother wither away, her body pumped full of drugs. She was in hell for the last months of her life. When she died, Moira, she didn't even know what season it was.'

'It was hard on you, wasn't it?'

'My dad used to bring her to visit me in the convent. She was so ill she could barely walk but she still came.'

'Yes, I remember.'

'Every visit she was thinner, weaker. The last time I saw her, my dad carried her in, as though she was a suitcase. Nothing more than skin and bone.' Mary-Jo paused for a moment. Her shining eyes gazed impassively at the water in the creek. 'It was like watching a skeleton.' Her voice dropped to a whisper. 'If only I'd been allowed out to nurse her myself.'

'Oh, Mary-Jo, so much of what we did in those days was wrong-headed. Scandalous, you might say. No one should come between a girl and her mother like that.'

'Oh, I'm not bitter.'

'The old ways are gone now, Mary-Jo. I understand your reservations. Especially with your mother's illness. But medicine's moved on since then. There are things they can do for you today that they couldn't hope to do for your mother.'

'Can they make us live for ever?' Mary-Jo whispered. 'Or help us die with dignity?'

'They can do a lot between those two points.' Moira searched the other woman's face, then nodded. 'I understand. Whatever you decide, we're here for you. Will you be coming back to the Mother House?'

'And leave here?'

'We'd be able to nurse you properly there. Everyone will be so pleased to see you again. You're a breath of fresh air to us stick-in-the-muds.'

'Moira, I think I want to die here.'

Together they walked over the marsh. 'You've worked it all out, haven't you, Mary-Jo?'

'Yes, I have.'

'You can come to us any time if you change your mind.'

'Moira?'

'Yes.'

'Will you look after Anne? I'll be all right. It's her that will need the help. She seems so robust, but I know her.'

'You'll have to take things easier yourself, Mary-Jo. Maybe you should stop working.'

'Oh,' she replied with a smile, 'there'll be plenty of time for stopping, Moira.'

They came to another creek, its exposed mud bloated as a tumour. 'You'll have to jump, Moira. Land on that stone in the middle and spring to the bank.'

'It's not quicksand, is it?'

'It could take you to the waist.'

'And then the tide comes in. A dangerous place, your marsh.'

'You have to treat it with respect.'

'Is that stone steady?'

'It was the last time I passed this way. Just follow me.'

They came up from the sunken creek and waded through a bed of buttercups. Slowly Mary-Jo's gaze travelled over the marsh. The brilliant blue sky diluted the presence of the encircling chemical works; the rays of the sun erased the drifting effluents. Amongst the acres of buttercups, the air was scented only with the perfume of the meadow.

'Isn't it beautiful here?' Moira said with some surprise.

'I want everything to be as normal as possible, Moira.'

'Yes,' Moira replied, still immersed in the sudden beauty of the place. When she saw Mary-Jo beside her, she closed her eyes.

'Don't be sad.' Mary-Jo took the hand of the Superior of her Order.

'Have you thought of a trip to Lourdes?' There was hunger in the question.

'A miracle?'

'We're all praying for one. We could get you to Lourdes tomorrow.'

'Yes, we're in a world of miracles. But I don't need to go to a shrine. Maybe I'll see the geese return again this autumn, that'll be miracle enough. Moira, I'll tell you something that I can't tell Anne. It would just upset her. You see, I'm ready to die.'

'Life as a trial for the afterlife, the bliss of the coming husband of death? I thought you'd thrown out the old ways with the old habits, Mary-Jo.'

'There's nothing new or old about the mystery of death.' Mary-Jo spoke without rancour. 'I've lived with it for so long now. Since the last operation, since my mother died. Moira. We all have to make the next journey. I'm lucky that I can prepare for it.' She held her face up greedily to the slight midsummer breeze. 'I want to know where the wind blows. Does that sound strange? You see, it's the breath of God, isn't it? It's the familiar things that carry the greatest mystery. The wind, the flowers. Moira, I'm ready to know why the geese return.'

Chapter Thirteen

'My God, Tom, I didn't know it was like this.' The Bishop turned from the rain-scarred windowpane. 'And that thing in the doorway, was that really a heroin needle?'

'Yes, it was.'

'We'll have to get you out from here before we end up with a real Blessed Damien on our hands.' The Bishop's smile moved seamlessly into a disapproving click of his tongue. 'I was remiss sending you here. I must apologise. Mea culpa, Tom. Mea *maxima* culpa.' As he continued to stare through the window, the prelate's eyes widened behind his glasses. 'Is that woman down there what I think she is, Tom? That woman under the viaduct?'

'A prostitute? Yes.'

'At four o'clock in the afternoon?'

'There's someone there most of the time.'

'In this weather too.'

'They use the doorways more when it rains.'

'And who's the down-and-out standing under the lamp-post?'

'Oh, that's just Kevin.'

'You know him? Will the car be safe?'

'I keep mine in a lock-up garage.'

'Well, I'd better not stay long then.' The Bishop came away from the window. 'Don't you hate it when it rains in July?' He grinned without mirth as he came close to the priest. 'And so, Tom, how's life under the stone?'

'I'm sorry?'

'That's what you said when we talked. You said that you were seeing life as though you had lifted up a stone and were looking underneath.'

'Maybe it's easier now.'

'Why's that?'

'Because I've come to realise that that's where I am too.'

The Bishop's fingers drummed his stomach agitatedly as he took in the appearance of his priest. The usually well-shaven cheeks showed a beard of a week's growth; the black clerical shirt, unbuttoned at the neck, had clearly not been ironed; his Roman collar was not straight. He spoke briskly. 'I think you were right after all, Tom. What you need is a proper sabbatical. Where would you like to go? There's a group going to Rome. I could get you a place. That's an idea, Tom, go and see the Holy Father before, God forbid, St Peter calls him. Take in Assisi as well. I know a place called Barga in Tuscany, I could fix you up there. Listen Tom, I'll shoot from the hip. You go away today, just drop everything, you've got my permission, we'll cover the port duties, they're not much anyway are they? You take your break and when you come back we'll talk about your future. You hadn't forgotten that I had you in line for a Monsignor, had you? I tell you what, when you're in Rome why not pop into Gammarelli's and get fitted up for the cassock. Now, what do you say?'

'May I stay here?'

'What?'

Tom stared down at his unpolished shoes. 'I think I might as well stay here.'

'Stay in this slum when you could be relaxing in Rome?' The Bishop laughed. 'This place wouldn't be passed fit for human habitation.'

The priest tried to smile but he could not raise his eyes. 'I've got used to it.'

'So what are you going to do, just moulder away in here like a rat?' The sudden rising of the Bishop's voice filled the room. The prelate forced himself back into an assumed levity. 'What do you think it'll be like in winter, Tom? Brass monkeys. It'll make seminary days seem like a rest camp.' The Bishop nodded at the priest with a show of camaraderie. 'Let me level with you, Tom. Asides from saying the odd Mass on a ship, there's nothing you can do here that a lay chaplain couldn't easily do.'

'I know that.'

'So why stay?'

'I don't know.'

'You must know.'

'Well, because I'm here.'

'That's not a very good reason, is it?'

'It's all I've got.'

'As your Bishop, I'm asking you not to throw yourself away here. And as a friend, I'm –' The prelate exhaled. 'Be honest with me, Tom. Is Frank staying here?'

'Yes, he is.'

The Bishop took a deep breath. 'How long has he been here?'

'A few weeks. I've lost track. Maybe longer.'

'You know how things get about. Did you really think that you could keep this little arrangement secret?'

'I haven't tried to.'

Again the Bishop's voice rose. His eyes widened with anger. 'Tom, are *you* a homosexual?'

Tom spoke levelly, looking the Bishop in the eye at last. 'No, I am not.'

'Then what's he doing here?'

'He hasn't got anywhere else to go.'

'So you thought you'd throw the presbytery open? What is it, some kind of hostel for the homeless?'

'He's been working as a volunteer ship visitor.'

'You'll be inviting that fellow outside to move in soon. The simple one standing under the lamp-post in all that rain.' The embryo of a smile on the priest's mouth froze at the Bishop's coldness. Tom lifted a hand to scratch his cheek and found that it was shaking. 'There's a scandal waiting to blow up here, Tom.

Do you really want to damage the Church? Is that what it's come to, when one of my best priests seems hell-bent on shooting us in the foot? Now come on. I know that's not you. Cut you in two and we'd find the grain of the Church.' Behind his glasses the Bishop's eyes grew piercing. 'Come with me now, I'll put you up for a few days if needs be, just until we sort out your sabbatical.'

'No.' Tom blinked as though surprised at the loudness of his own voice. He repeated himself, quieter this time, 'No, I'm not going.'

The Bishop took off his glasses. Without them he seemed greatly diminished. 'Some of the younger ones, it's no use telling them anything. They know I've so few priests that they can do what they want. But you, Tom, I never thought you'd do this to me.' He rose wearily and stared out of the window, wiping away the condensation from the pane. Suddenly he rapped against the glass, yelling, 'Get off the car!' Fumbling at the catch of the sash window, he snapped at Tom, 'Does this thing open?'

'Not very easily.'

'I think someone's trying to steal the bloody car.'

The Bishop rushed out of the room. He took the stairs two at a time, shaking the walls of the presbytery. Tom went to the window. Already the pane cleared by the Bishop had clouded over. He wiped it again. Down below he could see Kevin standing staring at the strange sight of a stationary car on the arches cruising route. The Bishop burst from the front door of the presbytery. Cowed, Kevin backed away. Getting into his car, the Bishop drove away quickly, spraying dirty puddle water.

The rain intensified. Drops drilled against the panes of the window well and on the roof above. Tom sat motionless, his breviary open on his lap. He heard Frank come in, scattering water from his umbrella before propping it up in the hall, but when his friend called for him, he did not reply.

The day went on, time measured by the shifting intensities of the rain. Then, as though recovering from a paralysis, Tom suddenly stood up. 'So you are in?' Frank said, emerging from his room when he heard him on the stairs.

'I'm just popping out.'

'Take my umbrella. It's cats and dogs out there. I've been on the *Australia Hope*; they've just set sail. They all sent you their best regards.'

But the priest was not listening. Without coat or umbrella Tom staggered out of the presbytery. Instantly he felt himself engulfed by the rain. Throwing his head back, he stared up into the downpour, the drops coursing down his chin and the back of his neck. His vision was blurred. The street was deserted. The rain had driven even the prostitutes from the arches, and not a single punter prowled the flooded street.

He walked quickly down Babbington Road, his step flaring to a trot as he passed through the narrow, empty terraces of Slaggy Island. The rain lashed against the grilles on the windows, rattled the loose roof slates and prodded the occasional children's toy abandoned in a doorway. Puddles were deepening on the uneven pavements and pooling against raised kerbstones. He urged his body into an untidy sprint.

At last he came to the community centre. It was an old Temperance Hall backing right on to the railway tracks. The strip lights within shone brightly in the darkness of the July rain. Hunched under the protection of a storm porch, breathless, Tom pressed the buzzer of the security door. 'It's Tom,' he said to the answering voice. 'Tom Carey. Is Mary-Jo there?'

'Is she expecting you?' There was suspicion in the voice.

'No.'

His own reflection, caught in the glass of the door, was superimposed on the receptionist as she peered at him over the space of the foyer. 'Well, what do you want her for?' the voice on the intercom asked.

'I just need to see her.' As he fought to capture his breath, Tom studied his reflection. His eyes were wide and staring, his unshaven face desperate. His chest rose and fell. Losing his nerve, he backed away. Beyond the ledge of the storm porch the rain closed over him again. Stumbling, he moved off. 'Hey! Hey!' He had gone about ten yards when he turned to see the receptionist at the open door. 'She says she'll be right down.'

Water dripped from him as he sat in the reception area. Self-consciously he lifted a hand to his sodden neck and straightened his Roman collar. The walls, freshly painted, were covered with community information posters. Amongst them he saw one which said *Rainbow People*. It was an art therapy class run by Mary-Jo for people with mental-health issues. At the sight of her name the priest rose and strode to the outside door, but before he could open it he heard her voice. 'Tom, nice to see you.' She was coming down a long corridor towards him; her voice travelled the distance effortlessly.

He attempted a greeting. No words came out. She wore a cotton-print dress with a pink cardigan. Her long hair was loose. He took deep breaths but his heart continued to thump. 'What happened, have you been for a swim in the river?'

'Sorry?'

'Did you fall off one of the boats?' she asked, arriving with a smile even brighter than he had remembered. 'You're soaked to the skin.'

'Oh that. No, I came out without a coat.' He tried to laugh but managed only a dry creaking.

'Well come on up, the class is almost over.' He followed her. 'Do you want a coffee?'

'Tea, please . . . If you have any.'

'And plenty of sugar, right?'

'Right.' The whole building was freshly painted. Hot pipes hugged the skirting boards. As he walked he tried to calm himself, falling, by an old habit, into a decade of the rosary. But the mystery he meditated on was her face. 'We've just secured new funding,' she explained. 'There's loads of things going on.' The corridor seemed without end. They passed a room in which teenage girls sat nursing dolls. 'Parenting class,' she said. From another came the babble of toddlers. 'That's the crèche.' Still praying the automatic words, he nodded. 'We're Slaggy Island's best kept secret, Tom. Now this is my room.'

It was an artist's studio. Paintings, plaster casts and busts hung from the wall. Objects dangled from the high ceiling. There were rugs, tapestries and a loom. Gentle music was playing on a tape recorder. A potter's wheel hummed softly. At the wheel, his hands kneading the clay, stood Kevin. Within walls his beard seemed to blaze even more powerfully, like the depths of a kiln. His foot turned the treadle rhythmically. One by one Mary-Jo introduced Tom to the ten members of her class, finishing with Kevin. After a furtive look at the priest, Kevin extended a hand to him. Tom glanced at the clay dropping from it, then took it in his own.

'I think you two are old friends,' Mary-Jo grinned.

The class was just ending. Slowly the group drifted away. They talked eagerly to each other about their work and chatted to Mary-Jo. Only Kevin didn't say a word. When they were alone, Mary-Jo filled a kettle from a sink. Tom stood with his back to her, looking at the pictures on which the paint was still wet. He knotted his fingers until they whitened. But the pain could not still the lurching of his heart. 'Do you like them, Tom?' Mary-Jo asked.

He did not turn. 'I suppose art is the one subject where what society calls insanity is a positive boon. Van Gogh's ear and all that.'

'Do you think insanity is a requirement for art, Tom?'

Tom's mouth had run dry. 'I've never really thought about it.'

'Look at what Kevin's been doing.'

Unclenching his fingers, Tom came over to where Mary-Jo stood at a drying board. He cleared his throat. 'It's a cup?'

She nodded. 'Now look at it again. Two hands cupped. Two hands touching. The simplest of human gestures, but the most profound. It's creation, isn't it? Sacramental.' Laughing, she broke off as though suddenly embarrassed by her own intensity. But the look of disturbed tenderness on Tom's face confused her. 'Do you like the music, Tom?'

'Yes,' he said quickly, trying to cover himself. 'What is it?'

'Hildegard of Bingen. A twelfth-century nun.' A constraint seemed to come over them. They busied themselves with the ritual of tea. 'What do you prefer,' she asked, handing him a number of individual sachets. 'Sweetener, white sugar or demerara?'

'I can't stand sweetener.'

'That was said with conviction.'

'It's one of the few certainties left in my life. I'll tell you what, I'll have demerara. It's ages since I had that. I used to have it on grilled grapefruit when I was a curate.'

'You got sugar? Luxury.'

'We even got jam at seminary.'

'You were spoilt.'

'And no public confession like you had to go through. Mind you, we had to wear shorts and caps even when we were sixteen.'

'Better than wimples.'

'You think so?' They looked at each other, and smiled. 'Where do you get all these individual packets from?'

'The sugar? I always take some of these home with me whenever I go to a café.'

'You steal it?'

She chuckled at his expression. 'I'd hardly call it stealing. I always think I'm entitled to two. We've got to do everything to keep costs down and my class usually have the sweet tooth.'

Tom paused in his stirring. 'Sugar in tea. Another sign of madness?' Looking at each other the smile became a laugh. 'Actually there's someone I know who's always on about Van Gogh. Either him or Stalin.'

'Bit of a difference.'

Taking too large a gulp of his tea, the priest burnt his mouth. His voice trembled slightly when he said suddenly, 'I really enjoyed it by the way. I mean, meeting you out of the blue like that at Saltburn.'

'So did I.'

'I just wish I hadn't had to leave so soon. I'm sorry, it must have appeared rude. It's just that with the seafarers I –'

'Well, we can do it again, can't we?'

The rain suddenly intensified on the roof. Their glances met again then fended quickly off. Sipping his tea, Tom barely noticed the damp shirt on his back. Walking to the far wall, he studied a glazed vase.

'Tom,' she said, 'I don't think I've ever seen Kevin shaking anyone's hand before.'

'Well, you said it yourself, Kevin and I are old friends. Mind you, the Bishop gave him a flea in the ear this morning. He thought Kevin was stealing his car.'

'The Bishop on Slaggy Island, we *are* honoured. I wondered why Kevin wanted the potter's wheel. He always likes clay when something's upset him.'

'Has he been coming here long?'

'For as long as I have. He's really talented, I'll show you his portfolio.' Rummaging in a cupboard, Mary-Jo brought out a fat bundle of paper. She spread out the individual pieces on a table.

Standing together, Tom felt her shoulder brush his, as softly as a butterfly. 'I had no idea he was capable of something like this. Does he always paint people running?'

'There are some self-portraits as well. Intense, aren't they? But tender in a way. Why was the Bishop visiting you, Tom?'

'He wants me to leave Slaggy Island. I think I'm in danger of becoming something of a loose cannon.'

'Are you in trouble?'

'I suppose I am.'

Tom glanced up from the pictures to find Mary-Jo looking intently at him. 'And are you going to leave?'

'I told him I wanted to stay. I . . . He wasn't very happy

about it. I can't believe it really. For the first time in my life I haven't done as I'm told. For the first time since I was a foetus I didn't roll when they said roll.'

'What does your saying yes mean if you never say no?'

'At seminary we were told that a bishop was a priest's oxygen.'

'You're still breathing, aren't you, Tom? Actually, I've been asked to leave too.'

'You?'

'Yes. My boss came to see me.' Mary-Jo went over to the tape recorder and switched it off. She swept up Kevin's papers and put the portfolio back in the cupboard. 'I told her I was staying as well, Tom. So we're a couple of rebels.'

His voice dropped to a murmur. 'I'm so glad we've met again.'

She looked at him. 'Yes,' she replied. 'Me too.'

'I . . .' began Tom, but he could not finish. He tried to scald his mouth on the tea again, but the drink had cooled.

'It's funny running into each other again like this, isn't it, Tom?'

'Yes, it is.'

When they had finished their tea, the rain had stopped falling but the clouds were still thick. Mary-Jo turned off the lights and all at once a twilight seemed to have fallen in the room. They looked at each other through the gloom. Mary-Jo spoke with sudden brightness. 'Tom, why don't you come for supper? Bring Frank. If you don't mind braving Anne a second time that is.'

'I will, thank you.'

Outside, the road was steaming. The indefinable, wonderful scent of drying tarmac filled their nostrils as they got into Mary-Jo's car. When the nun clicked in her seatbelt, the priest felt the tip of her elbow touch his own. He recoiled. Above the roofs of Slaggy Island, the sun had broken out and in the sky the grey was rolling back. Figures were stirring in the arches as they drove by the viaduct. 'You don't mind being in the middle of the red-light district?'

'Oh,' said Tom, waving airily, 'we diocesan priests aren't like you progressive nuns, we normally just go where the Bishop tells us.' Mary-Jo pulled up outside the presbytery. All at once, in the stillness following the turning off of the engine, the closeness of the car seemed to hold over them an offer of profound intimacy. Tom was the first to pull back. 'I ought to go and have a shave first.'

'I think it suits you.'

'A beard? It makes me look like a yeti.'

'A nice yeti.'

'There's no such thing. They're ferocious beasts who prey on lonely mountaineers.' Their smiles became irrepressible giggles. 'What is it, Mary-Jo?'

'What is it with you?'

'You say.'

'No, you.'

'I asked you first.'

'Well, I don't know.'

'Neither do I.'

Helplessly, like two children, they surrendered to the strange lightness that had come over them. Then, when it had gone as effortlessly as it had come, they both got out of the car.

He showed her into the parish room and went upstairs. Only when he reached the top did he realise that he had taken the stairs two at a time. Frank had gone out to the port again. Tom wrote a note and left it pinned to his friend's door. In his own room, he undressed hurriedly, throwing his wet things on to the floor. Mary-Jo was waiting for him at the foot of the stairs. 'I like it,' she said.

'What?'

'The new look.'

Instinctively Tom felt for the creases in his trousers, but his fingers encountered only denim. 'I see, the jeans.'

'Will the real Paul Newman now step forward. Seriously, Tom, I'm surprised you even own a pair. You were always a bit of a stickler for the formal look.'

'Actually I borrowed them from Frank.' As Tom descended the stairs self-consciously, Mary-Jo roared with laughter. He followed the direction of her pointing finger. 'They are a little bit on the short side, aren't they?'

'Just a bit.'

'What else can I do? I've run out of clean clothes.'

'Don't you have a washing machine?'

'Nope.'

Tom reached the hall. Abruptly Mary-Jo stopped laughing. 'I've never seen you without your collar before.'

His hand strayed to the neck of his short-sleeved shirt. 'Maybe it's time that this old dog was let off the lead.'

'You suit it,' said Mary-Jo. They held each other's glance for an instant then smiled. 'I bet there is one.'

'An old dog?'

'A washing machine. These presbyteries used to be run by housekeepers. Where's the kitchen?'

'Down the passage, through the parish room.' He followed her into the kitchen. It was dominated by a massive wooden table. 'Told you. No sign of a washing machine. If you're interested in catering for the Last Supper, or even the feeding of the five thousand, then we've got this table. But as for washing machines . . .'

'Have you cooked anything since you've moved in here?'

He grinned. 'We are a strange species. Half yeti, half holy priest and we exist almost entirely on beans on toast.' But as he pointed to the toaster and a single pan marooned on the draining board, the smile froze on Tom's face. 'Are you all right, Mary-Jo?' Without warning the nun had doubled up as though in sudden agony. Her hand, scrabbling over the table, knocked over the Saxa salt drum. The priest watched helplessly as the salt poured on to the floor. 'What's the matter?' Turning her back to him, she half-stifled a cry. He came over. Gasping for breath, she waved him away. Then as abruptly as it had come, the pain seemed to have gone. She straightened and smiled weakly. The running salt sifted the silence until Tom strode stiffly over and lifted the drum.

'Are you all right, Mary-Jo?'

'Of course,' she returned, only the slight huskiness in her voice testifying to the pain of a few moments before. 'It's just my back.'

'You seemed in agony.'

'It happens quite a lot actually. All those cold baths and wet habits when I was a girl. I must have put it out when I was lifting the easels this morning. I'll have to go to the osteopath.'

'Are you sure you're all right? It looked pretty nasty.'

'It's nothing really. Look, could I just use your bathroom?'

In the bathroom, Mary-Jo sat motionless on the edge of the bath. She stared numbly at the meagre possessions of the two priests on the glass shelf beneath the mirror. Then closing her eyes, she wept silently. Slowly the waves of pain grew less and less perceptible.

Tom was standing in the hall when she came back downstairs. She watched him for a moment then called down impulsively, 'Let's go for a ride.'

'A ride?'

'Yes.'

'Where to?'

'A mystery tour.'

'I've never been on a mystery tour before.'

'I can see I'm going to have to take you in hand. It's one of the best feelings, you know.'

'What is?'

'Running barefoot. Even yetis have to let their hair down.' She came down the rest of the stairs.

'But what about your back?'

'It really was nothing. Now, come on, close those eyes. Let's do things properly.'

The road steamed like a geyser as they drove over the railway bridge, pierced the spoil-heap acres and skirted the port. 'When can I open my eyes?' Tom asked.

She returned his laugh. 'Not yet.'

He breathed in deeply. Her scent was mixing with the freshness coming in through the open window. A profound peace settled over him. 'It feels a bit bumpy. Where are we going? It feels a *lot* bumpy. I'm glad it's not the suspension of my car.' They continued a little longer. 'We're slowing down. Why are we slowing down? What are you laughing at now?' he demanded playfully as the car came to a standstill. 'Can I open them then?'

'I didn't mean that you had to keep your eyes shut the *whole* time, Tom.'

For an instant he thought they were out at sea. She had driven along a spit of land extending into the mouth of the river. To their left was the river, to the right the little bowl of a bay and then the open sea. In front of the nose of the car, a knot of anglers congregated round a lighthouse, their hooks dangling where the fresh water was mingling with the salt. Brightly painted wooden shacks dotted the bay like large pigeon lofts. 'I'm glad you didn't drive any further, Mary-Jo. I don't think even you could persuade a car to be a boat.'

'It's Paddy's Hole. That's what they call it. I suppose because this is where the Irish labourers lived before they built your Slaggy Island. No one lives here now. At least I don't think so. They're just beach houses.'

Small boats bobbed gently in the bay. Getting out of the car, Mary-Jo eased down the stones of the peninsula to a jetty. 'Come on,' she called. 'You came to see where I work, now I want to see your office.'

Tom screed clumsily after her. Reaching the little wooden jetty he watched her jump neatly into one of the boats and untie the mooring knot. 'Is it yours, Mary-Jo?'

'Worried I'm stealing again? Don't panic, it belongs to a friend. He lets us holy nuns use it.'

Upstream on the north bank, a chemical-works' siren was

blaring. Tom tentatively lifted a leg. Losing his balance, he fell awkwardly into the boat. Still laughing, Mary-Jo handed him his life jacket.

'Just as well,' he said. 'I can't swim.'

'You're joking.'

'The baths were always so cold at seminary.'

'A port chaplain who can't swim? Does the Apostleship of the Sea know? I would have thought that it was the first requirement for the job.'

The boat lifted slightly as it powered over the calm water of the river. 'What do you think?' she shouted over the roar of the engine.

'I thought you said we were going to walk barefoot,' he yelled back.

'We are. We're walking barefoot on water. Remind you of anyone?'

Behind them their wake frothed and then dissolved. They passed under the Ore Terminal, its immense winching equipment poised patiently by the river like giant herons. The rust-coloured dunes of iron ore stretched endlessly from the dockside. They crossed to the other bank of the river and a solitary figure standing on the deck of a red-hulled chemical tanker waved. Painted in red letters on the white deckhouse above the figure was SAFETY FIRST. NO SMOKING. The hold of the tanker rose like a swollen stomach, the coiled pipes a maze of metal intestines. At full throttle they bounced up the river, Tom holding on to the gunwale with all his strength. Jumping and leaping they reached the Transporter Bridge, its steel shimmering in the late afternoon sun. The drops of water on the girders were countless gleaming gems, shaken into lights by the winching machinery hauling the ferry across the river. 'There!' Mary-Jo cried suddenly.

'What?'

'There.'

'Where?'

'Can't you see them, Tom?'

'Yes. Yes I can.' Tom pointed at the heads of three seals. Mary-Jo cut the engine. 'Aren't they beautiful, Tom?'

The seals bobbed in the water, staring curiously at them. 'You know, they look just like the surfers at Saltburn.'

'With whiskers. Don't shave for another week, Tom, and you could be one of them.'

They stared at the seals in silence, their boat drifting slightly. 'The Celts used to think that the seals were people,' Mary-Jo mused after a while.

'Plenty of blubber.' Tom grinned at Mary-Jo, but she did not reciprocate his frivolity. Her face was wrapped in wonder. 'I didn't know that the seals came right up the river.'

'This is a holy coast. The land of three rivers. It wasn't far from here that the otters used to come out of the sea to keep St Cuthbert's feet warm.'

'Do you really believe that?'

'Don't you?'

Tom sighed. His shoulders hunched as though taking back a heavy burden. 'I'm afraid I don't know what I believe any more. Still, I'm in good company. It's St Thomas's day today; patron saint of doubters.'

Turning from the seals, she scrutinised him. 'What's the matter, Tom?'

'What do you mean?'

'Are you all right?'

'Yes, of course. I –'

'I mean, deep down. It's just that I sense something. You seem, I don't know, heavy. I haven't known you for a long time, but you seem . . . Oh look, just tell me to mind my own business. Here we are, we haven't known each other again for five minutes and already –'

'No, no, I don't mind you asking.' He shook his head and smiled sadly. 'When we were at seminary they used to call me St Peter, but they would have been better off with St Thomas.'

'Doubting Thomas?'

'I'm not like I used to be. Nothing seems certain any more.'

'You're going through a hard time, aren't you?'

'Yes I am rather. I'm feeling a bit . . .' He looked out over the water, up the river to where it mingled with the salt. 'To be honest with you, I'm all at sea. No pun intended. The thing is, it's got so bad that I don't even know if there is a God any more.'

One of the seals rolled over and then shot under the boat. Clapping her hands, Mary-Jo cried out, 'It's playing!' Time and time again the animal swam under them. Once its back just touched the bottom of the boat and very gently tugged them along. Only when a huge bulk carrier passed up the river sending out a frothing wake, did the seals disappear, leaving just a string of bubbles. Mary-Jo turned to the priest with uncharacteristic solemnity. 'You know, everything will pass, Tom. The hierarchies, the buildings, all the orthodoxies, even the Mass itself. Everything from our religion will disappear. And the only thing left will be its mystical heart. That which we share with all the other faiths. Our dreams of God.'

Hunger gnawed the priest's features. 'But who is God, Mary-Jo?'

'God comes disguised as your life, Tom.'

'I don't understand.'

'Neither do I.' She laughed then narrowed her eyes. 'What I do know is that our buildings and institutions are empty. God chose the world to express himself or herself, Tom. The laugh of a child, the flight of a kingfisher, falling in love.'

Neither of them spoke for a long time. At last the priest broke the silence. 'Can I show you something?' He directed Mary-Jo down one of the slack waters.

'It's like a monster,' she said as they came alongside *Neptune's Booty*.

He glanced up anxiously at the rusting hull. He began to whisper. 'Some of the ships that come here are a disgrace. I haven't seen anything worse than this.'

'How could a rust bucket like this survive a storm?'

'It's been impounded. This is the ship I'd been visiting when I came to your house. The crew live in shocking conditions. I wonder, does God come disguised as their lives as well, Mary-Jo?'

Mary-Jo smiled sadly. 'Why don't you report it?'

'Who to?'

'Well, the authorities.'

'Who are the authorities? You see, properly speaking the ship is the floating territory of the flag under which she sails.'

'Well, what flag does she sail under?' They looked up to where a tattered, sodden flag hung lifeless from the pole on the bridge. The flag had a single star with red and white bars. 'What country is it?'

'I don't know. It'll be written on the stern.'

Mary-Jo eased the boat back down the ship. '*Neptune's Booty*,' she read. 'What's that other word? It's not very clear lettering.'

'Liberia. That means the boat's registered in Liberia. Look, come on, we'd better be going. I just wanted to show it to you.'

'Liberia?'

'It's a flag of convenience.'

'I think I've heard of that.'

'People on a ship are subject to the laws and protection of the country whose flag the ship is registered under. Unscrupulous ship owners rent the flags of countries with the poorest human rights record. These flags of convenience make it cheaper for them, no matter the cost for the crews. Poor devils, the crew of *Neptune's Booty* is subject to the laws and protection of Liberia.'

'That's terrible.'

'It gets worse. You see, the Liberian flag is licensed to an American company in Virginia; so there's someone making money even out of the dregs of shipping. Anyway, will you start the engine, please.'

'What a scandal.'

'You know, Mary-Jo, I used to think that sin was so easy to

recognise, but some things are just too big to fit in a confessional.'

'So what can *we* do?'

'In theory the port has some authority, but only concerning the condition of the ship. They're not usually worried about the crew. As long as they don't have a crowd of asylum seekers to deal with then they're happy.'

'That name,' said Mary-Jo, shaking her head.

'What do you mean?'

'Neptune's Booty.'

'What's so strange about that?'

'It's a Latin saying. Did they not teach you any Latin at that seminary of yours?'

'We didn't bother with the pagan stuff.'

'Neptune's booty is what's wrecked at sea. If a ship goes under, it belongs to Neptune; so do the hands lost at sea. Why on earth would anyone call a ship *Neptune's Booty*?'

'Well, the captain's a bit of a character.'

'The kind of character to invite a disaster?'

'He likes to joke. Remember, Christy talked about him.'

'Oh yes, the mafia man. Maybe it is a joke, but I thought seafarers were supposed to be superstitious. I wouldn't like to be one of the crew on a ship called *Neptune's Booty*. Still, your presence must mean something. I'm sure it helps to ease their burden a little.'

Tom's face clouded. 'Actually I've been avoiding *Neptune's Booty*. The thing is, we have to operate within the law and I've been on board without the captain's permission. I got rapped on the knuckles for that. I had a bit of a run-in with this Captain Cargo as well. Or at least, I think I did. The truth is, I'm a bit frightened of him.'

'Look, Tom,' said Mary-Jo, 'there's someone watching us. From *Neptune's Booty*.'

Tom looked up and saw a face staring furtively down at them. 'It's the bosun.'

'He's fishing.' Mary-Jo pointed at the line dangling in the water.

The priest gazed uneasily at the face of the seafarer. 'We'd better go, Mary-Jo. We'll be frightening off his fish. Please, Mary-Jo.' His voice sharpened. 'Please, just start the engine.'

They powered up the river, through the mouth of the Tees and out to sea on the freshet. Mary-Jo cut the engine again. Like a shaken rag, a flotilla of dirty seabirds flapped idly towards them from the lighthouse. Quarrelling bitterly with each other, they landed five yards from the bows. 'I didn't think there *were* any fish in the Tees,' said Tom.

'What are the seals after then? The salmon are running again. I love it here,' said Mary-Jo, 'just where the river runs into the sea.' The sun shone over the land, scintillating the dark ochre of the steelworks, whilst over the sea the storm clouds loomed like cliffs. 'You really were frightened then, weren't you? What happened between you and this Captain Cargo?'

'Oh, it doesn't matter.' Tom glanced at her. 'Well, it's just that something strange occurred after I left your house that night.'

'Strange?'

'Yes, after the meal at your house. Captain Cargo was waiting for me at the presbytery. I know he sounds a bit like a cartoon character; with the name and everything. Not forgetting his obsessions.'

'Obsessions?'

'Chess, genetics, seminaries. It's a long story. Actually, half of me is fascinated by him. I mean, who would have thought you could meet someone here who knows about Cardinal Newman. The thing is, that night somehow I agreed to go to Barnacle Bill's with him for a lock-in. Barnacle Bill's is the local pub; a lock-in is when –'

'I know. I know Barnacle Bill's and its lock-ins, but I can't quite picture you there somehow.'

'Neither can I. I can picture myself even less in what happened next. You see, after Barnacle Bill's we went on board the *Neptune's Booty*. I have to admit that I'd been drinking heavily. In fact I have never in all my life been so drunk. Is this too much like confession?'

'Your reputation as the Bishop's blue-eyed boy will never be the same again.'

He smiled uneasily. 'I know that this is going to sound far-fetched and I can't be certain, but I think he tried to knock me off the ship.'

'Captain Cargo?'

'As we were going up the gangway. At first I put it down to nothing more than a drunken scuffle, but something about it seemed deliberate. As though he was trying to warn me off or something.'

'Why would he want to do that?'

'Maybe he's got something to hide. As Christy always says, the world of shipping is a murky one. Earlier that day I'd gone on board to say a Mass for the crew without his permission and he obviously didn't like it. In fact it was that which seemed to drive him to threaten me.'

'He threatened you?'

'I don't know whether he did. That's the trouble. I really don't know. I was fuddled with drink. I'm afraid that it's all just like a dream. Or a nightmare. The funny thing was Kevin.'

'Kevin?'

'He suddenly appeared just when Cargo was jostling me. As though he . . .'

'As though what? Tell me, Tom.'

Tom smiled self-deprecatingly. 'As though he really was my guardian angel.'

The seabirds, having seen that there was no food on offer, were flapping querulously back to the lighthouse. Tom began to laugh.

'What is it?'

'If you'd told me six months ago that I'd be living in a

red-light district with an openly gay Frank, disobeying the Bishop, shaking hands with Kevin, and dangling from something called *Neptune's Booty*. . . How have I come to be in the middle of all this?'

Mary-Jo looked at him with great seriousness. 'Have you ever seen that film *Hud*?'

'I've always tried to avoid films with Paul Newman in them.'

'But you know the famous quote? Let me get the words right.' She closed her eyes in concentration. 'Right, that's it. Paul Newman's greatest line: *This world is so full of crap a man's gonna get into it sooner or later* . . .'

'Whether he's careful or not.'

'You *do* know the quote then?'

'I never thought I would have to apply it to my own life. By the way, your American accent is a great deal worse than Christy's, and that's saying something.'

They laughed until the boat rocked. The ripples sent over the sea slowed as they grew sober. The priest gazed back up the river. 'You know, lots of the crews I visit are lonely men. Far from home for months, and often working in isolation day after day, it's an occupational hazard, but I've never seen such loneliness as I did on *Neptune's Booty*.' He rubbed his unfamiliar beard. 'There's no lights on board, they have to use candles.'

'Maybe this is why you're here, Tom.'

'What do you mean?'

'Maybe you're here for this situation.'

'I'm here because I had nowhere else to go.'

'It doesn't matter about reasons or motives. If you don't speak up for those sailors, who will?'

'But I've been avoiding the *Neptune*. Anyway I can't speak for myself, let alone other people.'

'Maybe this is your destiny.'

'I have to be honest, Mary-Jo, I haven't understood half of what you've said today.'

She reached out and took his hand. The priest looked down

at the dried clay encrusted on his palm. 'The grime of the world, Tom.'

The boat bobbed gently. A lone fishing boat was setting out from Paddy's Hole. Cargo ships lined the horizon. When the priest glanced at Mary-Jo her gaze was far out at sea. There was a look of rapt bliss on her features. 'What are you doing?' he whispered.

'I'm regaining my tenderness,' she whispered.

'What do you mean?'

'It's another quote.'

'Not Paul Newman this time then.'

'No. An American poet called Theodore Roethke. *I regain my tenderness by long looking*.'

The sun continued to shine over the land. The storm clouds were emptying over the forlorn shipping lanes of the North Sea. And in the boat the priest gazed long at the woman beside him.

Chapter Fourteen

In the night the storm drifted back over the land, charged with electricity. The rain rucked the surface of the river and drummed the rusty metal carcass of *Neptune's Booty*. Tom woke with a jolt in the presbytery. A telephone was clanging.

He lay in the orange darkness as he had done so many times before. Just after going to bed the window well had sprung a leak and now the quick drops were loud in the deep pan the priest had placed there. The phone fell silent. Over the drilling of the rain came the unmistakable sound of a prostitute and her client in the presbytery doorway. Tom fumbled for his wristwatch; the fluorescent hands were motionless. For the first time in his adult life he had forgotten to wind his watch. The phone began again, ringing unendingly like the prayer of the rosary. As he forced himself out of bed, Tom staggered with weariness.

On the stairs all the different rhythms of the rain could be heard playing against the old building. A flash of lightning lit his way to the parish room. The thunder crashed out not long after. 'Hello?' Dropping the receiver, he fumbled it back to his ear. The lightning flashed in the room and Tom saw the old priest in the photograph staring down at him. 'Tom Carey here. Yes, Father Tom Carey, Teesport chaplain.' A clap of thunder reverberated through the parish room. The priest flinched instinctively. 'I'm sorry, what was that? Are you all right? You're speaking too quickly. Is that you, Bosun? I see. No, I can't come, not without . . . I'm not allowed to. Legally I . . . What's the matter? What about the captain?' With the rain had come a sultry heat and the sweat stood out on Tom's forehead. 'Speak slowly and clearly. No, I can't come on board *Neptune's Booty*.'

A void filled the priest's ear. He waited for it to refill with its human voice, then replaced the receiver. He climbed the stairs wearily. Two minutes later he emerged in his jeans and a white T-shirt that he usually wore as a vest. Tom had reached the little hall when a voice called to him, 'Where are you going?'

A lightning flash revealed Frank standing at the head of the stairs. 'The port,' Tom replied.

'These hours you're keeping. You might as well have stayed a parish priest.' The whole house seemed to shake under the impact of a thunderbolt. 'For those in peril on the sea and all that, Tom, but it's the middle of the night.'

'I know.'

'*Neptune's Booty* again?'

'It sounded like an emergency.'

'Like the last time?'

'It was the bosun.' Tom checked himself. 'At least I *think* it was the bosun.'

'Maybe it's Captain Cargo luring you on board to finish you off once and for all.'

'I told you about that incident in confidence, Frank.'

'Come on, you're not seriously worried are you? You said yourself you were pissed as a fart that night.' Frank tittered. 'All he probably did was to beat you at chess. You used to be a monster if anyone even got you into check.'

'Why am I having this discussion at this time in the morning during an electrical storm?'

'Look, do you want me to come with you? Every parish priest needs a good curate.'

'You get some sleep, Frank; but thanks, and sorry for waking you.'

'I was awake. I couldn't sleep. And it's me that should be thanking you. Not only have you taken in the homeless and outcast, but you've provided him with a social life as well. I really enjoyed it with Anne and Mary-Jo tonight.'

'Evidently you're the only priest Anne hasn't verbally assaulted.'

'And I think you're doing the right thing. Getting to know Mary-Jo again.' The flash and crack of lightning arrived simultaneously. 'I really wouldn't want to be out at sea on something like the *Neptune's Booty* tonight, Tom.'

'No.'

'I've just been lying in bed and thinking.'

'Bit dangerous that, Franky.'

'I suppose it is.'

'Much safer reading your breviary. Anyway, I'd better be going, Frank.'

'Shall I leave the toilet window open?'

Tom turned at the door. 'What do you mean?'

'You can't have forgotten that, Tom.'

'Oh yes. The eleven o'clock rule.'

A lightning flash caught Frank's grin. 'Woe betide the curate that stayed out after eleven. Many's the time you saved me with that toilet window.'

'Leaving it open for you at night used to give me terrible qualms of conscience.'

'I left it open for you as well.'

'Once. Anyway, for me at that time the height of sin was to sit in the pictures. To rub shoulders in a darkened room full of strangers.'

Frank giggled. 'It wasn't that different for me. What is it for you now?'

'Remember the time you climbed through the window and got your belt caught on the toilet chain? That was one heck of a high cistern.' Both men laughed as the thunder buffeted the presbytery. 'I found you hanging there like a hare in the butchers.'

'I was just so glad it was you. I thought old Fitz was coming down for a long session with the evening paper. He'd only have found out when he tried to pull the chain.'

'See you later, Frank.'

'Don't get struck by lightning, will you?'

'I'll try not to.'

Tom drove slowly down Babbington Road. Sheltering under the viaduct the prostitutes stared out mutely at the downpour, like faces behind net curtains. The drains were overflowing. Tom slowed his car to a walking pace. A figure darted from one of the arches. Before the priest knew what was happening, he heard his back door open and shut. A strong perfume, as sharp and unmistakable a reek as that made by the cows of his childhood, revealed the presence on the backseat. A dampness rose from the passenger. There was the click of a lighter. 'Do you mind if I smoke?' He shook his head helplessly. 'Mental outside,' she said. 'A proper storm.'

He looked in the driving mirror. Relief engulfed him when he saw that it wasn't the woman with the belly ring. 'How old are you?'

'Why, am I not young enough for you?'

'No, I didn't mean that.'

'I'm soaked.' She shivered despite the almost tropical warmth of the night. He drove on mechanically, blinking away a drop of sweat. 'What do you want to do then?' she demanded.

'Is it dry under the arches?'

'You want to go there?'

'No.' He cleared his throat. 'I don't want anything. I just want to know if you and the other women can keep dry.'

The girl sniffed. 'It's horrible under them arches. Stinks of piss. And shite. The winos all sleep there. It's my first night back on.'

'Back on?'

'Just had a baby.' She leant forward so that perfume, cigarette smoke and her dampness enveloped him, like an aura. 'I'll do you a milkmaid if you want. I let you drink from me boobs. Do you want to?'

'No, thank you.' He glanced up at the mirror and caught an expanse of white breast.

'I got the idea from one of the other girls,' she said, not covering herself up. 'She breastfed for as long as she could and got three times her usual whack. Some men really like it. Well, what do you want then? If you make it worth my while we won't use no johnny.'

'I don't want anything.' Coughing with the smoke, he opened the window. A shrapnel of rain smattered the shoulder of his T-shirt.

'Don't be shy,' she said. 'There's not nowt I've never seen before.'

'You just got in the car.' He paused. 'How old are you?'

'Why do you want to know that?'

'You seem so young to be on the street.'

'I'm older than I look. I've had a baby. I'm eighteen.' He heard her covering herself up. 'Don't tell me, mister, you've got a daughter my age.'

'I haven't got any children.'

'And I suppose you're going to say you're not married as well. Look, don't worry. I only got in because I wanted to get dry for a few minutes.'

'I live there,' he explained. 'That's why I was driving by.' The priest had driven in a loop round the tight, rain-flowing terraces. Reaching the presbytery again, he stopped.

'You live there?'

'Yes.' He pointed. 'In the old presbytery.'

'Oh, you must be Kevin's mate.'

'Kevin's mate?'

'That's what I've heard the other girls call them what live in there. Kevin's mates. You're not mental or nothing, like him, are you?'

'I hope not.'

'What's a presbytery then?'

'It's the house beside the church.'

'I thought that church wasn't used no more.'

He stared at the red-brick facades of the church and presbytery, almost completely dissolved in the rain. 'It isn't.'

'You want to go in there?'

'I don't want to go anywhere.'

The girl yawned. Her mouth opened so wide that she dropped her cigarette. The priest could smell the singed upholstery. Sweat beaded his brow. 'Sod this,' she suddenly said. 'I'm going home. I've got to feed that bloody baby. I'm dripping milk everywhere. Will you give us a lift?'

Tom drove over the railway bridge. The car headlights swept hazily over the rain-soaked slag heaps. 'What's your baby called?' he asked.

The young woman grinned. 'Florida.'

'That's an unusual name.'

'Well, you know how everybody calls their kids after the place where they had sex? Posh and Becks called theirs Brooklyn. The thing is, I couldn't call mine Slaggy Island, could I? So I did the next best thing, the place I would *like* to have been. Are you all right, mister?'

'I was just thinking about something that someone told me.'

'Your wife?'

'I told you, I'm not married.'

He looked up at the mirror. He saw his own face as well as that of the girl. His lips trembled as he murmured, 'God comes to you disguised as your life.'

'What?'

He steeled himself. 'I said, God comes to you disguised as your life.'

'God's in a bit of a fucking mess then, isn't he? You just turn left here.' She lit herself another cigarette from the end of the first. 'One of the God squad are you?'

'I suppose I am.'

'I hate God. Yeah, religion and that, I hate it. In one of the homes I was at there was this man, a real God-botherer. His

Bible-bashing didn't stop him fucking me brains out.' In the small window of the driving mirror, he saw her shake her head slowly and suck on her cigarette.

He dropped her off at a bedsit near to the Scandinavian Seaman's Church. When she opened the door he could hear the sound of a baby's cry perforating the din of falling rain.

The priest drove back to the river. The floodlights of the port were shrouded by the dense rain. There seemed to be no one in the security cabin. Water sprayed from the wheels as he skidded to the middle of the deserted space. Having parked, he ran to the cover of a section of the pipeline, the place where he had met Cargo for the first time. The thrumming rain sounded like thousands of whispering voices. He opened his umbrella.

The gangway was slippery. Halfway up he lost his footing and the umbrella shot from his grip. He stared down blankly at where the umbrella boated on the restless water between dock and rusting keel. Then slowly he continued, as painstakingly as someone crossing a torrent on a slim tree trunk. Stumbling on to the deck, there was a searing flash as lightning cracked above the river. *Neptune's Booty* was bathed in a scalding brilliance. In the violence of the exploding light, the priest saw the face of the bosun staring at him from beneath the corroded lifeboat. Without a word he followed him into the deckhouse.

Tom was taken down the dark, twisting maze. Washing still hung at face height, like the festoons of a jungle, and the heat grew steadily until the sweat was running constantly into his eyes. In the room where he had said Mass, the crew were standing expectantly in their shorts and flip-flops, taut faces beaded with perspiration. A lantern hung from a hook on the ceiling. The moment Tom crossed the threshold, a sickly-sweet stench punched him in the pit of his stomach. He gagged audibly. The crew shuffled aside to reveal a man lying in a makeshift bed. His face was bathed in sweat. Beside him squatted another man, mopping his brow and trying to make him drink. The injured sailor sighed with agony as the bosun peeled off a large, soiled surgical dressing from his leg. The flesh of the exposed wound was a putrid green. Tom's face creased with disgust. The squatting man reached into the wound and picked something wriggling from the suppurating flesh. He crushed the maggot between finger and thumb with an audible crack and a spurt of pus. 'Please, Father Tom Carey,' the bosun said. 'The wound is not healing.'

'It looks very nasty.'

'Yes, is nasty.'

The priest swallowed hard. Everybody was staring at him. The stricken man was making way for him to sit on the bed. The movement caused him bitter agony. A dander of putrefaction wafted over the priest. Swallowing back his gorge, he sat. 'And now,' whispered the bosun, 'he want to tell you his misfortune.' The bosun translated from the language spoken by the wounded man, whose voice rose and fell like the swell of a gentle sea. 'He say he is working in hold. Bottom of ship. You see it down there yourself, Father Tom Carey. He is chipping away rust. He say he no see the metal sheet is hanging by thread. He no see it fall. He no see it until he see it slice his leg.' The injured man shifted position slightly, showing a flash of bone in his wound. 'We find him unconscious,' the bosun continued. 'Much time ago, but the wound is not healing. And now we have no more painkillers.' The bosun handed the priest a box.

Stupefied, Tom stared at the box. 'He's been taking Lemsip for his leg?'

'Father Tom Carey, he is worrying. If he is losing his leg then he never sails again. If this happen, how is he to feed his family?' The injured man closed his eyes and leaning back began a quiet, mournful chant. 'He singing of his troubles,' the bosun explained. 'He trying to make his misfortune sound too bad so the spirits decide he have enough suffering.' The bosun dropped his head for a moment, and Tom suddenly saw his strain. 'You see, we are primitive people. He is from island far from Manila. Negros, the sugar-cane island. When you come before, we hope you drive away evil. But then the white maggots come. And we wait for next evil on *Neptune's Booty*.'

The bosun's last words echoed in Tom's head, his oriental accent holding the final note of the ship's name for a number of beats, like a singer. 'Does your captain know?' There was no reply. 'Is he on board? Cargo.' No one spoke. 'We must get him to hospital,' Tom said simply.

The bosun nodded and spoke to the rest of the crew in a language they all understood. An angry debate flared, stopping as suddenly as it had erupted. The bosun no longer looked the priest in the eye. 'Is not possible, Father Tom Carey.'

'Not go to hospital?'

'Is not possible.'

'For pity's sake, look at his leg. It's gangrenous.'

The priest's sudden shout reverberated violently around the small room. The bosun's inexpressive face twitched. 'Please to understand. He cannot leave *Neptune's Booty*.'

'He must.'

'Is not possible.'

'Look, I'm no doctor, but if he doesn't get medical treatment then I think he might lose that leg.' Sweat scalded Tom's eyes. 'It's boiling here. He's already got a raging fever and the infection will spread like wildfire.' The injured man continued his low monotonous chant. The rest of the crew averted their eyes from the suddenly angry priest. 'Tell them. Tell your friends that he might die if you don't get him to the hospital.'

'I already tell them.'

'Tell them again. And ask them how he's going to feed his family if he dies here.'

The bosun nodded and spoke to the other men again. None of them said a word in reply. He turned to the priest and shook his head. 'Is not possible.'

'Right, that's it. I'll get an ambulance myself.' Tom found his way to the door blocked. He could see fear on the averted faces of the men standing in his way. 'What's going on here?' he asked weakly.

'A doctor.'

'What?' Tom saw that the bosun was holding out a mobile phone.

'You know a doctor? He come on board. No questions asked.'

Tom felt for the sharp creases of his trousers and encountered the denim sodden with his own sweat. 'He needs a hospital.'

'Father Tom Carey, you not understand!' The shouted words struck the priest like a slap. He and the bosun stared at each other, the pores of their skin, opened and made greasy by the oily heat, only inches apart. 'Now, Father Tom Carey. Please to text message the doctor.'

'Text message?'

'No money for call. Why you laugh?'

'I'm sorry, I'm not laughing. It's just that I don't have a clue about things like text messages. I wouldn't know how to text message to save my life.'

The bosun paused for an instant. His eyes scrutinised the priest. Having spoken rapidly in his own language to the crew, he said quietly to Tom, 'Please to come up on deck, Father Tom Carey.'

'What?'

'You get signal there.'

The hand that gripped the priest's arm and propelled him to the door was surprisingly gentle. With his other hand, the bosun waved the mobile phone at the crew, who stepped aside uncertainly. Tom allowed himself to be led back up through the labyrinth of the deckhouse. In the bowels of the ship the storm had been strangely imperceptible, but as they stepped outside it broke over them. Hunched against the searing rain, they crossed the deck to the partial shelter beneath the corroded lifeboats. The lightning was probing above the chemical silos of the north bank. Alarms wailed, set off by the storm. The river was lit up from time to time in ghostly flashes. The nuclear power station cast a vast, momentary shadow. 'What's going on here?' Tom asked miserably.

'We are desperate men, Father Tom Carey, please to forgive. None of us want to treat a holy priest as we are treating you.' The seafarer closed his eyes and bowed his head. 'I am full of shame. Too full of shame. But, Father, fear is stronger than shame.'

'Is this something to do with your captain?' The sailor did not appear to hear. 'I said, is it something to do with Captain Cargo?'

'I not know what you mean.'

'For God's sake, stop playing with me. There's a dying man in there.'

'Play? You think we are playing?' Tom's burst of anger had been countered by a smouldering rage in the sailor. 'You think our lives are game?'

'No, I don't. I don't think that.'

'Our lives a game? What you know of our lives? You are not knowing anything of our lives.'

'I don't need to know anything about your bloody lives to know that that man is dangerously ill.'

The eyes that had angrily seized the priest dropped abjectly to the ground. 'And now I am shouting at you. I am so full of shame. I am sorry, Father Tom Carey, chaplain of Teesport. We are desperate men.' The bosun opened a fist, revealing the mobile phone. 'You are laughing at us again?'

'Far from it. In fact, I'm terrified. I'm laughing at myself.'

'Why?'

'What am I doing here?'

'We ring, you come,' the bosun answered simply. He shifted his feet uneasily. His upturned face looked suddenly boyish. 'Anyway, Father Tom Carey, you go now.'

'What?'

'This is why I bring you up here. To let you go. The others not want to let you go.'

'I don't understand.'

'You must go and never come back to *Neptune's Booty*. If there is nothing you can do, then go. Go, before is too late.'

'But –'

'Go!'

As he descended the gangway, all Tom could hear was the rain hissing on the metal of the boat. Reaching his car, the priest sat there for a while without moving, then sped away.

The Transporter Bridge was closed so he drove inland, crossing the river on the main road bridge and then weaving the intricate way between the petrochemical plants. Beyond the metal, the marsh was a seething rain-tortured darkness.

He stood hesitantly at the front door of the white convent, hunched in the rain. His first knock was too quiet. He tried a second time, and then, fighting against his own mortification, he knocked for a third time.

Anne came to the door in a towelling robe. 'What the bloody hell . . . Is that you? What are you doing, Mr Paul Newman?'

'I'm sorry for disturbing you.'

'Waking us up in the middle of the night, more like. Looking like a cowboy as well. Or a drowned rat.'

'I wouldn't bother you if it wasn't an emergency.'

'It must be one hell of an emergency.'

'Is Mary-Jo there, please?'

The smile evaporated on Anne's face. She stepped backwards. 'She's asleep.'

'I see.' The priest looked at the nun helplessly. 'Well, could you wake her please?'

'No, I couldn't.' Anne searched the priest's face. 'Hasn't she told you, Tom?'

'Told me what?'

There was a light tread on the stairs above them. 'What's going on?' Mary-Jo called down.

The priest looked past Anne to where Mary-Jo stood at the

head of the stairs and lifted his hands in a self-deprecating gesture. 'I was just telling Anne, I'm really sorry for getting you up, Mary-Jo, but there's an emergency at the port. I didn't know who else to turn to.'

Anne closed the door a few inches on the priest. 'Mary-Jo won't be able to help.'

'What is it?' Mary-Jo asked.

'It's a seafarer,' Tom called. 'He's hurt his leg.'

'I'll just get dressed. I'll be down in a moment.'

The door closed fully in Tom's face. Inside, Anne ran up the stairs. 'I'll sort it out, Mary-Jo. You go back to bed.'

'Don't be ridiculous, you haven't nursed for twenty years.'

'Neither have you.'

'Ten. I nursed in Africa.'

'Mary-Jo, for pity's sake.'

'What?'

'You can't go out.'

'Why not?

'Because you're ill.'

Without replying Mary-Jo went back into her bedroom. Anne waited for her on the landing. 'Mary-Jo,' Anne called, 'let me phone for a doctor.'

'What doctor would come out at this hour for a seafarer?'

Outside, Tom stood awkwardly on the step. All around him the drifting lightning blanched the chemical silos. The door opened. Anne stepped outside. 'Look, I'm really sorry,' the priest began quickly, 'I just didn't know where else to turn.'

'She shouldn't be doing this. Or going out in boats either.'

'What do you mean?'

Anne smiled sadly. 'It's always been impossible to tell Mary-Jo what to do. Look, Tom, get her to talk to you.' She seemed about to say more when the door opened. 'So you're going, Mary-Jo?' Mary-Jo tapped the little medical bag. 'But it's a monsoon.'

Driving, Tom's body tingled where his shoulder had rested against hers as they ran to the car together. 'What happened?' Mary-Jo asked. 'Is he badly hurt?'

'His wound looks gangrenous to me. Otherwise I wouldn't have bothered you at this hour.'

'Don't worry.'

'It's just that Anne said –'

'Oh, sometimes Anne has too much to say.' The nun leant her head back in scrutiny of the priest. 'You really did used to look like him, you know; everybody said, not just me.'

'I know. Ridiculous, isn't it?' He shook his head in utter disbelief. 'Of all the things in life to be saddled with.'

They drove along a length of electricity pylons, the cable humming with the rain. 'What kind of ship is he on, the injured man?' Mary-Jo asked.

'It's *Neptune's Booty*.'

'Captain Cargo's? I might have guessed.'

'Mary-Jo, something's definitely going on there. The crew is terrified. They don't want him to go to hospital. One of them even told me to leave the ship and never return. His actual words were *before it's too late*. I should warn you that technically we're not even supposed to be on the port at night. And I know for certain that we're not allowed to visit individual ships without the express permission of the shipmaster. We're breaking the law.'

'You'll be turning the tables over in the temple next.'

'I didn't know what to do for the best. I just saw that man's leg and I knew you'd been a nurse. But now I'm not so sure.' He pulled up on the side of the road. The windscreen wipers continued to flap urgently. 'No, I can't take you there. It might be dangerous . . .'

'I'm used to that.' Mary-Jo patted the medical bag on her knees. 'When I was in Africa I found myself in some pretty interesting situations. I was always having to do a doctor's job, and sometimes even a surgeon's. There wasn't always the opportunity for niceties. Come on, Tom, every moment might be crucial. Where's Captain Cargo in all of this?'

'That's the worst of it. He might pop up at any time.'

'We can't mess about at a time like this.'

Tom yawned savagely. Pushing the gear lever he drove off.

'Tired?'

'Shattered. Port duties are not as light as they may seem. And now all this. I'm just praying Cargo doesn't arrive back and see us.'

'Or smell us. You can't be wearing aftershave. What is it?'

'Funny, I thought I could still smell it too.'

'Smell what?'

'I had a girl in the back.'

'A girl?'

'She was sitting in the back, a prostitute.'

'A prostitute?'

'Yes.' He looked at her and even in the semi-darkness of the sodium lights lining the road she could see his sudden flush. 'Not like that,' he stammered. 'Not anything like that.'

'Like *what*?'

'She just got in. I couldn't stop her.'

'Don't worry, I believe you.'

But Tom was panicking. 'And when she was in, she looked so young that I felt for her. I didn't want to turn her out in the rain. She only wanted shelter from the storm. It seemed wrong somehow to push her out. But I never thought how it would look to others. God, what was I thinking?' His hands gripped the wheel tightly as he slowed at a red light. 'I think my brain's gone soft.'

'Hey Tom, I've told you, I believe you.' He looked down at the hand resting lightly on his arm. 'Anyway, Jesus used to hang about with prostitutes.'

'Now you're just laughing at me.'

'Sorry.' She smiled. 'It's just that I'd love to see the Bishop's face if you told him about how you've started spending your evenings.'

Having crossed the river upstream, they skirted the city centre, forlorn at this hour. The tight knot of streets unravelled itself in the docks. Out at sea the electric storm played like the aurora borealis. They parked by the pipeline, their shoulders touching again as they ran towards the tortured shape of *Neptune's Booty*. 'I'd better go first,' Tom said uncertainly as they reached the gangplank. His stomach lurched as it did every time he stepped off the quay, but this time the sickness of fear unsteadied him further. He gritted his teeth. 'And to think that once I used to worry about what vestments to wear.'

It took a long time to find the lounge. A dangerous murmur rose through the gathered crew at their arrival. 'She's a nurse,' Tom explained to the bosun. 'And a nun.'

The bosun translated. The men nodded, visibly relieved. Thick cigarette smoke mingled with the stench. Mary-Jo looked at the wound. 'Can we have some light?' The bosun reached up and lengthened the wick of the lantern. 'Clear the room, please,' Mary-Jo said.

The crew melted away behind dark cabin doors. The bosun remained with Tom in the corridor outside. They stood there in the hot darkness. Occasionally, through the door a thin moan could be heard, followed by Mary-Jo's soothing tones. The priest yawned widely. Beside him, the Filipino slid down on to his haunches. After a while, Tom did too.

He must have fallen asleep because the next thing he knew a small voice was waking him. 'Father Tom Carey?' Lifting a woozy head from his chest, Tom looked about in terror from where he had slumped to the ground. But it was the bosun squatting beside him who was whispering. The priest flexed the feet splayed in front of him. Both legs burned with pins and needles. 'Father Tom Carey?'

'Yes?'

'Sometimes I am wondering, will I ever go home?'

The priest glanced at his companion. All he could see was a pair of eyes, bright as moons. He licked his lips. His throat was dry. He craned his senses into the darkness but could make nothing out. 'Yes, you're a long way from home.'

'But whenever I close my eyes I am there.'

Tom tried to lift a leg, but couldn't. 'Is she all right, the Sister?'

'She still in there.'

'And no sign of your captain?'

'He will not come back for a while, Father Tom Carey.'

Helplessly, the priest flexed the unwilling leg. 'What's your home like, Bosun?' he whispered.

For a while, the man did not reply. Then he said, 'It is rural area.' Another long pause followed. 'Father Priest Port Chaplain? At home we are waking when the cocks crow and the hens are scratching the yard.' The voice murmured in the darkness like flowing water. Tom closed his eyes and listened to it. 'I wake first, after me my little boy, then my wife and the baby. My wife, she feed baby. When I am waking, I try and not move. I love to see the others sleeping. I love to see them resting, no trouble on faces.' The bosun broke off. Tom waited a long time for him to continue.

'I'm from a rural area too,' the priest said. When the bosun did not take the prompt, Tom continued, confiding to the darkness. 'My father was a farmer. Before I left to become a priest, I used to wake up to a cockerel. But he used to get confused; sometimes he'd crow in the middle of the day.'

'Yes, sometime that happen.'

There was a loud moan from the other side of the door. Opening his eyes, Tom leant back against the wall, his feet out in the middle of the corridor. He began to speak again. 'It's funny, even now sometimes when I wake up I think I'm back home. There's something in the country that you just don't get in towns.'

'Is right.'

'I mean, the slowness of the days. And their quickness. Do you ever feel that? Clocks and watches are not important when you're in the fields. I remember measuring from dawn to dusk by the task, each part of the day with its own ritual, like the old breviary. And always the birds singing. At dawn I remember there being such a peace it seemed that the world had been just created.' Tom faltered, his own voice sounding strange in his ears. He waited for the other man to speak, but he did not.

Just when he had become reconciled to the silence of their vigil, the seafarer broke it. 'My wife, she called Jocasta.'

'That's a lovely name. And your children?'

'The boy, he Xavier. And the baby we are calling Nancy.' There was a rustle beside him and, squinting, the priest saw that the bosun had brought something out from a pocket. He could just make out the shape of a photograph. 'Here, my family.' There was a click and the loose flame of a Zippo developed faces on the photograph. A slight young woman, who seemed nothing more than a girl to Tom, was holding a baby. A little boy with a dazzling grin stood between the woman and the sailor himself. They were standing on a bamboo veranda. A cockerel challenged the camera from the railing.

'Bosun,' Tom whispered, 'what is your name?'

For an instant the grin of the little boy appeared on his father's face. Then the flame was extinguished and only his eyes waxed large. 'My name is Jesus-Maria.'

'You've got a fine family, Jesus-Maria.'

Tom sensed the bosun putting his picture away, as though he were securing his very last banknote. When he spoke again his English words seemed startlingly clear. 'In my country we are very poor. I myself start a chicken business, but it fail. My baby, Nancy, she not want to come into the world. Jocasta have a difficult time with her. Baby come at last but how can I pay the hospital bills? I come to sea. Soon Xavier go to school. How will he learn to read? I come to sea again. This is the story of all of us on board here. Our only hope for life is *Neptune's*

Booty.' Once again the cadence of the ship's name rang in the priest's ear. 'Father?'

'Yes.'

'Please to pray for my family.'

'Of course.'

The priest closed his eyes tight. He saw the faces of Jesus-Maria's family as clearly as the photographer must have. The mother with her baby who had been sick, the young boy standing so proudly by his father, and Jesus-Maria thousands of miles from here in the beautiful valley of his home.

He could not say when he fell into a troubled sleep where different faces were waiting for him. His mother and father, Frank, and Mary-Jo, all seemed to peer expectantly at him, as though posing behind the lens of his camera. They faded, followed by a procession of others: the Bishop, Angela as she lay having her nappy changed, the albino motionless in his prison cell like an insect beneath a stone, the heavily made-up face of Marie during one of their long sessions, and Kevin, stretching out a clay-encrusted hand. Then came the only half-recalled faces from further and further in the past: members of his parishes from over thirty years, the men he had trained with at seminary, people that he could not even recall. They all began speaking to him at once until his sleep was full of their voices. He tried to talk back but could not. Suddenly silence fell and the crowd melted away. At last there was only one face left. It was bearded and haggard. Its lips were trembling with the difficulty of speech, its piercing blue eyes were searching. It was himself . . .

The priest woke with a start. The dream held for a moment then dissipated in an explosion of activity and light. A walkie-talkie was crackling. A team of paramedics stepped over his legs and opened the door to the lounge. Tom rose and stepped back clumsily. A few confused minutes later the paramedics re-emerged with the injured seafarer on a stretcher. One of them held a drip. A doctor came out behind them, with Mary-Jo.

As they passed, Tom flattened himself against the side of the corridor.

Dawn had broken and the sun was rising from the sea. The storm had passed over to Scandinavia. From underneath the dilapidated lifeboat the priest watched the ambulance drive away, its lights flashing. 'He said that if it had been left for another day we would have lost him.' Tom turned to see Mary-Jo standing behind him. 'The doctor. I had to call him, Tom. He's a friend of mine.'

'I fell asleep.'

'I know. Come on, let's go.'

'And you in all that danger. How did I fall asleep?'

'You were tired.'

'Where's Jesus-Maria?' Tom cast about the deck. 'The bosun, where is he?'

'I don't know. I haven't seen any of the crew.'

'What about Captain Cargo? He might have come back at any time, and I was asleep.'

She shrugged. 'No sign of any paper tigers.'

He followed her off *Neptune's Booty*. They were stopped at the security cabin. The guard's face peered suspiciously at them. He opened the window when he recognised the priest. 'What the hell's been going on, Father Tom? There's been flashing lights and mayhem.'

Tom drove off the port. 'Where are you going?' Mary-Jo asked.

'I'm taking you back home.'

'No, go to yours.'

'What?'

'I thought I might show you the nearest launderette.'

'Now? Aren't you tired?'

'Life's too short for being tired. If you're OK I might even take you to a supermarket.'

'You're doing all this for me, and I fell asleep. I would have been no use in the garden of Gethsemane.'

Slaggy Island was sparkling under a bright dawn sun. The arches under the viaduct were deserted. Tom mounted the three steps of the presbytery stiffly and pressed the key in the latch of the door only to find it swinging open at the first press. 'Frank's left it open,' he said with irritation. 'I'll just pop up and get my washing.'

'I'll wait in the car.'

Tom scooped up his dirty washing into two bin-liners. 'Frank,' he shouted, 'you've got two minutes to give me your dirty washing. We've had an offer we can't refuse.'

A yawning Frank appeared on the landing. 'What's the rush?'

'I'm going to a launderette. And by the way, did you know you'd left the front door open? Come on, Mary-Jo's waiting.'

'I can see the headline now: PRIEST AND NUN WASHING DIRTY LINEN IN PUBLIC.'

'Very funny.'

'How was *Neptune's Booty*? I see Captain Cargo didn't finish you off.'

Placing his bulging black bin-liners in the hall, Tom was just about to answer Frank when he heard a strange, sibilant groan. He followed the sound to the parish room. A figure sat slumped in the chair beneath the stern photographic gaze of the old cleric. Snoring loudly, he was in a deep sleep. Like a fox slumbering, snout in brush, his nose rested on his chest in the spread of his red beard. The stench of urine and sodden filthy clothes clogged the air.

The two priests met on the stairs. 'What the hell's Kevin doing in the parish room, Frank?' Tom hissed.

'Kevin in the parish room?'

'Yes, snoring like a train and stinking to high heaven.'

'*Kevin*?'

'Yes, Kevin, *Kevin*. Why do you keep on saying his name?'

They went into the parish room. 'So that answers that one,' Frank whispered. 'Kevin was the Mad Monsignor all along.'

'This isn't funny,' said Tom, retreating to the hall.

'What are you snapping at me for?' asked Frank, following.

'Because you left the front door open. Or does Kevin have his own set of keys to the place?'

'Me? I've been in bed since you left for the port. Strangely enough I was actually sleeping, until I was so rudely woken.'

Tom bit his lip. 'I see,' he said sourly.

'Look on the bright side, Tom. The presbytery's getting back to its full complement. The table won't feel so empty. Now all we have to decide is who are the curates and who's the PP.'

A bitterness twisted Tom's face. 'I'll ask him to stay, shall I? Then we can throw the door open to the rest of the dregs of society. I mean after all, this is a red-light district, we're bound to get a prostitute as housekeeper.'

'Sarcasm doesn't become you, Tom.'

'Of all the cheek, just walking in here bold as brass. Next thing we know, he'll be moving in.'

'Why not let him?' Frank asked simply.

'What?'

'We've got a grand total of ten rooms spare. He spends all his time standing under that lamp outside anyway so you might as well have him where you can't see him.'

'Jesus Christ.' There was no humour in Tom's blue eyes. 'Have we really sunk this low, Frank? I mean, I'm aware that the clergy's the butt of every Tom, Dick and Harriet's joke, but is this really what it's come to?'

'Don't take it like this, Tom.'

Tom's voice rose with the ferocity of an unexpected anger. 'How am I supposed to take it?'

'It was only a joke.'

'A pretty sick one.'

'Don't unleash the bull Carey now, Tom.'

'Frank, I'm not laughing.' Tom sat on the bottom stair and stared numbly at his hands. 'We used to be a priestly caste, a people set apart. Do you not remember that, Frank? It wasn't so long ago. We used to hold the keys to the Kingdom, for Christ's sake.'

'Pride comes before a fall, Tom.'

Tom's tone fell dangerously low. 'And what's that supposed to mean?'

'Nothing, Tom. Why are you so angry?'

'Tell me what you meant.'

'Well then, I will. It means *lo, how the mighty have fallen*. And I think that's probably just as well, don't you?'

'Maybe for you, Frank,' Tom said caustically. 'But I really believed in it all.'

Frank's voice rose in turn. 'Oh for heaven's sake, Tom. He was born in a stable to an unmarried teenager. Then he was a homeless refugee and eventually executed as a common criminal. Do you really think he wanted any of this?' Frank flung a hand over the solidity of the presbytery.

Tom stared as though his friend's hand had just conjured up the building and then knocked it down. 'Oh just . . . just fuck off will you, Frank?'

Tom drove through Slaggy Island in silence. He mounted the bridge and entered the spoil-heap meadows. 'What's the matter, Tom?' Mary-Jo asked.

'I'm just tired.'

From the launderette, they went into the supermarket. Piped music was playing. Tom pushed the trolley through the fruit and veg section. 'Are you going to tell me what it is, Tom?' Mary-Jo asked.

'You know when I was asleep on *Neptune's Booty*? I had a strange dream, Mary-Jo.'

'A dream?'

'Yes, not very appropriate, I know. Did the disciples dream at Gethsemane? We'll never know. It was all the people I've known. Staring at me. Talking. Telling me things. I wanted to touch them, speak back. Reach them somehow but . . .'

'What did you want to say to them, Tom?'

'Oh,' he shook his head. 'Everything.'

'What were they saying to you?'

He sighed. 'Things I couldn't answer. I've had it before. The dream. But this time I wanted to answer them. But I couldn't.'

'And is that what's got you so riled?'

He smiled sadly. 'No, it's not that. It's something else. A realisation I've just had. Mary-Jo, I'm a failure as a priest, there's no point pretending otherwise. As a person too. And I've just taken it out on Frank.' He sighed heavily. 'In fact I told him to F off.'

'Oh dear.'

'I've never said that to anyone else before.'

'Come on,' she urged softly, 'I have to show you something.' She looked at him solemnly. 'Tom, it will revolutionise your life.'

'What, here in the supermarket?'

'I've done a lot of thinking about this, Tom, and I've decided that you're ready. It's time for the leap.'

'The leap?'

'The leap of faith.' Taking control of the trolley, she walked with him in silence until they reached the cook-in sauces aisle. 'You see, you have to lose everything before you can have it. If your hands are already full then how can you bend down and pick up the pearl of great price? So come on, close your eyes. There's no joke this time.' With a deep breath he closed his eyes. She led him for a few, halting steps. 'Now,' she intoned, 'put your hand out.'

'It's something physical?'

'Haven't you realised by now that Christ revealed himself in the incarnation?' Tom put out his hand. He felt something cold and hard being placed on his soft palm. 'All right, open them.' The first thing he saw was a strangely familiar face grinning back at him. Then he realised that he was looking at the label on a jar. He read from the label. '*Paul Newman's Two Thousand Island Salad Dressing*?'

'Read that bit.' Mary-Jo maintained her seriousness.

'*Has twice as many islands as any other brand.*'

'That's right.'

There was silence for a few more seconds then their laughter rang out through the store, drowning out the voice advertising bargains.

Chapter Fifteen

Through the open skylight came the sounds of high summer: a child's voice rising and falling in laughter, the sleepy mid-afternoon contentions of a sparrow family, water from a hosepipe clattering the dusty leaves of a rose bush. Mary-Jo opened her eyes. She was sprawled on the carpeted floor of the little chapel. A guitar stood in the corner. Beside the wooden tabernacle, the red sanctuary candle fluttered slightly on the breeze that came through the skylight. From where she lay, Mary-Jo tried to detect the scents of the late July marsh. The pain, which had gripped a few minutes ago, sending her grovelling to the ground, was ebbing. A few more minutes passed and she was able to lift herself into a sitting position. On the simple, low table of the altar stood a Latin American cross, its bright wood multicoloured with a bird, a bush, a house and the rising sun. The nun closed her eyes again. If she were very, very still, she might be able to free herself for a few moments from the chains of pain that were constricting her a little more each day. By the sounds and scents rippling through the skylight she could picture the scene out in the garden. Little Hope was now running backwards and forwards through the jet of the hose as Anne tried to water the garden. The sparrow family was dust bathing. Mary-Jo waited breathlessly, but the pain did not return nor the coughing fit that had preceded it.

When Anne came in a long time later, Mary-Jo was sitting serenely on a cushion with a book of the psalms spread out before her. Having made the sign of the cross Anne sat down.

'What is it?' Mary-Jo asked after a couple of minutes. 'I mean, you've done nothing but sigh and twist and turn since you came into the chapel.'

Anne's voice was utterly miserable. 'We heard you coughing. Hope and I. We were in the garden. I told her you had a cold.'

'I'm sorry.'

'And what will I tell her next week?'

There was a long silence then Anne spoke. 'It's still not too late for treatment.'

Mary-Jo sighed. 'I thought we'd agreed –'

'Agreed what, Mary-Jo? You're supposed to be taking things easy, but you're behaving as though –'

'As though there's nothing the matter with me? How else am I supposed to behave?'

Getting up, Anne stood at the skylight. 'What about Paul Newman?'

'Tom? What about Tom?'

'Have you told him yet?'

There was a slight pause. 'No, I haven't.'

'Don't you think you should?'

'Why are you getting angry with me?'

'Oh, and thanks very much for the little chat from Moira.'

'What?'

'I had the full works from her. How was I coping? What was I going to do afterwards? Anyone would think it was me that was –'

'Why are you attacking me like this?'

'You haven't stopped to think what you're doing to other people, have you? Moira, Hope, poor old Father Paul Newman, God but he's in for a shock.'

'What do you mean, Anne?'

'Making him fall for you like that.'

'You're talking absolute nonsense.'

'Am I? Take a look at him next time he's with you. He's falling for you hook, line and sinker. It's obvious to anyone.'

'We're in our fifties. I'm a nun and he's a priest.'

Anne snorted. 'I've seen you together. You're like a pair of teenagers.' Her round face grew cruel. 'Are you sure it was only his hand you held all those years ago, or did you lead him a bit further up the garden path?'

'I can't believe you're saying this.'

'Mary-Jo.' Anne's voice broke. 'Mary-Jo, please don't die.' Softly, almost soundlessly, Anne began to weep.

Mary-Jo came to her at the skylight. 'It's as hard for you as it is for me. I know that.'

Anne forced her shining eyes to smile. 'God, I'm crying again. I've become a regular leaking pipe.'

They stood together in silence, the summer afternoon flowing past them outside, like a river. 'Remember when we built this place?' Mary-Jo said at last. 'When we started I never thought we'd manage it. It seemed such a big job. Building a chapel in a loft.'

'It was hard work.'

'But it was great doing it, wasn't it, Anne?'

Anne nodded. 'You and I can do anything, Mary-Jo.'

'I hope so, Anne, because what we've got to face is going to be even harder.'

'Where have our lives gone? It seems like yesterday that we were girls meeting for the first time.'

They stood together at the little window in the roof watching the blue sky of the untroubled afternoon. When Tom came to the white house, he had already knocked three times and was reluctantly walking back to his car when the front door opened. 'We were up in the chapel,' Anne explained.

'Sorry, did I disturb your prayer time?'

'I see you still don't know how to use the bell. How's things on Slaggy Island, Paul?'

'Oh, a far cry from Hollywood, Anne.'

In the chapel Mary-Jo could hear their voices. She smiled. She was relieved that no one was there to watch her descend the loft ladder. Her limbs were feeling increasingly heavy, she was liable to grow breathless with the slightest exertion.

'Look, if she's busy,' Tom was saying as Mary-Jo came down the stairs.

'If who's too busy?' Mary-Jo asked.

'Anne was just saying that you'd promised your neighbours –'

'Oh, we can do that any time,' Mary-Jo said airily. 'I promised I'd help you sort out your mum's things today and I will.'

'If you can't manage it, another week or so wouldn't harm.'

Mary-Jo smiled. 'Come on, Tom.'

Concealing the stiffness that had come over her upper body during the last seizure, Mary-Jo went round to the passenger door of the priest's car. A battered old-fashioned suitcase sat on the seat, like a dog. 'What's this?' she asked. 'Planning a holiday?'

'Oh that, sorry, just let me put it in the back. It's my bag of tricks. Stuff for the Mass, you know. I've carried it with me everywhere for thirty odd years. Funny thing is, it's been a while since I've actually said one.'

They drove along the river. The traffic was light and they were soon beyond the town limits. The moors rise dramatically from Teesside and very soon they were climbing above the metal chimneys and coiling river. The mile upon mile of the chemical industry flickered in the wing mirrors a few times and then they were motoring over open moorland. The empty acres of heather stretched endlessly on all sides. 'It's beautiful up here,' Mary-Jo said as her ears popped with the altitude.

'Yes, it is.'

'Is your farmhouse on the moors?'

'Yes. Well, it's down in one of the little dales.'

'Do you miss it? I mean, it must be so different from Slaggy Island.'

'I left it for junior seminary when I was eleven, but in the last few years of Mam's life I used to come back most Sunday evenings and stay until Tuesday if I could. I haven't been back since the funeral.'

'It's hard, isn't it? The loss of a parent.'

'She was getting very frail. I hated thinking of her all alone in the farmhouse. It's very isolated.' Ever higher they drove, then the road levelled on to a plateau. 'You asked me if I missed it. I never thought I did, but the other week I was talking to someone about it, a seafarer, Jesus-Maria from the *Neptune's Booty*.'

'Was that during your Gethsemane?'

'Yes it was, since that's what you insist on calling it.'

'I think it's a miracle that he didn't lose his leg, that seafarer. I'd never seen anything like it.'

'You must have seen some pretty harrowing things in Africa.'

'It's the other things I remember. The friends I made. The singing, the dancing. The sense of community.'

'Do you miss it?'

'Of course.'

'There's supposed to be no finer sight than an African sunset.'

'We lived by a lake and the sun used to sink into it. But you haven't lived until you've seen a Wilton sunset.'

'A Wilton sunset?'

'Where the big ICI plant is.'

The road dropped into a gully. The trees lining the steep sides were stunted. They climbed back out slowly. A large moorland bird hung in the thermals above them. 'I really appreciate this,' Tom said. 'Coming out here to help me sort everything out. I don't think I could face going through her clothes.'

'I'm enjoying the drive. What are you going to do with the place?'

'I don't really know. There's no land attached. Well, there's the garden and an orchard. We always used it as a lambing paddock; of course the trees are dreadfully neglected. The rest of the land Mam sold off bit by bit. I could sell it, I suppose. Then again I might retire there.'

'You're a bit young to be thinking of that, aren't you?'

'I suppose I am. The priesthood must be the only job where you're young in your early seventies.' The view on the other side of the gully was even more panoramic. In between the thick tussocks of heather grew grass, cropped to the sod by sheep. After a few more miles they turned on to a little-used road and as they drove over it they seemed to have the whole world to themselves. 'Actually there is something else I might do with it. I've been thinking about it for a while. Why don't you use it?'

'What?'

'You and Anne could use the farmhouse as a bolt hole; and anyone else who might need it. Mary-Jo, I've been wondering if it couldn't be somewhere for the disadvantaged to come to.'

Mary-Jo grinned. 'The disadvantaged?'

'I know, I'm not very politically correct. I mean, your neighbours. That little girl Hope would love it. People like Kevin.'

'You're getting fond of old Kevin, aren't you?'

'Well, I wouldn't have to be there with him, would I? I could just turn the place over to them.' Chuckling, he glanced at Mary-Jo. 'Who knows what we could do with it in the future, Mary-Jo. I mean it would need a lot of work and renovation but Anne's always saying how the pair of you converted your attic into a chapel.'

'Do you think the Bishop will allow it?'

'A fat lot you care about what the Bishop thinks. Anyway, maybe part of me would enjoy annoying him.' Stopping suddenly, he turned off the engine. All at once the great moors seemed to engulf them, deepening the silence of the intimacy. 'For the first time I've been starting to see more clearly. Think of what the future could be, Mary-Jo.' A little moorland bird called plaintively from its low perch on the heather. The ling was beginning to blossom; here and there the purple fire that would engulf the moors was beginning to crackle with colour. 'We should have a few sheep.' Tom nodded. 'Or a goat for the children to milk. We could bring seafarers as well; especially those who have been abandoned in port.'

'Tom,' said Mary-Jo quietly.

'Show them something a bit different from the inside of a bloody port.' Tom started the engine and drove off. 'Imagine what it would mean to them to come to a place like this. Six months cooped up at sea and in ports then you come out to this.'

'Tom.'

'I can't remember feeling so excited about anything. I'm serious, Mary-Jo. The more I think about it, the more –' When he looked at Mary-Jo, her face had clouded.

Sensing his scrutiny she found a grin. 'It's just the fresh air. You've grown light-headed. After all those months on Slaggy Island you can finally breathe again.'

'I know it's all just fine talk, all this about the farm, but who knows what we could do? And this is just the start.'

'Come on, Tom, we've a lot to do today. Let's just live for the present moment.'

'Please, Mary-Jo, let me talk. After years of silence all of a sudden I've got things to say. Things that I'd never dreamt of saying. You see, I thought I had nothing. And now all of a sudden there's a future. You wouldn't believe how lonely I've been. And empty, like a dry well. If other priests feel like me no wonder congregations are haemorrhaging. You don't draw from a well that's dry. But now . . . now, Mary-Jo, I can scent water!' Tom sighed heavily. 'You just wait, in a couple of years –'

'Don't, please, Tom.'

'We could have –'

Stretching across, Mary-Jo laid a finger over his lip to silence him. Slowly she removed her hand and looked away through the window.

'I was only going to say that we could have hens as well.'

Mary-Jo stopped. Closing her eyes, she spoke without turning. 'What about ducks? Ducks on a pond?'

Tom roared with laughter. 'Don't forget a donkey. We've got to have a donkey!'

From the seemingly endless plateau of the open moorland they plunged into a secretive valley where deciduous trees grew and a stream ran crystal clear. A single house stood by the road. 'I won't be a moment,' Tom said, springing out. Going round the back of the house, he passed from sight. Mary-Jo sat in the passenger seat, unmoving except for the hand that she had lifted to her mouth the moment Tom had disappeared from view, as though to stifle a gasp. She stared at the fast silver glimmer of the stream then, manipulating the little mirror, she rubbed the tears welling in her eyes.

The sudden explosion of wood pigeons from the trees advertised the priest's return. 'Just popped in on Agatha,' he explained.

'Agatha?'

'Our neighbour. She helped Mam a lot, especially at the end. She used to sit with her, do her shopping and washing, that kind of thing.' He went over and unhooked a gate with some difficulty. They drove on to a farm track, following the course of the stream. On the sides of the steeply rising valley, the roots of the trees showed like gnarled fingers. 'It *is* isolated here, isn't it?' Mary-Jo said.

'I kept on at her to come to Nazareth House where she could be looked after by the nuns, but she wouldn't leave.'

'Maybe it's better to be able to choose where you end your life.'

'Yes, I suppose it is.'

Two miles along its way, the track suddenly turned sharply and there, squatting on the wider, blunt head of the dale, was the farmhouse. Its ancient, weathered stone seemed to be a display of nature, like a jutting cliff or a landslide. A knot of beeches stood to the west of the house where the wind swept down from the moors. 'I didn't know places like this existed in England,' Mary-Jo said simply.

'Oh they do,' returned Tom. 'But you've got to know where to look.'

'No wonder she didn't want to leave.'

'The district nurse was very good and she knew how to ride Agatha's quad bike, which was just as well, given how the snow used to block up this road.'

The trees of the orchard were bearded with lichen, the boughs choked with dead wood. Acres of young conifer saplings stretched from the tumbled down drystone wall perimeter. 'That's all been planted up by the new owners of the land.' Tom pointed. 'They want the land for commercial forestry and grouse shooting. We get our water from the spring there.' Mary-Jo followed the direction of his finger as it traced up the stream. 'Its source is in the beech roots. When I was a kid we still used to have to carry it back in buckets. We had it piped to the house when my dad died. It's cold as ice all the year round.' Beside the main house crouched the outbuildings, a barn, a stable and a cattle shed.

Tom led Mary-Jo into the darkness of the stable. She ducked as something swept out above them. 'There's been swallows nesting there for as long as I can remember,' Tom said. He reached up to a hook on one of the rafters and brought down a huge key. They passed back into the light of day. The swallows were planing the short-cropped turf by the stream. The priest stood and watched them. 'It's a good omen. They say swallows won't nest in buildings deserted by people.'

The lock turned and the door to the house opened with a loud creak. 'Mind your head.'

'The lintel's low.'

'They were little people in these parts; stunted by the wind.'

'When was it built?'

'1680. See, it says above the door.'

'Oh yes. This door's so solid. No wonder you always give ours such a hammering. You'd practically have to blood your knuckles to be heard inside a house like this.'

Tom shrugged. 'People didn't have to lock their doors.' They went into a little hall. 'The whole house is on smaller proportions. When I went to seminary I thought I'd climbed a beanstalk and come to the giant's palace.'

Mary-Jo followed Tom through a latched door and over a raised threshold into a shuttered room. He lifted off the heavy wooden casements from the windows. It was a low-ceilinged sitting room with a huge fireplace. 'We always called this the parlour. Sorry it's a bit musty.' With a grunt of effort he opened the windows. 'The air will soon get in.'

'What a view,' said Mary-Jo, coming over and staring through the deep-set aperture. Past the effervescent ribbon of the spring fringed with watercress, and beyond the wall of the beeches, the valley rose to the moors. She stood beside him, gazing at the dramatic play of the land, her eyes narrowing in thought, like a genius on the verge of a discovery.

'What are you thinking about?' he asked a little later.

She did not reply.

At last the rattle of matches and tearing of newspaper caught her attention. Tom was lighting the fire. 'Just to clear the damp,' he explained. 'Look at these newspapers, the headlines, some of them twenty years old.' The flames spread over the handful of dried kindling. 'I chopped these,' Tom mused a few minutes later as he placed the logs on the flames. A rich white smoke plumed up the chimney. He breathed in deeply. 'Each different wood has its own scent.'

They went upstairs. The uncarpeted stairs were steep and narrow. 'I used to be terrified that Mam would fall down these.' Tom opened the latched door at the top. Then went into a bedroom. He took down the casements and threw wide the windows. The liquid moorland light flooded in, transfiguring the woman in the room with him. A great swell of emotion came over him. 'She died there,' he said, his hand resting lightly on the bed for an instant as he tried to conceal the strange, uncompromising joy of being here with Mary-Jo. He turned to her in confusion. 'Actually, it's the anniversary today. It's a year since she died. I can't thank you enough for coming. I'm not sure how I would have managed alone.' He went to the open window. 'She must have looked through here thousands of times. And her mother before that. A line of matriarchs. My dad was just a ne'er-do-well blow-in from Ireland, took the wrong turning at some crossroads in County Kerry. Came as a farmhand to the place where Agatha lives now. I've got no brothers, you know, or sisters. There's just me and then the family line dies out.' He looked about the room. 'That's why I want to do what I was saying before. Set something up of lasting value. A legacy, I suppose.'

'Kevin's holiday home?'

'Why not? Something tangible.'

'You sound as though you're on your last legs, Tom. Why talk about leaving and dying out on a summer's day like this?'

Tom tutted. 'Look at that. Now that really would have upset Dad. The sheep have broken the orchard wall. He used to love that orchard. He always said it was the best thing about England. Apple orchards don't thrive on the Atlantic coast. Look at it now, derelict. Half of the boughs won't be bearing fruit.' Tom's voice grew expansive. 'I'm going to restore this place.'

'Tom,' Mary-Jo cleared her throat, 'why don't you go outside, have a look round, inspect the trees, mend the wall, and I'll sort through your mum's clothes, if that's what you want?'

'I'm talking too much? That's the thing, after a life under the *magnum silencium*, all I seem to want to do is talk.'

After Tom had gone Mary-Jo stayed at the window. A cloud passed over the moors, hiding the sun for a few moments. Closer to earth, the white woodsmoke drifted into the blue air. Mary-Jo could smell a hint of it through the open window. She watched Tom walk through the overgrown orchard to the wall. His posture was startlingly straight amongst the crooked trunks and branches. As he lifted a fallen stone his body tightened under his white T-shirt. For the first time she noticed the strength of his arms. Turning from the window she went over to the wardrobe. She opened the heavy oaken door. The dresses were old and the material frail. She took one out and held it up; it was almost transparent in the sunlight. At that moment there was a breeze from the windows and the dress fluttered. Outside, a little moorland bird began to call. She listened to it as she sorted through the clothes. Some were beyond saving, others she put in a pile for a charity shop. The stringent smell of mothballs recalled the time she had sorted her own mother's effects as a sixteen-year-old girl allowed out from the convent for an afternoon. Sometime later a Tornado jet streaked over the dale, tearing the peace to shreds. Going to the window, she saw Tom waving reassuringly.

When she had finished with the clothes she went into the bathroom. The four legs of a heavy bath squatted on the tiles, the white porcelain grained with decades of scrubbing. A chain dangled from the cistern high above the toilet. On a glass shelf stood a bottle of Oil of Ulay, a jar of bath salts and a dish of shell-shaped soaps, whose scent still lingered in the air. A single toothbrush was propped in a glass; beside it lay the razor and shaving brush that Tom must have used on his frequent visits during his mother's latter days.

A floorboard creaked as Mary-Jo crossed the landing to another, far smaller bedroom. A model aeroplane hung from the low ceiling, a Spitfire; a globe stood on a child's desk. Over the bedhead loomed a large crucifix, every straining sinew of agony shown. Amongst the carefully arranged boy's novels on the bookshelf, including *Bevis, Jennings, Biggles* and *Tarka the Otter*, were many numbers of a magazine called the *Catholic Children's Realm*. Having played her finger over their spines, she reached out and brought down a clutch. Ordered in meticulous chronology, every month ceded to the next: five years in total. She picked through them carefully, as though looking for one in particular.

So engrossed was she in her search that she did not hear the tread on the stair, nor the creak of the landing floorboard. When she happened to look up he was standing on the threshold gazing at her. The shock dropped her to the bed. 'I'm so sorry, I didn't mean to pry,' she said. Looking at her, he did not reply. 'It's just that I used to get this as well.' She held up a copy of the *Catholic Children's Realm*. 'Look.' As Mary-Jo opened it for him on the children's poem page, their fingertips brushed. 'My first and only published work.' She smiled. 'In there. Look, let me show you.' He sat down beside her. The soft shape of the mattress brought their bodies together. 'It was a limerick about Mars.' Laughing, she pointed at the name printed in bold beneath.

'Bernadette O'Malley?'

'My real name. Mary-Jo is just short for Mary-Joseph, the name I took when I became a nun. When we were allowed to revert to our real names in the Order I suppose I'd just got used to Mary-Jo. Strange to see this poem after so long. And the name. Bernadette O'Malley. I didn't know she still existed.'

Tom lifted the magazine to a reading position, the slight movement bringing their bodies even closer so that he could feel the shape of her thigh.

'I can still remember it,' she said:

> There was an old woman named Sparrs,
> Who wanted to go to the stars.
> In a rocket she went,
> When the fuel was spent,
> She hadn't got farther than Mars.

'You know what, Bernadette O'Malley? I remember that one.'

'No you don't.'

'I *do* and it's stayed with me all these years.'

'I'd like to see *you* write a limerick.' She grinned. 'Seriously though, I never thought anyone else in the known universe got the *Catholic Children's Realm*. Me and my sister got ours from a teacher at primary school. Where did you get yours from?'

'Mam ordered them specially.'

'Did you ever read the Wopsy books?'

'*Wopsy the Guardian Angel*?' Tom pointed to a section on the bookshelf.

Mary-Jo laughed out loud. Tom felt her laughter vibrating over his own body, like a caress. 'I can't believe it. You've even got the Wopsy books.' He took the books down and handed them to her. 'It's all coming back to me,' she said, leafing through them. When she was finished, he replaced them exactly as they had been. 'You're really organised aren't you? And those books, all in immaculate condition.'

'I *used* to be an organised person.' He reached over to the shelf and straightened a spine fractionally. 'Mam liked to keep things tidy too.'

'Were you close to your parents, Tom?'

'I suppose I was.'

'Were they pleased when their only child wanted to become a priest?'

Tom looked up at the model aeroplane. 'It was all my mother ever wanted.'

'Is that why you became a priest, because of your mother?'

'Children always want to please their parents.'

'Did she keep your room like this?'

'How do you mean?'

'Well, the plane and books and things.'

His brow puckered slightly. 'Now you come to mention it, this room is exactly as it was on the day I left for junior seminary. It's funny.'

'What is?'

'What you said about why I became a priest. I've never really given it much thought, strange as that may seem.'

'Sometimes the most important decisions are like that. Our lives just seem to *happen*. We used to call it Divine Providence.'

The priest reached up and touched the model aeroplane back into life. 'I made this the summer before I went away.' He stared at the aeroplane. 'Why did *you* choose the religious life?'

'How could someone called Bernadette not become a nun?'

'Seriously. Was there not a moment when you knew that you wanted to join an Order?'

'Yes, there was actually.'

'Why are you laughing?'

'Because it was so stupid. Like all the reasons I've ever done things. Did you ever see *The Song of Bernadette*? The film about St Bernadette of Lourdes?'

'Of course I did.'

'Well, that's why I became a nun. *I did see her!*' Mary-Jo's American accent boomed in the room as she quoted from the film. '*Oh yes, I did see her, Maman. The blessed Virgin Mary did appear to me.* There, now you know my terrible secret, Tom. I became a nun because of a black and white film about St Bernadette of Lourdes.'

As she laughed he reached up to touch her face. In confusion he withdrew his hand. 'Look at that,' he said turning the hand palm upwards. 'A blister's forming.' He shook his head. 'My dad's hands told the story of his life; each nick and gash was a happening. What kind of life have I led when I get a blister after half an hour in the orchard?'

'What was your dad like, Tom?'

There was a pause. 'I was in the stable once and he came in. You know, where the swallows nest. He was holding something close in his hands. Like this. He opened them just a crack and I saw a pair of eyes peering out. It was a mouse. What Dad used to call "the little ones". He used to carry them from the stable into the long grass of the orchard to give them a better chance against the barn owl. But it wasn't the mouse that I was looking at.'

'What was it?'

'They were so callused and even then misshapen. A man who works with his hands can't stop every time he breaks a bone or sprains a joint. But it was the mud I noticed most of all. His fingernails were black, and when he let the mouse go I could see all the lines on his palm were ingrained with muck. His lifeline was encrusted with filth.' Tom looked at Mary-Jo. 'That's terrible, isn't it?'

'What is?'

'Becoming a priest so that you can keep your hands clean.' He exhaled softly. 'I was wrong. You don't lead a good life by keeping your hands clean. Anyway, my hands *do* tell the story of my life. They're untouched by the world. Forget St Peter, even St Thomas, I'm Pilate.'

'What's the matter, Tom?'

'Oh boy.' He smiled ruefully. 'The memories really are flooding in now.'

'What memories?'

'Just, things.'

'Tell me about them.'

'Some stones really are best left unturned.' He looked at her with a sudden intensity. 'Now this really does feel like something out of a film. But nothing Paul Newman would be in. Nothing like *The Song of Bernadette*.'

'You've got me intrigued now.'

His face darkened like a child's. 'No, it's not like that, Mary-Jo. It's not a good thing.'

There was a long pause. He reached up and knocked the aeroplane. The Spitfire recommenced its dogfight with an imaginary opponent, suspended more than forty years ago. 'I've never shared this with another living person.'

'Maybe it's time to start sharing.'

'It's not the kind of thing you can share with just anyone.' He narrowed his eyes as though bewildered by his own thoughts. 'I've always put it to the back of my mind, and now I realise that it's at the heart of it all. All these years it's been gnawing away at me, like the rats in a grain barn.'

'What has, Tom?'

He did not seem to hear her but getting up went to the little window. He stared out of it with a strange intensity, as though peering back through the years. 'When she was a little girl my mother saw a calf stand on an acorn. I don't know why she noticed it, but she did. She told me how the hoof split it.' Mary-Jo came over to the window. Across the yard, a twisted oak could be seen. 'That was the tree,' Tom whispered. 'We're like that. People. We carry our damage from childhood. We take our shape from it.'

'What happened to you, Tom?'

For a moment agony blunted the priest's features. 'It's so hard to begin to share, to break the real *magnum silencium*.' He faltered. The crucifix yawned balefully over them. The model aeroplane slowed its circling.

'Go on.' The murmur brought her lips within a hair's breadth of his head.

'I was getting ready for bed one evening,' he began. 'I can't have been more than five years old.' He bowed his head for an instant and swallowed. As he spoke he stared at the tree. His voice was without tone. 'I don't know how it was with you, Mary-Jo, but I was brought up never to touch my body. Especially, you know, down there. But that night as I was getting dressed my hand brushed against it; against my penis. I screamed for my mother at the top of my voice. You see, I'd been told that the devil would come for me if ever I touched myself. When Mam didn't come I grew hysterical. She was out milking the cows.' His hand clenched the windowsill. 'That's what they made of me. A little boy shouting for his mother in mortal terror; waiting for the devil to take him away because he'd touched his own body.' When Mary-Jo took his hand in hers, Tom began to weep. 'Is that what God really wanted?' Mary-Jo put her arm round his shoulder and brought him to her. His weeping became a naked sob. 'A priest?' he managed to stutter. 'I'm not even a man.'

Gently she kneaded his shoulder, then her head fell to rest on the other. 'Shh, shh.'

With a tortured shout he pulled away from her. He ripped

the crucifix from the wall and yanked open the window. 'What kind of thing is that to pester a child with?' he demanded. '*Look at what your sins do to him*, Mam used to say. *Look, look, look!*' He flexed his arm as though about to punch and then hurled the crucifix out of the window. It clattered over the flags of the yard, its body separating from the cross, and all at once his energy was drained. He leant heavily against the windowsill. 'What have I done?' he whispered.

'Shh,' whispered Mary-Jo. He turned. They opened their arms to each other. 'Shh, shh.'

Chapter Sixteen

The month of August was a seemingly endless litany of blue skies and sunny days. On Slaggy Island the prostitutes bathed in the warmth as they waited for the cars to cruise by at the arches of the viaduct, for a brief season the skimpy clothes of their trade a positive boon.

But already the days were shortening. Sitting at his desk in the window well of the presbytery, Tom had not noticed the light above him slowly change from afternoon to twilight to evening. Only when it was too dark for him to continue writing, did he stop. He stood and stretched. The street lamp began to flicker: unerring sign of night on Babbington Road. The priest half-smiled. In the gloom, he looked back at the page on which he had been writing, but all at once the words were mere shadows. A roaming gang of youths walked past below. Tom watched them from his attic room, flexing the legs which had grown stiff through long sitting. His stomach growled.

Tom was stirring a pan of baked beans in the kitchen when he heard the front door open. It was Frank coming in from the port. 'Tom,' he said entering the kitchen, 'I think someone's broken into the church.'

'The church?'

'Come and have a look. One of the boards covering the windows is loose.'

They went outside. 'See, that one there. It's been jemmied off. Do you think it's that group of lads who've been hanging about? I wouldn't want one of them getting inside and desecrating the place.'

Tom pulled the board back as far as it would go. 'You'd be lucky to get a cat through that.'

Frank sighed. He gestured at the beleagured facade of the church, the sign with the gold lettering. 'It's a pity to leave an old church derelict like this. Somehow it doesn't seem right, does it?'

'No, Frank, I think it's probably exactly right.'

'What do you mean?'

'What does it matter about bricks and mortar?'

'Who's this talking to me? We can't have St Peter coming out with lines like that. Where are you going?'

'I'm cooking. I've done enough beans for the Last Supper. Dinner will be served in two minutes.'

With a backward glance at the church, Frank followed Tom inside.

After their beans on toast they sat drinking tea, one at each end of the huge kitchen table.

'Will you do me a favour?' Tom asked.

'What?'

'I've been writing to the Bishop. I want you to check the letter over for me.'

'What is it, your formal acceptance of the Monsignorship?'

'Fat chance of that ever happening now.'

'I'll have to take it with me.'

'Take it with you?'

'I'm sailing on the *Baltic Queen* tonight remember? To Riga and back. I'll be away a week.'

'There's no hurry.'

'And before I go I have to take a minibus load of Poles to the mission centre for Mass.'

'Are you still saying Mass, Frank?'

'Yes, I am.' He flushed slightly. 'Why, do you think I shouldn't?' There was no reply. Frank studied his friend. 'Why don't you come with me? We could concelebrate the Eucharist. When was the last time you said Mass, Tom? Come on, you can't give up on it. What are we if we don't peddle the old magic?'

'Frank I . . . I want to go over the letter once more tonight.'

'You mean you're seeing Mary-Jo tonight? I bet you've arranged another trip to Saltburn tomorrow.'

Tom looked down the wide expanse of the table. The grain was stained dark, and despite the heat of the day, cool to his touch. He smiled. 'Get out before I double your rent.'

'Seriously though, Tom, shouldn't we check the church just to make sure. Maybe Kevin's in there.'

'He came in about four o'clock. I think he's asleep.'

Through the rest of the evening, Tom sat over his desk oblivious to the human traffic outside: the slowing of cars, the call of voices touting business, and the slam of passenger doors. Towards midnight, the priest stood up abruptly. He descended the stairs and after standing on the tiles of the hall for a while, went through into the parish room. The stench hit him as soon as he crossed the threshold. Kevin was in the bed they had carried down from a room upstairs and placed beneath the photograph of the old cleric. He slept as Tom always saw him sleeping, his nose deep in the red bush of his beard. As quietly as he could, Tom entered a number in the dial of the old safe and opened it. From within he brought out a bunch of keys. Kevin did not stir.

There was a locked door at the far end of the hall. By a long process of elimination the priest found the right key on the bunch. The lock was stiff and he had to use two hands to open it. It gave access to a small, musty chamber. Although the summer had been long and hot, here the air was still damp. It was the former sacristy. An old chest was discernible against one of the walls. He opened the top drawer and feeling inside brought out a box of matches. The first flare revealed a single candle, which had rolled to the back of the chest.

The light of the candle showed that there had been a soot fall in the old fireplace and the carpet was dotted with smuts. The rest of the stark room was empty. The drawers of the chest, which had once contained vestments, were riddled with woodworm. On the windowsill stood a single metal vase full of dried grasses.

It took him a long time to find the second key but at last the door in the far wall of the sacristy opened with a resonating click. Protecting the flame of his candle with a hand, Tom stepped into a greater space of darkness. There was a frantic explosion above him and he ducked instinctively: pigeons roosting in the rafters clattering to their escape crevices. Then silence. He was in the church. The flashing orange of the faulty street light splashed through upper windows.

The church had been stripped bare. Nothing was left to connect it to the ritual of the Mass: no pews, no statues, even the altar stone had been taken away. Much of the floor was covered in white pigeon droppings. The priest walked down what would have been the aisle, the candle fluttering feebly behind his hand. Dishes of rat poison had been placed below where the Stations of the Cross had hung. Mounting the old altar, he held up the candle above his head. Amongst the blackened bricks was a cruciform of a lighter colour. Here a crucifix had been attached to the wall for a century.

When Tom encountered the shape of the confessional box still standing in the side chapel, he stopped. The wood was strangely warm to his touch, the carved ornamentations swelling beneath his fingertips, but when he found the handle the sudden brittle chill of metal vibrated through him. He stepped back a few paces until the confessional lost its definition, the dark shape showing like the hull of an abandoned boat on a foggy shingle shore.

It drew him, this relic of Catholicism, and slowly he approached it once more. Opening the door at last, the loudness of the creak fluttered his heart. His shadow, cast by the candle, yawned over the wooden seat inside. He stepped within and sat down. The closeness of the box was filled with his own breathing. The grille separating priest from penitent was clogged with cobwebs which shattered to dust when he slid it across. The candle flared as he made the sign of absolution, something he had once practised endlessly at seminary. He eased himself back into the wooden chair, his body recalling the uncompromising shape of oak. 'Bless me Father, for I am sinning.' The priest shrieked at the sudden voice so close to him. In his shock, he dropped the candle. He fumbled helplessly after its rolling sound, the thick smell of waxy smoke filling his nostrils. The hidden voice spoke again, so close now that it seemed to be in Tom's own head: 'It is too long since my last confession.'

'Who's that?' Tom demanded, fear and anger mingling in his tone.

Forgetting the candle, the priest scrambled for the door handle, but the voice arrested him: 'So sorry for frightening Priest Port Chaplain.'

Straightening, Tom peered at the grille. In the darkness he could just make out the whites of a pair of eyes.

'Is Jesus-Maria, bosun on *Neptune's Booty*.'

'What are you doing here?'

'Where else can I go?'

'What do you mean?'

'Father Tom Carey, I claim sanctuary.'

'Sanctuary?'

Urgency metalled the bosun's tone. 'I come to your church for sanctuary and confession.' There was a pause as the two men gazed at each other through the grille. 'Bless me Father for I am sinning, it is more than two years since my last confession.'

'Don't.' Tom's word was soft.

'What do you mean?'

'I'm not the right man for this, Jesus-Maria. Go to a better priest.'

'I not understand. You are my priest. You are Priest Chaplain of Teesport.'

'You deserve more than me.'

'I no follow.'

'Please, just see someone else.'

'Who else?' Jesus-Maria's voice reverberated in the box. '*You* are knowing the names of my children.' A wave of pity broke over the priest, like a sickness. 'Father Tom Carey, I need forgiveness.'

Tom lifted a hand wearily and formed the sign of the cross. 'Whenever you want to begin.' He waited as the penitent's lips mumbled in fervent prayer. 'Go on,' he coaxed, as he had done so many times before. 'Unburden yourself.'

'Father, you know how it is that one time I start a chicken business and it fail?'

'Yes.'

'Everything we try, it fail. Is how we live. Like chicken, always pecking the ground for tasty morsels, always hungry. But when I see my baby ill I feel not like chicken, but like tiger.' The bosun's breathing became tangled.

'Our Lord is listening, Jesus-Maria. He loves a sincere penitent.' The old words returned to Tom so easily. He seemed to be watching himself, as though the situation was an example being outlined at seminary.

The moonlike eyes narrowed suspiciously. 'You are a holy priest? You not say to others what I am going to say?'

'I'm under what we call the seal of confession. I cannot tell another living soul.'

The eyes seemed satisfied and waxed large once more. 'Then I say all. But it is a great crime.'

'A crime?'

'Yes. A terrible crime.' Tom's heart lurched. The sickness of his compassion was spreading through his veins like fear. 'Father Tom Carey, *Neptune's Booty* is a place of great evil.' The name of the ship echoed in the confessional. 'The *Neptune's Booty*, she a people smuggler.'

'A people smuggler?'

'We pick up people, hide them in cargo hold and take them.'

'Take them where?'

'Anywhere. Great Britain, America, the middle of the ocean.' Jesus-Maria's voice was without tone. 'I not know about this until we come up coast of England and I see Captain Cargo make drop.'

'What do you mean, make a drop?'

'He not see me. I should not see him, but I *do*. This is what happen. It is night and all others are sleeping. Captain Cargo send the watch to bed. I am the watch, why he want to send me to bed? If there is accident, I am to blame. So I not go to bed. I see a small boat come alongside us. She no have lights. I hide and watch as Captain Cargo open hatch and bring out men on deck. These are not crew. I have not seen them before. They climb down to waiting ship and are gone. But I see them.' The priest lifted a hand to rub his face. 'That night in bed,' the penitent continued, 'I thinking of my family so far away and it feel like my heart it break. I stare through porthole at stars, but Father Tom Carey, your stars are not those at home above the failing chicken farm. At home the night sky is like diamond. Just to look make you feel rich. Father Tom Carey, I give anything to see again the stars shining over our valley.' There was a pause. The priest waited. 'Father Tom Carey?'

'Yes?'

'I am not telling whole truth. And I must tell the truth or there is no forgiveness.'

The priest's heart throbbed as he whispered, 'And what *is* the whole truth?'

'The truth is I am angry tiger. The truth is even when we are back in Malacca Straits I know that *Neptune's Booty* she a people smuggler. How I know? Because I see Captain Cargo make people jump into sea, South China Sea. And no boat wait for them there. Perhaps they not pay enough. *If you see too much*, is proverb, *then you must see nothing*. But who else will see them if I do not? What is the sound of a human falling into sea from a container ship? Just a flea jumping from tiger's back. Those men in the Malacca Straits,' Jesus-Maria fought against a sudden trembling in his voice, 'maybe a shark eat them. I know all this, but I stay on *Neptune's Booty*. Why I stay? If I not see through contract then I get black mark against me in manning agency in Manila. Then how my family live? This is my sin. I see murder and do nothing. I see others' suffering, and close my eyes.'

Tom waited for the Filipino to continue, but he said nothing more. 'Jesus-Maria, I absolve you in the name of the Father, and of the Son and of the Holy Spirit.' His hand sketched the cross on the air again. 'As your penance I want you to say three Hail Mary's.'

Disbelief caulked Jesus-Maria's voice. 'Is that all?'

Tom tried to calm his voice. 'You haven't actually committed a crime, Jesus-Maria. It's just a sin of omission. I mean, did you actually throw the people overboard yourself?'

'No.'

'Did you profit from it?'

'No; my contract is for bosun.'

'Exactly.'

'I am seeing now what you really think, Father Tom Carey.'

'What are you talking about?'

A cold rage suffused the bosun's voice. 'You think because I am poor I have no choices to make. You think because I am poor I have no free will.'

An unfathomable answering anger swelled within the priest. 'How can you possibly say you know what I think? I have prayed the words of absolution over you. You are forgiven. What more do you want?' The last words rang out in the empty church. His temper cooling as soon as his shout had died away, Tom waited. 'Jesus-Maria?' The priest peered through the grille into the gloom but there were no white eyes. He climbed out from the confessional box. The penitent's door was open. 'Jesus-Maria?' Tom walked quickly through the church. In the shadows the altar seemed to rise before him like a hill. He gazed numbly up its steep height.

He had mounted two altar steps when Jesus-Maria spoke, his voice close again. 'Now you give me sanctuary.' Tom looked down, the Filipino was kneeling. 'I say my penance.'

'Come into the presbytery. This isn't the place for any of this.'

'You give me sanctuary,' the bosun returned with gentle obstinacy.

'Jesus-Maria, this isn't the Middle Ages.'

'You hide me, Father Tom Carey? You see, Captain Cargo, he want to kill me.'

Tom paused only for a moment. 'The presbytery counts as the church,' he said, adding airily, 'under canon law, that is.'

'Sanctuary in presbytery?'

'Yes.'

The priest led him through the sacristy and up the stairs to the attic room. 'Is like the bridge,' Jesus-Maria smiled.

'The bridge?'

'Like on ship, the room at the top of the house.' The bosun went over to the window well and wedging himself in it, lifted himself up nimbly. 'A good place for the watch.'

Tom sat heavily on the bed.

'Father Tom Carey? I am sorry for involving you in my shame. And in my danger. I know, you are wishing you never see me.' Neither spoke for a while. It was the seafarer who broke the silence. 'When Nancy was born the frangipani trees bloom.'

'Your daughter?'

'My Nancy. The frangipani trees all bloom.' Jesus-Maria smiled to himself. The smile remained for a moment, then vanished, like a bird alighting on a blossom branch only for an instant. He gazed through the window. 'Babbington Road is not like my valley. Is like Manila, whores, drinking, drugs. Why a holy priest live here?

'You look exhausted, Jesus-Maria.'

'I am not sleeping for many night. Now I am always on watch.'

'Well, the one thing we do have is plenty of room. Why not have a sleep? Then we'll talk.'

'You give me sanctuary?'

'I'll arrange a bed for you.'

'Are you not frightened, Father?'

'Do you want a wash? You can have a bath. Here, I'll get you a towel.'

When the priest came back, Jesus-Maria was standing in front of the Rembrandt print. 'Father Tom Carey, what is that?'

'The picture?'

'Is a picture of God?'

'It's the prodigal son. You know, from the gospel.'

'Yes, I know.'

'Are you all right, Jesus-Maria?'

'I am happy now Jesus forgive me.'

When the Filipino looked away from the picture, the priest could see that his cheeks were glistening with tears. For a long time the bosun stood with his back to the priest. When he turned, there was no sign of his grief. He looked at the desk on which stood the priest's fountain pen, a bottle of black ink and a notepad. Beneath it was a waste-paper bin filled with sheets darkened by close, neat writing. 'You are writing a book, Father Tom Carey?'

'Just a letter to the Bishop.'

'I could write a book about what I see. Maybe I should be a writer.' He nodded eagerly at the priest. 'Yes, I am doing a course. A correspondence course from the Commercial University of Central Missouri in United States. If you finish it they say you are writer and earn up to ten thousand dollars a month.' A profound longing narrowed Jesus-Maria's eyes. 'Then my Nancy get well and my Xavier go to school. And I not have to leave them any more.' The longing disappeared. 'But I can no afford to finish the course.' He broke off and looked about the room. 'You have a shipshape cabin,' he said with a smile. 'And so many books. You are very clever man.'

'I can't remember the last time I read a book.'

'You have Wilbur Smith?'

'Wilbur Smith? No, I don't have any Wilbur Smith, I'm afraid.'

'I am liking Wilbur Smith. He in Tagalog.'

'Tagalog?'

'Language in Philippines.'

'It's mostly non-fiction. I never was very imaginative.'

'I can look?'

'Of course.'

Jesus-Maria went over to the shelves. He reached up and brought out a heavy book. It was an atlas. Slowly he flipped through it. Selecting a page, the seafarer's finger travelled across a blue sea sifting through a gravel of islands. 'Father Tom Carey, here is failing chicken farm.'

The priest looked over his shoulder. 'And the frangipani tree, Jesus-Maria.'

The two men's eyes met. 'Yes, it is there also in my Philippines. Where is your home, Port Chaplain?'

'My home?'

'Your farmhouse, with confused cockerel.'

'Oh yes. I told you about him, didn't I? I'll show you exactly where the farmhouse is.' Tom reached out to a shelf full of maps and selected one. He unfolded it. 'Here we are.' His hand rested on the River Tees for a second then lifted over the moors like a bird. A finger ran along the track that the priest had driven on with Mary-Jo. The stream was a thin blue line. 'Here's the farmhouse . . . with the confused cockerel.'

'Is remote?'

'Yes, by English standards. The nearest neighbours are two miles away.'

'And who lives in your farmhouse?'

'No one. It's been empty since my mother died.'

Jesus-Maria blinked. 'I am sorry your mother die.'

'It was over a year ago.'

'Is beautiful place?'

'I'm sorry?'

'Your farmhouse? Is a beautiful place?'

'Yes. Especially when the apple orchard blooms.'

'Apple bloom?'

'A little like your frangipani.'

'My mother she die after Nancy is born. No money for her hospital bills.' Jesus-Maria looked up from the map. 'And now, Father Tom Carey, it is my turn to die. Captain Cargo, he is mafia. Father Tom Carey, mafia own the sea.'

There was a pause; Tom folded the map. Through the corner of his eye he could see the sailor's fingers drumming the map of the Philippines in restrained agitation. 'Jesus-Maria,' he said quietly, 'you must go to the police. This is too big a matter for me.'

The seafarer looked pityingly at the priest. 'Still you not understand. If I go to police, he kill my family. He break their necks easy as chickens. Captain Cargo, he a violent man. He already threaten one of our crew, and soon he is killing him.'

'Who?'

'The one with the bad leg.'

'I heard he was in hospital again. Why did he discharge himself in the first place? The leg won't heal properly that way.'

Jesus-Maria shook his head. 'He back on *Neptune's Booty*. He discharge himself again.'

'Discharged himself *again*?'

'Captain Cargo, he make him.'

'But why?'

'He want to kill him. You see, this man is watch with me when I see drop. He see it too and so Cargo is killing him.' The seafarer sighed. 'You not know the world, Father Tom Carey. Maybe you are great saint.'

'I'm just scared. And very confused.'

'Like your cockerel.'

Tom closed his eyes and clenching his fists drummed his head lightly. 'Jesus-Maria, are you telling me that Captain Cargo is a member of the mafia, a people smuggler and that he's going to kill the man with the injured leg and then you?'

'Yes.' The word resonated. 'Yes. He will come looking for me soon. And now you must promise you not call police.'

'But that's why you must go to the police, Jesus-Maria. How can you be safe without the help of the police?'

The seafarer's voice broke. 'Only you can help me.'

When Jesus-Maria was in the bathroom, Tom went over to the window. For a while he scanned the street. Then he stood in his bedroom, listening to the sound of the running water, staring at the framed Rembrandt print.

'Worked out who you are yet?

Tom looked round. 'Oh, it's you, Frank. I thought you'd gone.'

'Expecting someone were you? Well, I've packed for my trip to the Baltic. Have you got that letter?'

'Here it is.' Tom went over to the desk and handed Frank a large envelope.

'Some letter. What is it, an Epistle to the Apostles?'

'If you must know, it's about the farmhouse. You know, Mam's old place. I'm planning to turn it into a diocesan resource centre. A retreat for the disadvantaged. Actually, I'm hoping that Mary-Jo and I can run it.'

'Well, I hope the Bishop will agree. Tom, what's the matter?'

'Look, close the door and come over here.'

'What is it?'

Tom dropped his voice below the chatter of the filling bath. His anxiety engulfed him. 'Jesus-Maria's in the bath.'

'Who?'

'You know, the bosun from *Neptune's Booty*. Frank, he's claimed sanctuary.'

Frank giggled. 'Sanctuary?'

'Keep your voice down. You were right before about the

church being broken into. It was Jesus-Maria. He's claimed sanctuary.'

'God, won't the Bishop just love it? Welcome to the alternative presbytery. One poof, one down-and-out, one priest carrying on with a nun and a sailor boy claiming sanctuary to boot.'

'This is serious, Frank. He's in trouble.'

Frank clicked his fingers in triumph. 'At last I've solved the mystery. It's you that's been the Mad Monsignor all along.'

'It's not a laughing matter.'

'Well, claiming sanctuary, isn't that a touch melodramatic, Tom?'

'Someone's trying to kill him.'

'Don't tell me: Captain Cargo.'

'Yes.'

'It's not a letter you've been writing, Tom, but a novel.'

'He says that Cargo will kill him and his family in the Philippines as well.'

'The ability to be in two places at the one time, eh? What is he, some kind of evil Padre Pio figure?'

'The captain is a member of a mafia people-smuggling operation.'

'Tom, don't you think that it's all a little far-fetched?'

'Quite honestly, I don't know what to think. This is uncharted territory. He's also said certain things in confession.'

'I see.' Frank narrowed his eyes. 'Look, he's under stress. From what you and Mary-Jo say, all that crew must be stretched to breaking point. I mean, life on good ships like the *Baltic Queen* is hard enough. What's it going to be like on a rust bucket like *Neptune's Booty*? Maybe he's had a breakdown or something.'

'So what are you saying, that I should just send him on his way?'

'No. Listen to him. Talk. You've heard his confession. That'll have done him a power of good.'

'You think so?'

'Don't you, Tom?'

'Does the absolution of a man who no longer believes in forgiveness mean anything?'

'I'm surprised, Tom. I thought you of all people would understand reconciliation. Would believe in second chances.'

'What do you mean?'

'I mean I would have thought you'd understand what it means when you're allowed to change. Anyway, what *are* you going to do with this bosun?'

'I'm going to have to go to the police, although he doesn't want me to.'

'Isn't it a crime, wasting police time?'

'Now isn't the time for joking, Frank.'

'What, and you think the police will give you a better response when you roll up at the station and tell them about Captain Cargo and the mafiosi?'

Tom sat down heavily at his desk. He hid his face in his hands. 'I'm . . . I've got myself involved in something. I'm not up to this, Frank.'

'Do you want me to stay, Tom?'

'Oh no, you go. I know how much you've been looking forward to the voyage.' He looked up. He seemed to come to a decision. 'You're probably right. It's all a storm in a teacup. You go. I'll manage.'

They listened to the running water. 'He likes his baths deep.' Frank's giggle became a hoot. 'This is turning into a farce. Can I play the Norman Wisdom character?'

'I think I've already collared that one.'

'Kevin sleeping in the parish room, a sailor in the bathroom. Maybe you're more like Damien than I ever gave you credit for.'

'Damien risked everything, Frank. He didn't wait for them to come to him, he went into the heart of the leper colony.'

When Frank had gone, Tom went round to the front of the old church. With a hammer and a few nails he had brought from the farm, he secured the hoarding back in place. One or two of the women gazed down from the arches. Constantly he scanned the street. Back inside, he sat on the bottom stair, staring at the tessellated tiles. Then he went to the phone. As he waited for the person on the other end of the line to pick up, the priest noticed that his hands were shaking. 'Hello, Anne,' he said, speaking quietly so as not to wake the sleeping vagrant. 'It's Tom. How are you? I was just wondering if Mary-Jo . . . What? What is it?' Tom's face puckered with puzzlement. 'I don't really understand what you're saying, Anne. Are you talking about Mary-Jo? Anne?' He rang back, but the phone was engaged. For a long time he stood there, ringing the number, but each time the engaged tone sounded in the earpiece. Kevin turned over in his sleep.

When Tom reached the top of the stairs, the bathroom door was open. The tap was still running; steam filled the landing. Water was lapping on to the floor. 'Jesus-Maria?' There was no answer. After a moment's hesitation Tom plunged into the bathroom. He clawed through the steam, yanked out the plug and switched off the taps. He ran to his attic room, then checked each room in turn. Getting a torch, he went into the church. The pigeons had returned to roost and as he strode across the old aisle the explosion of their wings echoed in the large building. 'Jesus-Maria?' The confessional box was empty.

Backing the car out of the garage, Tom drove along the viaduct. As he was passing Barnacle Bill's, he thought he caught sight of Captain Cargo going in. Panicking, the priest drove on. But he did not mount the bridge; instead he circled round the cobbled streets of Slaggy Island a few times, searching for the slight figure of the bosun. Returning to the pub, he bumped the car on to the pavement. He paused on the threshold of the pub, breathed in deeply, then entered.

Barnacle Bill's was heaving. A pool tournament was in progress. Cigarette smoke blued the air. The priest pushed his way through the crowd gathered round the pool table. Spotting him, the landlord called: 'Drink, Reverend Father?' Tom nodded and elbowed his way to the bar. The landlord glanced over his shoulder at him as he filled the glass at the optic. The hard chock of striking pool balls rang out, followed by the thirsty glug-glug of one of them rolling down the pocket. There was an explosion of cheering.

'I'm looking for the captain,' Tom heard himself say in a voice far more commanding than he felt himself to be. He followed the landlord's pointing finger to the pool table. In the middle of the pressing throng, Captain Cargo was lining up his shot. Cigar in mouth, leg raised jauntily, he potted a ball with ease. There was more cheering. Ten-pound notes were waved like ticker tape. The shipmaster was wearing his usual black leather jacket and his cheeks remained darkly unshaven. His blond hair and eyebrows had been dyed black. His gold earring glistened under the pool table lights.

'On the house,' the landlord said, placing the large cognac on the bar with a wink that Tom could not fathom.

Head low over the table, with a sudden spectacular flourish, Captain Cargo potted another ball.

Tom sat in a corner. In the company he recognised one or two of the prostitutes. Yawning, they nodded at him. When he reached out to take a drink from his glass, he realised that his hand was shaking so violently that he had to steady his grip with a second hand. There was a sustained roar from the pool table then the crowd moved to the bar, like a single creature of many heads and shoulders. When he looked up again Captain Cargo was standing above him. He was holding out a pool cue. 'You are on next I think, my fellow seminarian.'

'I'm sorry?'

'One of team has pulled out. You are replacement.'

'I don't play pool, Captain Cargo.'

'You want disappoint all these people?'

The blackened hair and eyebrows had markedly changed the way the shipmaster looked, like a carrion bird in winter plumage. The priest reached out for his glass. 'Captain Cargo, I've come for a chat.'

Cargo continued to stare penetratingly at him, then roared with laughter. 'We can talk as we play.' With a growing sense of disbelief, Tom followed him to the table. He chalked the end of his cue. When he gripped it tightly with both hands he found that it stilled his trembling. 'It is a pity that we meet on the green baize,' the captain said, and the priest realised that he had been drinking heavily. 'I would have preferred the chessboard as our swords. And playing with bishops is, perhaps, more your game.'

'I think a pawn more appropriate.'

'Doesn't every pawn dream of being a bishop?'

'I believe it's the other way round, Captain Cargo.'

Cargo chuckled. 'Such philosophical discussions, just like seminary days.' Wielding his cue carefully, Tom broke clumsily. The balls clattered over the table, two were drunk thirstily by the holes. 'Two stripes,' the captain said approvingly.

'Beginner's luck,' said Tom, but he potted the next ball too.

'I of course should have expected it from a man of talents like my Vincent Van Gogh. Is this not just like our old seminary days?'

'You must have gone to a strange seminary, Captain Cargo,' said Tom as he lined up his next shot.

'Why you say that? What did you discuss at yours?'

'Oh, things like what to do when someone comes to you with a great crime on their conscience.'

'And what did you decide should be done?'

'Well, not play games with them, that's for certain.'

'And what are you doing now?'

'This is no game.'

'Careful my friend.' Tom's shot cannoned fruitlessly off a cushion. 'I hope you not continue to play as recklessly as you talk, my fellow seminarian.'

'Why do you call your ship *Neptune's Booty*, Captain?'

The captain lowered himself over the table. 'And what else are we other than Neptune's Booty? People like you and me, we are lonesome driftwood, castaways; people for whom no one waits at home counting the days until their return. My friend, it makes no difference to the world whether we sink to the bottom of the ocean. We are Neptune's Booty.'

'Do you really think that?'

'Don't you?'

'Do you believe in God, Captain?'

'Do you?'

'I'm asking you.'

'Never ask a question that you will not answer yourself.'

'Where's Jesus-Maria, Captain?'

'I was hoping you could answer that for me.'

The captain potted his ball. Hardly bothering to line up his next shot, he struck successfully. Tom's voice cut through the hum of the crowd. 'Are you a member of the mafia, Captain?'

'Now you are sailing in very dangerous waters.'

'More dangerous than the Malacca Straits?'

'There is nowhere more dangerous.'

The shipmaster's next shot was a violent crack. He potted, but the cue ball ran into a cluster of stripes. 'You've snookered yourself,' Tom said, not hiding the glint in his eye.

With a casual shrug of his shoulders, the shipmaster played. He narrowly missed off the cushion. 'Two shots to you.' As Tom bent down for his shot, the captain, chalking his cue, came so close that the priest could feel the dark whiskers bristling against his cheeks. But his own face was equally unshaven, and he did not give way. The earring was cold on his skin. The sailor's voice became a menacing whisper. 'You think because you are priest you can poke your neck into a noose. But the noose tightens for all that.'

The priest's shot was a harmless slice. Despite the unmistakable menace in the captain's voice, he smiled in return. 'Maybe it's because I'm a priest that I can do that. You see, I have no family to threaten.' Without replying, Captain Cargo manoeuvred his cue into position. Tom looked at him uncertainly. 'I think it's my shot.' The other showed no sign of hearing. The thick end of the sailor's cue cocked like a rifle bolt. After some hesitation, the priest grabbed it. 'You missed, remember? That means two shots to me.'

The seafarer glowered at the priest, then burst into laughter. 'There is no cheating your genes.' He waved a hand airily. Most of the crowd had drifted away. The bar was a milling machinery of backs and shoulders. A few people remained round the table, talking as they watched. 'My friend,' Cargo said, 'sometime when I am in Barnacle Bill's, I think I am in the house standing on the edge of the world.'

'Do you?'

'Yes, yes,' the captain said briskly. 'The sailor's life is as lonely as cosmonaut's. What is the sea but an emptiness as vast as space? Sometimes, when I am at sea, the albatross follow me for days. Now he look in one window, then the next, as though he is looking for something. But what can I give him? He has wings, all I have is Barnacle Bill. A Barnacle Bill in every port all over the world. No wonder my crew make a habit of coming to Babbington Road.' At these words Tom miscued but the striped ball rolled towards the far pocket. Its momentum seemed spent but still it travelled in the right direction. Over the rumble of the glug-glug, he drank from his own glass, his back turned from his adversary to hide the shaking hand, but he found that it was steady. His head felt suddenly, coldly clear.

'For jig-a-jig, I mean,' the captain continued, glaring at the pocket down which the priest's ball had dropped. 'Why else they come to Babbington Road?' As Tom lined up a shot his cue was nudged. The ship captain was coming near again. 'My fellow seminarian, what I want you to understand is that when you see the life of a sailor it is easy to understand how a good man can do bad things.'

Tom cleared his throat. 'When a good man does evil does he remain a good man?'

'You asked me before if I believed in God. I will tell you a story. There was once an old priest. People thought he was very holy, a living saint. They came from far away to see him. *What is the secret of your holiness*? they asked him. This is what he said: *I struggled all my life with the devil, it's been hell at times, but now we've grown old together and these days we hardly bother with each other. So you are at peace now?* they ask. He shook his head: *Now I've begun my struggle with God. And what's that like?* they demanded. He looked at them a long time before answering. *That, he said at last, that is much harder.'* Without pausing or changing the tone of his voice, the captain added, 'Did he warn you not to go to police when he came to see you at Babbington Road?'

Tom closed his eyes to try and ward off the buzzing resonance produced in his ears by the way the captain said Babbington Road. It struck him as forcibly as the way the bosun pronounced *Neptune's Booty*. All at once the desperate bravado that had brought him to the pool table at Barnacle Bill's had evaporated. The clarity had been stirred to murk. It was as though he had suddenly woken up to find that a nightmare was real. 'I'm sorry I . . . I don't know what you're talking about.'

'Oh you do, my seminarian. I know you and you always know more than you say.' The priest's next shot fluffed tamely into the D; before he had time to rechalk his cue, Captain Cargo had potted twice. 'Did he say I was a mafioso?'

'He told me nothing about you, Captain.'

'Do not be embarrassed on my account. He is a desperate man and will say desperate things.'

'Are you a desperate man?'

'God only knows how you have survived to play this game. I was certain he would kill you when he went to all that trouble to lure you to bottom of ship.' The shipmaster potted twice, striking with the speed of a snake. There was only the black left on the table. The cue ball rolled into an unpromising position. The whole pub, which had seemed intent on its own business a few moments ago, fell quiet at the intensity of the moment. His face wreathed in concentration, Captain Cargo raised his cue. He lined it up through one eye and then fired like a sniper. The black ball missed the intended pocket, but its power carried it to the opposite one. It sank and for a moment the shipmaster's single smile was an elemental gloat of triumph. But the white ball was still running. It reached a middle pocket then disappeared into it. The captain stared as though in disbelief, his lips lifting into a snarl. The arm he threw round the priest's shoulders squeezed so tightly that it took Tom's breath away, but when the priest saw the face lowering over his own it was smiling good-naturedly. With his arm still around him, Captain Cargo led him through the back of the bar to the landlord's living room. The landlord got up immediately and brought them a bottle of cognac with two glasses. They were alone. The muffled sound of voices and the cash register could be heard from the bar.

As Captain Cargo poured them both a large bumper of spirits he spilled the liquor over his own hand without seeming to realise. It was then that the priest realised just how drunk his opponent was.

'Now we have a proper talk, my fellow seminarian. Our friend, the saintly Jesus-Maria, is a, how you say, multiple homicide. He's a people smuggler and a drug trafficker. This surprises you? Does it surprise you even more to know that Jesus-Maria does not even exist? His real name is Eduardo Marcos.' The captain plunged a hand into his jacket and brought out a folded sheet of paper. He held it out. The priest took it feebly. Cargo watched Tom as he unfolded the paper and began to read. 'It is *Neptune's Booty*'s crew list. See? Jesus-Maria is non-person. Look there. Bosun Eduardo Marcos.'

The priest could not conceal the tremor in his voice as he read the name of the captain. 'Vasily Shukshin,' he said slowly.

'At last you know what even my father never knew.' Captain Cargo sighed. He peered levelly at the priest. 'The Snakeheads are no Boy-Scout pioneers. You lift a finger against them, they cut the whole arm off.' He mimed the incision with a powerful chop of his hand against his own arm.

The priest flinched. 'Snakeheads?'

'Eduardo works hand in hand with Chinese Snakeheads. Ah, my fellow seminarian, did you not know that?'

'Snakeheads?'

'The Snakeheads. Ulo ng Ahas. They make Stalin and KGB look like tea party. And it means even though I am no Van Gogh I will lose more than an ear.' The captain sighed. 'Eduardo knows he can kill me whenever he wants me. That is for certain, whether my genes want it or not. He will kill me tonight, maybe tomorrow night. So you see, fellow seminarian, after all we must settle for the game of pool, inferior though it is to chess, and say farewell just as we are coming to be on first-name terms.' Looking at the captain through the river-bottom murk of his cognac, Tom was confounded to see genuine fear on the face of the other man. Cargo drained his glass then leant forward with a philosophical raising of his eyebrows. 'Ah, my friend, you have come too late for my friendship.'

'And what about the other one?' the priest heard himself ask timidly. He gathered his small store of courage. 'The man with the injured leg. How is he?'

'What are you talking about?'

'The one too scared to get a doctor. The one in and out of hospital, discharging himself.'

The captain smiled sadly. 'A little knowledge is a dangerous thing, my friend. Shipmaster only in name, I act under orders. It is Eduardo, he holds, how you say, whiphandle. Ulo ng Ahas rules the waves.' Before Tom could answer, the sailor reached out and wafted the conversation away as though it were an unpleasant smell. 'But tell me, my Cardinal Newman, how is the woman you love?'

Enveloped in the sense of unreality that had been growing since the game of pool, Tom picked his way through the still crowded pub. The landlord said something to him as he passed, but he could not make out the words.

The human traffic along the viaduct was at its busiest. A peep show throbbed luridly from the church doorway. Tom hardly seemed to notice anything as he drove by. He mounted the bridge and sped down the other side through the slag-heap ring. He skirted the port. As the Transporter Bridge crossed on its low-slung platform, he got out of the car and stared at the slowly approaching lights of the petrochemical plants on the far bank.

There were cars gathered outside the convent. The priest had to park further down the road. A full moon was climbing above the marsh, scattering its silver over the darkness. The priest broke into a trot as he passed the cars. Having knocked at the door he waited. A sudden sickness in the pit of his stomach nauseated him.

A strange woman answered. She stared at him without saying a word. Her eyes were red-rimmed with weeping. 'Tom,' he said, his breath coming out jerkily. 'Tom Carey.' She stared back without replying. 'Father Tom Carey,' he added. 'The port chaplain.'

He saw her look for his collar and then rest on his jeans and T-shirt. 'Anne?' the strange woman called over her shoulder uncertainly. 'There's someone here.'

Anne was in the hall. She was just about to go up the stairs. 'What is it, Moira?'

'A Father Tom Carey?'

'What's going on, Anne?' the priest asked.

Anne stared blankly past the Mother Superior at Tom. 'She never did tell you, did she?'

'Tell me what?'

'I think you'd better come in.'

Chapter Seventeen

When he was a boy Jesus-Maria once watched a wasp fight with a spider. The spider had had eight long, jointed legs, the wasp only the single, inflexible tapering sting. At first the two creatures had not engaged with each other. The spider had stood there, its eight-legged muscle-memory hesitating in the face of the wasp's motionlessness. Seizing this instant of confusion, the wasp had struck, puncturing the spongy abdomen as the terrible legs fumbled for a grip. Jesus-Maria had watched the wasp fly away leaving the spider writhing in its death agony. At first he had felt a profound relief, then a deep, unfathomable sorrow. Against all the odds the wasp had escaped. From where he now hid on the dark deck, Jesus-Maria stared up at the moon. It was full. His thumb rested on the keenness of his blade. He shook the sweat from his brow. It trickled into his mouth, breaking on his tongue with the saltiness of blood. The same moon shone on his home so far away. How he longed to see his family sleeping safely, each face bathed in the moonlight streaming through the gaps in the bamboo roof. From the heights of the moon, he looked back down to the top of the gangway, his ears straining for the sound of boots on metal. The captain would be back any moment.

Just then Jesus-Maria heard the door of the deckhouse open. It was the injured man from Negros. His crutches tapped as he moved across the deck. Jesus-Maria was about to call out when he realised that someone was mounting the gangplank. He melted back into the shadows. The shipmaster came into view, his full stature picked out by the moon. The bosun was startled by the blackened hair.

Throwing aside his crutches, the injured man fled. As though momentarily mesmerised by his rapid hobbling pace the captain only moved when the injured man had reached the accommodation. Then he clicked into life, sprinting after him. In those few moments the bosun had spotted a fatal flaw. Although the coiled power remained in his legs, it was clear that the captain had been drinking. The knife glinted in the moonlight as Jesus-Maria followed them.

The injured man descended flight after flight of stairs, moving with the speed of a crab over rocks. Jesus-Maria crept silently to the top flight and peered into the gloom below. He could hear that the captain was no longer hurrying. 'Why you run?' the shipmaster asked in a heavy, seemingly unconcerned voice. 'I no hurt you. I look after you. I no hurt you.' The repeated words were spoken in a deliberate pidgin, mocking the oriental accent. The stricken Filipino was desperately entreating for mercy in the language of his island. Under cover of the sound Jesus-Maria stole after them. 'Yes, yes,' the captain said airily. 'Jabber-jabber. And what am I to do about your jabber-jabber?' The injured man's words became a piteous swirl as they echoed in the bowels of the ship. The captain, unruffled, descended slowly. The Filipino ceased to plead. Crouching low on the stairs, Jesus-Maria could hear his fellow countryman's terrified breathing as he clambered down the ladders into the very bottom of the vast ship. He slipped silently after them, his knife severing the gloom through which he passed.

By the time the bosun arrived, Captain Cargo had already struck. The injured man was propped up against the side of the cavity. Like an artist, the shipmaster seemed to study his victim for a few moments through the perspective of his knife, then, lowering his blade, he hurled himself against him a second time. Helplessly, Jesus-Maria watched. When the two bodies disengaged, the man from Negros was left crushed against the metal side. Like a swatted fly, he held there for a few moments then fell to the ground. Fatally stabbed, he began to gurgle. The moon shining down from the gash in the hull above them glinted on the knife in the Filipino's chest. But as the shipmaster went to pull the knife free, he stumbled. He clutched at his own shoulder in confusion. His jacket was glistening with blood. His probing hand found a rent the size of an index finger. He himself had been stabbed. Puzzled, he pulled out his blade from the body of his victim. He felt it rasp against a rib before coming free. Stepping away from the dying man, Captain Cargo stumbled again. He grunted in bafflement.

Jesus-Maria crept towards him until he could smell the leather of the captain's black jacket, and the sour tang of alcohol. Fighting against a nauseating fear, he coiled himself. Then he sprang. The instant Jesus-Maria attacked, the shipmaster became aware of him. With one hand he knocked the bosun's wrist aside; with the other he bludgeoned him to the ground. Jesus-Maria heard his blade skittering across the metal. He had landed beside his dying shipmate.

'This is no good,' Captain Cargo said, calmly regarding him. 'One of us has to die and my genes will not allow it to be me, my friend.'

'I not your friend.'

'Then that makes you my enemy. You have seen too much, my friend. As someone once said, only dead men don't talk.'

'Do not kill me,' Jesus-Maria said simply.

'You are begging for your life?'

'I have wife and two children.'

'And do I not have a life worth saving for anything?'

'All you have is *Neptune's Booty* –'

It took Captain Cargo an extra instant to realise that the bosun had snatched up the knife of the dead man, but no sooner had the shipmaster registered the attack, than he had moved to dodge it, whilst striking with his own terrible sting.

Chapter Eighteen

After the morphine injection the dark film of pain began to lift from Mary-Jo's vision; in its place came a haze. Through this haze peered faces that she recognised, the doctor, Anne, Moira and other members of her Order.

Tom waited numbly downstairs in the room where he and Christy had eaten supper. That evening when the late spring twilight had flowed in through the windows seemed so long ago now. The room itself had not changed. The same accordion of books played itself over a shelf, the same screen was placed in front of the fire, and the same statue stood in a corner. Flowers from the marsh still filled vases.

When he had first been shown up to see her, her skin, stretched painfully over her face, had unforgivingly revealed the shape of her skull. The zigzag of a blue vein had pulsed on her temple, like the water running beneath a frozen stream. Black bags had bunched beneath her eyes. The fingers he had watched fluttering on the outside of the sheets had been as white as the asbestos scattered in the hold of *Neptune's Booty*. Mary-Jo had not been able to talk. He did not even know whether she had recognised him; and then he had been ushered away by others who apparently had better reasons for being there. All at once he had found himself a stranger to her again, tolerated only in his capacity as a priest.

Towards three o'clock in the morning he was called for to administer the last rites. Her eyes still held the drugged look of half recognition, but the curtains of pain were closing again. As though robbed of free will, he performed the Anointing watched over by the women gathered there. Members of her Order, he realised, people who had known her for so long. He felt himself to be an interloper.

And now his presence was no longer required. He wandered out on to the marsh. The moon glimmered above him, large enough to cast his shadow. A bird of the night called from along the hawthorns, the hedge of those ancient trees a compelling silhouette. The legs of his jeans were quickly soaked with the heavy dew of the pre-dawn. Heedless of the damp he sat for a long time in the middle of the pastureland watching the different coloured flares from the chimneys of the chemical works: blue, orange and green. All around him the refilling of the tidal creeks was the gentlest of whispers.

When he came back to the house the light in the living room had been lowered to a single standard lamp and the nuns, sitting on the sofa and chairs, were gathered. Some clicked rosary beads in silent prayer, others slept. He found Anne in the kitchen, staring through the window over the moonlit marsh. 'I thought you'd gone,' she said.

'No.'

'Look at you, you're soaking.'

'Yes, it was damp on the marsh.'

'So that was you out on the marsh? I thought I saw a figure.' Tom tried to speak but found himself unable. Anne stared back out through the window. 'She wanted it this way. You know, lead a normal life until the end.'

'The end?' Tom asked. Anne nodded tightly. 'How long has she got?'

'I don't know. Weeks at the most. Probably just days.'

'Days?'

The despondency in his voice caused the nun to turn. Her face softened. 'Why don't you go up, Tom? The doctor said there'll still be lucid moments.' The priest went to the door. 'And Tom?'

'Yes?'

'She thinks a lot of you, you know. Maybe that's why she didn't tell you.'

The old nun sitting at the bedside wore a plastic apron. The room was foetid with the sweet sickliness of death. Mary-Jo seemed in a deep sleep. Her eye sockets were bruised as rotting fruit. The nun looked up at the priest as though puzzled by his presence. 'Sister Anne sent me up,' he mumbled.

'There's no change, I'm afraid.' The old nun smiled. 'Ah, look at her there. What a life she led. People have always loved her. They loved her in Africa. And look at what she's achieved here. Some of our Order said that Mary-Jo and Anne were wasting their time when they came here. Communities like this one would never accept a pair of nuns. No sense of the Church, you see. But since she's been ill the door's hardly stopped with people bringing flowers and prayers. One little girl brought a whole carrier bag full of wild flowers. She was a gift to us in this world, Father.'

Tom fell asleep eventually in the kitchen. He had just meant to sit down for a moment and the next thing he knew the cool wood of the table had spread through his body. He lifted his head blearily from where it had been resting. The cold ashes of morning were turning blue at the window. The house was silent. 'I imagine you feel as useless as me.' For a while Tom could not locate the voice that had spoken to him. Then he saw the doctor standing sagging against the units.

'I'm sorry?'

The doctor wiped his face with a hand. 'There's little either of us can do now.'

Tom nodded. His head was aching sickeningly. He rose from his chair on stiff legs. Half-heartedly he stretched his knotted shoulders. From where he stood at the sink, he could hear people mounting the stairs on tiptoes. The loft ladder creaked. A little later the low hum of praying voices began from the chapel. By the rhythm he could tell that it was the rosary. He mumbled his own prayers but the unvarying drone from above began to lull him and he felt his eyelids growing heavy. When he opened his eyes again, the doctor had gone.

'Where are the cups, then, and the bowls?' a woman asked some time later.

Tom pointed uncertainly at the units. 'Probably in there.'

The woman opened the double doors and bent inside the cupboard. 'How many of us are there?'

'I don't know.'

Silently she brought out a great pile of plates and bowls.

The grass on the marsh was still sodden. Tom walked numbly through it. A lark rose. The herd watched him with mild eyes then returned to their grazing. He crossed creek after creek, the mud beds hissing as the tide ebbed. When one lark fell silent another began its singing ascent. He came to a thick scrub of birch trees through which the faintest of trails led. He followed the promise of a path and found himself on a beach. Behind him, up the coast, the nuclear power station towered almost as high as a lark's flight; in front of him the river flowed into the sea. Beyond was the open salt water into which a heavily laden container ship was sailing.

Crossing a shingle bank, the pebbles seemed to clatter beneath his feet. A flock of little wading birds rose dense as gnats. On the wet sand his feet sank to the heels. Seals viewed him from a rocky promontory. Having reached the very lip of the foreshore he stared down the coast. The rusty steelworks rose from its unearthly terrain of ore dunes. He gazed beyond that, his eyes straining. The golden sands of Redcar curved, indistinct with the glare of the eastern morning sun. Further, a faint line lay on the sea, as if drawn by a pencil, and he believed for a few moments that it was the pier at Saltburn. All he could make out with any certainty was the cliff. After a long time he realised that the flashes he saw showing out like the lights of lanterns from a smugglers' coast was the sun catching the windows of the trams as they rose and fell on the heights. Gradually, as the tide ebbed further and further at his feet, he followed after it. Without noticing, he came too near to the seals, who, losing their nerve, creamed away through the water.

Silently a ship was coming down the river to the mouth. It was a chemical tanker. Its wash soaked him to the knee. Unbidden, memories of what he had been taught at the seminary about the final sacrament flooded through him. Extreme unction; they had called it *the last journey*. No one could make it with you; you had to go it alone. He had been told that although it was a time of great human sorrow, it was also a moment of sublime joy. The soul was going home. Tom looked up. The ship was crossing the bar and entering the open sea.

'There you are,' Anne said when he came back to the house at last. She was weeding in one of the flowerbeds. She worked with a quickness that did nothing to conceal her preoccupation. 'Christy came round. There's been some trouble at the port.'

'Trouble?'

'The police are wanting to talk to anybody who might have any information. Your trousers are soaked again.'

'What trouble, Anne?'

'It isn't urgent. An open-and-shut case; that's what Christy said. It's happened before. Two men killed in a fight with each other apparently.' She glanced at him rapidly. 'When I told him about Mary-Jo he said that the police may not even want to talk to you.'

'I see.' The priest blinked. 'How is she?'

Anne shook her head. He stood there helplessly as she went back to working the soil. When she looked up again she was surprised to see him still there. She rose with difficulty. 'Did you manage to speak to her?'

Tom shook his head. 'She didn't recognise me.'

'Look, Tom, go home and have a sleep.'

'I don't want to leave.' His voice was a whisper.

'I know. Go back to Slaggy Island for a bit of rest, then come back here. Stay . . . until the end. She'd want that. I'm with her tonight, I'll call you if she can talk. If I think she can recognise anyone, I'll call you.'

The beautiful summer day passed achingly slowly. Tom wandered the quiet roads of the petrochemical district. A dust, long undisturbed by other pedestrians, rose from his feet. Reaching the Transporter Bridge, he travelled back and forth on the ferry. The sun grew hot but the girders of the bridge remained cold. He walked home. On foot, the isolation of Slaggy Island showed itself as never before: the old spoil heaps, now grassed over, ringing it like a sea, the railway bridge rising to form a causeway. One or two prostitutes were smoking drowsily in the arches. Tom stood in the parish room watching the untroubled peace of a sleeping Kevin. Towards evening he returned to the convent, footsore and numb.

In the small hours he felt a hand gently stirring him. He had fallen asleep in the kitchen again. Anne was nodding at him and he followed her up the stairs.

Mary-Jo was lying propped up and smiled when she saw him. But to Tom the smile was like a crack that runs along the circumference of a pot. 'Hello, Paul Newman.'

'Hello, Bernadette O'Malley.'

She smiled again. 'Or should I call you St Peter with that beard?' He lifted a hand to his cheek. The whiskers had indeed become a beard. 'Thanks for coming, Tom.'

'I . . .' Tom tried to speak, but there were no words.

He sat down on the chair beside the bed. 'I'm sorry, Tom,' she said at last. 'For not telling you.'

'It doesn't matter –'

'It does. I've hurt you.' Mary-Jo pursed her lips and there was a light gargling sound. Tom realised that she was laughing. 'Brings it back,' she whispered.

'How do you mean?'

'In Nazareth House, remember? When we sat round the bed.'

There was a catch at the back of the priest's throat. Another long pause followed. She closed her eyes and a dreadful panic came over him. When she opened her eyes again, the skin of her face seemed almost translucent. 'Tom?'

'Yes.'

'Will you forgive me?'

'Forgive you? There's nothing to –'

'I've been so angry with you.'

'Why?' The word was a murmur.

'You made me want to live, Tom.' She began to cough and the priest cast about helplessly. He handed her the glass of water standing on the bedside table but she shook her head. Slowly he waited for the coughing to pass. 'Maybe you were right first time.'

'Ssh, don't upset yourself.'

'It would have been easier. If you'd pretended you didn't remember me. For you as well as me.'

'Oh, Mary-Jo.'

There was a long pause. When she started to talk once more, each word was an effort. 'Before I met you again I was ready to go. You pulled me back.' She lapsed into silence, exhausted. But just when he thought he should get Anne, she had mustered herself. 'Turn off the light,' she said huskily. 'Pull back the curtains and open the windows.'

'But –'

'Please, Tom.'

He rose stiffly. A cooling breeze sprang into the room and the nun sighed happily. The moon was bright. Its silvery light softened the look of death that already pinched Mary-Jo's features. Fighting back a sob, the priest found himself able to look at her now without flinching. The silence stretched between them as they gazed at the framed stars. 'What's that?' she said at last. 'That orange star.'

'Mars,' he replied.

'Oh, good. It's so bright. I thought it might be the lights of a plane.'

'It's the closest Mars has been for sixty thousand years.'

'How far away is Mars?' Mary-Jo asked a little later.

'Oh, it's a long way. But they think they can land astronauts on it. One day.'

'Come nearer, Tom.'

He moved his chair closer so they were within touching range. Mary-Jo took his hand. The grip was so firm that it hurt him. Her voice was little more than a torn whisper. 'And what do you think about God these days, Tom?'

His breath shredded. 'It's you I think about, Mary-Jo.'

'That's not so bad is it, to lose God if you find love?'

'No, it's not so bad.'

Still hand in hand they lapsed into a silence. All at once a shimmering seemed to fill the air. Baffled, Tom looked about but no one had entered the room. The sound increased. It was musical, a song whispered by many voices. When he looked back at Mary-Jo her face was ecstatic. Her hand tightened in his own. 'You heard them as well, Tom.' The priest nodded, deeply disturbed. 'The geese,' she said simply. 'They've arrived earlier this year. You see, they always winter on the marsh and I didn't think I would see them.' She closed her eyes in pleasure. Tom did not see them open again. Slowly the pressure from her grip ebbed, like the tide in one of the marsh creeks, until it was only the priest who kept hold.

When Anne came in, Tom left the room. He walked down the stairs and straight out of the front door. Above, Mars twinkled in the sky. On the marsh the coloured steam drifted mutely, like a wearied harlequin.

Chapter Nineteen

The heather was in full bloom on the moors. Above, the wide sky was slate grey. A change had come in the weather. It was cold and damp. On the wind blew the breath of autumn.

He drove without looking at the horizons, the purple all around nothing but a blur on the edges of his vision. From time to time a grouse crossed in front of the car, flapping wildly before plunging complainingly into the sea of flowering ling. He passed a shooting party: beaters in tweed plus fours, spaniels prancing at thick green socks, guns held broken over arms. Turning on to the minor road he did not slow down. When he reached the gate, he got out and called on Agatha. A few minutes later he was driving down the farm track. The sight of the clear waters of the stream seemed to sear his eyes.

Apples were swelling in the orchard. He walked under the trees, checking the repairs he had made to the drystone wall and fencing on his last visit. Everything was as it had been and when he straightened and looked over at the house to see the window at which she had stood watching him, his heart lurched. They would be burying her about now in the London cemetery owned by her congregation of nuns.

Entering the darkened stable, he ducked as, one after another, the family of swallows shot out. There were two parent birds and a brood of four youngsters. Over the yard the young birds wheeled in ungainly flight. When Tom reached up to bring down the key, he stared at the rafters above him. They were streaked with decades of bird droppings. Feathers lined the mud cup of the swallows' nest. The thick cobwebs were choked with dust. Just then one of the youngsters flew in, followed by the others. Darting like fish in the pooled shadows of the stable, they settled on the rafter and stared at the man below them, chirruping their late summer song. Scarcely daring to breathe, he watched them. Each beak opening in turn to describe a trilling joy. When he left, they shot out with him. They were preparing for the long journey.

In the parlour of the farmhouse he opened the casements, disturbing a cloud of dust motes, and a sudden ricochet from his loss hit him under the ribs. How many times had he pictured them sitting in this room together through the long years of the future? He stood there until every gnat of dust had settled.

It was just as he heard a sound from upstairs that he noticed the ashes in the grate. When he had been there with Mary-Jo he had meticulously cleaned the fireplace before leaving. Someone had been burning a fire. The noise he knew well from childhood: the floorboard in the middle of the landing. Someone had crossed from the bathroom above to his bedroom. 'Who's there?' He opened the latch door and his voice reverberated up the steep stairs as he called again: 'Who's there?' Slowly he began to mount the narrow stairs.

The same floorboard creaked as he walked over the landing and came to the door of his own bedroom. He stood there listening but could hear nothing. 'Who's there?' he whispered, and all at once he could feel the hairs lifting on the back of his neck. Then, suddenly, when he could stand it no longer, he roared, his jugular vein thickening with the effort. Yanking up the latch, he kicked open the door with all his strength. But it was empty. Only the model aeroplane drifted above him in a nosedive, animated into defeat by the gust from the door. The books and magazines stood exactly as he had left them. The splintered pieces of the crucified Christ lay on the bed beside his cross where Mary-Jo had placed them that day.

He passed from room to room, roaming through the emptiness of the house. When he came back down the stairs and entered the parlour, Jesus-Maria was standing in front of the fireplace facing him. The Filipino spoke first. 'Father Tom Carey, now is time for me to make second confession.'

'How long have you been here?' Tom managed to mumble.

'Five nights.'

'Five nights?'

The Filipino's voice shook and all at once the priest saw his abject terror. 'Five nights.'

'Jesus-Maria, the police are looking for you.'

'Police?' The seafarer's face sharpened with suspicion. 'I not want police.'

'But they want to speak to you.'

The words were as rapid as a stabbing. 'No, no, no.' The bosun ran to the door.

'What are you doing?'

'Police coming. I must go.'

'But they're not.'

'Must to hide. Must to run.'

'Jesus-Maria, they don't know you're here.'

'Not know?'

'Why should they know?'

'You not bring them?'

'I haven't spoken to them.'

Jesus-Maria lowered his hand from the latch of the door. His eyes were bloodshot. He moved stiffly back to the fireplace as though the sudden burst of movement had robbed him of his last energy.

'I'm afraid I've had other things on my mind, Jesus-Maria.' Tom pictured the proud young father in the photograph he had been shown on *Neptune's Booty*. Now Jesus-Maria had become like an old man.

'What you do now, Priest Chaplain of Teesport?'

Tom sat down heavily on the battered old sofa where he had

sat so many times with his mother, where he had hoped to sit so many times again with Mary-Jo. 'Have you been all right here?'

The Filipino's reply was a whisper. 'Yes. Is cold at night.'

'It's almost autumn.'

'After *Neptune's Booty* I am too happy to be here. Father Tom Carey, you are right. Is a beautiful place, your farmhouse. At the night there are stars and the moon. I hear the geese fly over. But the wind it blow. Is not good for a chicken farm, I think.'

'No.'

'Chickens, they not like wind. Not like rain. The pullets, they die.'

'Yes, it can get chilly at night here. I'm glad you used the fire. There's plenty of firewood outside. In the shed.' The priest's own words struck him as ridiculous.

'Even now you still smiling?'

'Jesus-Maria, I am afraid I don't think I have ever been further from laughter.'

'Your cockerel, I look for him, but he not here. Is me. I am the one who is confused.'

'So am I.'

'Where is frangipani?'

'I'm sorry?'

'You say at farmhouse is trees like frangipani bloom.'

'I see, the apple orchard. Well, the trees don't bloom at the end of August.'

'All those trees are orchard? When they bloom like frangipani?'

'April.'

'Father Tom, I like to be here in April.'

'Yes, it's very beautiful then.'

Taking out a tube of wine gums, the priest offered it to Jesus-Maria, then selected an orange sweet for himself. They sat there chewing.

'I came here with her,' began Tom in nothing more than a murmur.

'Who?'

'A friend of mine. And the thing is –' Tom shook his head as though unable to believe his own words. 'Well, you see the thing is, she's died, Jesus-Maria. And I thought that we would return here together many, many times. But now I have to understand that my friend will never see the apple blossom come. And I don't know whether I can bring myself to believe that.' He half-smiled. 'But I'm sorry. You've got enough to worry about.' Tom stared blankly at the cold ashes in the grate.

'Father Tom Carey? I so sorry your friend die.'

Tom wrenched his sight from the wintry vacuum of the cold hearth. 'But tell me what happened, Jesus-Maria. How did you get here?'

The bloodshot eyes flickered with exhaustion. 'Was a big fight. I run off ship, through port. Nobody see me. Father Tom Carey, as I run I pray to God I never see *Neptune's Booty* again. All night I run. All night, streets, houses and then fields. In morning I come to road. A lorry standing there. Driver eating sandwich from diner. I smell the bacon. I read name of town on side of lorry. I remember it.'

'Remember it?'

'I get in the back of the lorry and hide with sheep. When lorry stop, I get out. Then I am walking. Not long, a few hours, and I here.'

'But I don't understand. How did you know the name of the town? How did you find the farmhouse?' The Filipino held up an object. It was the map that Tom had shown him in his room at the presbytery.

'Please to have back. One less sin to confess.' The priest took the map from him and laid it on his knee. 'Father Tom Carey, I wish stealing map is my only sin.'

'Jesus-Maria, they're both dead you know.'

'I could not save him.' The seafarer bowed his head and began a low chant. The priest opened the map out. The endless inches of brown-ringed contours, green woods and place names scrambled together in his vision. He had reached the door when Jesus-Maria called after him.

'Where you go?'

'I need to see something.'

The tremor had returned to the bosun's voice. 'You not get police?'

'No, I'll not get the police.'

Tom returned to the orchard. He walked slowly through it. Then, in a sudden rage, he picked up a dead bough and smashed it against a trunk. The stick broke with a brittle crack. Falling against the tree, the priest pressed his cheek against the lichened bark. Entwining his arms around the trunk, his lips mumbled as though in silent but passionate prayer. A dry sob ran out through the orchard, louder than the crack of the dead bough. Closing his eyes, he bowed his head and wept bitterly.

For a while the pattern of the bark continued to stain his cheek where it had pressed against the trunk. Slowly it faded as he walked to the car and opened the boot.

'You must be hungry,' the priest said as he came back into the house with two carrier bags. 'There was no food in the house.'

'You not ring police?' the seafarer demanded from the parlour, staring through the window suspiciously.

'How? The line's been cut off.'

'You make call on your cellphone?'

'Don't you remember, Jesus-Maria? I don't even know how to use one.'

Having placed the bags on the kitchen table, Tom lifted out the groceries. He began to heat some soup. Like a hungry animal overcoming its own fear, Jesus-Maria lurked at the door. They sat at the huge cold slab of the kitchen table. Tom cut one of the large loaves and handed it to Jesus-Maria. 'There's butter here as well.' At first the seafarer ate slowly, spreading the butter with almost exaggerated care. Tom cut him a second slice and then a third. The more he ate the hungrier he became until he was stuffing the food ravenously into his mouth. He drank the soup straight from the lip of the bowl, not spilling a drop. All the while one of his eyes glared at the door as though he expected it to open at any moment. 'I've brought sausages,' said Tom. 'And this.' He held up a bottle of red wine. When he drew the cork it popped loudly.

He fried eggs and sausages in a huge black pan and then piled them on a plate for the seafarer. The wine was ruby in the old glasses.

'Father Tom Carey, why you not eat?' Jesus-Maria asked halfway through the mound of food, his mouth full.

'I'm not hungry.'

'You so sad today. Is because your friend not see bloom in orchard?' Tom did not reply. 'Father Tom? Will you say Mass for me; and maybe for soul of your friend also?'

Tom looked at the broken loaf and the wine. 'I think I already have, Jesus-Maria.'

A little later, he felt a hand resting lightly on his arm. 'Father Tom Carey, please to hear confession now.'

'What?'

'You hear confession.'

The priest nodded.

They sat in the kitchen, the table between them thick with the remnants of their meal, ancient pans dangling above from the beam. 'I tell you something, Port Chaplain, is the first time I eat and not think of my family. Now I must think of my own soul. You see, I kill him.'

'Who?'

'Vasily Shukshin.'

'You killed Captain Cargo?'

'Yes. He kill Romeo.'

'Romeo?'

'The man who injure leg. He kill him and then he try kill me.'

'You acted in self-defence?'

The bosun shook his head. 'Still you not understand. I go back there to kill him. I go to *kill*. Is murder, Father Tom Carey, Chaplain of Teesport.'

'Is it really murder?' The priest sighed. 'I used to think sin was so certain. Like a questionnaire you could tick the boxes. But now . . . Why did you kill this man, Jesus-Maria? You did it for your family. Did you have a choice? If Captain Cargo was the kind of man you say he was, I don't think you need forgiveness.'

Jesus-Maria spoke slowly, painstakingly. 'Then, if you are saying truth, what I need is alibi.'

'An alibi?'

'Is right word, alibi?' The seafarer's bloodshot eyes glimmered, like a starving man seeing a scrap of food. 'Father Tom, you not talked to police?'

'No, I haven't.'

'Then you can say I with you when they die.'

'I don't understand.'

The bosun's fingers drummed on the table. 'What you not understand? Is simple. You give me alibi.'

'You're asking me to lie for you?'

'No lie. Is alibi, alibi!' The seafarer's voice grew excited. 'Romeo, he already stab Cargo one time before I get there. I use Romeo's knife. Cargo try to kill me after Romeo if I not kill him. Yes, yes, as you say, is self-defence.'

Tom passed a hand over his face. 'You should have stayed on the boat. Christy told me that until they discovered that you had gone the police were treating it as an open-and-shut case.'

'Open-and-shut case?'

'No need for investigation. The men had killed each other fighting. A drunken brawl, nothing more. I suppose their suspicions were aroused by your sudden disappearance. There was a crew list, you see. Why didn't you just stay on the boat?'

'Does the wasp stay in the spider's lair?'

'I'm sorry?'

'This is what happen. I have plan worked out. But Romeo come. He not in plan. My mind go blank. All I can think of is kill Cargo before he kill me, then pick up knife and run. I no want to kill, but what choice is there?' The seafarer's voice had grown breathy, as though after great exertion. He stared unblinking at the priest. 'Father Tom Carey, now I go to police and hand myself in. Say I with you when killings happen. Say I steal map and run because I hear about killing on radio and think they are coming for me.'

'Who?'

'Police. And then after the police, mafia come for me.'

'Hold on, hold on. I can't follow. It's all a bit confusing. I'm not sure the police would believe you. I mean about the mafia.'

Jesus-Maria moaned. 'Alibi, Father, you must give me alibi. They must see I no do it. If mafia think I kill Cargo then they kill me *and* my family.' Jesus-Maria fumbled in the breast pocket of the old suit before bringing out his photograph. He held it out to the priest. 'Father Tom Carey, please to have this. You keep picture of my family, then maybe I will see them in flesh again.'

Tom pushed the photograph away, but the seafarer pressed it on him. He took it reluctantly. 'But they have all sorts of ways of establishing the truth these days.'

'What you mean?'

'DNA. Just a stray hair, a speck of blood. Genetics reveals the truth.'

'Now you are sounding like Captain Cargo.'

Tom blinked. 'The police are looking for someone called Eduardo Marcos. Is that you?'

The bosun did not answer for a while. The hope which had been flickering in his eyes began to die. 'You think Captain Cargo only one to use false name?'

'I don't know what to think.'

'Father Tom Carey, you can help.'

'You're asking me to lie.'

'I am asking you to help me and my family.'

'Why do you ask *me*?'

'Who else I ask?'

'Your friends.'

'Who are my friends?'

'The Snakeheads. The ones you call Ulo ng Ahas.'

The two men held each other's glance. Jesus-Maria was the first one to look away. 'You not know what you say.'

'Is it true that you're involved with the Snakeheads?'

The bosun shook his head. His hands writhed on the table. 'Ulo ng Ahas? I am a failing chicken farmer. That is all. I no member of any gang.' He studied the priest closely. His face was pained. 'Father Tom Carey, you really think I am Snakehead?'

'No. Not really. Even in all the confusion, I never really believed that.'

'Then listen. If mafia think I kill Cargo then they kill my family. Only you can save them.'

The priest's voice was a whisper. 'And what will happen to me if I lie? Not only will I run the risk of becoming an accessory to a crime, and that means prison, but what kind of priest would I have become? A perjurer, a common liar.'

'Please help us. You say I not need forgiveness, so why you not help us?'

Tom's agonised shout rang out in the kitchen. 'Is this all that's left of me?' He rose to his feet, upturning his chair. It clattered loudly against the flagged floor.

Hope died for the seafarer. 'You no give alibi, Father Tom Carey, Chaplain of Teesport.'

When the priest turned round he saw that Jesus-Maria had snatched up the bread knife. He held it high, like a poised javelin. Tom began to laugh. He turned his back again. 'You know, at seminary I used to imagine myself as a martyr. Even someone like me held those delusions. But it was never like this. There is one thing that's the same, mind you. I always thought that when it came to it I wouldn't care if I lived or died. And now it's *really* like that. Not that I'm a martyr. I mean, at this moment, Jesus-Maria, I don't care if you kill me. I'm already Neptune's booty.' His last words were a whisper.

When Tom looked round again he saw that the seafarer was holding the blade of the bread knife at his own throat. 'I no kill *you*,' Jesus-Maria said. 'I kill myself.'

'What?'

'I no kill holy priest. I no kill a good man like you. There is too much killing. And now I add to sin by getting angry and asking you to lie for me. It OK if I kill myself. If I kill myself no one know I kill Cargo. I a bad man. No alibi? What chance I have? I go to prison and mafia kill my family.' He gripped the knife handle more tightly. 'Is trade off. My soul go eternal perdition, my family live. I burn, Father, but they live to see frangipani bloom.'

Chapter Twenty

Snow came one night in December. The gale that had been rushing across the moors for days suddenly became a blizzard. When Tom woke in the morning, the dale was white.

The wind had dropped just before dawn and the silence that met the priest as he crossed the yard was as blinding as the pale, bitter sunlight reflecting from the drifts on the ground. The trees in the orchard were swollen with rime and snow. A single red apple that he had missed when gathering the fruit in October hung like a lantern. The pile of dead wood, which he had painstakingly gathered beneath the trees, was a smooth mound.

He was working in the stable. Already he had replaced the old roof and was now clearing out the stalls. He did not notice the passing of time. When he came and stood for a moment in the doorway, steam rose in great clouds from his mouth. A buzzard was gliding across the frigid sky. The moon was a wisp in the blue. Before he went back to work he examined his hands. They were pitted with the dark mud of the dale. His palm was callused. A thumbnail was black where he had accidentally struck it with a hammer.

The afternoon was waning when he heard the sound of an engine. The snow creaked under him as he walked over the yard. It was later than he had thought. In the west the belly of the sky was slashed red. The engine grew louder, a din rattling the ice-silence. Then it came into view. A quad bike was bouncing over the blocked farm track. The identity of the two riders was hidden until the vehicle pulled up alongside Tom. One of them was Agatha, but the priest was amazed when he saw the passenger pull away the scarf and hood from his face. It was the Bishop.

'Tom, Tom,' he said, levering himself uncomfortably from the back of the four-wheeled bike. 'I barely recognised you. Long time no see.' Stumbling, he peeled off his thick gloves and thrust out a hand. They shook. The Bishop hastily removed his. 'The horny hand of toil, Tom, I see. When you submitted the plans I didn't know that you were actually going to start implementing them.' The Bishop's grin was lost in the vigorous rubbing of a cold nose.

'It's just a few bits of preparation, that's all.'

When Agatha had left, the two clerics went into the farmhouse. Tom blew the embers of the fire back into life and boiled the kettle. 'The mugs are chipped, I'm afraid,' he said, handing the Bishop his drink.

'First class, first class.' The Bishop wrapped his hands round the mug. 'It was pretty cold on that quad bike. There was no snow when I left Teesside, but you're adrift in it here. That's some beard, Tom. At first I thought you were Saddam Hussein. They found him, you know. Hiding away in a hole in the ground. Anyway I was just passing so I thought I'd pop in.'

'Just passing?'

'Well, I was visiting Ampleforth.' The Bishop couldn't quite conceal his unease. 'I don't mind telling you I had a bit of a shock, Tom. When I knocked at the door and Agatha answered. You see I thought that *that* was your farmhouse. Thought you'd shacked up with some woman.' The Bishop's laugh boomed through the parlour. 'No blondes hiding under one of the beds, are there?'

'I've been alone here.'

'We joke, we joke, but these days you don't know what to expect. I don't mean with you. You're one of my few trusties.'

'Frank visited for a few days.'

The Bishop's blink was a wince. 'Ah yes, Frank. That's a grand fire you've got there now, Tom.'

Taking a sip of his tea, Tom peered over the brim of his mug at the prelate. 'He's been shortlisted for a job.'

'Has he?'

'Port chaplain up on the Tyne. As a layman.'

'I see.'

'I hope he gets it. He'll be first class.'

'Of course, of course.'

In the silence the wood cracked. Its heat was beginning to spread over the men. 'Now, Tom,' the Bishop began again, his voice businesslike. 'I'll shoot from the hip. You've had a rough time; what with the sudden move from St Wilfrid's, and that awful business on the ship at the port. Not to mention the house on Babbington Road. The presbytery from hell, as my secretary terms it. When we went to close it up again we found that it had become some sort of brothel. Or at least, those women from the arches were using it to shelter. There were down-and-outs. We couldn't move this fellow with a red beard. What you must have been through.

'Tom, no one deserves time out more than you do. Now, it's been a few months already, hasn't it?' Tom nodded. 'I know we talked about a six-month sabbatical, but what about four? How about if we have you back in the New Year? Truth is, we're desperate. I need another finger for a hole in the dyke. If you could cover the port full-time and relieve the prison chaplain, you know, how you used to. There's no question of Babbington Road of course. I happen to know that there's a nice house on the north bank. It's empty. It belonged to those nuns. I've contacted their Order and they're willing to lease the house to us. It backs on to some kind of nature reserve. Did you ever come across them? There were two of them there. And as for this place, the farmhouse, well I accept your kind offer to use it as a diocesan resource. Mind you, I'm not sure how much we can afford to spend on it so you'd better not go around tearing down walls or hatching any eggs just yet. And oh yes, before I forget. These are for you.' The Bishop handed over some envelopes. 'We collected them from the dreaded Babbington Road. What a nightmare that whole affair was. With you being questioned by the police like that. They're going to destroy that boat, you know. They haven't been able to find its owner. It was registered under Liberia but the American firm in charge of leasing the Liberian flag have no record on their registery. So they're going to scuttle it. What was it called again?'

The priest had to lick his lips to reply. '*Neptune's Booty*.'

'That was it. I knew it was something odd like that. Anyway, there's something very strange about it all. It's supposition of course, but people are saying it had something to do with George Bush's visit to the area. Some kind of terrorist threat. Al Qaeda, or that kind of thing. I suppose we'll never get to the bottom of it. What have you got there, Tom? Oh, the postcard, yes, I saw that. A nice picture on the front. Where's it from? Can I have a look? The Philippines; how beautiful. I was at a conference in the Philippines once. Very Catholic country; quite inspirational to us old hacks. Aren't those frangipani blossoms? Very striking.'

The Bishop brought out another letter. 'Since I'm playing postman, here's one from me. Or from Mother Church rather. I was going to post it, but as I say, since I was in the area . . . It's good news, Tom. Confirmation of that little matter I mentioned previously. Yes, when you come back to work with us, it'll be goodbye to plain old Father Tom Carey and hello to the Monsignor. Well, congratulations, aren't you going to shake my hand? What's so funny? Come on, Tom, share the joke then.'